Dear Reader,

I love writing stories set in the fictional town of Dundee, and this story was no exception. Maybe it was a little more difficult than most, because Liz, the heroine, had such a complicated background, and because the relationships among this particular group of people are a bit complex. But life is complex, so it rang true to me. And I was glad to give Liz her own happy ending—even if it was with a guy who at first surprised me. I hadn't originally intended Liz to fall in love with the man she chooses (for those of you who have written me about this, notice I'm not giving away his name!), but I think they're perfect for each other. He needs her as badly as she needs him (even if he's a little slow to realize it).

And now it's back to work on my next romantic suspense novel. I'm in the middle of a brand-new series, which begins with the August release of *Dead Silence* (from MIRA Books). It's actually quite a bit like the stories I've set in Dundee—there are a lot of interesting relationships, small-town intrigue and drama—only, these new books focus on a man who went missing eighteen years ago and the family who knows exactly where he is (a secret they're willing to guard with their lives).

On a completely different note, drop by my Web site at www.brendanovak.com and check out my online auction for juvenile diabetes (my youngest son has this disease). Last year I raised $35,000 for research—this year I'm shooting for $100,000. I should reach it, too. I'll be auctioning off more than six hundred items (some of which you can't find anywhere else), so don't miss out!

For those without Internet access, please feel free to contact me at P.O. Box 3781, Citrus Heights, CA 95611.

Here's to making a difference!

Brenda Novak

THE OTHER WOMAN
Brenda Novak

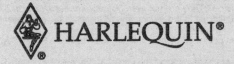

HARLEQUIN®

TORONTO • NEW YORK • LONDON
AMSTERDAM • PARIS • SYDNEY • HAMBURG
STOCKHOLM • ATHENS • TOKYO • MILAN • MADRID
PRAGUE • WARSAW • BUDAPEST • AUCKLAND

ISBN 0-373-78089-3

THE OTHER WOMAN

Copyright © 2006 by Brenda Novak

All rights reserved. Except for use in any review, the reproduction or utilization of this work in whole or in part in any form by any electronic, mechanical or other means, now known or hereafter invented, including xerography, photocopying and recording, or in any information storage or retrieval system, is forbidden without the written permission of the publisher, Harlequin Enterprises Limited, 225 Duncan Mill Road, Don Mills, Ontario, Canada M3B 3K9.

All characters in this book have no existence outside the imagination of the author and have no relation whatsoever to anyone bearing the same name or names. They are not even distantly inspired by any individual known or unknown to the author, and all incidents are pure invention.

This edition published by arrangement with Harlequin Books S.A.

® and TM are trademarks of the publisher. Trademarks indicated with ® are registered in the United States Patent and Trademark Office, the Canadian Trade Marks Office and in other countries.

www.eHarlequin.com

Printed in U.S.A.

Books by Brenda Novak

HARLEQUIN SUPERROMANCE

HARLEQUIN SINGLE TITLE

HQN BOOKS

Don't miss any of our special offers. Write to us at the
following address for information on our newest releases.

Harlequin Reader Service
U.S.: 3010 Walden Ave., P.O. Box 1325, Buffalo, NY 14269
Canadian: P.O. Box 609, Fort Erie, Ont. L2A 5X3

To my Aunt Judy

When I was a child, coming to stay with you was an absolutely magical experience—the new houses, the new cars, the dinners, the diets, the giant Cokes and candy bars, the movies, the hours of playing our homegrown version of Pictionary, and especially the sledding. I'll always remember those times with great fondness. I still smile when I think of your laugh.

CHAPTER ONE

ELIZABETH O'CONNELL WASN'T sure she could tolerate another minute. This was her fifth blind date in as many weeks, and each of them had been significantly worse than the one before.

"I heard what happened with your ex-husband." Carter Hudson, the tall, dark-haired man seated across from her at the new Dundee Inn and Steakhouse reached over to touch her hand. "It must've been a terrible ordeal."

With light-brown eyes and strong, rugged features, Carter wasn't unhandsome. But the way his thumb rested against the pulse at her wrist gave the impression he didn't care so much about what she'd suffered as he did about pretending to commiserate with her—to make sure this night ended in as friendly a way as it could. Besides, his New York accent grated on her nerves. Almost everything about him grated on her nerves.

Looking for a distraction, she glanced around the dining room to see if she could spot someone she knew. She'd lived in Idaho for less than two years, but Dundee was a town of only fifteen hundred people, and she'd already become acquainted with many of the locals.

Unfortunately, it was a Thursday in late May, the

height of the tourist season. She saw no one familiar. City slickers and yuppies drawn to the area by the Running Y Ranch, which offered visitors an authentic western vacation, filled the steak house.

Liz, while stubbornly keeping her smile in place, wished the waitress would arrive with their dinners and tried to focus. "It wasn't easy," she said. "But it's over now. Thank God."

Carter didn't take the hint. "And yet you're on friendly terms with him. Wasn't he on the phone a moment ago?"

Keith, her ex, was attempting to fix the wall at her new store. She knew she probably shouldn't allow him to do her any more favors. But she'd relied on him for so long that it was still easier to accept his help than refuse it. And he was the father of her children. If The Chocolaterie proved as successful as she hoped it would, they all stood to benefit. With Keith working at the hardware store, it wasn't as if he could provide her with much child support. "Yes."

"You spoke to him as if you are good friends," he marveled.

It seemed that every man she dated either wanted to discuss his past relationships or hers. And once what had happened to her was out in the open, she faced a million questions.

She used the excuse of taking a drink of water to shift her hand. "I don't see any reason to be the stereotypical ex-wife."

Carter relaxed in his chair with easy grace. Judging from his build, he could move with impressive coordination and speed. But Liz doubted Carter ever really exerted himself. "That's pretty forgiving. I'm sure it doesn't sound very nice, but if I were you I'd make him pay—whether I was being stereotypical or not."

Her grip tightened on her glass. Her emotions were complicated when it came to Keith, and Carter's negativity wasn't helping. "Why, when we have so many friends and loved ones in common? Maybe it'd be different if we lived in a big city. But in a town like this, we have to deal with each other every day."

"You're serious? You can take what he did as though it was nothing?"

"We have two children together," she said, hoping he could understand the point of that, if nothing else.

Carter reacted with a snort of incredulity. "From what I've heard, he has three more with your brother's wife."

Liz told herself to count to ten. She itched to get up and walk out. Without an explanation. Without a backward glance. But she couldn't. She loved Senator Garth Holbrook and his wife, Celeste, who'd set up this dinner date. She didn't want her behavior to reflect poorly on them. Maybe if Carter was only a casual acquaintance of the senator's, she wouldn't have to be so careful. But he'd just opened a field office for Garth and still worked with him. "She wasn't my brother's wife at the time," she said.

"No, you were both married to Keith."

The waitress approached, carrying two plates, and Liz sat back in relief. But the arrival of their food didn't distract Carter. He simply dodged the waitress's movements and continued to talk. "How long did he lead this double life—wasn't it close to eight *years?*"

Liz couldn't imagine Senator Holbrook sharing such information with someone she didn't know. Not when his daughter Reenie had suffered because of Keith, too. "Who told you about it?"

"Everyone who gets the chance," he responded, adjusting the napkin on his lap.

"You're talking about Keith, aren't you?" the waitress said.

Liz had met this woman at the salon when she was getting her hair cut, and had seen her around town several times since. Her name was Mandy something, and she always stopped Liz to marvel over what had happened as if they were good friends when, in reality, Liz barely knew her.

"What an incredible story," she went on before Liz or Carter could respond. "That he was able to maintain two separate families without giving himself away is amazing. I still can't believe he didn't go to jail for what he did."

"The state has too many violent criminals to spend money prosecuting someone like Keith. He didn't marry me to commit fraud, and he's always taken care of his children."

"Still. It's amazing."

"Yes, it is," Carter said dryly.

Liz ground her teeth. These people had no idea what she'd been through—or why. "Maybe if you knew Keith, you'd understand. He was gone half the time because of his job. I had no reason to suspect him of being unfaithful."

Carter drew forward in his seat. "Unfaithful? He had a whole other family."

"He wouldn't strike you as the type of person to do what he did."

"You were *living* with him," he pointed out.

The waitress, who'd been struggling to light a candle on the table finally managed to succeed. "Yeah, but she and Reenie were two states apart. Otherwise, they probably would've found out sooner." She put her lighter back into the pocket of her burgundy apron and smiled engagingly at Carter. "By the way, I love your accent."

Liz had no patience left and ran over Carter's polite acknowledgment as she tried to make her point. "Keith has a strong sense of responsibility. That's partly what got him into trouble."

The waitress toyed with the salt and pepper shakers in a rather obvious attempt to stick around, but when Liz leveled her with a meaningful look she finally seemed to realize she had no business there.

"I'll check back in a few," she said, belatedly snapping into work mode.

"Thank you," Liz said and picked up her fork.

Mandy hurried off and Carter cut into his steak. "If you ask me, lying and cheating is what got your ex-husband into trouble."

There had been a time when she wouldn't have attempted to justify Keith's behaviour. But now that she'd put some emotional distance between the revelation that had caused her divorce and herself, she could almost understand how her ex-husband's particular strengths and weaknesses had combined to turn a simple affair into an even bigger mistake. In any case, she felt more loyalty to Keith than she did this stranger. Had Keith not married her, Mica wouldn't have had the family she'd known for the first eight years of her life and Christopher never would have been born.

"How can I blame Keith for loving Reenie, when my own brother couldn't resist her?"

"Your brother married her almost as soon as she was divorced from Keith, right?"

She bit back a sigh. "Right."

"So you came first?" Carter asked. "He met the senator's daughter after?"

Liz cleared her throat, struggling with the shame that so often engulfed her. She hadn't come first. Keith had already been married to Reenie for three years when Liz met him on that plane. She hadn't been aware of this, of course. She and Reenie had lived in parallel universes, unknown to each other until Liz's brother had uncovered the truth eighteen months earlier. When Isaac spotted Keith at the airport, traveling to Idaho the very day he was supposed to be in Phoenix, her world had come crashing down around her.

"No. But I had no idea he was already married." She'd been pregnant with Mica and head-over-heels in love.

"It came as a complete shock." Carter continued to look disbelieving.

She nodded.

"Wow." He wiped his mouth with his napkin. "You're remarkably forgiving to be on speaking terms with him."

Liz could feel Carter's disapproval, despite the fact that his remark appeared to be a compliment. "You've never been married, have you?"

He held his fork halfway to his mouth. "What makes you think so?"

His inflexibility had given him away. He still believed he could call all the shots in a relationship, live in a world of absolutes and straightforward decisions. If she had her guess, he'd never been deeply in love or deeply hurt. So he had the luxury of believing he didn't have to compromise.

"A good guess." She swallowed her bite of garlic mashed potato without tasting a thing. He'd learn someday, she told herself. She didn't have to worry about it. This man wasn't right for her. She wanted to steer the conversation back to neutral ground until they could part ways amicably.

Evidently, however, her tone had revealed more irritation or been more challenging than she'd intended, because his expression darkened and became guarded.

"Senator Holbrook said you're from Brooklyn," she said, trying to fill the sudden silence.

"That's right. I grew up there."

"How are you surviving in such a small town? It's got to be a shock."

"It's different." He shrugged as if he accepted the shift in topic, but the wariness that had become so noticeable following Liz's comment about marriage clung to him like frost. "I'm not convinced it's all bad."

"You've only been here a few weeks."

"Are you telling me it's going to get worse?"

She couldn't help wishing his Dundee experience wouldn't be *entirely* positive. "You haven't been through a winter yet."

His lips, which she would have found beautifully sculpted had she been willing to admire them, quirked. "Do you *mean* to give the impression you're trying to get rid of me?"

"I'm just doubtful you'll like it here, that's all," she said, as if her feelings were really that simple.

He started to eat again, chewing slowly, his actions deliberate. "You're from Los Angeles. How do *you* like it?"

It had taken a significant adjustment. If not for the desire to see her children grow up with their father nearby, she would've returned to L.A. long ago. But now...

She surveyed the familiar dining room. She didn't want to tear Mica and Christopher away from Keith, and she couldn't imagine leaving her brother, Reenie or Reenie's three girls. She was also afraid of what she might do if she were to go back. Trouble waited for her there in the form of her former tennis coach.

Briefly, she wondered if her infatuation with Dave Shapiro, seven years her junior, was the cause of her less than enthusiastic response to the much more eligible men she was dating in Dundee. "It's becoming home."

"You don't think the same thing will happen for me?"

"I doubt it." She pushed at her potatoes with her fork, avoiding his gaze. "I'm guessing you're too ambitious for these parts, too interested in climbing the ladder of success. Which means you won't be staying long."

"You say that as if ambition is bad."

"Not necessarily. As long as you don't mind temporary relationships."

"Dundee's not a real hot spot," he agreed, washing down another bite of meat with a sip of wine. "But there's nothing wrong with temporary relationships. People pass in and out of other people's lives all the time. You never know what you might learn from someone, how a particular person can enrich your experience, even if they don't become a permanent fixture."

She chuckled softly. At least this guy made no apologies for who or what he was. She had to respect that. "Your words sound an awful lot like that country song, 'Lot of Leavin' Left to Do.'"

He laughed out loud. Feeling triumphant at seeing through him so quickly, she was tempted to let her lips curve into a smile. But she suspected that his motivations weren't quite that simple. He just wanted her to think so.

She buttered a sourdough roll. "How'd you meet Senator Holbrook in the first place?"

"When I went to college—"

"Where'd you go?"

"Harvard."

Liz refused to let that impress her.

"Anyway, I thought I wanted to go into politics, so I interned for a state senator in Massachusetts. After I graduated, he hired me full-time and I ran his first campaign."

"But then?"

"But then I took a different career path. When I eventually decided to get back into politics, I contacted him. He didn't have an immediate opening, but he asked around and almost before I knew it, I was flying out here."

"I see. So you're looking for someone to help stave off the boredom while you're in Dundee? Is that it?"

"I'm interested in company," he said with a shrug. "I'm not sure about anything else."

"By anything else...you mean a relationship?"

He chewed thoughtfully before answering. At last, he said, "Probably."

"Well..." She gave him a confident smile. "You don't have to put *me* on notice."

"I don't?"

"No."

A dimple flashed in his cheek, seeming rather out of place amid the hard planes of his face. "Interesting you think so."

"Why?"

"What I've heard so far wouldn't lead me to believe that."

Her knife scraped against the surface of her plate. "Because my husband cheated on me?" she asked, forcing herself to stay calm.

"He was husband and father to another family through your entire marriage and you never suspected it. That's a pretty big thing to miss."

Senator Holbrook's new right-hand man certainly didn't sugarcoat his thoughts. "If you're intimating that I didn't see the truth because I didn't want to, you're wrong." Liz was tempted to tell him how devoted Keith had been, how he'd never even shown interest in another woman when he was in her presence. Reenie hadn't suspected, either. But why waste her breath? She wasn't ever going out with this man again.

"If you say so."

"Are you *trying* to offend me, Mr. Hudson?" she asked.

"I'm trying to figure you out."

She forked another bit of potato into her mouth and swallowed without tasting. "Don't bother."

He poured her more wine. "Too threatened by taking a hard look at yourself?"

She felt her eyebrows draw together. "Excuse me, but this is a first date."

He studied her. "And that means what?"

"I'd rather pretend I'm having fun."

She expected him to be offended. But her words seemed to have the opposite effect. He actually chuckled as though he approved of her response. "So you do have a backbone."

"You were checking?"

"I was curious. Something has to explain what happened."

"That's it." She nearly spilled their drinks as she shoved her chair away from the table. "I'm finished here."

"Just because I won't play according to the rules, *Ms. O'Connell?*"

"The *rules?*" she echoed, standing over him.

He didn't bother getting up. "Stick to tedious small talk. Never say anything that evokes an emotional reaction. Be as solicitous and fake as possible. Those rules."

"Maybe I like playing by the rules."

"Then you're smart to call it quits, because I value my time too much to waste it on superficial encounters."

She blinked, surprised that he'd come right back at her. Earlier, she'd been halfway convinced he wanted to take her home with him. She'd had no plans to comply, but his willingness to let her go so easily still came as a shock. "That's it?"

"If it's all you can handle," he said.

She stared at him. For the sake of her friendship with Reenie and Reenie's parents, she knew she should sit back down. But she couldn't. She had more than enough to worry about, getting her new business up and running. She didn't need this.

"Fine, no problem," she said and stalked off.

KEITH WAS BUSY TAPING the wall he'd just fixed when Liz came in through the back of the shop.

"Hey, that's not bad," she said.

The surprise in her voice made her ex-husband scowl. "You didn't think I could do it?"

"You've never been known for carpentry. But most computer guys aren't," she added.

"I've been working at the hardware store ever since…Well, for a while," he said, obviousy choosing not to refer to the reason he had given up a $190,000-a-year job with Softscape, Inc. to work for twelve dollars an hour in Dundee.

Liz was grateful he hadn't reiterated what had caused the destruction of the life she'd previously known. She didn't need to be reminded of the fact that he'd abandoned her in an effort to save his marriage to Reenie. Carter had already done that.

"I'm getting the hang of being a handyman," he added.

She didn't think he'd ever be much good at manual labor. It wasn't in him. But she was grateful for his efforts, all the same. She'd sunk every dime from the sale of the house they'd shared in California into her new candy-making business and she didn't have money left over to hire extra help.

"You're learning." The improvements to the premises she'd leased three weeks earlier lifted her spirits despite her frustration and anger toward Carter Hudson.

Pausing from his work, Keith ran his eyes over the simple coral-colored linen dress she'd worn for her date this evening. "You're back awfully early."

Liz didn't want to admit that her encounter with Senator Holbrook's new aide had been a flop, so she shrugged off the comment. "I'm tired."

"You cut the evening short?"

She met his gaze. Dating was relatively new to her. Only in the past six months had she felt sufficiently recovered from her divorce to meet other men. "We'd already had dinner." *Part of it, anyway,* she added to herself.

"So you didn't like him."

Her ex-husband's apparent relief made her supremely conscious of how much Keith seemed to want her back. Sometimes she was tempted to relent, to do what she could to rebuild their relationship. With his chiseled features, deep brown eyes and dark blond hair, he'd always appealed to her on a physical level. He appealed to her in a lot of other ways, as well. Memories of better days occasionally teased her into wondering if she could reclaim what they'd once had.

But then she remembered that he'd loved Reenie more—that he'd been willing to give up Liz and their two children if it meant he could keep his other wife— and she couldn't summon the trust. With Keith, she'd always be second best. He was only hoping to get back with her because Reenie was no longer available.

"I liked him fine," she lied.

He wiped his hands on a pair of faded, holey jeans. "Garth acts as if Hudson's the most brilliant man in the world."

He was a Harvard graduate, which was impressive. "He's candid and confident."

"Do you think he's handsome?"

She pictured the dark-haired man she'd left at the steak house. "He's okay, I guess."

Keith squatted to scrape the edge of his trowel against the lip of the bucket at his feet. "Reenie claims he's one of the best-looking men she's ever seen."

Wanting to make sure the plumber had installed the new sink, Liz went into the small bathroom in the back corner. "Reenie's a lot more enthusiastic about him than I am," she called.

Evidently he heard her, because he answered right away. "Why?"

"He has a New York accent."

"You said that as if he has an unsightly mole covering half his face. What's wrong with an accent?"

She wasn't sure. It was just something she'd focused on. Maybe it was easier not to find him appealing if she dwelled on the blunt, unfamiliar feel of his voice and language instead of his attractive features. "It's pretty strong."

"I heard he grew up in Brooklyn. What else would you expect?"

She didn't answer. She was too busy trying out the new sink.

"What does he look like?" Keith called.

Satisfied that the sink worked, she came out of the bathroom. "Do we have to talk about Carter?"

"I'm curious," he insisted.

"Okay, he's tall."

Keith flicked some plaster off his forearm and stood. "Taller than me?"

She quickly tried to compare the two. "Maybe by a couple of inches."

"That would make him nearly six foot four," he said, skeptically. "He's not *that* tall, is he?"

Hearing the jealousy in Keith's voice, Liz grabbed a broom and started sweeping up the dust and dirt left behind when they ripped out the old cabinets. She didn't want to analyze Carter Hudson. Especially with her ex-husband. She had a lot to do if she hoped to open The Chocolaterie by Memorial Day. Although a candy shop had been Liz's idea, when Mary Thornton, who'd recently opened a gift store next door, had heard about it, she'd decided to sell chocolate, too. Mary was busy building her business while Liz struggled to finish the improvements to her space.

"Is he?" Keith prompted.

"I don't remember. He's a big man, okay?"

"Big as in *fat*?"

With a sigh, she faced him. "No. Big, as in muscular. Big, as in he has broad shoulders, a well-defined chest and a flat stomach. Big, as in—"

"Okay, okay, I get it," he grumbled, holding up a hand to stop her. "Jeez, I thought you couldn't remember."

"You wanted details," she said, and could've given him a few more. She hadn't mentioned that Carter had a soccer player's build, with nice long legs and large, rugged hands. Or that, judging from the golden color of his skin, he spent a fair amount of time outdoors, which she definitely hadn't expected from a political aide. But she'd said enough.

"Have you heard from Mica and Christopher?" she asked, changing the subject.

"No, was I supposed to check on the kids?" He wiped a bead of sweat from his temple.

"Not necessarily. I'm sure they're fine. They love it at Reenie's."

"You'd know, since the two of you are such *good* friends," he said flippantly.

The pique behind those words confirmed what Liz already knew. Keith resented the closeness between Liz and his other ex-wife. Liz supposed she could understand why. After having the love and attention of both women for so long, he was suddenly the odd man out, and that wasn't likely to change. Not now that Reenie had married Liz's brother. It probably didn't make the situation any easier for Keith that Isaac was also the man who'd found him out and revealed his duplicity. Liz considered it ironic that, prior to Isaac's spotting Keith at the airport catching a plane to Idaho when he was supposed to be in Arizona, Isaac hadn't really been involved in their lives. He'd spent much of the previous eight years researching pygmy elephants in Africa. And when he was in the States, he'd lived in Chicago, where he taught biology at Chicago University. If not for that fateful visit to Liz and Keith's home in L.A. following one of his research trips, Liz might still be married to Keith and living in California, believing it was only her husband's job that took him away.

"Reenie and I are more than friends. She's my sister-in-law, remember?" Liz said, using a dustpan to empty her sweeping into the wheelbarrow Keith had brought with him.

"I'm not likely to forget," he mumbled. Dipping his trowel into a bucket of compound, he smeared more taping mixture on the wall. "Is this Carter guy planning on running for office someday?"

"I don't know." Liz's mind had already shifted to what remained to be done at the shop. "I hope the other display case I ordered will be big enough."

"You didn't ask?" Keith said.

"About the display case?"

"Whether or not Carter Hudson is someday planning to run for office."

Carter again. Liz propped the broom against the wall. "No, I didn't ask. Thanks to you, we talked mostly about me."

The hand holding the trowel stopped moving, then began to scrape along the mended Sheetrock. "What'd he want to know?"

She gathered up the ceiling tiles they'd torn down. "Like everyone else, he was curious to know how you managed to get away with having two families for so long. And how you and I could still be friends."

"That's none of his business," Keith snapped.

Liz ignored his response. "But he's not as generous as some people," she continued. "He seems to think I'm a fool for not realizing I was being duped."

"Then, it *didn't* go well between you."

That was all that registered from what she'd shared? Closing her eyes, Liz shook her head. "No," she finally admitted. "It didn't go well."

"Good. Maybe, even though he's *big*, as in muscular and well built, I won't be as easy to replace as you thought."

"Keith—"

He lifted his arms as if her pointed stare was a gun. "That's all I'm saying."

"You've said it before. As much as I wish it wasn't so, it's too late for us."

"With a little forgiveness, it doesn't have to be," he murmured.

The look on his face might have stirred something inside her once. It had been a long time since he'd touched her—since any man had touched her. In a way, she wanted to turn back the days and months, to feel the old excitement. But as handsome as Keith was, she had so little feeling left for him.

"Thanks for fixing the wall," she said. "I'd better go pick up the kids."

Keith let her slip out without saying another word, for which she was grateful, relieved. But when she reached her brother and sister-in-law's small farm, she found the porch light on and a note taped to the door.

Liz—We're at my parents'. Stop by, okay?

"Great," she grumbled, crushing the paper in her hand. She was going to have to give an account of her date to Senator Holbrook and his wife before she could take her children home.

CHAPTER TWO

WHEN LIZ REACHED the Holbrooks', she saw a metallic-blue Jaguar parked next to Isaac and Reenie's minivan. The Jag was a beautiful vehicle, and one that always garnered attention. Which was why she immediately recognized it.

She would have turned around on the spot and headed in the other direction, if not for her daughter, Mica, and Reenie's middle daughter, Angela. They were playing in the hanging swing on the front porch and had already spotted her.

"Mom!" Mica called, running down to the sidewalk, waving. "We were wondering when you'd get here. Mr. Hudson came a long time ago."

Evidently, Mr. Hudson had no shame. How could he drive directly to the Holbrooks' after treating Liz so poorly at the restaurant? Or had he dropped by so he could blame her for their failure to get along?

"I'll be right there." Pulling up in front of the house across the street, the one she'd rented when she and Isaac had first moved to town, Liz shut off the engine. That house reminded her of some of the darkest hours of her life. She was glad she'd moved across town six months ago, when her lease had expired. She was living in another rental house, but her situation was improving. Maybe not her love life, but…other aspects. And she was going to make sure that trend continued.

Mica crowded the car door as soon as Liz opened it. "Did you have fun on your date? Did you like him?"

Liz refused to meet her daughter's eyes. A gifted child, Mica would likely guess the truth if given half a chance. Fortunately, the purple of dusk had deepened into darkness, which provided Liz with some cover.

"We had a great time," she said, averting her face as she leaned across the seat to get her purse. The sensible sedan she'd bought when she could no longer afford the Cadillac Esplanade she'd leased while she'd been married still had a comforting new-car smell, but it wasn't half as good as the vehicle she'd lost.

Angela peered over Mica's shoulder. "He really likes you, too."

Masking her skepticism, Liz turned off her headlights. "What makes you think so?"

"He said it," Mica replied.

From what Liz had gathered so far, Carter Hudson didn't tell many lies. So this surprised her. "He did?"

"Yeah. When he first got here, he told Mrs. Holbrook you're attractive." Shoving her glasses higher on her nose, Mica gave Liz a smile. "He also said I'll be as pretty as my mother someday."

"How charming," Liz said, but she was hardly convinced of Carter's sincerity. The man she'd met wasn't the type to compliment a gangly ten-year-old girl. "But he's wrong."

Mica blinked at her with wide, owlish eyes. "He is?"

"Yes. You're both already far prettier than I am." She pecked her daughter's cheek while giving Angela an affectionate squeeze.

They laughed and held hands as they crossed the street. "We'll tell everyone you're here," Mica hollered back.

Liz opened her mouth to stop them. She wanted to ask Mica to go in, collect her brother and quietly mention to Reenie that they were leaving. But she knew it would look odd if she didn't put in an appearance, so she said nothing.

Striding up the walkway, she followed the girls past the tall, heavy door they'd left standing open. "Hello?" she called. "Mind if I come in?"

"Liz, is that you?" Reenie's voice could be heard somewhere out back. "We're in the yard."

The entryway smelled of exotic flowers. After taking a moment to admire the floral arrangement in front of the large gilded mirror, Liz proceeded through the house.

Her heels clacked on the marble floor as she passed a tall table topped with a glass bowl full of marbles. The kitchen, with its center island and shiny copper pots dangling from hooks near the ceiling, came next. Beyond that, French doors opened onto an elaborate brick patio illuminated by tulip-shaped yard lights. Senator Holbrook, Celeste, Reenie, Isaac and Carter were out there, relaxing in lawn chairs.

"Here she is," the senator said, getting up to kiss her cheek. "I told you she was special, didn't I?" he said to Carter.

Carter's eyes lifted momentarily to Liz's, and she thought she recognized a hint of amusement in their depths. "Yes, you did."

"Can I get you a drink?" Celeste asked.

Liz raised a hand. "No, thank you. I won't be staying long. I'm just here to pick up the kids."

"What happened to your dress?" Reenie asked. She and Isaac sat across the patio at a circular table.

Liz did her best to wipe dust and taping mixture from her dress. "Oh, I stopped by the shop."

Her brother stretched out his legs and toyed with the stem of his empty wineglass. "How's it coming over there?"

"Good," she said. "Keith's almost finished repairing the wall that was damaged when LeRoy ripped out the television."

"I think LeRoy will regret moving," Senator Holbrook volunteered, nursing what appeared to be a brandy.

"Why do you say that, Dad?" Reenie asked.

"Folks have been going to his barbershop for years. They won't like the change."

"You're the one who doesn't like it," Celeste corrected with a soft chuckle. "Because it means you'll have to drive somewhere in order to get your hair cut."

"With all the new shops going in on either side of him, I think he made the right decision," Isaac said. "His rent was going up, and there wasn't any good reason for him to pay the extra. At this point in his career, he has all the business he wants from regulars. Tourists aren't really his target market."

The senator winked at Liz. "At least it created a nice spot for a candy store. That makes me happy."

Liz smiled at Reenie's father. With his dark hair and strong chin, he looked exactly like Reenie and her brother Gabe. The only feature Reenie and Gabe seemed to have inherited from their mother was the shocking blue color of their eyes. "Now you'll have to walk over to get some fudge instead of a haircut," she told him.

"You bet I will." He pulled out an extra chair. "Here, have a seat."

"I can't stay. The kids have school tomorrow."

"It's only nine o'clock," he said. "Why not give them fifteen more minutes? They're downstairs playing pool. They won't be happy if you drag them away so soon."

"You generally don't put them to bed until nine-thirty, anyway," Reenie added.

Liz glanced from father to daughter. She wanted to refuse. But she couldn't tell them she didn't enjoy Carter's company. Neither could she say she was in a hurry to get home so she could call a friend in L.A. Reenie and Isaac would both know exactly who she was talking about.

"I guess I've got a few minutes." Slipping into the chair Senator Holbrook held out for her, she helped herself to a cookie from a plate on the table. If she had to join the fun, she might as well indulge. It wasn't as if she'd eaten much dinner.

"Are you excited about opening the shop?" Celeste asked.

Liz dusted a few crumbs from her lap. "I am," she said, without adding that she was worried about the competition from Mary Thornton, now that Mary had had a two-month jump on attracting chocolate-loving patrons. "But I was hoping to be ready in time for Memorial Day."

"You're not going to make it?"

"No."

"Why not? Keith promised he'd help you," Reenie said.

"You know him." When she said this, Liz could feel a spike in Carter's interest level, and she figured he was sizing up the relationship, wondering how she and Reenie could be so friendly. Liz knew it was remarkable that they had overcome the past. But Reenie was a remarkable woman, and what had happened wasn't her fault. "He doesn't know enough about carpentry," she explained. "And I'm having trouble finding someone else I can afford."

"What about me?" Isaac said.

Liz shook her head. Isaac wasn't any better at construction than Keith, and besides he was always so busy. "You already have your hands full."

"There's Gabe," Celeste said. "You've seen his furniture. He can build anything."

"He and Hannah should be back from Boston in a few days," the senator added.

Liz exchanged a quick glance with Reenie. They both knew her brother and his wife, Hannah, wouldn't be home for some time. They'd met a doctor in Massachusetts who thought he could restore some of the mobility in Gabe's legs, maybe even get him out of his wheelchair. He was scheduled to have surgery a week from now but because of the risks, he'd made Reenie promise to keep it a secret from his parents and Hannah's sons. Her two boys were staying at home—when they weren't at the Holbrooks'—since Kenny at nineteen was old enough to care for his ten-year-old brother.

"Maybe I'll talk to him when he gets back," she said noncommittally.

"Meanwhile, Carter could get you started," the senator said. "He grew up building homes with his dad. Didn't you, Carter?"

Carter put his drink on the table and sat back. Liz could feel his eyes on her, but she refused to look directly at him. She sensed he knew she and Reenie were harboring some kind of secret, even if the Holbrooks didn't. He seemed to have an uncanny ability to cut through pretenses. "What is it you need?" he asked.

She was reluctant to tell him. Even if he had the ability to help her finish the store, she didn't want his assistance. She'd find someone else eventually—or muddle through on her own.

"Liz?" Reenie prompted.

"Just a few improvements," she said at last. "Flooring, paint, some shelves and display cabinets. But please don't trouble yourself. I'm sure you're far too busy to be bothered."

"The job should probably wait for Gabe," he agreed.

Carter didn't like her any more than she liked him, Liz realized. That was apparent. But he'd said Gabe's name with enough emphasis that she shot Reenie another glance. Did he *know?*

Reenie managed a tiny shrug to indicate she had no idea.

"Or someone else," Liz muttered.

"Why wait?" the senator asked. "Besides taking a few calls, there's not much Carter can do for me until the computers arrive. And we're a week away from that at least."

Carter's forehead creased. "I was thinking about driving to Boise to work out of the capitol office until we were up and running here."

The senator bit into a chocolate-chip cookie. "Don't bother driving to Boise," he said. "There're too many people at the capitol already."

"But the painting might be difficult," Liz interjected. "I was hoping to create a marbled effect."

The senator brushed some crumbs from his mouth. "You can create a marbled effect, can't you, Carter?"

"I've never done it before."

"Don't you have a book or magazine on it?" Senator Holbrook asked Liz.

Reenie and Isaac knew she did. She'd shown it to them. "Yes."

The senator finished his cookie. "Carter?"

"I suppose I could take a look at it," he said.

"Good. Help Liz for the next week or so, then we'll see where we're at with the office."

Liz waited for Carter to refuse. She guessed he wanted to. But he managed a pleasant voice when he answered. "Okay." He shifted his gaze to her. "What time would you like me to meet you there tomorrow?"

There was no polite escape. She'd thrown out a problem and the senator had solved it. "How about six?" she said, still hoping he'd balk.

One eyebrow slid up. *"Six?"*

"I thought we'd get an early start. But if you'd rather sleep in…"

"No. Six is fine."

Liz knew there was a lot going on behind the unaffected mask he wore, but he gave away nothing.

"Carter would work around the clock if I let him," the senator said. "He's amazing."

"Yes, he is." Liz held her breath when her voice came out a little flat, but Isaac immediately jumped in to cover for her.

"Sounds like you've done a variety of things in your life, Carter. How'd you get into politics?"

Carter finished his drink. "I considered it as a profession years ago. I'm just coming back around to it."

"Do you think you'll ever run for office?" Liz asked, remembering Keith's question to her.

"No."

Reenie's chair scraped cement as she scooted forward to reach the cookies. "Why not?"

"I don't have the right makeup."

"What kind of makeup does it require?" Liz asked.

He smiled as if he understood that she was tempting him into making a blunder. "Diplomacy. The ability to call your enemies friends. My enemies are simply my enemies. But a politician doesn't have the luxury of living in black and white."

"You can say that again," Holbrook said with a laugh. "Problem is, in politics your friends and enemies are never clearly defined in the first place. That's why I need someone like Carter to help me keep them straight."

No longer enjoying her cookie, Liz set the last of it down on a paper plate. "So you'd call yourself a particularly good judge of character, Carter?"

"I'm...cautious," he said. "It's necessary in my line of work."

"There's nothing wrong with being cautious." Isaac took Reenie's hand, in a casual gesture but when Carter wasn't looking he shot Liz a glower that told her to back off a bit.

For the sake of politeness, she wanted to—but she couldn't. Not when she had him cornered. "How so?" she asked.

He pinned her to her seat with an unswerving gaze. "I'm a strategist of sorts. I keep an eye on the playing field, attempt to figure out who will do what under a certain set of circumstances and go from there."

Liz folded her arms. "So you draw assumptions about people based on limited information."

Reenie's mouth fell open and Isaac cleared his throat—another attempt to warn her she was being rude. The senator and Celeste shifted uneasily in their seats. But Liz was too intent on making her point to change course. She didn't even blink as she waited for his answer.

"Don't we all?" he countered.

Liz thought she could guess at the assumptions he'd made about her. Past events didn't paint her as particularly astute or perceptive. "Innocence can make people blind."

"I wouldn't argue with you there," he responded.

"Maybe that's not a bad thing," she said. "Maybe there are too many cynics in the world already."

He scratched his head. "From what I've seen, the innocent rarely survive."

"Some people might be tougher than you think."

"That's definitely a more pleasant surprise than finding out the opposite is true." He rose to his feet. "I'd better go. It's been nice chatting with you, but—" he offered Liz a brief smile "—I've got an early day tomorrow."

After coaxing Carter to take home a plate of cookies, Celeste showed him out.

In the silent aftermath, Liz squirmed against the pointed stares of everyone who remained.

"What?" she said.

The front door closed and Celeste's footsteps echoed across the entry.

"What'd he do?" Reenie asked, sounding a little shocked.

"Nothing," Liz said.

"But you never act like that. You're soft-spoken, well mannered, reserved. *I'm* the temperamental one."

"You went after him like a piranha," Isaac added. "Why don't you like him?"

Liz offered Reenie's father a feeble smile. "I do like him. Really."

"He comes highly recommended," the senator responded. "He used to work for a state senator who is now a congressman, and even though Carter's very discreet about the past ten years or so, according to Congressman Ripley, he's honest, straightforward, fiscally responsible and hardworking. I've seen a lot of that in him myself. I wouldn't have set you up with him otherwise."

"I know." Liz patted his arm affectionately. Since her own father had remarried eight months after her mother's death and basically dropped out of her life, she regarded the senator as a sort of replacement, even though she'd only met him eighteen months ago. She hadn't meant to be rude to his aide. The frustration she'd felt at dinner, and the disappointment she was experiencing with her love life, had simply boiled over. "I'm sorry."

"You don't have to apologize," he assured her. "Carter has a few rough edges, I can see that. Go ahead and challenge him, make him think." He sat back and smiled. "If anyone can handle it, he can."

LIZ WASN'T HOME fifteen minutes before Reenie called. "Are you okay?" she asked.

"Of course. Why?" Carrying the cordless phone with her as she moved through the house, Liz began to straighten up. This part of the day was typically the most difficult. Once the kids were in bed and the place had fallen silent, she rambled, feeling more alone than at any other time and looking for ways to fill the void Keith had left behind. In recent weeks, creating lists and projecting financial statements for The Chocolaterie had given her fresh purpose, but she was too agitated to concentrate on her lists tonight.

"You seem stressed."

She was stressed. She feared her investment in her new candy-making enterprise might be a mistake and she wasn't sure what she'd do if it failed. She didn't want to go back to working at Finley's Grocery. There, she couldn't earn enough to squeeze by. And in such a small town there weren't many better jobs available for a former flight attendant. "I'm just overwhelmed, trying to launch my own business and all that."

"You need to slow down and relax. Isaac and I are worried about you."

Liz's brother had always been there for her. When they were young and their stepmother had been making life so miserable for Liz, it had been Isaac who had defended her, supported her, given her a shoulder to cry on. He'd helped her through the rough time right after she'd found out about Keith, too.

"Tell him I'm fine. You two have enough to worry about with Gabe. Have you heard from him?"

"Yesterday. They've postponed the surgery."

"Why?"

"They're still running tests."

Liz picked up her son's sweatshirt and hung it on a hook in the coat closet. "I wish he'd play it safe and come home."

"So do I," Reenie said. "If the operation goes badly…" She drew an audible breath. "It'd kill my parents."

It would affect Reenie and Isaac and a lot of other people, too. Since the car accident that had ruined Gabe's NFL career three years earlier, he had been coaching football at the high school. Most of his players worshipped him like a big brother. "He'll be okay," she said.

There was a brief silence before Reenie continued. "Mica seemed happy tonight. She talked a lot about the store. She's so proud of you."

A candy shop had been Liz's mother's dream. And now it was hers and Mica's, too. At Mica's insistence, Liz had driven by the store on the way home so she and Christopher could see the progress and say good-night to their father. "The kids are doing well."

Liz felt certain she'd done the right thing in following Keith to Dundee. He was a good father, despite what he'd done, and her children were thriving. She had to keep her mind on that, on what really mattered, or the loneliness would drive her crazy. Reenie and Isaac tried to support her, but they were caught up with their own family. And now, with surgery for Reenie's brother looming in the near future, they were more preoccupied than usual.

"So...was it Keith?" Reenie asked.

"Was what Keith?" Liz replied absentmindedly.

"Did he say something that upset you tonight?"

"I wasn't upset."

Silence met this response, which compelled Liz to elaborate. "I was frustrated."

"Over what?"

Where did she start? Eighteen months earlier, she'd been devastated to find out that her husband had another wife and three children living in Idaho. When he'd left her to try and save his first marriage, Liz had followed him from L.A. in order to keep her children near their father. Mica, now ten, and Christopher, seven, desperately loved Keith, but the change had been a shock to Liz. Especially when she'd had to deal with Keith's first wife so much.

Fortunately, that was behind her now. She loved Reenie and, for the most part, she'd made her peace with

Keith. But life still wasn't easy. She was going from blind date to blind date, denying herself contact with Dave, who was the only man she really wanted to be with, and investing every dime she possessed in a business that could break her if it didn't succeed. She'd known hard times before but she'd never felt so insignificant or overlooked, or so immature and guilty for feeling insignificant and overlooked.

"I want to call Dave," she said simply.

"Liz, I know you're homesick for California and probably a tad lonely—"

"A *tad?*" she interrupted.

"That's what makes it so hard to say go ahead," Reenie told her. "At this point, you're too vulnerable."

"Oh, so I could call him if I didn't need him?"

"He's only twenty-five. If you fell in love with him, would he marry you? Be a good stepfather for your children?"

Wearily, Liz ran a hand through her hair. "I don't want to hear that tonight."

Reenie's voice rose. "At least one of us has to be realistic."

"It'd still be nice if once in a while you asked if he makes me feel attractive. Or if I'm happy when I'm talking to him. Or even if I think he's good in bed!"

"You've slept with him?"

Liz silently cursed her own big mouth. She hadn't told anyone about meeting up with Dave three months ago. She'd simply explained to Keith that she was going back to L.A. to visit her friends and flew to Vegas on a weekend when he had the children. But as much as she and Dave had enjoyed their time together, she regretted that trip. It had started them thinking more seriously about their relationship, and Dave had been after her to meet him again ever since. "It was just one weekend."

"Liz, how long could you reasonably expect a relationship with him to last?" Reenie asked. "You told me yourself that you've never seen him with the same woman twice."

It was true. The Dave she'd known in California had definitely been a womanizer. But that was a while ago. He seemed different now. Besides, how much danger could there be in establishing a relationship when they lived a thousand miles apart? Maybe there were times she wanted to meet him again. But she hadn't given in, even though he offered to pay for the flight.

"There's no *real* risk. He'd never move here, and I can't go back to California. Not until the kids are older."

"So why get involved with him?" Reenie argued.

Maybe he wasn't the perfect fit. But she enjoyed him. That was better than nothing, wasn't it? "He gives me someone to talk to, someone to dream about."

Reenie sighed into the phone. "Don't settle, Liz."

"That's easy advice for you to give. You're remarried and happier than ever."

"It can happen for you, too."

Liz put in a load of laundry. "Oh yeah? Who do you have in mind?"

"What's wrong with Carter?" Reenie replied. "He seems like a good candidate."

"You barely know him. What makes you think he's any more suitable than Dave?"

"He's local, for one."

"I bet he won't stick around for long."

"He might. And he's older, more mature—"

"There are no guarantees."

"My dad doesn't get enthusiastic about people unless they deserve it, Liz. He's really impressed with Carter."

Reenie's father hadn't always been such a good judge of character. He'd once had an affair that had resulted in a child, a girl, who'd shown up in Dundee as an adult and nearly cost him his marriage. Gabe, Reenie's brother, still resented her. But Liz wasn't about to bring up the past. Everyone made mistakes and, all in all, Garth was one of the best men she'd ever known.

Using her shoulder to hold the phone to her ear, she unloaded the dishwasher. "Does your father even know what Carter has done for the past ten years? He could be an ex-convict, for Pete's sake."

"Congressman Ripley wouldn't have recommended an ex-convict. Carter's a straight arrow, and Dad says he'll be one hell of a campaign manager."

"Campaign manager?" Liz paused with a stack of clean glasses in her hand. "I thought he was an aide."

"Only until the next election."

She finished putting away the glasses. "Your dad doesn't need a high-powered campaign manager to retain his seat in the state senate. He's a shoo-in."

"You're probably right," Reenie agreed.

Silverware jangled as Liz pulled a basket from the dishwasher. "So you're telling me he's thinking of running for congress again?"

"I'm pretty sure he has his eye on a national senate seat this time."

"That could be a tough race," Liz said. Considering the scandal that had ensued when Lucky returned to town and everyone had found out who her father was.

"He always aims high. You know that," Reenie responded. "And Carter can help get him where he wants to go."

Liz opened the silverware drawer. "He seems capable enough. But on a personal level, he's…"

"What?"

"Too standoffish, impatient.…I don't know."

Reenie hesitated. "You got all that from one dinner?"

"How long do you think it takes?"

"Are you sure you read him right?"

"I'm sure." Finished unloading the dishwasher, Liz wandered into the living room and sank onto the sofa. "Did he comment on our date?"

"Not much. We asked him if he enjoyed dinner, and he said you were good company."

Liz raked her fingers through her long hair. At least he hadn't used what had happened to make her look bad. That brought him up a little in her esteem. "We have conflicting personalities."

"I've never known you to conflict with anyone."

A call-waiting beep interrupted their conversation, causing a prickle of excitement along Liz's spine. Was it Dave?

She checked her caller ID. Sure enough. She didn't have to decide whether or not to phone him. She only had to decide whether or not to answer. And regardless of all the reasons she shouldn't, she already knew what she was going to do. "I'm tired. I'll let you go."

"Liz, I heard that beep and I know what it means—"

"Talk to you tomorrow," she said and switched over.

CHAPTER THREE

"THERE YOU ARE," DAVE SAID. "Where've you been? I've been trying to reach you for days."

Liz had been avoiding his calls and refusing to return his messages—a futile exercise. Despite her resolution to forget him and find someone better suited to her needs, she was right back where she'd been before, wanting to hear his voice, see him, be with him.

"I've been busy," she said, choosing to keep the truth to herself.

"Getting your chocolate shop up and running?"

"Trying to."

They were talking about innocuous things, but the tension that had slowly built between them since she'd left California—tension that had definitely spiked since Vegas—made Liz nervous. The last time she'd called him, he'd talked almost nonstop about wanting to make love to her again. That was partly why she'd decided to bail out while she still could. Those words hung over everything else they said.

"What's left to do?" he asked.

His deep voice felt like a caress. Briefly, Liz wondered if he'd have been a temptation when he coached her, had she been less dedicated to Keith. While she'd been married, she hadn't allowed herself to admire Dave's muscular physique, engaging smile or laughing eyes. She'd been too in love with her husband, too intent on protecting her family.

Not that it had done her any good. Her marriage hadn't lasted, despite her commitment to it. When Keith had flown off to "work," he'd actually been traveling to Dundee to be with Reenie and their three children.

The depth of Keith's betrayal sometimes crept up on Liz and nearly swallowed her whole. Tonight it was the power of those emotions that eroded her resolve.

Dave made her feel desirable, and that had to count for something. After the toll divorce had taken on her ego, Liz craved the attention.

"A lot," she said, finally answering his question. "I'm beginning to think it'll never be finished."

"And you want to open next week?"

"It would be nice. Winters will be lean. It'd be smart to capitalize on the tourist season as much as I can."

"We have mild winters here in California. Lots of great weather."

She grinned at the enticement in his voice. "We weren't talking about the weather," she said. "We were talking about tourists."

"We have lots of those, too."

"I remember," she said with a laugh.

"Come on. Don't you miss it here? Isn't it time to come home?"

"I can't."

"The longer you stay in Idaho, the more difficult it will be to move."

He had a point. She and her children were growing attached to this place. But Liz didn't feel she had a choice about staying. Not when leaving would have a negative impact on Mica and Christopher. "I can't take the kids away from Keith or their half sisters."

"*Ever?*"

"Maybe when they're older."

There was a slight pause. "Will I be gray by then?"

She laughed. "No, but *I* probably will be." She couldn't help pointing out the difference in their ages. The gap between them had to bother him on some level, didn't it? She always expected him to wake up and realize how easily he could get someone younger, someone less encumbered. But he usually ignored such references, as he did now.

"I can't compete with a mother's dedication to her children."

"Single mothers have to make tough decisions," she said.

"And you owe it all to Keith."

Leaning back, she stretched her legs over one arm of the sofa. Dave was like a bouncy puppy—always warm and friendly. Unlike Carter Hudson, who reminded her of a shark, gliding silently through deep waters. "If Keith hadn't done what he'd done, we wouldn't even be talking."

"Good point." He became more cheerful. "So…is he helping you get the shop ready?"

"He's trying. It's just not coming together as quickly as I'd hoped. Today I wanted him to meet me as soon as he got off work, so he'd have time to patch a wall and make some progress on the painting."

"And?"

"Angela wanted him to take her on a bike ride, so he showed up two hours late."

"Sounds to me like he's dragging his feet."

"Why would he do that?"

"Maybe he'd rather not see you open this business."

Liz changed the phone to her other ear. "Why would he care?"

"Didn't you tell me he wants another chance?" Dave asked.

"That's what he says."

"The more independent you are, the less likely you'll be to give him that chance."

Liz had never thought of the situation in quite that way. She hadn't considered Keith's take on her actions at all. She'd simply wanted to start her own business and stop punching a time card and collecting a small wage from someone else. "The more I make, the more secure Mica and Christopher will be. Which will mean less pressure on Keith to help support them."

"Doesn't he need to find a better job, anyway?" Dave asked. "He can't work at that hardware store indefinitely."

"He's looking, and doing some projects on the side. But it isn't easy to find a software development company that will let him telecommute from Idaho. That's why he can't go back to Softscape. They've moved their offices from Boise to L.A. and want him to live there. But he won't move."

"There's got to be other opportunities in Boise."

"Even that's too far to go."

"Why?"

"I think it's because he's afraid he'll lose his Number One Dad status with Jennifer, Angela and Isabella. The competition he feels toward Isaac has made him even more determined to remain a central figure in their lives."

"Aren't divorces fun?" Dave said. "Suddenly parents are competing for their children's affection and admiration, instead of acting like adults."

She knew he'd grown up in a broken home. She could tell by the conviction in his words how much he'd hated it. His mother had packed up and moved out of state almost as soon as the divorce was final, and left him with his father. Liz sometimes wondered if he liked older women because he was searching for a mother figure to replace the one he'd lost when he was young. She wanted to ask but was positive it wouldn't go over very well. "You're speaking from experience."

"I am. My father tried to become my best friend, instead of just being my parent. It was pretty damn embarrassing to see him dressing like a kid my own age."

"It's tough to keep what's really important in mind when you're reeling emotionally," she said, trying to be fair.

"I know. That's why I admire you."

Liz wasn't sure how to respond. She didn't expect any praise for trying to hold up her end, but the compliment felt good. "Thanks," she said softly.

"What do you need in order to finish the store?" he asked.

"Someone who knows what he's doing," she replied with a laugh. "And a few more hours in each day. I've been checking out chocolate suppliers, experimenting with ideas, buying the pots and equipment I need, and getting the proper licenses. I haven't had enough time to focus on the actual improvements. Now I know it won't happen unless I push a little harder."

"I wish I was there to help you."

"Do you know much about carpentry?"

"No. But I'm good at other things."

"Like…"

His voice turned as thick as honey. "Rubbing the tension from your shoulders."

Liz covered her eyes and imagined him bending toward her, brushing his lips softly across hers.

Pushing herself upright, she redirected her thoughts. It was that kind of reverie that made her realize she had no business remaining in contact with Dave.

"You won't even miss me as soon as you get another woman out on the court who has a better pair of legs," she said.

"Are you kidding?" he replied. "There *is* no one with a better pair of legs."

"I bet you say that to all the girls."

There was a slight pause.

"Dave?"

"What?"

She could tell by his tone that she'd upset him and regretted going so far. "I was only joking."

"Very funny. You say stuff like that almost every time we talk."

It was true. She supposed she was trying to remind herself of the risks involved in letting this relationship grow. "I'm sorry. Maybe if you were older, I could take you more seriously."

"Here we go again."

Liz rubbed her left temple. "It's just—"

"Who cares about the difference in our ages?" he interrupted. "It's only seven years. If I was older than you, no one would think twice about it."

Liz turned off the lamp overhead. She preferred to sit in the dark when talking to Dave. "It's not only that," she said. "It's the fact that I have two children."

"So? I'm good with kids. Do I have to be thirty before you'll introduce me?"

"Of course not. If we lived closer, you could meet Mica and Chris." She wasn't sure that was really the case. Setting herself up for disappointment was one thing; doing it to her children was another. But she didn't want to argue.

"I bet if I was there, I could make you forget about the age difference."

"No, you couldn't."

"I proved you wrong once. Should I come for a visit? See if I can do it again?"

Liz blinked in surprise. They often talked about their trip to Vegas and the possibility of another meeting. He'd been pressuring her to return to L.A. for a few days. But even though Dave had a cousin in Boise, this was the first time he'd ever mentioned venturing into *her* world.

She guessed that would be a little too much reality for both of them.

Knowing if she could just put him off now they'd

probably never address the issue again, she said, "It'd be better to come in the winter when you're not so busy at the club, wouldn't it?"

"Winter is pretty far away."

"Mommy?"

Liz spun around as if she'd just been caught doing something wrong. Christopher was standing in the doorway, rubbing his eyes. "What's the matter, honey?"

"I can't sleep," he complained. "Will you lie down with me?"

Liz bit her lip. She wasn't ready to end the conversation. But as she looked at her son's sleepy face and thought of how quickly he was growing up, she knew what she needed to do. "I've gotta go," she said into the receiver.

"Call me later?" Dave asked.

"Tomorrow," she said and hung up.

CARTER HUDSON WAITED impatiently beneath the old-fashioned sign that identified Liz's new store as a chocolaterie. He'd never heard of a chocolaterie, but she was the one who had to worry about making this business a success. His only problem was that he had to spend a whole day with her, which wasn't going to be easy because she reminded him so much of Laurel.

He remembered the feel of Liz's slim fingers, the flutter of the pulse at her wrist. When he'd touched her hand at the restaurant, he'd wanted to close his eyes, block out the restaurant and everyone else in it, and simply count the steady beat of her heart. How he craved just one more moment with Laurel, the chance to say goodbye...

He'd been too aggressive with Liz. But he didn't

care. The whole encounter had been illogical. Besides, he wasn't planning on getting to know her in any meaningful way, so it didn't matter. Which was good, because they weren't off to a better start this morning. After dragging him out of bed at the crack of dawn, she was late. The only shops open this early were those that catered to the ranchers—the diner, the feed store, the hardware store and the old-fashioned doughnut shop.

Wishing he'd stopped for a cup of coffee, Carter wandered over to Belinda's Bagels two doors down, then frowned at the sign in the window. The place didn't open until eight. Evidently bagels, at least in Dundee, were a tourist item, and tourists typically didn't venture into town until later in the morning.

He considered walking back to the doughnut shop—it was only a few blocks away—but ultimately decided not to. He'd grab a cup when the bagel shop opened. He'd need that coffee even more in a couple of hours. Last night he'd had another terrible nightmare. After jerking awake in a cold sweat, it had taken at least ten minutes to convince himself he'd just been dreaming.

Laurel…

The sudden, hollow ache in his chest nearly made him sick. He knew the pain would ease eventually. He'd had plenty of practice dealing with that. He just had to keep his mind occupied.

Dropping a quarter into the newspaper bin next to the curb, he removed a copy of the *Dundee Weekly* and sat down at one of three small outdoor tables. If Liz didn't come in the next fifteen minutes, he was going to head home. Helping her finish the inside of her chocolate shop wasn't actually in his job description. He would've said so the night before, but the supportive, helpful attitude of the people around here inspired him. Dundee was so different from the big city. So…rejuvenating.

He needed the change, whether he wanted to admit it or not.

Of course, the helpfulness he so often encountered here had a downside. It sometimes bordered on nosiness, even outright interference. But at least these folks typically meant well. At least they cared.

He gazed down the ribbon of street that split the small town in half. Would it have made a difference if he'd brought Laurel to a place such as this?

The question crept unbidden into his consciousness but, with some effort, he shoved it out of his mind. Second-guessing wouldn't help. There was nothing more he could have done. And now he had no choice except to square his shoulders and face each new day as it came.

He shifted his attention to the newspaper and, slowly, the ache subsided. He found no stories of rape or murder. No missing persons. Nothing violent or ugly. The headline read Crab Feed Raises $10,000 for Schools. He couldn't call the accompanying article riveting, but it was comforting to know that a crab feed could still be front-page news.

Laurel would've liked that….

Annoyed with himself, he made another attempt to control his thoughts by moving to the article directly below the one he'd already read.

City Council Bucks Rodeo Improvements

Is it time to improve the rodeo grounds? According to Councilwoman Foley, it is. But with Mayor Wells out of town, the council voted 3–2 last week against appropriating the necessary funds. Fortunately, the opportunity to make your opinion heard hasn't been lost. The mayor is back and calling for another vote. If you'd like to see…

The beep of a horn brought up Carter's head. Liz had arrived. At last.

Tucking the paper under his arm, he stood and waited for her to park.

Her keys rattled as she slipped them into her pocket and hurried over. Dressed in a red T-shirt, blue denim shorts, tennis shoes and a gray zip-up sweatshirt to ward off the morning chill, she'd pulled her long blond hair into a ponytail. She hadn't bothered with makeup, but then she didn't need any. Large hazel eyes watched him from above a narrow, well-defined nose and high cheekbones. As much as he hated to acknowledge it, she possessed a delicate sort of beauty. Like Laurel's. But her mouth was all her own. Too expressive for a woman who looked so reserved and sophisticated, it added an accessible human touch to a face that, without it, might have almost appeared too perfect—more like white marble than flesh and bone.

"Have you been waiting long?" she asked as she approached him.

He sent her a pointed glance. "Since six."

"Right. You were on time. Of course." She cleared her

throat and shifted a roll of blueprints from one arm to the other. "Sorry about that. I had trouble rousing Keith's mother. She'd forgotten she agreed to get the kids off to school for me."

"No problem." Trailing her to the shop, he waited as she unlocked the door. Then he followed her inside to find the gutted remains of a retail establishment, which he knew from the conversation the night before, had previously been a barbershop. He eyed the well-worn floor, the freshly patched wall, the wheelbarrow in the corner. A door at the back led to what appeared to be another room. "Storage?" he asked, waving toward it.

"It used to be a small apartment, which the previous owner leased out. When we're done it'll be my kitchen and pantry."

He rubbed his chin. "So we're starting from scratch."

"Basically."

"What's the goal here? With the improvements, I mean?"

She unrolled her plans on the lone display case and let Carter take a look. "Have you ever seen the movie *Chocolat?*"

"Never heard of it."

She stared at him. "It was nominated for several Academy Awards, including best picture."

He was busy already noting what would have to be done, trying to estimate how long the work might take him. "When?"

"I don't know exactly. Several years ago."

The biggest part of the job would be the kitchen. The

showroom needed little more than flooring and paint and the placement of some additional display cases and shelving. "Does this movie have any karate fights?"

"No."

He glanced up at her. "Explosions?"

She scowled. "It's not that kind of movie."

"Then I probably didn't waste my money on it," he said, a shrug in his voice.

He was teasing, but if she understood that she didn't crack a smile. "Your loss," she said, sounding slightly offended. "It's fabulous. Almost as good as the book."

Having studied the plans, Carter crossed the floor to make sure Keith's patched wall was dry enough to paint. "I'm guessing there's a tie-in?"

She put down her purse on top of the plans, to keep the paper from rolling back into a scroll. "There is. I'm trying to re-create the atmosphere of the shop in that movie."

"Which was a choco-later-ie?"

"That was a poor attempt even for a Yankee," she said, making a face. "It's pronounced *chocolaterie*. The movie is set in a provincial French town."

He'd slaughtered the word on purpose, but he didn't bother to point that out. "Just like this small western one, huh?"

At last she seemed to realize he was baiting her. Her mouth twitched as if she might smile, but she frowned instead. "I can only do so much. Anyway, Vianne, who owns the chocolate shop in the movie, has traveled widely and brings a bit of her mother's

Mayan heritage along with her. I want to decorate this shop the same way."

"I'm not familiar with Mayan decor," he said, facing her.

"Think decadent and sensually appealing, with a South American flavor."

Carter hadn't found anything sensually appealing in a long time, regardless of the "flavor," but he pretended otherwise. "It's *starting* to sound good."

Too caught up in her vision to be interrupted, she ignored him. "You see, Vianne is serving more than chocolate to the locals—"

"And now it's getting even better."

She spread her hands in exasperation. "Would you quit?"

Satisfied he'd already made himself look like enough of an ass, he became more serious. "Okay, so what's she serving?"

"Love, acceptance, change—a rebirth. I find the whole concept incredibly...uplifting."

As much as he'd decided he wouldn't let himself like Liz—nor let her like him—he couldn't poke fun at that. Her sincere words seemed to echo around the hollow space inside him, making him crave those very things.

"Are you actually making the chocolate?"

"No, Vianne crushed cocoa beans and made her own chocolate. But there's no need for me to do the same. Generally, only really large companies do that. I buy my chocolate from San Francisco."

"Ghirardelli?"

"No, Guittard. For some of my truffles, I also incorporate European chocolate to produce my own unique flavor."

"So they ship it to you from California?"

"Exactly. It comes in boxes of five ten-pound bars, which I temper and then use to create various decadent candies."

"Temper?"

"Melt in a particular way, to keep it shiny and smooth."

"What kind of candies?"

"Candies made with pretzels, Oreos, marshmallows... Strawberries, bananas and raisins dipped in chocolate. I also make fudge and truffles, even cakes and frosted brownies. But like Vianne, my signature is going to be rich hot chocolate."

The passion and excitement in her voice again summoned memories of Laurel. Turning away, Carter pretended to examine the walls, making note of the nicks and gouges that remained. "We should really patch a few more spots."

"Probably," she said. "Old LeRoy wasn't much for maintenance or housekeeping. The dirt and grime in this place was unbelievable when I got here."

No longer interested in conversation, Carter let her comment go. "Do you have the supplies we'll need?"

Her eyebrows inched up a notch at his brisk tone, but she responded at once to the question. "I should. Keith brought over a lot of stuff last night. It's all in the back room. If we need anything else, there's always the hardware store down the street. And the good news is that we finally have a sink that works, which should help with rinsing out trays and so forth. I just had the plumber install it yesterday."

Carter glanced in the direction Liz had pointed. The bathroom door was only partially open. He couldn't see the sink well—but it didn't look right. Walking over to the doorway, he poked his head inside. "Did you say he already installed it or he's going to?"

Liz came up behind him. She didn't answer; she didn't need to. The shock on her face, when she saw that the sink had been torn from the wall, said everything.

CHAPTER FOUR

L<small>IZ</small> STOOD AT THE BACK of the hardware store, trying to keep her voice low enough that Keith's boss, Ollie Weston, wouldn't hear them arguing.

"It had to be you," she said vehemently.

Keith stepped closer, looming over her. His anger and indignation etched a deep V between his eyebrows and almost made Liz retract the accusation. He didn't *look* guilty. But he'd been the last one to leave her shop the night before. Who else would have had the time or opportunity to cause the damage she'd found?

"Why would I do that?" he demanded, his voice rising. "I spent three hours there last night trying to *help* you!"

Ollie glanced at them from the cash register in front, and Liz felt her cheeks grow warm. When she'd first come to Dundee, she'd caused a huge scandal simply by virtue of being the Other Woman. Because Reenie had grown up here and was a popular figure, folks had felt protective of her, and they'd whispered about Liz, even stared at her, as though she'd purposely destroyed Reenie's marriage.

A private person to begin with, Liz didn't want to draw attention to herself now that she was feeling comfortable in this place. "Be quiet, will you?" she said.

"You're accusing me of something I didn't do," Keith snapped.

"Who else could it have been?"

"Anyone!" He threw up his hands. "Christopher was playing with the key you gave me and lost it. I couldn't lock up last night."

"*What?* Why didn't you call me?"

"Because I didn't want to wake you. I didn't think it was a big deal. The place isn't even fixed up yet."

Again, Ollie angled his head to see if he could hear what was going on, but Liz turned her back to him. "I paid a small fortune for all the supplies that are lying on that floor," she said in a half whisper.

"So? This is Dundee. Who's going to steal them?"

"I grew up in L.A., where people lock their businesses."

He straightened a sack of fertilizer that had fallen from the shelf. "You've been here for a year and a half, Liz. You know what it's like. The worst crime we ever see is drunk-and-disorderly. Why would I worry about not being able to lock the door? Especially the back one?"

Liz tucked the hair that was falling from her ponytail behind her ears. If Keith hadn't caused the damage at her shop, was it some sort of hate crime? Vengeance from someone who blamed her for wrecking Reenie's first marriage?

She couldn't imagine anyone holding a grudge over that. Especially since she hadn't done it intentionally and Reenie was so obviously in love with Isaac. Watching him and Reenie for two seconds revealed how happy they were together. The only people who weren't pleased about their relationship were Keith and his family....

Narrowing her eyes, Liz stabbed a finger into Keith's chest. "Your brothers would never do this, would they?"

"My *brothers?* Cal lives in Boise, for crying out loud. Do you think he'd drive up here just to wreck your sink? And Luke's still in Texas. He's staying at Baylor for summer term."

"What about your father?"

Keith gave the fertilizer a kick because it had tipped again. "Come off it, Liz."

"Your folks have never liked me, Keith. Even now that they help out with the kids, they barely speak to me."

"They're still struggling with what's happened. You can't blame them for that."

No, she couldn't. What had happened was entirely Keith's fault. Which was one of the reasons she could never reconcile with him. As hard as she tried, she couldn't completely forgive him for the devastation he'd wrought in her life. And she couldn't imagine trying to belong to a family that resented her as much as Frank, Georgia, Cal and Luke did. She was the physical embodiment of the disappointment and embarrassment they'd all suffered over Keith's deception.

"Are they struggling so much that they'd try and make me fail?" she asked.

His jaw dropped as if he couldn't believe she'd even suggest it. "Of course not. They're better people than that."

Liz wanted to think so. But she wasn't entirely convinced. *Someone* had torn the sink from the wall.

"Maybe it was Mary Thornton," he said.

Liz bit her lip. She and Mary had exchanged words, but…"She wouldn't go that far."

"Why not? You know she's upset that you're opening a chocolate shop right next to her candy store."

"When I leased the space, she wasn't selling candy. She had a card-and-gift shop!"

"That's my point. She's green with envy. Grant Nibley did that big write-up on you in the paper and how you're basing your shop on the movie and all that, so she copied you, and still her shop didn't make the paper."

"At least her store is open."

"But not doing particularly well, from all indications."

Pressing her fingers to her forehead in an attempt to ease the headache pounding behind her eyes, Liz sighed. "She's just disappointed that she didn't think of a chocolate shop."

"I agree. She feels you've outdone her, and yet she has as much riding on her business as you do on yours. She quit her job at Slinkerhoff's law office to make this big career change. She's a single mother. Her ex-husband has been a total flake—"

Liz didn't want to hear it. She didn't feel sorry for Mary. Maybe Mary's ex-husband paid his child support in fits and starts and rarely came around, but Mary had it better than she liked to portray. "Are you kidding me? How stressed can she be when she's still living with her parents? When they're helping her raise her son and filling in with anything else she needs? It's their money behind that shop, not hers."

"No one our age likes accepting help," Keith said. Liz knew his parents had had to come to his rescue a time or two during the past eighteen months. Keith hated needing help. But that didn't mean Mary Thornton felt the same. She *used* her parents.

"So why doesn't she move out? Make it on her own?" Liz asked. "Like the rest of us?"

Because of her stepmother, Liz had run away from home at seventeen and had never returned. She'd graduated from high school while living with a girlfriend, spending most her weekends hanging out with Isaac at college.

"I don't know," he said. "I'm just saying that if you're having trouble at the shop, Mary could be behind it."

Liz stared at him. Was her neighbor really trying to cause trouble?

"Listen, I'll pay the plumber to reinstall the sink, okay?" Keith said. "Then maybe you won't think *I* caused the damage."

Liz didn't want him to pay the plumber. Because of what Dave had suggested earlier, Liz had accused Keith without any real proof, and now she felt terrible. "Thanks anyway, but...I'll take care of it."

She started out of the store, but Keith caught her arm. "Liz."

"What?" she asked as she turned.

"You believe me, don't you?"

She noted his earnest expression. "I believe you. I'm just scared," she admitted. She was putting everything she had into the shop—all her money, her hopes, her dreams.

"It'll be okay," he promised.

There was a time when Keith's words would have encouraged her. But her trust in him had been destroyed when Isaac had revealed his infidelity.

She nodded, but he still held her arm. "There's something else," he said.

"What?"

"When you first came in here, I thought...Well, since you haven't mentioned it, I'm guessing you don't know."

The seriousness of his tone made her leery. "*What?*" she repeated.

"Your father's in town."

"No!" The word came out far too loudly. Ollie frowned at the two of them, but Keith ignored his employer.

"Yes. I ran into him at the gas station on my way to work. He looked a bit rumpled around the edges, as though he'd driven all night, but it was definitely the man I've seen in your childhood scrapbooks. I spoke with him briefly and tried calling you afterward, but no one answered."

"I was at the shop," she said numbly.

"I went by there."

"Then I must've been at your parents' house, dropping off the kids."

"I figured you were in transit. And since you don't have a cell phone..."

Cellular coverage had improved to the point where people in Dundee could now get service. But local reception wasn't the best, and Liz couldn't afford it. Keith didn't have a cell phone, either. Since he'd left Soft-scape, they'd both been forced to tighten their budgets.

She blinked, wondering how she could even be thinking about cell phones.

"Are you okay?" he asked.

She took a deep breath, trying to dispel the shock. "What does he want?"

"You haven't talked to him recently?"

She shook her head. The past two Christmases, she'd sent her father a card containing a few photos of the kids. In more than ten years, that was the extent of their contact.

"That would explain why he didn't know we were divorced." A muscle flexed in Keith's cheek. "It was pretty damned embarrassing."

"Embarrassing?"

Regret filled his eyes. "Right before we got married, I called to see if he'd meet us in Vegas. He gave me some flimsy excuse, which made me mad, so I told him not to bother. I said you didn't need a bastard like him, that I'd take care of you." An uncomfortable-looking shrug followed this admission. Keith didn't spell it out, but Liz knew what he was thinking. When he'd spoken to her father, he'd already been married to Reenie. It had only been a matter of time before he'd broken both their hearts.

But another thought surfaced on the heels of the previous realization. Was the way her father had responded part of the reason Keith had gone ahead with the marriage? In addition to the fact that she'd been pregnant with Mica? "You never told me you were going to call him," she said.

"After I'd spoken to him, I was glad I hadn't told you."

The heat of the day seemed to grow worse, become stifling. A large fan whirred in the corner, but Ollie was too conservative to use an air conditioner in May. "What does he want?" she asked, wondering why her father's actions still hurt so badly.

"He and Luanna have split up."

Liz's heart leaped into her throat. How many times had she prayed that her father would separate from the woman who'd made her life so miserable? How many times had she dreamed of reclaiming his love and approval?

"Is he here to see me or Isaac?" she asked.

"I'm guessing he wants to see both of you. Who else does he have, now that Luanna's out of the picture?"

There was Luanna's son, Marty, but he was Liz's age and on his own. Liz couldn't imagine her father being attached to him. Luanna had spoiled Marty so terribly that hardly anyone could stand him. But maybe he'd changed. Liz couldn't say for sure what kind of man he'd turned out to be. She hadn't been in touch with him either since she'd run away.

"Liz…"

She lifted her eyes to his. "What?"

He sighed. "You look devastated."

"I'm fine." After all, she'd had eighteen months to recover from the previous blow.

"You're not fine." Gently tugging her up against his chest, he kissed her head. Liz would have resisted, as she always did these days, but she wasn't thinking straight. The news he'd just delivered felt like a knockout punch.

Keith smelled good. Familiar. Comfortable. Not so long ago, he'd meant the world to her. Certainly one moment in his arms wouldn't hurt. Resting her head against his shoulder, she tried to decide what to do about her father.

"I know you're under a lot of pressure right now, and you don't need this." Keith's hands caressed her back, reassuring her with their strength.

Liz knew Ollie was watching, and that word of the embrace would probably spread. But she stayed where she was, too shocked to pull away.

"Do you want me to ask him to leave town?" Keith asked.

"No."

"Why not?"

Because it was no longer Keith's responsibility. He had no right. "I'm sure Isaac will take care of that," Liz said. Her brother felt angrier toward their father than she did, even though Luanna had treated Isaac much better. His presence in the house hadn't threatened Luanna in the way that Liz's presence had.

"I wonder what happened to their marriage," she said, still trying to come to terms with her father's sudden appearance in Dundee.

"He said he got tired of Luanna's bullshit. But—" Keith brought her chin up "—I got the impression it was Luanna who left."

The sting of this particular detail surprised Liz. Had she hoped, after all these years, that her father had finally come to his senses?

What did it matter? It was too late, anyway. The girl who'd needed him so badly was an adult, now.

Straightening up, she disengaged herself from her ex-husband's embrace. "So he's here because he has no better place to go."

Keith's sympathy reminded Liz that he wasn't quite as bad as she sometimes liked to tell herself he was. "I'm sorry, babe," he said.

She smiled sadly and said, "Thanks. But don't call me *babe*, okay?" Then she forced her feet to carry her out into the dazzling sunshine.

AS SHE EMERGED from the hardware store, Liz nearly bumped into Carter.

"You've already started?" she asked when she noticed the cranberry-colored paint that speckled his hands and hair and even the soft T-shirt that made the most of his muscular build.

"Was I supposed to wait?" he replied.

"No, it's just that I was going to help you. But—" She shook her head, trying to order her scrambled thoughts. She felt like a punctured balloon, in the process of deflating. "Did you figure out the marbling?"

"Yeah. It's easy."

"Okay, well, I'll be there shortly."

"I could use a more expensive roller," he said. "This one won't last an hour. And I figure I might as well get a few of these while I'm here." He showed her a tiny screw that he carried in one large hand. "We'll need them when it comes time to reattach the light plates."

"Light plates?" she murmured, unable to immediately picture what he was talking about.

"The face plates that go over the outlets and light switches?"

"Oh, right." She waved a hand halfheartedly. "Tell Ollie to put whatever you need on my account."

He peered more closely at her. "Is something wrong?"

She stole a glance down the street. "No, why?"

"You seem a little dazed."

An old truck came rattling by. Holding her breath, she tried to identify the man behind the wheel....

It was Hawthorne Cawley, one of the longtime ranchers who lived in the area. The vehicle was probably one he didn't bring to town very often, which was why she didn't recognize it. Letting her breath out slowly, she said, "It's nothing."

"You're sure?"

"I'm sure." She began to step around him, but he cut her off. "What'd you find out about the sink?"

Anxious to get to her car and head for the high school, where she hoped to find her brother, she rubbed the palms of her hands on her shorts. "It wasn't Keith."

"You're sure?"

"I'm sure."

"How do you know?"

She pulled her sunglasses out of her purse and took refuge behind the dark lenses. "He said so."

Carter's smooth forehead rumpled with impatience and disbelief. "You're taking him at his word?"

At this point, Liz wasn't as concerned about the vandalism as she was about the next twenty-four hours. How long would her father stay? What would she say to him? And how would he treat her children? He'd never even met Mica and Christopher. "I guess."

"We're talking about the same man who lied to you your entire marriage."

She managed to give him her full attention. "Listen, I'm grateful for your help at the shop, and I'll do what I can to compensate you."

"But…"

"I don't need any of your cynical bullshit right now," she said and walked away.

She knew he stared after her, that she'd surprised him once again. But she couldn't find it in herself to care.

CARTER HAD QUIT HIS JOB with the Federal Bureau of Investigation shortly after Laurel's funeral. He knew he'd never go back. But he was still a cop at heart, and that made him reluctant to allow the mystery of the vandalized bathroom to go unsolved. *Someone* had been inside Liz O'Connell's chocolate shop; *someone* had caused the damage. He intended to find out who was responsible—and he doubted he'd have to work very hard to do it. The way Liz had muttered, "Keith!" before she'd stormed out and marched over to the hardware store told him she had reason to believe it might be her ex-husband. Which meant Keith probably had a solid motive. And a solid motive made him Carter's best suspect. Maybe Liz's ex denied ripping the sink from the wall, but any man who could lead the double life Keith had led had to be one hell of a liar.

Carter hated liars almost as much as he hated petty

thieves and vandals. In seven years with the bureau, he'd learned that small crimes stemmed from the same lack of regard for others that fostered larger crimes.

"Can I help you?" An old guy with spidery veins covering his ruddy cheeks stood at the cash register.

Carter paused long enough to hold up the screw. "Can you tell me where I can find these?"

He took a moment to peer at it. "Aisle nine."

"Thanks." Carter moved on. He hoped to run into Liz's ex while he shopped. But he found a new paint roller and the right screws without meeting anyone else, so he wandered about the store until he heard voices coming from the nursery that leaned against one side of the building.

Sure enough, there was a tall dark-blond man inside. Judging by his T-shirt, which had Ollie's Hardware written across it in red, and by his approximate age, Carter guessed he'd found Keith.

Taking a well-worn dirt path that snaked through the plants, Carter drew closer and listened as Keith spoke to a middle-aged woman and her teenage son. They wanted advice on getting rid of snails in their garden without using pesticides.

Carter paused while Keith answered, using the time to examine a stone birdbath in front of him.

Finally, the teenager hefted a bag of potting soil over his shoulder, and he and his mother headed out of the nursery.

Carter sauntered closer.

"Can I help you find something in particular?" Keith asked.

Carter took in the sharp angles of the other man's face. Keith appeared to be fit and healthy, and Carter guessed most women would find him attractive. But the way his clothes hung on him suggested he'd lost weight recently. Was he depressed? Skipping meals? Experimenting with drugs?

Carter wished he could ignore such details, the way most other people did. But it was the minutiae that made the difference in an investigation. Noticing had become second nature to him. "You're Keith O'Connell?"

Keith's eyebrows shot up. He wasn't wearing a name badge, probably because there wasn't any need for it. In a town this size, most folks would already know who he was. "Have we met?"

"I'm new in Dundee. I work for Senator Holbrook."

"Oh, right." He looked Carter over thoroughly. "I hear you went out with my ex-wife last night."

"I went out with one of them," Carter corrected.

His pointed allusion to Keith's past prompted a tightening about the mouth and a quick retaliation. "Yeah, well, from what I hear, she wasn't very excited about your dinner together."

Keith's dig bothered Carter, and that surprised him. He hadn't cared about anything for a long time. But he'd made no effort to endear himself to Liz and he knew he couldn't expect any better. Anyway, he had no real interest in a woman with emotional baggage. He had too much of his own. "I guess I'm not very good at small talk," he said.

"I can see that," Keith replied. "It's almost as if you came here just to piss me off."

Carter held up the new roller he meant to purchase. "Actually, I came to get a few supplies, too. Otherwise, I couldn't make the improvements at the chocolate shop."

Keith's jaw dropped. "The what?"

"You heard me." Carter suspected he was being too combative. He didn't even know Keith. But since the numbness that set in after Laurel's death had worn off, the darker emotions simmering beneath his skin sometimes got the best of him—especially when he found a target as deserving as a man who'd cheated and lied to the extent that Keith had done.

"Did Liz *ask* for your help?"

"The senator suggested it."

Liz's ex stepped closer, giving Carter the impression he wasn't the type to back down from a fight. "Well, you can forget about it. She doesn't need you. She's got me."

Carter eyed Keith's hands, which had nearly doubled into fists. He waited to see if Keith would take a swing at him, but when Keith made no move, he said, "Evidently it's not happening fast enough."

"I'll get to it."

"No need," Carter said. "The place will be painted before you can get off work."

"That's all you wanted to tell me? That you're helping Liz—and that you can get it done quicker than I can?"

"No. There's one more thing."

Keith's nostrils flared. "What's that?"

"If you're the person who ripped her sink from the wall, you'd better not try that shit again," he said and stalked off.

"Who the hell do you think you are, you arrogant son of a bitch?" Keith called after him.

Carter didn't respond. He'd already made his point. Besides, he wasn't arrogant. He was angry.

CHAPTER FIVE

LIZ WRUNG HER HANDS TOGETHER as she stood at the door of Isaac's classroom, barely able to resist the urge to barge in while he was teaching. She wasn't sure what she expected him to do about their father's unexpected arrival. But she wanted to warn him. Isaac hadn't spoken to Gordon for years, hadn't even bothered with a Christmas card. Liz had encouraged him to do what he could to improve the relationship, but Isaac had no patience for any talk of reconciliation. He couldn't understand how Gordon could have allowed Luanna to do what she'd done to Liz.

To be honest, Liz couldn't understand it, either. Her father had probably been lonely and in love, she told herself. He had needs, too. But Luanna had been downright cruel, at least to Liz. And Gordon hadn't interfered.

At last, the class bell rang, tinny and loud enough to rattle Liz's nerves. Taking a moment to regain her composure, she threaded her way through a crowd of high school students surging past her.

She spotted Isaac sitting on the edge of his desk, wearing a pair of chinos and a blue short-sleeved shirt. He was speaking with a female student. "You're making it more difficult than it has to be," he said calmly. "The number of electrons surrounding the nucleus of an atom is equal to the number of protons inside."

The girl scrunched up her nose. "Always?"

"Always," he replied. "And the number of the element on the periodic chart is the number of protons in that element's nucleus."

She smacked her forehead. "*Now* I get it."

"It's that easy." Catching sight of Liz over the girl's head, Isaac started to get up.

The student grabbed his forearm. "But what do I use to build my model?"

"Anything you want." He gently extricated himself, as if he'd had ample practice slipping out of the clutches of overenthusiastic teenage girls. "That's the fun of it. You can be creative."

"I like this class." The adoration in the student's voice indicated she was far more interested in her handsome teacher than in the subject he taught.

Liz raised her eyebrows at her brother and Isaac blushed. The student's crush obviously embarrassed him. "You'll do fine," he said as he shepherded her to the door. "Model's due on Monday. Don't forget."

The girl cast a jealous glance at Liz before stepping outside. Clearly she wasn't pleased she'd lost her audience with Isaac so soon. If not for her own preoccupation, Liz would've laughed. Isaac handled the attention he received so well. If Liz hadn't witnessed this little scene firsthand, she knew he never would've mentioned it.

"Evidently you have another female admirer," she said when the door clicked shut.

He shrugged as if he'd barely noticed. "The only female admirer I care about these days teaches next door."

Although Isaac wasn't the type to cheat on his wife, especially with a student, he was human and had more opportunity than most men. After what Keith, who'd once seemed equally devoted had done, Liz thought it was probably good Reenie worked so close.

"What's up?" he asked, folding his arms and settling back onto the corner of his desk. "The last time you showed up here, you'd just quit your job and leased a thousand square feet of retail space. I'm almost afraid to hear what's happening next."

"This isn't about the store."

When she didn't crack a smile, he grew serious. "Are Mica and Christopher okay?"

"They're fine. It's…" She cleared her throat "It's Dad."

Isaac stiffened slightly but showed no other emotion. "What about him?"

"He's in town."

He sat perfectly still for several long seconds, then sighed. "Did he call? Stop by? What?"

"I haven't seen him yet. Keith bumped into him at the gas station a couple hours ago."

"I guess it's too much to hope that it was a chance meeting? That he was only passing through?"

"Probably." Liz turned to examine the handmade rockets that covered one table. She didn't want her brother to read the mixed emotions on her face. He was good at remaining aloof, at shutting off whatever he'd once felt for their father. Liz wished she could do the same, or channel her emotions into something simple and all-encompassing, like hate, but she wasn't built that way. "Luanna has left him," she said.

"No kidding." When Isaac added a curse, Liz glanced up. "She would wait until now," he explained. "She probably hung on for so long just to spite us."

Liz toyed with the zipper on her sweatshirt. "What do you think we should do?"

"Ignore him until he goes away, I guess."

"That's not realistic."

"Why not? He ignored us for years. Or he took Luanna's side in every argument."

"She was his wife, Isaac," she said.

Her brother moved toward her. "I don't care. She was in the wrong."

Liz couldn't argue with that. Luanna had constantly found fault with her, even in the beginning when Liz was still trying so hard to please. *How long can it take to do a simple batch of dishes?…I swear you'd forget your head if not for your neck….I don't know what's ever going to become of you….Stupid girl…I'd be humiliated if you were my daughter….*

That voice came to her even now, every once in a while, undermining her confidence. She'd heard a bit more of it than usual since she'd decided to take the risk of starting her own business. But that was between her and Luanna. Isaac wasn't part of it. Or in any case, he didn't have to be.

"I don't want you hating Dad because of me."

"I don't hate him because of you. He's *earned* my derision."

Liz couldn't believe it wasn't because of her. When they were growing up, it had been Isaac who'd tried to protect her. She knew a lot of what he felt had to do with how she'd been treated. "It's in the past."

"He treats you like shit for years and years, and then one day he shows up out of the blue, and you're ready to welcome him with open arms?"

It's in the past was easy to say, but not so easy to act upon. She was nervous, frightened, hopeful—and those were just the emotions she could identify. "I guess I'm willing to give him an audience, and see what he has to say."

"If you think he's come to make you an apology, Liz, I wouldn't get my hopes up. He won't admit he did anything wrong. I've tried talking to him about it before. He says you and Luanna didn't get along. As if the problem could be summed up so simply. As if he had no responsibility in the matter."

"Maybe I wasn't as good a girl as I thought."

Isaac rolled his eyes. "No. I was there, too. You were sweet and innocent and…It wasn't fair."

But Liz must have done *something* to make Luanna target her. Isaac was treated with a mild sort of neglect, but he was never berated. "Okay, say our stepmother was completely to blame and our father let me down—"

"Which is true."

"I'm thirty-two years old." She slipped into the desk in front of him. "I can't hang onto the resentment forever. I have to let go."

"Can you?"

That was the big question. Liz wasn't sure. She hadn't expected to be faced with this decision, not right now and not after so long. Her father hadn't even cared enough to stay in contact with them. So why was he here?

"What if he's willing to be a better grandfather than he was a dad?" she asked instead of answering Isaac's question. "It might be good for Mica and Christopher to know him."

Isaac's long fingers tapped the top of his desk. "And what if Luanna takes him back after a week or two, and things revert to the way they were? How will you feel then?"

Cheated. Betrayed. Like before.

She wasn't up for it, she realized. Not when she had so much going on in her life.

She stood. "You're right. It's not a good time for me. Maybe in a couple years—"

The door opened and a male student sauntered in. Liz knew many more would arrive in a matter of minutes.

"Never mind," she said. "You've got another class coming up. We'll talk about it later."

Isaac followed her to the door. "You can tell him to leave you alone if you want to, Liz. Remember that."

"Right. I'll remember," she said.

"Who, Mr. Russell?" the student asked.

"No one you know," he responded.

The boy's eyes lit up. "Is someone *stalking* your sister?"

Liz noted the kid's black hair, black pants, black T-shirt and black fingernail polish. A quick glance at the cover of his notebook revealed numerous drawings of skeletons, vampires and graveyards.

"Nothing quite so dramatic, Devon," Isaac said with a chuckle. "This is still Dundee, remember?"

"How can I forget?" The boy slumped into a desk in the back row. "I'll die if I don't get back to Detroit soon. I'm tired of watching the grass grow."

"There's always homework."

He slouched even lower. "Yeah, right."

Isaac flashed Liz a smile as he held the door for her. "Call me after he's caught up with you, okay?"

"How do you know he's here to see *me?*" she asked as she stepped outside.

"Because he knows enough not to try and contact me," he replied and waved as a sea of arriving students surrounded him.

"WHAT'S A *CHOCOLATERIE?*"

Carter paused from painting long enough to look down at the unshaven but well-dressed man. Liz's father, who'd identified himself as Gordon Russell, had his arms crossed over a lightweight V-necked sweater and stood gazing out the front window. He'd appeared almost as soon as Carter had returned from the hardware store. Since then, he'd asked several questions about Liz— where she was, how he could reach her, where she lived.

Carter didn't have any of that information. But he probably wouldn't have shared it even if he did. His background occasionally made him too secretive, he knew, but he found it pretty strange that a father wouldn't be more familiar with his own daughter.

"Evidently, it's a chocolate shop," he said, focusing on his work.

The man's expensive Italian loafers made barely any sound as he wandered over and stood beside the ladder. "Why doesn't she just call it that?"

Carter reloaded the paint on his roller. He remembered what Liz had said about the movie, and he liked the idea. But Russell's condescending attitude made him undeserving of an explanation. "I guess she doesn't want to."

At the coolness of his response, Liz's father propped his hands on his hips, splaying well-manicured fingers—one of which sported a large diamond. Either he had money or he liked to pretend he did. Carter was betting on the latter.

"Who did you say you are?" Russell asked.

"A friend of a friend," Carter responded.

"So you know Keith?"

"Not really."

"In a town this size?"

"I'm new."

Russell had to be nearing sixty, but the years had been kind to him. If not for the crow's feet at his eyes and the subtle lines around his mouth, he could easily pass for ten, maybe fifteen years younger. He certainly took care of himself. Judging by his muscular physique, he worked out often. And he went to the added trouble of coloring his hair. It stuck up a bit as if he hadn't showered after rolling out of bed this morning, but it was completely brown, without any hint of gray.

"How well do you know Liz?" he asked.

"Not very well," Carter admitted.

"You two aren't dating, are you?"

Russell said it as if he wouldn't be pleased to see his daughter fall for a mere painter. Carter took exception to the implication but refused to reveal how much it bugged him. "No, we're not dating." He didn't bother to explain that they'd had dinner together last night. One evening didn't qualify.

Liz's father consulted the thin gold watch at his wrist.

Carter sensed that his visitor was growing impatient, but Russell didn't leave. He walked into the back rooms, poked around, used the restroom.

"Maybe I should go back to the diner down the street," he said when he returned. "The waitress who told me Liz would be here might be able to give me directions to her house."

"Probably," Carter said. "But I don't think your daughter went home."

"There're only so many places she could be in this Podunk town." With one foot, he tapped the wrapper of Carter's new roller. "To be honest, I don't know how you stand it."

"It has its benefits," Carter said.

Russell didn't appear to be convinced. "Really?"

"Sure. Depends on what you're looking for, right?"

"What are *you* looking for?"

Carter needed the space. He'd lost the idealism that had once characterized him so strongly—the belief that good would eventually prevail. Because of that, he didn't have the patience he'd once possessed, the kindness, the diplomacy or the understanding. Hell, he didn't even have the *desire* to be close to anyone.

Charles Hooper, who was now spending the rest of his life in prison, had seen to that.

"A crab feed on the front page of the newspaper," he mumbled.

"Did you say *crab feed?*" The deep grooves in Russell's forehead revealed his confusion at such an answer, but he didn't have time to question Carter further. The door swung open and Liz walked in.

"Sorry that took so—"

Her words trailed off as soon as she saw her father.

"Surprise!" Crossing over to her, Russell swept her into his arms.

Liz didn't push away, but neither did she respond to the embrace. She tolerated it—at least that was Carter's interpretation.

"Keith told me he saw you in town," she said, her voice breathless and wispy.

"Can you believe it?" Russell's response was a little too loud to sound completely natural. "Me, all the way out here? I'm already going nuts without a Starbucks on one corner and a golf course on the other. What made you move to the boonies?"

He acted as if Liz's relocation was something that had just happened. But Carter was fairly certain she'd been living in Dundee for over a year. Maybe two.

"I like it here," she said simply.

She didn't mention what Keith had done to her—that she'd only come because of her children. Anyone even remotely connected to her knew about *that* scandal. So how was it her father didn't?

"To each his own, I guess." He waved toward Carter.

"Your painter wants a crab feed on the front page of the paper. He doesn't ask for much, eh?"

Liz offered Carter a quick, apologetic smile. "He's not my painter."

"No?"

"He works for Senator Holbrook. He's just helping me out."

"There's a senator in the area?" Russell said. Obviously that was the part that impressed him most.

"A *state* senator," Liz clarified. "He's Isaac's father-in-law."

At the mention of Isaac, there was a strained silence, but Russell's pleasant expression remained stubbornly in place. "Isaac married, huh?"

"Yes. A year ago."

"Good for him. Sounds like it's about time I came out. We've got a lot of catching up to do."

Liz clutched her purse to her side. She hadn't taken a single step from where she'd been when her father had hugged her. "Where are you staying?"

"I'm not sure," he said. "Is there a motel around here?"

Liz's father must've passed the Timberline on his way through town. Carter guessed he was hinting—hoping Liz would put him up.

"There is," she said. "But..."

"The Timberline's only sixty-five bucks a night," Carter volunteered.

Russell blinked at him, but Liz made the offer anyway. "I guess you could stay with me. For a few days," she added quickly.

Carter shook his head. He couldn't protect people from themselves. He'd learned that the hard way.

"A few days ought to be enough," Gordon said. "I'm just here to meet those kids of yours."

Had this guy been out of the country? Carter wondered. Liz's children had to be six and nine, at least. Maybe older.

"Right," she said, but she seemed more confused than anything, and immediately launched into a series of questions. "So you're retired now? You've sold your law practice or…or closed it down?"

"I sold out to my two partners, coupla years ago. Got a good price, too. It's nothing but traveling and golf for me. A whole new life."

"And Luanna?" Liz asked.

A shadow fell over Russell's face. Carter told himself to keep painting, that the scene unfolding beside him was none of his business. But he hadn't felt so much tension crackling in the air since he'd arrived in Dundee. He slowed his paint strokes so he could hear clearly over the spin of his roller.

"We split up."

"Does that mean it's over? For good?"

"That's right. She's too difficult to live with." He grinned conspiratorially. "You of all people should know that."

Liz didn't answer, but Carter got the impression she had plenty to say.

Her father clapped his hands, obviously eager to put the subject behind them. "So what should I do with my bags?"

Liz looked at Carter. When he saw the uncertainty in her eyes, he couldn't help getting involved again.

"You might prefer to stay at the Running Y," he said. "It's a nice resort. They have eighteen holes out there. Hunting. Fishing. Horseback riding. Scenery's beautiful."

Liz turned expectantly to her father. But he shook his head. "That's okay. No need to waste good money when I've got family in town, eh?"

The knuckles of Liz's fingers grew white on her purse. "Right," she said. "Well…in that case, why don't you follow me over to the house?"

"Sounds good. Nice meeting you," he added, but Carter could tell he didn't mean a word of it.

"Same here," Carter replied, equally insincere.

Liz's polite smile disappeared as soon as her father moved ahead and could no longer see her face. Her chest lifted, as if she was attempting to summon more strength, then she began to follow him. But as the door swung shut behind Russell, Carter reached over and managed to catch a piece of her sweatshirt.

"What are you doing?" he asked, keeping his voice low.

He thought she'd tell him to mind his own business. She definitely had reason to. But she didn't. "I have absolutely no idea," she murmured, shaking her head.

"Maybe you should rethink this one."

"How can I?" she said. "He's my father."

Carter frowned as he watched her go, wishing she'd let him take control of the situation. But then he cursed himself. Why did *he* care? Maybe blocking his emotions made him more of a robot than a man, but at least he could still function.

Drawing in a deep breath, he returned to his work. Mr. Russell's appearance wasn't a life-or-death situation, certainly nothing like what Carter had faced in the past. He had no moral responsibility in this, and he could safely go on with his day as if the situation didn't exist.

But Russell's arrival seemed pretty catastrophic to Liz.

CHAPTER SIX

LIZ WALKED STIFFLY through the four-bedroom house she rented on a month-to-month basis. When she first moved from the Holbrooks' neighborhood, she'd considered purchasing. But buying a house had felt far too permanent. She was staying in Dundee for her children's sake, but she was comforted by the knowledge that she could escape with relative ease if she wanted to. Maybe that was what made Dave's calls so titillating. There was always the possibility she could pick up and go. That was true, even with the store, since she'd signed only a six-month lease.

Of course, she'd lose her initial investment, which was significant. But that was another story. She had an out, if she needed one.

"So…how long have you been living *here?*" her father asked.

Liz cringed at the subtle emphasis he placed on the final word. Her father had always cared so much about appearances. Seeing the old ranch house through his eyes embarrassed her, made her wish she'd been more successful in life. She'd had a nice home in L.A. She'd had a happy marriage, or so she'd thought; elegant clothes and jewelry, an expensive car, even a club membership that enabled her to play tennis three or four days a week. Her father would have been impressed.

But he hadn't bothered to come around then. He'd waited until she'd been stripped of almost everything, even her pride. "About six months."

"Do you own or…"

"I rent." She opened the linen closet in the hallway and grabbed a fresh batch of sheets. Although the house had four bedrooms, only three were furnished, so she'd have to put Christopher on the couch and give her father his room.

"Where does Isaac live?" he asked.

"On the other side of town, a little farther out. He and Reenie own a small farm."

"They have animals?"

"A couple of horses, a pig that Jennifer's raising—"

"I thought his wife's name was Reenie."

"Jennifer's one of Isaac's stepdaughters."

"How many does he have?"

"Three. Jennifer's eleven, Angela's nine and Isabella's seven."

"Any children of his own?"

"Not yet."

Her father acted as if he had more to say, but the pictures on the wall caught his attention. He stopped, and Liz turned to see him staring at a photograph of her mother.

"Where'd you get this?" he asked.

Luanna hadn't allowed any sign of Chloe Russell in her house. On the night Liz had run away, she'd gone to the attic to find this photograph in the boxes containing her mother's belongings. "I took it when I moved out."

She wondered if that admission would bring up the past, if her father would finally ask her why she'd left. But he didn't. He pulled his gaze away from Chloe's pretty face and smiled expectantly, as if he was ready to see his room.

Didn't he get it? Liz wondered. Didn't he realize they'd lost far more than a wonderful wife and mother? More than they'd needed to lose?

If he understood, he gave no indication. "I've got to get back to the store and help with the painting," she said, sliding some of Chris's LEGO creations out of the way so her father could wheel his luggage into the room. "And I've got to go by the police station on my way."

"What do you have to do at the police station?"

"File a report. Someone tore the sink out of a wall at the store."

"I saw that."

"It was probably a random one-time occurrence and nothing I can do much about. But I figure I should report it, just in case."

"That's a good idea."

"Why not grab a nap here while I'm gone or—" she wasn't sure what he'd do, why he'd even come "—or take a look around town, if you're up to it."

"Where are the kids?"

"They don't get out of school until three."

"And Isaac?"

Liz had started changing the bedding. Hesitating, she glanced at her father. The way he'd said her brother's name made her wonder if Isaac was the real goal.

Or was that jealousy talking?

She was tempted to tell him Isaac didn't even want to see him. But loyalty to her brother wouldn't allow it. She could see why Gordon loved Isaac. Everyone loved Isaac. Especially Liz. "He teaches science at the high school."

"Maybe I'll go by there."

"It might be hard to talk to him while he's in class."

"When will he be out?"

She finished making the bed. "He has a prep hour at one," she said, hoping to save Isaac the embarrassment of having to react to the sudden appearance of his father in front of a room full of students.

"I guess I can wait a couple hours."

Why not? Liz wanted to snap back. *You've already waited* years.

"Towels are in the bathroom," she said. "There's plenty of food in the kitchen." At least she hoped there was. She'd been so busy with the new store that she hadn't kept up with the shopping as well as she normally did.

"Thanks," he said. "Do you have any plans for dinner?"

"I promised the kids we'd have pizza at the shop tonight. I'll be working late."

"When do you open?"

"I'm shooting for next weekend. Now that I have Carter, that might actually happen. He seems to know what he's doing, even if I don't."

"Maybe I'll stop by later and lend a hand."

"Sure," she said. "If you want."

"Great."

She stalled a moment longer. It was awkward, leaving her father alone in the house. Especially when she hadn't seen him for more than a decade. But she had so much to do. She was beginning to feel extremely guilty for abandoning Carter while she ran around taking care of her personal problems.

"Okay, I'd better go," she said.

He nodded. "I'll see you this afternoon."

He'd see her this afternoon.... He stated it so casually. For years she'd doubted they'd ever speak again. Yet suddenly he was staying with her. And the strange thing was, deep down she was happier about his presence than she'd ever dreamed she would be.

NOW THE CREAK OF HIS OWN footsteps was the only sound as Gordon Russell returned to the hall. Chloe's picture drew him close, the one that used to grace his desk until he'd remarried.

Chloe had been a beautiful woman. Prettier than Luanna. More refined. But weaker, too.

He sighed, telling himself to turn away. He'd been driving for eighteen hours. He needed some sleep.

Yet he remained transfixed.

When he looked at his first wife, he felt so much. Pain. Loss. Betrayal. Regret. Admiration. He'd spent years trying to forget what he'd learned two weeks after she'd died. He flinched with the memory of it even now—and yet the truth resonated through every cell of his body. He believed it; he had believed from the beginning.

Was it time to tell the truth? To lay out all the secrets of the past?

He wasn't sure. Especially because he doubted it would make a difference. Chloe was gone. She couldn't do anything by way of atonement. He couldn't even hear her side of the story.

"SO WHY DID YOU DO IT?" Carter asked above the song playing on a small, battery-powered radio that sat in the corner.

Liz kept her paintbrush moving. She knew what he was referring to, but she didn't want to admit it. Except for the music on the radio, they'd been working together in silence for almost thirty minutes. She didn't see why that pattern shouldn't continue.

"I don't know what you mean."

The masking tape screeched as Carter ripped off a long strand. "Yes, you do."

"I already told you. He's my father. I couldn't turn him away."

He fixed tape to the windowsill to protect Liz's white trim from the darker cranberry they were using on the walls. "You wanted to."

That wasn't entirely true. Liz was afraid to let down her guard. She didn't need to be disappointed again. But she'd meant what she'd said to Isaac. She was thirty-two years old. If she wasn't going to forgive Gordon now, when would she? When she was forty? Fifty? Never? What good would it do to carry a grudge?

"My mother's death couldn't have been easy on him, either," she said.

He finished taping the window. "How long has it been since she passed?"

"They discovered her heart problems when I was thirteen. Then, she had a heart attack and died when I was fourteen."

Most people said, "I'm sorry to hear that," or offered some other words of condolence. Carter made no comment. At least for several seconds. Then he said, "I'd tend to think that would make you and your father draw closer."

"No, he changed." She remembered how quickly he'd withdrawn from her, how the love he'd always lavished on her had dried up like a shallow puddle beneath a burning sun. Because she was the family baby, she'd always secretly believed she might be his favorite. But it was Isaac who'd become his favorite after that. She'd often wondered if it was that she reminded him too much of Chloe.

"It was as if they both died," she went on. "And then he married Luanna." She toyed with the paint in her pan, watching rich-looking cranberry drip from her brush.

"You had an evil stepmother?"

Straightening her shoulders, she went back to work. "I did. But that happens to a lot of kids. So who am I to feel singled out?"

"Having a mean stepmother isn't what makes you different," Carter replied. She could hear him moving around as she continued to paint. "It's the fact that your father hasn't met your children that seems a bit odd to me."

It seemed odd to her, too. How could Gordon have let her go so easily? Her own children meant the world to her. "Can we talk about something else?" she asked.

"Like what?" He moved his ladder to the wall with the window.

"I don't know. You, I guess."

He turned up the radio. But she wouldn't let him put her off that easily.

"What was it like growing up in Brooklyn?" she asked.

"Not so bad."

"You weren't particularly poor?"

"I don't have any sad stories about my childhood. My father was an electrician, but he owned his own business and did quite well. We were definitely middle class."

"What did you do before you came here?"

When he pretended not to hear her, she lowered her arm to let the blood flow back into it, walked over and turned down the radio again. "I wouldn't expect that to be a difficult question."

His eyes flicked her way, the light-brown irises contrasting markedly with the darkness of his hair and the olive tone of his skin. "A little bit of everything."

"So you didn't have a specific profession?"

His roller began to squeak, as if he'd increased the pressure. "I didn't say that."

"You didn't name one."

"No, I didn't."

Obviously he didn't plan to, either.

She went back to painting a section of the wall she'd left half-finished, but curiosity got the better of her earlier reticence. "Does your family still live in Brooklyn?"

"No."

"Where are they now?"

"I have a younger sister in upstate New York, on a dairy farm. My older sister married money and lives on a large estate in the Hamptons."

"And your parents?"

"My mother recently sold her house and moved into a cottage on my sister's estate."

"Sounds very English," she said. "Are your parents divorced, then?"

"My father died in a scuba-diving accident when he was sixty-four."

Several drops of paint fell from Liz's brush. She jerked back to avoid getting any on her clothes and in the process nearly fell off her ladder. "I'm sorry to hear that," she said when she was sufficiently recovered. "How old were you when you lost him?"

With one eyebrow cocked, he'd watched her teeter. "If you ever have to make that decision again, choose the paint."

"What?"

"When you're weighing things in the balance. A drop of paint on your shorts or a broken arm. Choose the paint."

She made a face at him. "It was an instinctive reaction, okay?"

"That's what worries me. Some people can't seem to avoid getting hurt."

"I'm not one of them."

"I'm betting you are."

She gaped at him. "You're not always very nice, you know that?"

He seemed unconcerned about her accusation. "Because I'm telling you not to break your fool neck?"

"Call me sensitive, but I think it's the 'fool' part I find objectionable."

When he chuckled and didn't say anything, she shook her head. His responses always ran opposite to what she expected, to what she'd get from any other guy. She thought they were arguing, when actually he was enjoying himself.

"Have you always had such a big chip on your shoulder?" she asked.

"Chip? What chip?"

From the amusement in his voice, he knew it existed, but she let it go and repeated her earlier question. "How old were you when your father died?"

"My father has nothing to do with the chip on my shoulder."

"The one that doesn't exist?"

"Exactly."

"So you were older."

"Twenty-one." He gave her a pointed look. "Any chance you'd like to listen to the radio now?"

"Not yet."

His ladder creaked as he shifted his weight, and she thought she heard him murmur something about Pandora's box. But she didn't care. He was the one who scorned meaningless small talk. That opened him up to almost any query. "Do you have children?"

No response.

"A little boy? Maybe a girl, as well?"

"Did I bring any children to town?" he asked.

"They could be with their mother."

"You were certain, at the restaurant, that I've never been married."

"Some men have children without ever marrying."

"Not me."

She considered his answer. "That's admirable, at least."

"Glad you approve."

He didn't give a damn whether she approved or not, and she knew it. "Why won't you tell me what you did before returning to politics?"

No response.

"Are you being secretive on purpose?"

"What do you think?" he asked.

"I think so. Definitely. And that makes me ask why? Why are you so guarded about your past?"

His eyebrows gathered into a glower and he swiveled to face her. "Forget about it."

She grinned at the strength of his accent as he uttered that classic Brooklyn pronouncement. "Perhaps you're beginning to reconsider your low opinion of polite conversation," she said sweetly.

He moved his ladder, to start another section of wall. "Not really."

"Good. Because you've made a believer out of me."

His gaze slid her way. "I'm happy to hear you're experiencing some personal growth."

"Thank you. I have a few more questions."

"Ask what you want," he said. "I can't promise I'll answer."

He'd already proven the truth of that statement.

She eyed his dark hair and skin, the beard growth that already shadowed his jaw. "What's the big secret?"

"I don't know what you're talking about."

"What happened between growing up in Brooklyn in

a middle-class family and winding up in Dundee to run a campaign?"

"Nothing."

"That's a ten- to thirteen-year gap. Were you part of the mafia?"

She was teasing, of course, but he seemed to take the question at face value.

"No."

"You could pass for Italian," she said, still speculating.

"My mother's Greek."

"That would explain your coloring." She addressed a section of the prepped wall where the masking tape was peeling away from the molding. "Okay…maybe you don't have a past, at least one that you can talk about. Are you in the witness protection program?"

"Wrong again."

"That was still a good guess."

He balanced his tray on top of his ladder and descended. "Why don't you tell me something?"

"What's that?"

"Why would your ex-husband want to tear the sink from the wall?" he asked, bending to retrieve a jug of water he'd brought in from his truck an hour or so earlier.

She stepped back to admire their progress. "Because he doesn't want me to succeed?"

He opened the spigot on his Thermos. "You don't sound completely convinced."

"I'm not. A friend of mine mentioned it, that's all. He was guessing Keith wouldn't want me to make it on my own because it'd diminish the odds of me taking him back."

When he'd finished drinking, Carter set the Thermos back on the ground. "Your ex hopes to reconcile?"

"Now that Reenie's off the market, he acts quite sincere about how much he loves me."

He wiped his hands on his jeans, which hugged him in all the right places. "What're the chances?"

"Not very good."

A slow smile curved his lips. "Maybe you're smarter than I thought."

"That's supposed to be a compliment?"

"Coming from me." He climbed back onto his ladder. The view of his washed-out denims was even better from behind. Since she didn't really like Carter, since he wasn't a threat to her, Liz let herself enjoy the view. "Keith isn't the type to be vindictive."

He turned and caught her admiring him. Recognition sparked in his eyes, making her believe he might call her on it. But he didn't. "Who else might've had a motive?"

She quickly anchored her attention to the wall in front of her. For not liking him, he was having a strange effect on her. "Motive? You make it sound like there's been a murder."

"Okay, let me put it another way. Who'd want to set you back?"

"Keith thinks it's Mary Thornton."

"Who's that?"

"She owns the shop next door. She pokes her head in almost every day, just to take note of my progress and secretly wish me bad luck." Liz stretched her back, which was beginning to ache. "I'm sure you'll meet her soon enough."

His paint roller made a continuous *warp, warp, warp* sound. "Why would she vandalize your property?"

"It's a long story."

"I think we've got time."

He was right. According to her watch, the kids wouldn't be out of school for another two hours. Besides, she was suddenly far too aware of him and she needed a distraction. "Two months ago, just before Mary opened her shop, she intended to sell cards and gifts. She was very excited about her plans and told anyone who would listen exactly what the business would be like. Then word got out that I was going to open a chocolate shop, and Mary was so afraid I'd hit on something better that she started selling candy along with those cards and gifts, including a whole range of truffles and chocolates."

"I can see where she might be unhappy about you copying her," he said.

Liz's jaw dropped, but a flash of straight white teeth told her Carter was joking.

Rolling her eyes, she slid her paintbrush carefully along the edge of the tape that protected the molding. As contrary as Carter could be, she was beginning to find him a *little* appealing. That smile…It was rare enough to make her feel as if the sun had just come out.

So he had a sort of dark allure, she told herself. Maybe she got that now. But it was like the beckoning call of craggy rocks at the bottom of a high cliff. A woman would have to be crazy to get involved with a man like him.

And yet she could almost understand the temptation….

"What is it?" he asked when he realized Liz was staring at him again.

"I was thinking."

"About…"

"Have you ever heard of that book, *Men Who Hate Women and the Women Who Love Them?*"

His expression revealed his doubts about this most recent shift in conversation. "No. But I can imagine what's inside. What brings that up?"

She'd read it, wondering if she might find some key to understanding her father's behavior. She'd decided the definition didn't apply to her dad, but Carter seemed like a possible candidate. "I'm wondering if you're the type."

"To hate women?"

"Yes."

He shook his head. "Let me save you the guess-work. I'm not."

"You could be," she mused, pursing her lips as she studied him. He was brooding, bitter. He didn't go out of his way to attract female attention and he barely responded to a friendly word or gesture. He said and did exactly as he pleased, as if he longed to tell the whole world to go to hell—

"I don't hate women," he snapped, as if he could read her mind. "The rest of my family consists of three females."

"Your mother and sisters don't count," she replied. "In any case, I just realized something else."

"Do I want to hear it?" he asked with a scowl.

She told him, whether he did or not. "You weren't coming on to me last night."

He straightened, still on the first step of his ladder. "You thought I was?"

"I thought perhaps you were hoping to get lucky. But now that I know you better, I can see you weren't really interested."

She could tell he didn't quite know how to take her frank appraisal of the situation. "I'm not sure I'd go that far," he admitted.

A strange sort of energy hummed in the room. Liz could feel it. Whether she wanted to acknowledge it was another story entirely. "You didn't even try to make me like you."

No response. She imagined he was tired of the conversation, but when she turned, she discovered him looking at her legs. "I would've taken you home, had you asked nicely," he said.

"*Asked?*" she scoffed. But she couldn't deny that the tension level in the room had just edged up another notch.

He produced a crooked grin. "I'm not opposed to providing a lonely divorcée with a little pleasure."

Now it was getting *very* warm, and Liz's heart was beginning to hammer against her chest. "Who says I'm lonely?" she asked, trying to appear nonchalant as she stripped off her sweatshirt.

"You're not?"

A denial hovered on her lips but in the end she didn't see any point in pretending. With Carter, she didn't have to be anyone other than who she was. She didn't even have to be polite. Just herself. Real. Honest. Like him. "Okay, maybe I am," she admitted.

His grin turned slightly wolfish. "Let me know if it gets to be too much for you."

With that he reached for his roller. But when Liz stood as though transfixed, actually contemplating the possibilities, he hesitated. "I guess you're lonelier than I thought," he said, his smile disappearing in favor of heightened interest.

Liz's heart pounded faster. She remembered what it was like to have a man's hands on her body, what it was like to be a woman instead of only a mother. For the briefest moment, she was tempted to admit that the life she'd been living for the past eighteen months was already too much for her.

What would happen if she gave the word? Would he take her here, on the floor? Would it be the hot, sweaty, whirlwind kind of sex she'd always been too inhibited to experience?

His gaze fell to her breasts, the tips of which tingled as if he were already touching her. Maybe if she let him satisfy the terrible craving welling up inside her, she could keep her life in perspective, look at Dave and her other options more objectively.

At this moment, the notion of a one-night stand, which she'd held in such contempt the night before, seemed like the perfect solution. She and Carter had nothing in common, nothing except the inexplicable crazy-hot desire curling through her veins like smoke. So...

"No strings attached?" she whispered, thinking of her children.

"No strings attached," he promised.

She anticipated the satisfying weight of his body. "And no one else would ever have to know?"

"Who would I tell?"

Carter wasn't the type to brag. She knew that instinctively. He wouldn't even be around all that long. They could lock the doors and the next fifteen minutes would cost her nothing, not even the threat of ruining a good friendship.

"Do you have birth control?" she asked, almost unable to recognize her own voice.

His eyes widened, as if he hadn't really expected her to capitulate. "No."

Then it could cost her something, after all. More than she was willing to pay.

She drew a deep, steadying breath. "I'll keep your offer in mind," she said and turned away.

CARTER COULD NO LONGER concentrate. He went back to painting, but he was only going through the motions. He wasn't even sure he was covering new space. All he could think about was what might have happened a few seconds earlier had he been better prepared.

He'd gone nearly two years with barely a thought about sex, hadn't touched a woman since Laurel.

And then this. Why?

Liz's footsteps crossed to the bathroom, but Carter refused to let his gaze trail after her. He knew what would show on his face. He longed to lose himself in the mind-numbing frenzy she offered him—yearned for the release, the escape, no matter how temporary.

Even when Liz left the room, he could pick up the

scent of her perfume. He'd barely noticed it an hour
before; but now he could smell nothing else.

The bathroom door shut, and she reappeared. When
her ladder creaked, Carter took a quick glance over his
shoulder, then forced himself to turn immediately back.

"I'll buy condoms tonight, in case you change your
mind," he said.

CARTER TRIED TO IGNORE the animated conversation taking
place in the back rooms of the chocolate shop and keep
to his painting. But he was still grappling with a surplus
of testosterone. And the brief snatches he happened to
hear between Liz and Reenie Russell made him even
more curious about Liz's relationship with her father.

*At the school?...He just left....How did Isaac treat
him?...Wouldn't even speak to him. What did you expect?...I thought he might soften....I'm not sure he ever
will...Was it terribly awkward?...Are you kidding? I
almost felt sorry for him....People make mistakes,
Reenie....Mistakes that last eighteen years?...Maybe
he had his reasons....How can you justify that? Where
was he when you needed him? And now you're laying
your heart out there again. I don't want to see you
hurt....I'll be fine....That's what you say, but Isaac's
worried. He doesn't know whether to send him packing
or let you handle this on your own....I'm an adult. It's
my decision.*

Obviously, Liz's brother didn't get along with
Gordon Russell any better than Liz did. And he wasn't
happy to hear that Liz was harboring the enemy.

"As long as you're okay...." Reenie said, her voice

growing louder as she started to walk toward the front room.

"I'm fine," Liz insisted, trailing after her.

"I've got to run. The girls are going home with a friend so Isaac and I can tutor a few students today. I just couldn't wait any longer to talk to you."

"I appreciate the support, Reenie," Liz said. "Really. But…"

Reenie slowed and let Liz catch up with her. "What?"

"Tell Isaac I want to give Dad a chance. I have to. Just in case."

"I'll tell him," Reenie said with a sigh.

"Now that Luanna's finally out of the picture, maybe Isaac will be able to forgive Dad, too. Eventually."

"I doubt it. Not after so long."

"He sent me a Christmas card two years ago, with some money in it for the kids," Liz said, as if that somehow redeemed her father completely.

"Didn't you send him a card first?"

Liz didn't reply.

"See?" Reenie hesitated at the door. "I'm afraid he's here only because his wife left him. I have no respect for that."

"Neither do I," Liz admitted. "And yet…" She nibbled at her bottom lip. "Never mind."

"Say it," Reenie prompted.

"Maybe this will be the beginning of something good. Our relationship was…interrupted somehow, like a power line someone cut. I can't help wanting what we used to have."

"Someone did sever your relationship. Luanna. And

your father made no attempt to stop it, which is just as bad as cutting you off himself. He married another woman and then failed to stand by his own child."

Liz pushed around the dust on the floor with one foot. "Occasionally I wonder if there wasn't some other element at play."

"Like what?"

"I don't know. But sometimes he looked at me so strangely, almost as if the sight of me caused him pain."

"Don't create excuses for him. He was selfish, pure and simple."

Personally, Carter agreed with Reenie. What had happened to Liz happened all too frequently, as she'd said. But he had something more immediate and personally threatening on his mind: he didn't want to see her get hurt. Despite his efforts to remain detached and aloof, he already cared about her.

How? Why? When? He'd only met her the night before!

"Hell no," he muttered to himself, and picked up the pace of his painting. He could finish the improvements to the store in a matter of days. Then he wouldn't have to witness the continuing drama in Liz's life, wouldn't run the risk of getting involved emotionally. She had been fine before he'd come to Dundee; she'd be fine after he left.

What was that old cliché? A rolling stone gathers no moss? As much as it betrayed everything he'd once believed, everything he'd ever tried to do, he was now a rolling stone....

Life sometimes did that to a person. But he'd never dreamed it would happen to him.

CHAPTER SEVEN

CARTER WAS REMOTE after Reenie left, but Liz didn't try to draw him out. What had passed between them was daring enough to be a little frightening. It had come out of nowhere—and had sparked and flared in about the same amount of time it would have taken to light a match.

Liz had never had such a strong reaction to someone who was almost a complete stranger. But she didn't want to dwell on it. If she did, then she'd probably have to acknowledge that she still felt like melted butter inside. And that the idea of no expectations, no obligations appealed to her far more than she thought it should. She wanted to experience what she'd been missing for so long, to believe she was still the same vibrant, whole person she'd been while she was happily married and not "second choice" for the rest of her life.

People pass in and out of other people's lives every day. You never know what you might learn from someone, how a particular person can enrich your experience, even if they don't become a permanent fixture. He'd said that at the restaurant. Why did it sound so much better today?

Liz considered the weekend ahead of her, now that her father was in town. Maybe a bit of fantasy would provide an escape....

She watched Carter through her lashes as he tilted the paint can to refill his tray, imagining how his short, thick hair might feel between her fingers.

"You stare at me that way much longer, and I won't have time to get to a drugstore," he said without looking back at her.

Embarrassed by her own transparency, Liz's first impulse was to blush furiously and dive back into her work. But this was Carter. He didn't play by the rules and that meant she didn't have to, either.

Lifting her chin, she gave him a challenging smile. "There's one right down the street."

His eyes locked on hers. Had she really said that out loud?

Dropping his roller in the tray, he strode over to her. She nearly backed into the freshly painted wall in her effort to keep some distance between them, but he didn't pause until he was mere inches away. "Don't say something that provocative unless you mean it."

She'd meant it. At least, part of her had. She could easily imagine how good he'd be with his hands. There was a deft efficiency to everything he did.

But the other part of her couldn't ignore the reality of her situation. She was over thirty. She was divorced. She was the mother of two children. She'd only slept with three men in her whole life—her high-school boyfriend, Keith and Dave. She'd be crazy to ask for trouble by becoming intimately involved with a virtual stranger.

"Sorry," she said, deciding, at the last moment, to play it safe.

His eyes focused on her mouth, as if he was tempted

to see what she might do if he tried to kiss her. She hoped he would. She only needed the smallest excuse in order to let go of the caution that was holding her back.

She suspected he understood that, and yet he wouldn't exploit it. "Let me know when you're ready," he said, and returned to his side of the room.

Following that close encounter, Liz didn't dare look at him. She was intensely aware of every move he made, of all the things being said without words. But she was careful not to provoke him into crossing the tenuous line between them.

When she realized how quickly they were completing work that had seemed so daunting before, however, she couldn't help breaking the silence long enough to thank him. They'd already finished the front of the store and had started working on the kitchen and pantry. "It's really good of you to help me," she said over the noise of his hammering as he nailed a piece of baseboard to the wall. "I appreciate it."

"No problem."

His response was clipped, but Liz didn't let that bother her. The shop was taking shape exactly as she'd envisioned it. "You're obviously a good carpenter. Do you think you'll ever build houses again?"

"No."

That was it. No explanation. No reference to their earlier conversation. No acknowledgment of the suppressed desire that hung in the air as thick as the melted chocolate that would soon fill her new vat.

As Carter switched on the saw to cut another length of baseboard, Liz told herself his self-control was a good thing. Maybe it wasn't too late to master whatever it was that had come over her.

She checked her watch: it was two-thirty, and she was hungry. Carter had to be famished, as well. He hadn't stopped working since he'd arrived.

"You ready for lunch?" she asked.

"Maybe in a few minutes."

He was obviously someone who finished whatever task he set himself. No excuses. No wimping out. Liz found this extremely appealing. Keith had said he'd make the improvements, but the night before was the first time he'd tried to accomplish anything at the shop. More often than not, he'd excused himself for one reason or another. "Breaks are allowed, you know."

Carter hammered the new baseboard into place. "I know."

"I'll buy a pizza while I'm out. What kind would you like?"

"Don't worry about me. I'll fend for myself."

"I'm picking up the kids. I have to feed them anyway. Besides, it's the least I can do in return for all your help."

As he stretched to reach into the corner, the muscles of his arms and shoulders strained against his T-shirt and Liz's mouth went dry.

"Whatever you bring will be fine," he said, as the whine of the saw shattered the air again.

"I might be in trouble," she muttered as she headed out, trying to convince herself she preferred a leaner build than Carter's. She'd thought so just a day ago. But at the moment, even Dave's body paled in comparison.

The door opened just as Liz reached it, and Mary Thornton strode in as if she owned the place. She was wearing the same kind of business suits she'd worn when she'd worked at the law office. She'd always prided herself on her professional attire. But her smile was as artificial as her nails. "How's the work coming along?" she shouted above the racket.

Liz tried not to grimace at this unwanted intrusion. "Fine, thanks for asking. But I'm on my way out."

"I won't stay long." Mary turned to inspect the new paint. Then the saw fell silent and she angled her head to see who'd been running it. "Who's here with you?"

At the sound of their voices, Carter ducked his head into the open doorway.

"This is Carter Hudson, Senator Holbrook's new aide," Liz explained. "Maybe you've met him."

"No, but I've noticed him driving around town." Mary said this as if she'd marked those occasions well. But Mary being Mary, Liz wasn't sure if she was impressed with Carter or with his car. In any case, Carter was no longer visible. He'd gone back to sawing and hammering without so much as a word of greeting.

Perhaps the fact that he hadn't spoken to Mary was rude, but Liz was slightly gratified. Mary tried to win the heart of every single man she encountered, although she'd risk her own on only a sparse few—chiefly those with thick enough wallets.

When Mary glared in the direction of the sawing, Liz knew she'd expected a warmer reception. "Friendly, isn't he?" she said.

The saw stopped as abruptly as it had started, but Liz

spoke up anyway. "Blunt trauma to the head will do that to a person."

Mary's mouth formed an O. "He's been in an accident?"

"That's my guess," Liz whispered loudly. "He's not telling."

Carter reappeared in the opening, his scowl indicating he'd heard at least part of the conversation.

Liz gave him a sweet smile, then turned her back on him. Doing and saying exactly what she pleased had its benefits. She wasn't sure it'd save her from spending the night with him. Now that certain statements had been made, she couldn't seem to think of anything else. But she felt more liberated than she had in a long while. That was some consolation. "What can I do for you, Mary?" she asked.

"I came to get your e-mail address."

"It's Liz@chocolaterie.com. Why?"

"I was hoping we could go in together on a newspaper ad or maybe some other promotional ideas, and I wanted to send you the details. Will you be open next weekend for Memorial Day?"

Liz remembered the torn-out sink. Mary wasn't happy about competition from The Chocolaterie. Liz had known that for some time. But had she stooped to vandalism? "It's possible," she said.

"You don't know?"

"I've run into a few problems that might delay my schedule."

"Like what?" Mary threw back her shoulders and Liz suspected she was trying to give Carter an excellent view of her generous profile, should he look up. But he was far too busy hammering.

"Someone yanked my sink from the wall," she said, watching carefully for Mary's reaction.

But Mary gave nothing away. "Here? In the shop?"

Liz nodded.

"And?"

"And what?"

"Is that all?"

"Isn't that enough?" Liz asked.

Mary shrugged. "At least the damage will be easy to fix."

Easy for *her*, maybe. The only plumber Liz could afford was Sam Brown and he refused to work unless he was broke and needed money to buy booze. When she'd called him on Carter's cell phone earlier he'd said he'd be out as soon as possible, but since she'd already paid him for the first installation, she knew it could take a while. Unless Carter could do it. But if that was the case, he probably would've mentioned it when she'd asked to borrow his phone. "Nothing happened to *your* store, did it?" she asked.

Mary rubbed her hands together. "Nope. Store's perfect. Business is good."

Liz couldn't believe business was *that* good. Rarely did she see many customers in Mary's shop, which made her worry that she'd soon be facing a similar dearth of sales. But she allowed Mary her pride. Right now, Liz was more concerned with the man hammering in her back room, because already she'd nearly stripped off her clothes for him and she still felt the same compulsion. And there was the issue of the vandal. If she was the only one being targeted, it probably meant one of two things. Either the act was completely random. Or whoever had caused the damage had a grudge against her personally.

"How'd he get in?" Mary asked, without acting too concerned. It was the improvements that seemed to interest her more than the actions of Liz's vandal.

Liz watched Mary's face as she took in the marbled walls. "Do you like what we've done?"

"It's nice." Her voice held no real enthusiasm, but Liz suspected that by next week Mary would have her own shop painted the same way. "How'd this person get in?" she asked again.

"Keith left the back door open after he finished patching the wall last night."

When she said this, Liz knew she had Carter's attention, too. The hammering and sawing had stopped, and she could sense him listening.

"*Keith* was the last one here?" Mary said.

So far, everyone had jumped to the same conclusion. "I don't think it was him, Mary."

"Divorces make people crazy, Liz. And Keith lost more than most."

"You say that as if *he* was the victim. He got what he deserved."

"He did. But I'm sure he doesn't look at the situation the same way. Heck, he probably blames you for breaking up his marriage to Reenie. Everyone knows how much he adored her. Even now he can barely pass her without glancing longingly in her direction."

Liz didn't want to hear this. Her self-esteem had already taken a direct hit because of Keith's obvious preference for his first wife.

"Never mind," she said, but Mary continued, heedless, as usual, of her own insensitivity.

"Even if he doesn't blame you, he might resent you," she offered as an alternative. "In the beginning, your presence in town made his life infinitely more difficult. Had you stayed in L.A., he might've been able to talk Reenie into staying with him, even though Isaac had already blown his big secret."

"Nice of you to mention it," Liz said, gritting her teeth. "But I did what I thought was best at the time." What would Mary have done in her shoes? When Keith realized Reenie had discovered his deception, he left L.A. without so much as a coherent explanation. Liz couldn't let her marriage end that way. She'd *had* to come to Idaho, to fully understand what had happened to the man she loved, to finally accept that her husband was really walking out on her and their children, and to face the worst part of all—that he wasn't coming back. Without seeing for herself how he treated Reenie, without witnessing firsthand how much Reenie meant to him, Liz might have clung to her marriage longer. She'd probably be holding out hope to this day.

Of course, if she had the past eighteen months to live over again, she probably wouldn't make the same decision. She hoped she wasn't that much of a masochist.

"I don't think he blames me," she said. "At least not anymore. If anything, he blames himself."

"Then maybe he's jealous because you're getting onto your feet faster than he is," Mary suggested. "He's still working at the hardware store, isn't he? That's got to be embarrassing."

"It's an honest living," Liz said, her syllables clipped.

"But look where he came from. He had a wife in Idaho and California. He had homes in both places, and a job that was paying him the big bucks. Now he lives alone in the house he once shared with Reenie, he drives a beat-up old truck in place of his new SUV and he makes an hourly wage. Tell me that wouldn't be a bitter pill to swallow."

"I don't want to talk about it anymore," Liz said.

"You can tell at a glance that he's suffering. He's lost at least thirty pounds."

"I've got to get my kids, Mary."

"You should confront him about the sink. See how he reacts."

Liz told herself to leave Mary and just walk out. What could the other woman do with Carter in the shop? If she bothered him, he'd likely ask her to leave.

But Liz had already confronted Keith, and so Mary's suggestion called for a response. "I *did* ask him about ripping out the sink. He said he didn't do it."

Mary slid her purse higher onto her shoulder. "Who else could it be?"

You, Liz wanted to say. But she had no proof. "Who knows?"

"Well, it's definitely not anyone who really wants to hurt you."

"How do you know that?" Liz kept her hand on the doorknob in anticipation of her escape.

Mary waved an arm toward the mostly empty space. "Because someone who was truly vindictive wouldn't mess with this. They'd smash up your house or steal one of your children."

A chill ran up Liz's spine. "Don't even say that," she whispered, her heart pounding.

Mary gave her a mysterious smile. "Relax. You're in Dundee. Those things don't happen here, remember?" And with that, she brushed past Liz and swept out.

Liz didn't follow. Her legs felt like lead. She stood for a moment, trying to convince herself that Mary's words were meaningless. But she couldn't forget the sick feeling in the pit of her stomach when she'd seen her sink torn from the wall. If something that small could make such an impact...

She turned to see if Carter had heard Mary and found him watching her.

"Stay as far away from that woman as you can," he said.

LIZ TRIED TO TALK MICA and Christopher out of going to their father's. But they wouldn't even entertain the idea. They'd been promised a slumber party with their half sisters, including movies and popcorn and candy, and they weren't about to miss out. Especially when the alternative was spending the evening with their grandfather Russell, who'd smiled and nodded when they'd been introduced but otherwise appeared not to know what to do next.

He was a stranger to them. And not particularly good with children. Liz couldn't blame them for going to Keith's. She just wished their absence didn't mean she'd be alone with Gordon.

"Mica and Christopher are great," her father said, turning down the television. They'd finished a supper of spaghetti and garlic bread and were watching the news while eating ice cream. "I'm glad I was able to meet them."

Shifting as she sat on the couch, Liz forced a smile and bit back what she really wanted to say. *Why didn't you come before? What stopped you? Could Luanna have meant that much more to you than me?* "Thanks," she said. "I'm proud of them."

"You're a good mother. I can tell. Completely devoted."

"I appreciate you saying so."

The volume went up on the television, and she stood to carry the empty dishes into the kitchen. But her father caught her arm. Besides that brief, overwhelming hug at the chocolate shop, this was the first time he'd touched her in years. His fingers seemed callused in places she didn't remember. She didn't know if she wanted to throw herself against his chest, hoping he'd press a hand to her head as he had when she was small. Or if she wanted to recoil from his touch, which had become so foreign to her.

"What happened between you and Keith?"

She knew the kind of questioning she'd undergo if she told him the truth; she didn't want to go into it. "Personality differences."

"Marriage can be tough," he agreed. "How long have you been divorced?"

"Eighteen months."

"Keith told me he has family here."

"Yes."

"But you broke up almost as soon as you arrived?"

"How did you know—"

He answered before she could even get the question out. "Your last Christmas card is the only one with an Idaho address."

"Oh, right. Of course."

He seemed to grope for something more to say. "What do you do for fun in a town like this, now that you're single?"

The bleakness of her social life embarrassed her, so she covered her discomfort with a smile. "I go down to the Honky Tonk every now and then. I like to dance."

"I'm glad you have *some* fun. You've got to take care of yourself, too, you know. Just because you're divorced, doesn't mean you should live exclusively for your children."

Was that what she was doing? If so, she hadn't learned it from him.

"What about men?" he asked. "Are you seeing anyone?"

She thought of Carter, who'd left the shop a few minutes before her. He'd barely said good bye, but after she'd locked up she'd found a slip of paper stuck beneath the windshield wiper of her car. The only thing on it was a telephone number.

"I'm sort of in a relationship," she said, referring to Dave.

"Really?" Her father pushed the mute button and seemed to relax in his chair, as if he'd finally hit on something they could discuss without any danger of approaching one of the many uncomfortable issues that existed between them. "Is he from around here?"

"No. He lives in L.A."

"Are you considering moving back?"

"I can't. Not until the kids are older."

"You're not getting any younger. Why wait?"

"I don't want to take them away from their father." He scowled.

"Then you must not love him very much."

"I love my children," she said, the coolness she'd been trying to hide from him evident in her voice.

Gordon focused on the silent moving figures on TV. The awkwardness between them had surfaced again, twisting Liz's stomach and making her long to escape her father's company. "You're a good mother," he repeated.

"In any case, I'm not necessarily in love," she said, belatedly hoping to soften her response. "Just a little infatuated." She wasn't even sure about that anymore. Today she'd scarcely thought of Dave. She hadn't been able to think of anyone other than the darkly handsome Carter Hudson.

Sex appeal could make up for a lot, she decided. Carter wasn't the type of man to grin and flirt, to woo a woman with wine and flowers and compliments. He guarded his thoughts, and stared right through Liz with eyes as fathomless as a still, deep lake. She shouldn't be attracted to someone with such hard edges. And yet there was something raw and sensual about him that caused a strong physical response.

It was the danger that drew her, she guessed. The

thrill. The promise of feeling young and reckless. What she'd been through had probably thrown her into a midlife crisis ten or fifteen years too early.

"Considering the distance between you, you're probably smart not to get too wrapped up in him," her father was saying.

She agreed wholeheartedly. But she was no longer talking about Dave. There was distance between her and Carter, too—just not in the physical sense. "Right."

"What does he do for a living?"

She moved into the kitchen and started rinsing off the plates. "He's a tennis pro," she called back. "Works at an exclusive club."

"I love tennis." Her father said this as if she didn't already know it. He didn't mention that he'd been the one to introduce her to the sport when she was only seven years old. They'd spent hours on the court every week. Liz remembered how proud he'd been of her ability; how he had bragged to everyone that she'd play at Wimbledon some day.

But that was before her mother had died. They hadn't played together since.

"What's his name?" her father asked.

The hot water felt comfortable, familiar, running over Liz's hands as she worked. It was easier when she didn't have to face her father, when she went about her business as if it weren't odd to have him in the house. "Dave."

"Is he as good a player as his position would suggest?"

"He is, actually."

"How'd you meet?"

She stacked the dishes in the dishwasher. "He was my coach."

Now there was no getting around their past involvement in the sport. "I thought you gave up tennis."

She had, for a while. She'd been waiting for him to resume interest. It was what they did together. It was *their* thing. But he'd put her off every time she'd asked, until she'd realized that she'd lost that part of her life as well as losing her mother.

"No, I joined a league in college, and kept playing as a hobby when I started working for the airlines. But I didn't play a lot until after I married Keith and we joined a club near our house."

"And now?"

"I don't get out on the court much these days. Not since I moved here."

"Why? Don't they have the facilities?"

"They have some really nice courts at the Running Y, if you don't mind the drive. And the locals have an old court in town. It's behind the community center over by the cemetery. But it doesn't see much action. The problem is finding someone other than Keith who plays on my level. Tennis isn't a popular sport here. We have more barrel racers than tennis players."

"Maybe we should go over and play a set in the morning," he suggested. "See what you've got."

Liz imagined serving him a perfect ace and smiled. She'd be happy to show him. But morning seemed a long way off. Especially with Carter's phone number waiting like a secret treasure in her pocket.

CHAPTER EIGHT

LIZ SAT IN THE SEMIDARKNESS, smoothing the slip of paper she'd found beneath her windshield wiper. The clock on the wall across from her kitchen table ticked loudly in the cool, otherwise silent room. Steadily. Inexorably. It was getting late—almost eleven—and that damn clock wouldn't let her forget it.

Her father had gone to bed at least an hour earlier. She knew she should retire, too. But she couldn't close her eyes without seeing Carter Hudson standing before her, looking at her with an intensity that could forge steel.

Sighing, she picked up the phone and dialed Dave's number, her fingers quickly punching in the keys of the already familiar pattern. She'd tried calling him earlier in the evening, hoping a diversion would see her through the night—Dave suddenly seemed much safer than Carter—but he'd been out. Normally, she would have wondered where he was, maybe even obsessed over who he was with. She used those frequent late-night absences to prove to herself he was far too young to be ready for the type of relationship she'd require if she ever fell completely in love with him. But none of that seemed particularly important right now. She was more concerned with her own temptations.

Hello. You know who you've reached. Call my cell if you need me. Otherwise leave a message. I'll get back to you.

At the beep, she hung up and tried his cell. As a rule, she didn't call him on his cell after ten o'clock, just in case he was doing something she'd rather not know about. He deserved his privacy, and she didn't want to hear the giggle of another woman in the background. But she was getting desperate. She kept imagining what it would be like to slip out of the house and drive to Carter's, to have him open the door wearing that unfathomable expression that could mean he was absolutely dying to touch her—or he was completely ambivalent and simply taking what life offered at the moment.

This is Dave. My coaching schedule is full for next week, so if you want an appointment call the club. They'll add you to my waiting list and I'll squeeze you in if I can. If you want to talk, text me. I can't hear in this place.

That gave her some indication as to where he was. Out dancing or drinking, having fun.

After disconnecting, she tapped her fingernails on the table in keeping with the rhythm of the clock. Another five long minutes passed. Finally, in the dim light falling into the room from the hallway, she squinted to make out the numerals on Carter's note and picked up the handset.

Her stomach filled with butterflies as she dialed. The phone began to ring, but she didn't give Carter the chance to pick up. She lost her nerve almost immediately. Quietly setting the phone on its cradle, she shoved away from the table and headed down the hall to change.

She couldn't sit alone any longer, couldn't unwind enough to sleep and couldn't let herself go to Carter's place. She needed a fourth option.

So she decided to follow Dave's example and went out.

CARTER DIDN'T SEE LIZ COME IN. He didn't even know she was at the Honky Tonk until he circled the pool table, looking for the best angle for his next shot, and bumped into the guy who'd challenged him to a game.

"Excuse me," he said, irritated that his companion hadn't stepped out of the way as he'd expected. But Jon Small, who'd introduced himself as *Councilman Small's son*—as if small-town connections mattered to Carter— still didn't move. He was too busy gawking at the dance floor. "Man, she's got a body."

Turning, Carter spotted Liz dancing with a cowboy he didn't recognize. She was dressed in a sleeveless white sweater and a short denim skirt, nothing particularly revealing. But that simple skirt, in combination with her high heels, showcased a pair of the most beautiful legs he'd ever seen.

Carter felt an instant reaction, but he bent over the pool table to take his shot. He preferred not to acknowledge the effect she had on him. He wasn't the type of man to use a woman.

But in his present state, that was the only kind of intimacy he was capable of. And he was beginning to suspect she wanted to use him just as badly. *She* was the one who'd said "no strings," as if that were a prerequisite.

"Keith told me you got to help her at the shop today," Jon said, still staring at Liz.

Carter noted the appreciation in his opponent's face and the envy in his tone. "You can help her tomorrow, if you like," he said, hoping Jon *would* take over. Ducking out of Liz's life would probably be best for both of them.

"I will, if she'll wear that skirt when she climbs up one of those ladders," he said, laughing. "Preferably with some sort of thong underneath."

He grinned as he mimicked sliding his hands up under the back of her skirt, and Carter immediately changed his mind. Jon needed to stay as far away from Liz as possible. *He* needed to stay away from her, too. And yet he'd left his phone number on the windshield of her car and had stopped by the drugstore on his way home.

"Shit," he grumbled, not particularly pleased to realize that he couldn't ignore her as he wanted to.

"What?" Jon asked without looking at him.

"Nothing."

Since Jon didn't seem to be in any hurry to resume the game, Carter gave up and joined him in watching Liz. She tossed her long hair back and smiled at her companion as she moved to the rhythm of the music. Until she spotted Carter. Then her lips parted and her eyes widened as if he'd kissed her—and he knew it wasn't any use fighting the attraction. They'd make love. Tonight.

But in order to salvage his self-respect, she had to come to him, he told himself. And she had to convince him that the encounter wouldn't leave her disillusioned or jaded. She'd insisted he didn't have to worry about breaking her heart, but he hadn't been joking when he'd said she seemed particularly vulnerable. Despite what her ex-husband and her father had done—or not done— she still believed in love, acceptance and change. She'd told him she wanted to provide those things along with her chocolate, hadn't she?

God, she was idealistic. But he wouldn't destroy that. His grudging admiration of her resilience wouldn't allow him to. Why make her cynical, too?

THE ALCOHOL MADE HER light-headed. Liz didn't drink very often. Usually, when Keith had the kids, she spent her time experimenting with different chocolates or making new candies—her latest achievement was the best chocolate-covered cinnamon bears she'd ever tasted—and not hanging out at the town's most popular bar. She had so much to do that she didn't see much point in wasting the time. But she was having fun tonight. Especially now that she'd spotted Carter. Although meeting up with him was exactly what she'd hoped to avoid by coming here, she couldn't leave. Not when the evening was finally becoming interesting.

She liked the way he watched her while he played pool. Sexual energy radiated from him in waves, lapping around her like warm water, trickling down the front of her shirt and swelling up her bare legs.

"Having fun?" Pat, her dance partner, wanted to know.

She nodded and closed her eyes, losing herself in the moment and refusing to let anything else intrude. Her father was asleep at her house. She'd have to face him again in the morning. She'd also have to bear the burden of everything happening at the shop, call the plumber a second time to get him back to fix her sink, start on Mica's costume for the end-of-year school play, buy some groceries so she could make healthier meals this week than she had the week before—to ease her guilt over working too much—and pay the bills. The list was overwhelming. But she had a few hours before she had to go back to her life. It could wait that long.

Heather Parkinson waved from the table where Liz had been sitting. Liz smiled and waved back at her and her twin sister, Rachelle. Heather and Rachelle were five years younger than Liz. They had red hair and freckles, and they worked at the Running Y. Heather wanted to get married and have babies, but she didn't have a boyfriend. Rachelle had a boyfriend, but she wasn't ready to settle down. Liz had little in common with either one of them, but they rented a house down the street from her and came over quite often to borrow eggs or a cup of sugar. In recent months, they'd become fairly good friends.

The song ended and Pat escorted Liz to her seat. She glanced over at Carter as she reclaimed her drink, hoping he'd ask her to dance. She wanted to feel his arms around her, his body undulating against hers. But he had his back to her as he took his turn at the pool table.

"I think Pat really likes you," Heather said as he made his way to the bar.

"I like him, too," she said.

"That sounded pretty neutral. I don't get the feeling

we're talking about the same kind of like," Rachelle said with a laugh.

"He wants to hook up with you," Heather clarified.

"No he doesn't," Liz replied. In any case, Pat was Dave's age, maybe even younger, and there weren't any sparks between them.

"Sure you're not interested?" Rachelle asked, peering at her more closely.

"You're flushed," Heather accused.

"I'm overheated," Liz said.

"Where're the kids tonight?" Rachelle wanted to know.

"At Keith's."

Heather toyed with her wineglass. "That's convenient."

Liz grimaced. "Not really. I miss them when they're gone."

"Tonight you might be glad of the break," she said with a suggestive smile. "There's a man in the corner who's been watching you. Do you know him?"

Liz met Carter's gaze. When he didn't glance away but continued to stare, she curved her lips in a slow smile. She'd been married for more than eight years and divorced for eighteen months, and yet she'd never felt anything quite so erotic as the way he looked at her.

He didn't return her smile or come toward her, but he seemed to register every detail of her face and body before he went on with his game.

"He's Senator Holbrook's new aide," Liz said shortly, her pulse still racing.

"Oh." Rachelle shivered. "He makes me sort of uncomfortable, you know? I mean, he'd be handsome if he wasn't so...*intense*. Would it hurt him to smile once in a while?"

Rachelle was right. Carter needed to lighten up. A smile could transform him from simply "rugged" or "masculine" to darn near perfect. But there was that chip on his shoulder....

"Something's made him angry," she said, feeling the need to defend him.

"I don't think so," Heather said. "I've seen him in here before. He always looks that way."

"I think he always feels that way."

"What could be wrong?" Rachelle wanted to know. "We're out dancing and drinking, for heaven's sake. Why not let go and have some fun for a change?"

"Like me." Liz took a bolstering sip of her margarita. This definitely wasn't her usual behavior.

"Exactly," Heather agreed.

Liz wiped her mouth with her napkin. "Whatever's bothering him must be pretty bad."

"How do you know?" Rachelle asked.

"From what I've seen, he can handle almost anything."

She watched Carter bum a cigarette off Jon and head out the back door, and stood as though it was some sort of cue to follow him.

"Where are you going?" Heather called after her.

"Just to talk," Liz said. "Nobody should be that alone."

Heather snorted disbelievingly behind her, but Liz didn't turn around. She didn't want Carter to be alone. *She* didn't want to be alone anymore, either.

CARTER LEANED AGAINST the gritty bricks of the building and took a deep drag on the first cigarette he'd had in ten years. The night overhead was cool and dark and boasted a blanket of stars he'd scarcely noticed until he'd moved away from the bright lights of the city.

It was beautiful, he thought, not wanting to think about anything other than the night sky. Not the noise or heat of the bar. Not Jon Small, who irritated him with his stupid, sexist comments and pointless pretenses. Not the past, and not the future.

Especially not the future. One day at a time. That was his motto.

The door beside him opened and Liz stepped out.

"Ready to go?" he asked as if he'd been expecting her. Part of him still wanted to offend her—whether to keep her from taking a risk or to deny himself, he didn't know.

She didn't fall for the line, though. She simply stared at the sky, as he'd been doing a moment earlier.

He took another long drag on his cigarette, hoping the tobacco's bite would clear his head.

"I didn't know you smoked," she said.

"I don't."

"Right. I can see that." She fell silent again as Carter flicked his ashes to one side.

"You're up late, considering you wanted us to start work at *six in the morning*," he said.

She shrugged off the comment. "No need to sound petulant. I let you talk me into eight."

He chuckled at the fact that she still seemed disappointed to have lost that battle. "The shop means a lot to you."

"My future is riding on it."

He didn't want to contemplate the likelihood of seeing her fail. Fortunately, if that happened, he'd probably be long gone. "Tell me about chocolate."

She took her time answering. "What do you want to know?"

"Why this particular kind of shop? It can't *all* stem from a movie, can it?"

"*Chocolat* was also a book, but you're right. My mother had her own special fudge recipe, and she used to sell her candy in order to make a little money on the side. She dreamed of opening a shop one day, and I've wanted to do the same thing ever since I inherited that recipe. When I saw *Chocolat* I decided to get busy."

Carter was stalling for time, trying to be certain there was no way to avoid taking what he wanted. He was fairly sure there wasn't, but he wanted to give Liz plenty of time to decide. "How'd you choose which chocolate to use?"

"Research. Chocolate is an acquired taste, which comes as a surprise to most people. It's like wine. Some wineries produce a better-tasting product than others, and those outstanding wines are direct reflections of the areas in which the grapes were grown, right?"

It was a rhetorical question, so he merely nodded.

"It's the same with cacao beans. They're grown in tropical climates. West Africa. Indonesia. Brazil. Malaysia. Each region produces its own flavor, according to the variety of bean, the soil and the climate."

"Are you enough of a connoisseur to tell the difference?"

"Not yet, but I'm learning. West African beans typically have a slight coffee flavor. Ecuadorian Arriba beans are floral. Cacao beans from Venezuela and Trinidad have a fruity flavor."

Carter took another drag from his cigarette. "What's the best?"

"The Madagascar Criollo. These beans are difficult to cultivate, but they're considered the nobility of all cacao beans."

He let the smoke curl through his lips. "You seem to know your stuff."

"Like I said, I'm learning."

"Who were those women you were sitting with inside?"

"Heather and Rachelle Parkinson. They live down the street from me. We go out occasionally."

"You didn't come with them tonight."

"No. I got a late start."

"Your father hold you up?"

"Not really. I wasn't planning on coming in the first place."

Once again, Carter filled his lungs with smoke. "What made you change your mind?"

"It beat sitting by the phone, thinking about calling you," she said. "But now I see I would've been better off if I'd done that instead."

He smiled. "Better off? What are you afraid of?"

"I'm not accustomed to this kind of encounter. I was hoping to keep my head."

"Then drinking might not be the ideal solution."

"I haven't had much," she said. "Coming here was merely a distraction. And it would've worked, except…"

"I was here, too," he finished. "Interesting how fate steps in."

She kicked a small rock, which skittered across the pavement toward the garbage cans. "That's what you'd call this? Fate?"

"No, I'd call it basic animal attraction."

She tucked her hair behind her ears. "How long do you expect to be in town?"

He tossed his cigarette onto the blacktop and ground it out with his foot. "Six, seven months."

The shadow of the building obscured her expression. But he could make out the gleam in her eyes. And he could sense the conflict inside her. He had his reservations, too. Only he knew when he was beat.

"If I go home with you, will you still help me finish the shop?"

"Of course. I wouldn't leave you hanging with all that high-quality chocolate." He grinned devilishly.

"Relations won't be awkward between us afterward, will they?"

His eyebrows went up. "Relations?"

"You know what I mean. I don't want to feel uncomfortable around you."

"Why would you feel uncomfortable? We both understand what's going on," he said, even though he wasn't completely sure he understood anything. He'd dated occasionally since Laurel had taken her life. After the first few months, he'd even tried to find someone to grab onto, to keep the world as he'd once known it from slipping away. But no one had been able to rouse him from the indifference that had descended the day he'd found Laurel dead in their bed. These days, if a woman showed interest in him, he felt mild annoyance and nothing more.

What made Liz so different?

He suspected it was partly how much she reminded him of his late wife—in looks, in manner. But that wasn't any reason to feel guilty, was it? They could each have their own reasons for what they were about to do. They were only asking for one night's reprieve from the emptiness that had swallowed them whole. One night wouldn't hurt anybody.

"We're adults," she agreed. "We'll be fine in the morning. Friends, right?"

He made no reply. He couldn't say how they'd come out of this, whether or not they'd maintain any type of relationship.

"You could help me out with a few assurances here," she said sarcastically.

"I'm not going to talk you into anything."

Moonlight hit the side of her face as she stepped forward, lining the curve of her cheek in silver. "This is my decision?"

"Completely."

She lowered her voice. "Okay, but I want you to make me one promise."

He wished he had another cigarette. He didn't feel half as calm or in control as he wanted to. "What's that?"

"When it's over, it's over."

He considered her request and couldn't see any problem with it. "I promise."

"Pick me up around the block," she said and ducked back inside.

CARTER'S CAR SMELLED like he did—mostly of leather and good cologne. But the inside wasn't as immaculate as Liz had imagined it would be. Books, filing folders, newspapers and several bags from a sporting goods store filled the back seat. Old coffee cups sat in the cup holders, the ashtray was open and full of change, and Carter was still trying to move his camera and some empty packaging out of the passenger seat when she opened the door and peered inside. "Maybe it'd be smarter for me to follow you, so you won't have to bring me back later," she said.

He reached out to hold the door. "Don't worry about that."

Being whisked away in his expensive sports car was much more in keeping with the fantasy she'd been spinning in her mind, so she didn't argue. Sliding into the passenger seat, she stretched her seat belt across her lap. "Where do you live?" she asked, expecting Carter to give her a location in town.

Instead he said, "I have a small cabin twenty minutes into the mountains."

The setting sounded private, which was a relief. She didn't want anyone to see them and guess what they were doing. But twenty minutes would be a long drive at three or four in the morning. Liz had moved her car so that Heather and Rachelle would assume she'd gone home as she'd told them, but she didn't see any need to make Carter come out again, later, when she was capable of driving herself. Especially if she didn't have to worry about her car being spotted in front of his house.

"Wait," she said as he pulled away from the curb.

He put on the brake. "What?"

"If it's that far, maybe I should get my own car."

"There's no need. It's dark and the roads are narrow and windy," he said, speeding up again.

She leaned forward to catch his eye. "Do you think I'm too drunk to drive?"

"If I thought you were drunk, I wouldn't be taking you home with me."

Had he been any other man, she might have doubted the truth of that statement. But Carter was so blunt she couldn't imagine him lying. "That doesn't explain why I shouldn't bring my own car."

"I'd rather not have you get out of my bed to drive home alone, okay?" he said in exasperation.

Evidently, he was more of a gentleman than she'd expected. "Okay."

She settled back in her seat as he selected a CD tucked behind his sun visor, and a few seconds later the voice of Bob Marley filled the car. The traffic light turned green and the buildings that had become so familiar to Liz over the past eighteen months began to fly past her window.

"Do you do this type of thing very often?" she asked.

"No."

"How long has it been?"

"Since I've made love?"

"Yes—providing it's not a national secret, like some other parts of your past."

"Two years." Now that they were in the car together, he seemed less guarded, less remote.

"*Really?*" she said in amazement. "That's even longer than it's been for me."

A pair of headlights coming from the opposite direction painted a yellow stripe across his face. "You haven't slept with Keith since your divorce?"

"We were together once, right after I came here. But too much had changed. I couldn't go back, couldn't access what I'd felt before. I didn't like it."

He made no comment.

"Anyway, my love life hasn't been completely dismal." She knew she and Dave had no commitments between them, but she felt as if she should at least mention him. "There's this guy from California named Dave. He calls me a lot."

"Calls you?"

"Would like to pursue a relationship."

"You think you'll ever get together?"

"He's been talking about coming out here, but I doubt it."

"Why not?"

"He's only twenty-five." She pictured Dave at a typical L.A. hangout and wondered if he was going home with someone, too.

"How'd you meet him?" Carter asked.

"He was my tennis coach. He used to flirt with me

quite a bit, but I didn't pay much attention to him until I got divorced."

Herb Bertleson's new real-estate office sat at the edge of town, a final outpost. Liz glanced at the squat building with its wide gravel parking lot, feeling as if it marked her last chance to change her mind. They'd be into the mountains next, and Carter would be well on his way home and not simply cruising down Main Street.

"How long has it been since you picked up someone at a bar?" she asked, turning from the window as Herb's office disappeared from view.

"I've never picked anyone up in a bar. Why?" he replied.

The town fell away behind them, shrinking to a tiny pinprick of light she could see in her side mirror before winking out altogether. "This is a first for me, too."

He cocked an eyebrow at her. "We didn't meet in a bar. I took you out to eat last night, remember?"

"Still."

"It's not the same," he said.

"A one-night stand is a one-night stand," she insisted.

"Not exactly. Consider the differences." He ticked them off on the fingers of one hand. "I work for a man you know and respect, and he's done an extensive background check on me."

"He doesn't know anything about the past ten years," she grumbled.

"Believe me, he knows enough not to worry. Besides, we've been together all day. That has to equal at least five cursory dates."

"Which means what?"

"We're not total strangers."

"It's only been about thirty hours since we met!"

"During which time we've shown admirable restraint."

She couldn't help laughing. "You're kidding."

"Not completely," he said.

She got the impression he was trying to put her at ease, but she wasn't sure that was possible. The slight margarita buzz she'd felt at the Honky Tonk was gone, so there was nothing to take the edge off her nerves. And Carter had just rested his hand on her leg.

CHAPTER NINE

THE REMOTE CABIN Carter had rented was nestled in the middle of a forest. It was small but cozy, with two bedrooms, a loft, a living room, a kitchen area and one bath, and it smelled of fresh cut wood, a stack of which was piled in the corner by the fireplace. With dated furniture and only a few simple decorations, the cabin appeared to be a typical vacation rental. Except for the moving boxes that cluttered almost every room. Because they were open and partially ransacked, it looked as though Carter had unpacked only what was absolutely necessary for day to day living—as if he wasn't really moving in so much as holding over.

While he built a fire, Liz stood on a large rug in the middle of the living-room floor, trying to remember just how long it had been since Carter had arrived in town. Two weeks? Three?

"Would you like a glass of wine?" he asked. The fire had begun to flicker and burn, but it wasn't yet throwing off heat.

"That'd be great." She hoped another drink would help warm her. As sunny as the spring had been, it could still get chilly in the mountains—downright cold at night. The trepidation she felt over what she was about to do probably didn't help.

But the kitchen didn't appear to be stocked. "Are you sure you have wine?" she asked, eyeing the empty countertops.

"There's a bottle in the fridge." He started going through boxes. "Glasses might be more of a problem."

"Don't worry about it," she said, but he'd already pulled two wineglasses out of a box beneath the breakfast bar, as if he'd known where they were all along, rinsed them out and filled them with a light chardonnay.

"What kind of music do you like?" he asked, as he handed her a glass.

"Pop, hip-hop, R & B, classical."

His stereo was one item he'd unpacked. It sat on an end table beside an extensive CD collection.

"Wow, you really like music," she remarked as he put on Sheryl Crow.

"Music and photography," he replied.

She didn't see any photographs on the walls, or set out on the empty side tables. But he'd had a camera in the car, and it had looked like an expensive one.

He pulled a few candles from another box, arranged them along the edge of the counter and lit them. Then he flicked off the lights.

Liz felt better in the semi darkness, less exposed, which was probably Carter's goal. He turned up the music just loud enough that they'd have to raise their voices to speak, relieving her of the need to make conversation. Along with the cabin and surrounding mountains, the candles and music combined to create an

ambience Liz found almost intoxicating even without
the wine. The boxes, which reminded her that he was
only a temporary addition to the community and that she
had no business being with him, seemed to disappear,
leaving only the sensory input for which she was so
hungry.

"Do you see it?" he asked, and she realized that he
was now standing very close. His arm brushed hers,
sending a tingle through her as he pointed at something
beyond the window.

"What?" she replied.

"The moon, reflected on the water."

"There's a lake nearby?"

"A large pond. Right there." He turned her head a few
inches to the right and she finally saw the water.

"It's lovely."

"I could almost get used to living here," he said, his
voice a promising sound in her ear.

She opened her mouth to ask him why he ruled that
out as a possibility. He could stay anywhere he wanted,
couldn't he? But he'd lifted her hair and started kissing
the nape of her neck, causing her to catch her breath. He
must have set down his wine, because he wasn't holding
it when both hands slipped around her waist and coaxed
her to lean into him.

Liz closed her eyes and let her head rest on his
shoulder as his lips grazed her skin, lighter than the
brush of a butterfly's wings. His mouth moved to the
line of her jaw and a moment later he flicked his tongue
inside her ear, alternately using his teeth to tug gently
at the earlobe.

Within moments, she wasn't sure she'd have the strength to remain standing.

She wanted to do something about her wineglass, but Carter didn't give her a chance. He was too focused on exploring, cautiously discovering all the places that made her gasp.

Liz had thought the initial contact would be awkward. She couldn't imagine how they'd touch each other without feeling painfully self-conscious. But her inhibitions were burning away as quickly as the paper he'd used to light the fire. She felt her hesitation being sucked up the chimney and blown down the mountain by the wind outside. She was still fully clothed, but that only made the craving for real contact stronger.

The sensations bombarding her as Carter familiarized himself with her body swept Liz into a euphoric state she hadn't known for ages. Gone were the worries that had nagged her for so long, the painful memories, the knowledge that she'd have to deal with her father tomorrow, along with a myriad of other concerns. There was only Sheryl Crow, crooning in the background, filling her head with voice and song and beat; the cool cabin air swirling against her suddenly feverish skin; the flickering of the fire and the candlelight, causing the shadows to dance all around her in glorious celebration.

And there was Carter lifting her skirt, sliding her panties over to one side, and taking his exploration to a far more intimate level.

When Liz cried out, Carter froze, steadying her with one arm around her waist. "That's it," he murmured approvingly.

Finally taking her wineglass, he set it aside. Then he pressed her down onto the couch, where he gave her a roguish grin, spread her knees and bent in front of her.

BIRDS TWITTERING in the trees roused Liz. Slowly she opened her eyes, feeling languid, content, heavy-limbed. The sheet that covered her slipped easily over her bare skin as she moved, but Carter, still asleep beside her, slung out an arm to keep her in place, as if he was afraid she'd leave before he was ready to let her go. They'd made love several times and had planned to do so again. That was why he'd carried her into the bedroom. But by then they'd been too exhausted to act on the desire. Resting for what Liz thought would only be a moment, they'd fallen asleep and—

Coming to her senses, Liz bolted upright. What time was it? The vanilla scent of the candles still lingered in the air, bringing back steamy, sensual memories she wanted to examine more closely. But later. For now, fear overrode everything else.

Clearly they'd overslept. The sun drifted through the uncurtained window, revealing another room full of boxes. It had to be well past dawn.

Carter groaned and rolled the other way when she got up and pulled the sheet along with her. She needed to find the clock she'd noticed on the nightstand several hours earlier. But it was gone. Where?

Searching the floor, she finally found it where they must've knocked it. The glowing numerals read seven-thirty. Damn! She'd told her father they'd play tennis at seven.

"Carter, I need to get out of here," she said.

He mumbled something incomprehensible, his face far younger in repose.

Instead of touching him, she jiggled the bed. "Carter, you have to take me to get my car."

"It's still early," he muttered, lifting his head and squinting at her, his hair tousled. "You said we don't have to be at the shop until eight."

She righted the alarm. "That doesn't mean I can stay all morning."

"Why not? Your kids are with Keith."

"There's still my father. He'll be wondering where the heck I am."

"Can't you call him and tell him you're with me?"

She hiked the sheet up higher. "Are you *joking?*"

"You're right. Bad idea. He won't be happy to hear it."

"He's not the only one," she said. "I have enough to worry about without risking a backlash."

He lifted himself onto his elbow, and she tried not to notice what a beautiful specimen he made, lying there completely nude. Maybe she shouldn't have taken the sheet—but then she'd be naked. "What kind of problem could there be?" he asked with a scowl.

"This isn't the big city. You can't sleep with someone and expect people not to talk about it. And if word gets back to Keith... Well, if he's the one who vandalized the shop, I don't need to provoke him."

"I thought you didn't believe it was him."

"I'm not sure. It could be Mary. Or it could be someone else. But...just in case, you know?" The sheet dragged along the floor as Liz went into the living room to gather her clothes, which seemed to be strewn, along with Carter's, throughout the cabin. Additional memories bombarded her—she actually blushed at some of them—and then she told herself simply to concentrate on getting home. "Keith might be angry enough to say something to my children," she called out in the direction of the bedroom. "Use it to make me look bad."

"I'd have to break his jaw if he did that," Carter yelled.

"I'd probably hit him, too. But that wouldn't fix the damage. It's better not to give him any ammunition. Especially since what happened last night will never happen again."

Carter didn't answer. Liz imagined he was getting up and trying to pull on some clothes. She was trying to do the same. But she couldn't find her panties. Reluctant to ask him where they might be—after all, he was the one who'd been holding them last—she pulled on her skirt, her bra and her shirt before continuing her search in earnest. It was much easier to move when she didn't have to worry about holding up that darn sheet.

When she found only her shoes on the floor, she began to peek into the open boxes nearest the sofa. She discovered even more CDs—unbelievable—and a tripod, along with some other camera equipment. A second box contained books. "Are you coming?" she called, hoping to hurry him along.

"I'm considering it." The floor creaked as he came out of the bedroom, wearing only a pair of boxer briefs. Traipsing into the kitchen, he took some orange juice from the refrigerator and poured himself a glass. Then he held the carton up to her.

She kept her eyes well above the impressive contours revealed by his underwear. "No thanks. I'm in a bit of a hurry, in case you can't tell."

His lips pursed as he considered her. "I guess it's taking me a little longer to shift gears. We're already at the part where we pretend we were never naked together, right?"

Liz cleared her throat and averted her gaze. "That was the agreement."

"And you think we're really going to be able to do that?"

The skepticism in his voice troubled her, but they had agreed to a plan in order to avoid future problems, and she didn't see any reason not to stick to it. Maybe moving on as if they didn't know each other quite so intimately would require some acting ability and a lot of self-discipline, but she couldn't let herself be drawn into a full-blown affair. "Why not?"

No response. After draining his glass of juice, he returned to the bedroom, and Liz went back to checking boxes. She didn't find the black lacy panties she was searching for, but a picture frame caught her eye. Thinking it might contain an example of Carter's photography, she picked it up and then sank onto the sofa. It wasn't a snapshot of a beautiful river, a sunset or a still wood, as she'd expected. It was a wedding photograph of a stunning blonde, wearing an elegant white dress and veil. Carter stood beside her in a black tuxedo.

"Let's go," he said from behind her.

Liz quickly shoved the photograph back into the box and stood. He hadn't gone to a lot of trouble to get ready, but at least he was dressed. He wore a pair of torn jeans, a clean T-shirt and a ball cap.

Carter's gaze dropped to the edge of the frame, which glinted in the sunlight, before rising to her face. He didn't speak for a long moment. When he did, he didn't mention it. "Ready?"

Nodding, Liz hurried out ahead of him. She had no idea where her panties had gone, but she no longer wanted to look for them. What she'd just found had knocked her off balance. She'd thought she had Carter pegged. She'd thought he was a tough guy who'd never give enough of himself to enter into a deep, fully committed relationship. But after their night together, she had to admit that sex with him hadn't been nearly as detached as she'd expected. And from his expression in that photograph, he'd not only been married at some point, he'd been deeply in love.

So where was his wife? And why hadn't he spoken of her?

ON THE RIDE BACK TO TOWN, Liz barely spoke, and Carter said even less. She studied him through her lowered eyelashes, wondering how the woman she'd seen in that photograph fit into his life, and how he could be so warm and responsive while making love when he was normally standoffish and aloof. But she couldn't allow herself to get tangled up in all the contradictions that made Carter Hudson who he was. He wasn't what she needed or wanted. He'd hurt her in the end, if only because he was hurting so badly himself.

"What are you thinking?" he asked, adjusting his speed as they passed Herb's real-estate office on the edge of town.

"That you're an incredible lover," she said honestly.

His eyebrows went up, as if her candid response surprised him. "And yet you won't be returning to my cabin."

"No."

"Because…"

The Arctic Flyer ice cream parlor came up on her left. "I don't want to get attached to you."

He didn't argue. He drove several more blocks before she directed him to the neighborhood where she'd parked her car.

Liz sank low in her seat, hoping no one would spot them together. If she could get out of Carter's car without being seen disheveled and wearing the outfit she'd had on the night before at the Honky Tonk, she could continue with her life as if nothing had happened.

As he pulled in behind her Toyota, she put her hand on the door handle.

He caught her wrist. "I hear what you're saying about getting attached," he said, "but there's always the other school of thought."

She glanced nervously at the houses surrounding them, afraid someone she knew might come out to retrieve a newspaper or leave for work. Fortunately, no one stirred. "Which one is that?"

"Taking advantage of something while it lasts."

She clung even tighter to the keys she'd dug out of her purse, worried that her father would be up and know she wasn't at home. "We got away with it once," she said. "Why invite trouble by asking for more? I'll see you at the shop later, okay?"

"I'll be there."

"I appreciate it." She felt as if she should say something else. Carter had been an unlikely savior in several regards. But she didn't know how to express her gratitude for his help at the shop when it was all jumbled up in what had passed between them overnight. "I owe you for your help," she said.

"You heard the senator. I'm on salary, but there's not a lot to do until we get the office up and running," he replied. "I think he's glad to be rid of me for a while, so don't worry about it."

She smiled. "Thanks." She started to close the door, but he leaned over and stopped it midway. "Liz?"

"What?" she asked from the curb.

"Last night was good. Better than good," he said, and closed the door.

LIZ COULD SMELL COFFEE. Her father was up, and she had no idea what she'd say to him. She wanted him to approve of her again. At last. She'd wanted that since her mother had died. So why couldn't she have hooked up with Carter *after* her father left town? Or come home last night instead of falling asleep?

And yet those early morning hours with Carter had been arguably her favorite part of the whole experience. Especially when he'd smoothed the hair off her face and kissed her cheek. Who would've thought he could be so tender?

"Hungry?" her father called.

Evidently, he'd heard the door. "Not really." She forced one foot in front of the other until she reached the kitchen.

Dressed in a pair of running shorts, a tank top and tennis shoes, he turned from the stove, holding a spatula. Two eggs popped and spit in her new frying pan. "I went to rouse you for our game this morning." He eyed her smudged makeup and tousled hair, her wrinkled clothes. "Where have you been?"

"Nowhere important," she said.

He pursed his lips. "You didn't go over to the shop, did you?"

The shop? She dropped her keys onto the counter, where she typically left them, and poured herself a cup of coffee. On the ride home, she'd decided that she wouldn't offer him any excuses. She was thirty-two years old. As much as she wanted to gain what she'd lost so many years ago, she no longer had to account for her actions. At least not to him. But she now realized that the vandal had given her the perfect explanation for her absence. "I stopped by the Honky Tonk and had a drink with some friends, then spent the night at The Chocolateric."

"Why didn't you come back here?"

She told him about the person who'd torn her sink from the wall, embellishing the story at the end with her own imaginary attempt to catch whomever it was by staying at the store.

"If Keith's the one who left the back door unlocked, he should pay to fix the sink," her father said.

"He offered. But—"

"You won't let him?"

"He's pretty broke," she said. "Even with the jobs he takes on the side—"

"Doing what?"

"Developing small business software. Anyway, child support takes almost everything he makes. And when we divorced, he let me keep the equity from the house we owned in California. That's what's financing The Chocolaterie in the first place, so I don't feel I can be too hard on him."

"You should've made *him* stay at the shop last night. Or told me about it. I would've gone."

The protectiveness inherent in those words raised all the questions Liz had wanted to ask her father for so long. And she was just tired and emotionally ragged enough to be incapable of holding them back. "What happened to us, Dad?" she whispered.

His scowl deepened. "I don't know what you mean."

"Stop pretending," she said. "I have to know."

"What?"

"What I did wrong! How I lost your affection. I was fourteen years old, for crying out loud. What could a fourteen-year-old do to suddenly destroy her father's love?"

He stared down at his eggs. They were beginning to burn, but he didn't remove them from the stove and Liz didn't offer to help. She couldn't. She stayed rooted to the spot, awaiting an answer that would finally explain everything. But he said nothing.

"Dad?" she murmured. She hated the beseeching quality in her voice, but the desperation she'd felt for so long filtered through in spite of her efforts to squelch it. "We were close, once. Do you remember?"

"I remember," he said, but he was hanging his head and it was difficult for Liz to make out his expression.

"Was it your grief over losing Mom that separated us?"

Nothing.

"Was it the fact that Luanna and I didn't get along?"

Still no response.

"A combination of both?" she offered.

He made no reply, but Liz refused to fill the gaping silence. He owed her the truth. If, all of a sudden, he was going to be a part of her life and her children's lives, she had a right to know.

"It was grief," he said at last. Dumping his fried eggs into the sink, he set down the pan and went to his room.

Liz stared at the blackened remains of her father's breakfast, then covered her face. Even now he couldn't give her what she needed.

CHAPTER TEN

CARTER'S CELL PHONE RANG as he sat at Jerry's Diner, having a quick breakfast before heading over to The Chocolaterie. When he'd left New York, he'd almost cancelled his service. He didn't want anyone from his former life contacting him. But he moved around so much these days that it didn't make any sense to rely on land lines. Besides, his mother needed a dependable way to reach him. There were times when she grew frustrated with his sister and needed to vent.

This caller had a blocked number. Because of that, he was tempted to let the call go to voice mail. Anyone who wanted to reach him could damn well identify himself. But then he accidentally hit the talk button while trying to silence the ringer.

Biting back an irritated curse, he held the phone to his ear. "Hello?"

"Carter Hudson?"

"Yes?"

"It's Johnson."

Carter had already recognized the deep, raspy voice of the supervisory special agent who'd run the field office from which he'd worked. "What do you need?" he asked. His relationship with Johnson hadn't ended on the best of terms. Johnson wouldn't be calling him without a reason.

"We could use your help."

Carter glanced around to make sure no one could overhear his conversation. The diner was starting to fill up, but he'd taken a booth in the far corner and no one was in the immediate vicinity. "You don't need anything from me," he said.

"Charles Hooper wants to talk."

Just the mention of Hooper's name was enough to contaminate the life Carter was now living, like a toxic chemical leaking into a pure lake. Bar fights and rodeos were about the most violent events that took place in this quiet town. Certainly folks in these parts had never seen the things he'd seen; they'd probably never imagined the half of it. "Answer me one question," he said.

"What's that?"

"Is he still in prison?"

"Of course. He'll be there for the rest of his life. You know that."

"Exactly. And that's all that matters to me."

"He claims there are more, Hudson."

Carter knew what "more" meant. But he refused to let Johnson draw him in. He was through with trying to save the world. There were too many sick bastards out there. And even once they were caught, there was no way to neutralize what they'd done.

"I don't care what he claims," he said. "It'll be a cold day in hell when he gets me to jump at his command."

"I don't blame you for feeling the way you do,"

Johnson replied. "No one does. He's not worth the money it takes to feed him."

Carter couldn't help noticing how carefully Johnson avoided any mention of Laurel.

"But you wouldn't be doing it for him," he went on. "You know that, don't you, Hudson?"

"I'm not doing it for *anyone*," he said.

"We think there are three."

Three. Carter scrubbed a hand over his face, struggling to contain the rage building inside him. Why did Johnson have to call him on the first morning he'd felt human in twenty-four months? "He can tell you anything he can tell me," he said.

"But he won't. He's made that very clear. He says you're the only one he'll sit down with."

"I don't give a rat's ass what he says!"

The waitress who'd delivered his steak and eggs turned to gape at him. So did the two cowboys sitting at the table nearby, where she was pouring coffee.

Bowing his head over his plate, Carter lowered his voice. Hooper must've heard what had happened to Laurel and wanted the opportunity to gloat. Why else would he ask for him?

"He's a psychopath, Johnson. He manipulates people. I won't let him manipulate me. As far as I'm concerned, he doesn't exist."

"What about the families of his victims, Hudson? They deserve some closure. You know what it's like for them, and for us. How hard we work. Can't you help us out here?"

No, he couldn't. Hooper had cost him too much. His

whole philosophy of life. His love of police work. His belief that he could make a difference. And, most of all, his wife.

A vision of Laurel lying as pale as a ghost on the bed flashed before his mind's eye, making his heart pound as if he'd just found her. He opened his mouth to tell Johnson to go to hell, but Johnson cut him off before he could say anything.

"Don't give me an answer right now. Think about it and we'll talk more later, okay?" he said and disconnected, leaving Carter in a cold sweat.

"YOU NEW IN TOWN?"

Gordon Russell glanced up to see a man on the other side of the gas pump. Wearing a straw cowboy hat with the edges rolled up, he was leaning against a dusty old pickup. The sleeves were torn out of his wool shirt, revealing beefy arms folded across his chest as he waited for the rolling numbers to indicate that his tank was full.

Gordon was standing next to his own vehicle, engaged in the same activity. But he wasn't interested in conversation. "No, not really," he mumbled. "Just passing through."

The man shoved off the flare of his wheel well. At full height, he stood at least three inches taller than Gordon, and he was probably seventy pounds heavier. After depositing a pinch of snuff inside his cheek, he pocketed the can and made himself comfortable again. "Where you headin'?"

Gordon didn't know. After Liz had left for the shop, he'd simply packed his bags and loaded his car. He'd made a mistake coming to Dundee. He couldn't close the gap between himself and his children. He'd devoted his life to other pursuits for too long. One year had stretched into another and another, leaving him no way to reclaim what he'd lost. He was crazy to have thought he could reverse the process in one trip.

But with Luanna and her new boyfriend living in his house, he didn't want to go back to L.A.

He told himself he should see the world. He had nothing better to do. These were his golden years, right? But the world was feeling like a damn lonely place at the moment, making travel seem a bit overrated. "Here and there," he answered vaguely.

"What brings you out this way?" the man persisted.

An error in judgment... "My son and daughter live here," he explained.

"Who are they? Maybe I know 'em."

"Isaac and Liz Russell."

"Of course. I see the resemblance." The man spat on the ground. "They haven't been around that long, but I remember when they first got here. Your girl caused quite a stir, thanks to Keith. Terrible what he did to her, ain't it?"

Terrible? Gordon peered at the man a little closer. "These days, divorces happen all the time. It's not always easy to place blame."

His new friend gave him a funny look. "It was pretty damn easy in this case. If you ask me," he added.

"And you are..."

"Tim. Tim Downey." He motioned to the sign on the side of his truck. "I'm a cement contractor. Been living here my whole life."

Mr. Downey pulled the nozzle away from his tank. "Have a good one," he said and climbed into his truck.

Gordon watched him drive off, staring after him until the racket of the truck's large engine faded to silence. What had happened between Keith and Liz? She'd cited personality differences.

His pump gave a final chug and shut itself off, but Gordon wasn't in a hurry to get out of town anymore. Mr. Downey, a cement contractor in Dundee, Idaho, knew more about Liz—and probably about Isaac, too—than he did.

As difficult as it might be to stay, if Gordon left, that situation would never change.

LIZ FOUND HERSELF WATCHING Carter whenever she thought he was too preoccupied to notice her doing so. Memories of the night before were still so fresh in her mind, it was difficult not to dwell on them. And she couldn't believe how much her opinion of him had changed. At the steak house, she'd been absolutely ambivalent about his appearance and she'd hated his accent. Now, only two days later, she thought he was one of the handsomest men she'd ever seen, and she strained to hear him when he talked on his cell phone simply because she liked his accent so much.

This was a crush, she realized with sudden clarity, recognizing all the typical signs. She now had a crush on the man she'd gone home with last night. Which was exactly why people like Liz shouldn't do what she had done, she told herself fiercely. She just wasn't a woman who could separate sex from love. In the past, they'd been one and the same to her.

But that was when her relationships had begun with attraction and progressed toward commitment. Whereas her involvement with Carter certainly hadn't started with attraction, nor was it going to develop into commitment.

"You're frowning," Carter said.

Liz blinked. She'd stopped painting. "I was wondering how much longer it might take to finish," she lied.

He rested a hand on the counter he'd just installed and assessed their progress. "We should be done by Monday evening."

"With everything?"

"With everything."

"So I can have the cooler and confectioner's stove installed on Tuesday?"

"They won't be on the concrete floor, but in case someone inadvertently steps where we don't want them to I'd wait until Wednesday. The cement will take time to harden."

The smile she'd forced a moment earlier was suddenly effortless. She was about to say how fabulous that would be when the bell jingled over the front door.

"Sounds like we have a visitor," she said, setting aside her paintbrush.

"Mary Thornton?" he asked, with little enthusiasm.

"Probably," she grumbled.

But it wasn't Mary Thornton. It was her mother-in-law. Liz still didn't feel entirely comfortable around Georgia O'Connell. When she'd married Keith, he told her his parents were both dead as the result of a tragic automobile accident. So Georgia and Frank had been a surprise—one of the less than pleasant surprises waiting for Liz in Dundee, along with Keith's *other* wife and *other* children. Despite the fact that they'd now known each other for eighteen months, Liz could sense Georgia's resentment. It was almost as if she blamed Liz for ruining Keith's life.

"Hello, Georgia," she said, reminding herself to be nice.

Georgia had once requested that Liz call her *Mother*, for Mica and Christopher's sake. She was their only grandmother, after all. But most of the time Liz avoided calling Georgia anything, at least in front of the children. And when the kids weren't around, the two women interacted on a more formal basis.

"The work's coming along," Georgia said, adjusting the scarf tied around the crown of her wide-brimmed hat. She was one of the few women in Dundee who still wore such a fashion accessory, except for the cowboy hats favored by the cowgirls, of course.

"Yes, it is," Liz said.

"Will you be able to open as planned?"

"It's possible."

Georgia seemed cheerful, but her eyes darted around as she talked, missing nothing. "You've had some help, then?"

No doubt Keith had mentioned Carter. Keith wasn't pleased to have another man take his place. He'd made that clear when Liz had dropped off the kids the night before.

"Carter Hudson has been kind enough to put some elbow grease into this place."

"Nice of him," Georgia said, but her tone was too flat to be sincere. "Maybe you'll introduce us. I've been told he works for Senator Holbrook, but other than that he's a mystery to me. And to Keith, evidently," she added under her breath.

Liz didn't want to include Carter in her network of friends and family. He was temporary, unrelated to her long-term goals. And she was willing to bet he'd rather not be disturbed, especially by someone he'd probably describe as a nosy old lady. But she couldn't see any polite way to avoid an introduction now that Georgia had asked to meet him. "Sure, come on back," she said, waving her hand to indicate that the older woman should follow her.

Georgia minced her way past the paint supplies, drop cloths, balled-up plastic and miscellaneous debris as if she was afraid she might run her panty hose. "The marbling effect of the paint is quite nice," she mused, taking that in along the way.

"Thank you. I like it, too. Carter's done a great job."

"Keith could do as well," she said. "He just hasn't had the time. You know how hard he works."

"Yes," Liz replied, but as far as she was concerned, Keith worked harder on maintaining his relationships with Jennifer, Angela and Isabella than he did on anything else. He didn't have male competition when it came to Mica and Christopher, so they received less attention.

"What will you put in the front window?" Georgia asked.

They entered the kitchen, where Carter was installing new cabinets.

"I'm going to do my best to recreate the shop window from the movie."

"Right down to the window dressings?"

Clearly, Georgia didn't share Liz's vision, but Liz wasn't about to let that sway her. She knew what she wanted, and she was going to stick to it. "For the first month. It'll change weekly. At some point, I'll have a chocolate fountain right in the middle. I guess it's inevitable that the shop will take on more and more of my own personality. But the overall feel should always remind you of Vianne's shop."

"A chocolate fountain. Now I've heard everything," Georgia said. "I don't know how you manage to stay so thin."

Hoping to guide the conversation away from the recurrent theme, toward which it was drifting dangerously close (the added pounds Georgia couldn't seem to shed despite dieting), Liz motioned to Carter, who set his hammer aside.

"This is the man I have to thank for it all," she said.

Georgia looked mildly annoyed at such a flattering introduction but she managed a tight-lipped smile. "How do you do? I'm Georgia O'Connell, *Keith's* mother."

Liz dug her fingernails into her palms as Carter's eyes lit first on her, then shifted to her ex-mother-in-law. He had to know why Georgia had come—to determine the threat he posed to her son. So Liz didn't know how much forbearance she could expect on Carter's part. But he surprised her.

"Nice to meet you," he said, giving Georgia a polite nod.

"Likewise," she replied stiffly. "I've heard a great deal about you."

"Don't tell me I'm developing a reputation already." He found his feet, grinning devilishly.

Liz couldn't miss the captivating warmth of his response. She wasn't sure why he'd go to the trouble of charming Keith's mother—but she nearly laughed out loud when the full brunt of his smile seemed to make Georgia forget she wasn't supposed to like him. Pressing a hand to her chest, Liz's ex-mother-in-law smiled broadly.

"Oh boy, I'd better warn you, Liz," she said.

"*Warn* me?" Liz echoed.

"This man is trouble. I can tell already."

"Not for me," she replied confidently. It was, of course, wishful thinking. But she hoped to convince them both. Otherwise, once Georgia returned to the real world and was no longer dazzled by Carter's charm, she'd remember her loyalties to her son and start drawing up battle lines. Liz didn't need any additional meddling. Neither did she want to hear Carter say anything that might tempt her back to his cabin.

"You think you're immune to his charisma?" Georgia wanted to know.

Carter and Liz locked gazes; Liz looked away first. "Have you ever read Tennyson's poem, 'The Lady of Shalott'?" she asked by way of an answer.

"The lady of what?" Keith's mother responded, but she wasn't really paying attention. She was too busy preening for Carter.

The easily flattered side of Georgia was one Liz hadn't seen before. "Forget it," she said. "It's not important."

Carter seemed unperturbed. "I'm afraid I'm not familiar with Tennyson," he said. "But a line from *Hamlet* comes to mind."

"*Hamlet?*" Liz asked. She hadn't expected him to respond with a reference to Shakespeare.

"Something about protesting too quickly," he replied.

"That's protesting too much," she corrected, pretending he hadn't just revealed her lie for what it was.

His smile turned slightly mocking. "Exactly."

The undercurrent in their conversation seemed to break the spell over Georgia, causing her expression to darken. Drawing herself up straight, she cleared her throat. "Word has it you're in town only for a few months," she said to Carter.

"The senator hasn't even announced his candidacy yet, and you already know I'm a short-timer?"

"There are no secrets in Dundee."

Carter's eyes again flicked Liz's way, and she felt her cheeks flame. She certainly hoped there was one secret in Dundee—and that it'd stay that way.

"I'll be here through the election," he said.

"Here today, gone tomorrow, hmm?" Georgia challenged.

"Are you making a point, Mrs. O'Connell?" He grinned as he asked this, softening the question, but Liz could sense the steely edge lurking beneath the surface of his words.

"I'm simply saying that seeing you leave so soon

would be a pity for anyone who might find herself attracted to you."

"Then, I'll let you be in charge of warning off the ladies," he said, glossing over Georgia's words with a wink.

"I just did," Georgia said and checked her watch, before heading for the door. "I've got to go. Frank's waiting for me at the bank."

"Mrs. O'Connell?" Carter said, calling her back.

Liz couldn't believe he'd detain her.

"Yes?" she replied.

"Is this the first time you've seen the shop?"

"No, Liz showed it to us the day she leased it."

"And you haven't been back since?"

Georgia's eyebrows knitted. "Not until now, why?"

He hesitated. "How do you like it so far?"

"It's nice," she said, but her tone was definitely grudging, even guarded.

He studied the improvements. "We're almost done. Then we'll just have to get the plumber back out."

"For what?" Georgia asked.

He studied her for a moment. "A few odds and ends."

"I see. Well, good luck with it," Georgia said tightly. Then the bell jingled over the door and she was gone.

"So what do you think?" Liz asked Carter when the silence was complete.

"She's not the one," he replied.

"Who tore out my sink?"

He nodded.

"She's sixty-three years old and my children's grandmother." She didn't mention the fact that the thought had crossed her mind, as well, and that she'd asked Keith about the possibility of his parents sabotaging her efforts.

"So?" He shrugged. "She's pretty protective of her boy."

"But not that strong."

"Where there's a will, there's a way," he said simply.

CHAPTER ELEVEN

CARTER OFTEN HAD DIFFICULTY sleeping. Because of the physical nature of the work he'd performed in Liz's shop—not to mention being up most of the previous night—he'd hoped to have better luck this evening. But at twelve-thirty he found himself wandering around the cabin like a ghost, feeling utterly detached from the rest of humanity.

He told himself he should finally unpack his belongings and settle in. He'd already been here for three weeks. So he poked through a few boxes, but without any real commitment. What was the point of putting it all away? It didn't matter how he lived. He had only himself to please. Besides, if he left his belongings the way they were, it'd be that much easier to move on after the election.

Shoving the items he'd disturbed back where they'd been in the first place, he made his way eventually to the spare bedroom he used as an office. It was the only room in the cabin uncluttered with boxes. Here, he'd set up his computer and organized his desk and files so he could work from home. Beyond what he did for Senator Holbrook, Carter also did some consulting on other small-time campaigns, which he managed via the Internet or telephone.

Generally, he felt comfortable here. As comfortable as he felt anywhere these days. But tonight he couldn't seem to settle into any specific project. The moon had slipped behind the tall trees that surrounded the cabin, doing little to dispel the inky-black void beyond his windows, and the darkness seemed to press in on him from all sides, reminding him of another dark night— one he longed to forget.

The conversation he'd had with Johnson came back to him. *We think there are three more.* The remains of three women. Johnson had implied that Carter could put the families of those women out of their misery by making it possible for them to say good bye to their daughters or sisters, wives or mothers.

But that would mean meeting with the man who had, in effect, killed Laurel. Maybe Hooper hadn't actually done the deed, as was the case with his other victims, but the end result had been the same. Carter had had only a brief few years during which he thought he'd saved Laurel.

Rubbing his eyes, he bowed his head over the file of "issue position" letters he'd been editing for the senator. He'd already read the top one twice, but it hadn't registered, and the third pass made no deeper impact than the previous two. The image of Charles Hooper continued to intrude—his blond head and slightly protruding forehead, his gangly build, his awkward gait. Carter had never hated anyone more than he hated Charles Hooper, and that animosity brought anger, which alienated him from everyone, even the man he used to be.

Give it a rest. In an attempt to seize upon something

real enough to bring him back from the black hole of swirling emotions that threatened to suck him in, he focused on Liz. Leaning back, he pictured her body, milky-white in the moonlight, lying beneath him. He remembered the slight arch of her back as he took her, heard again her soft sigh of release. Last night had provided the first peace he'd known in two full years.

He craved more....

Picking up the telephone, he dialed her number, thinking it might help if he could hear her voice. When he was talking to her, the past couldn't crowd too closely. She was current, unrelated, stimulating. But he'd made her a promise at the Honky Tonk: when it was over, it was over.

He chuckled mirthlessly to find himself struggling, only a day later, with a promise that had seemed so easy to make at the time. He might have found some way to justify calling her in spite of those words—if she hadn't tried so hard to put some distance between them today. When Georgia had stopped by, Liz had nearly given away the nature of their relationship simply by insisting too energetically that she had no interest in him whatsoever.

The lady doth protest too much, methinks. He'd referred to that quote. But she'd said something significant right before. Something about a poem by Tennyson. What was the title of it?

Lady of shallow or...

Signing onto the Internet, he entered "Tennyson Lady of..." into Google.com, which immediately pulled up "The Lady of Shalott." It was a poem about a woman who lived in a castle tower upstream from King Arthur's Camelot, sewing a tapestry and watching, in a mirror, the reflection of those who passed by outside. Forbidden, as the result of a spell, to look directly at the world around her, she seemed content to live in the tower— until she saw the reflection of the handsome Sir Lancelot. Then she looked out the window at him, the mirror shattered, and the lady left her castle, only to lie in a boat and drift down the river to Camelot, singing a final song before she died.

"Uplifting," he muttered and exited the site. He didn't even want to think about what Liz had meant by the reference. He didn't like the poem. It was a little too close to his own reality. But Liz didn't know that and, as he delved back into his work, he couldn't forget her or the Lady of Shalott.

Switching to e-mail, he used the address he'd heard Liz give Mary Thornton the day before and sent her the following question: You'd rather remain safe in your tower and let life pass you by while watching in a mirror?

LIZ HAD TOLD CARTER TO TAKE Sunday off. She felt too guilty having him work his *entire* weekend, especially since he was helping her more as a favor than anything else. But she thought she'd go to the shop in the afternoon, and see what she could accomplish on her own. Her kids had called to see if they could stay with their father until after dinner. Keith still had Jennifer, Angela and Isabella there, and they were planning a barbecue. So Liz figured she might as well take advantage of the fact that Mica and Christopher were happy and well occupied by pushing forward with her own plans. She would've headed to The Chocolaterie directly and put in the whole day, but her father had convinced her to play tennis with him. They'd barely spoken since their encounter in the kitchen the day before, but he'd approached her the moment she'd gotten up this morning, and now here they were, facing each other on the court.

"You ready to show me what you've got?" he asked.

Liz stood diagonally to him in anticipation of his serve. But when he issued his challenge, she let her racket dip. Her father had said the same thing to her when she was fourteen years old, right before lobbing the ball softly over the net.

Today, however, the ball came hard and fast, catching her off guard. She stretched to connect with it, but it whizzed past the tip of her racket, hitting the corner of the court and going out of bounds.

"Too tough for you?" he asked with a grin.

It wasn't his serve that was too tough. It was seeing him wield a racket again after so many years. It was recognizing the subtle signs of age in his face and body and knowing the changes in her were even more dramatic. It was remembering. And most of all, it was forgiving.

"I can handle it," she said and emptied her mind, keeping the bulk of her weight over the balls of her feet so she could move more quickly.

The next serve came, and this time she was able to return it. Her swing didn't have the power she would've liked, but it forced her father to rush the net. He barely dinked the ball, hoping to catch her while she was still out too far, but she'd anticipated his strategy. Racing forward, she sent the ball rocketing past him before he could get back into position.

"Not bad," he said, watching it go, and she could tell that any thoughts he might have had about going easy on her were now officially history.

He got ahead after that. But she won the next point. Then they volleyed back and forth three or four times until he maneuvered her to the far right and placed the ball to her extreme left. It flew out of bounds before she could reach the centerline.

"You're better than I expected," she said, impressed.

He seemed surprised by her words. "So are you."

Although her father went on to win the first game, Liz came back to take the set. Gordon had great technique, but he grew winded before she did. Soon it became apparent, at least to Liz, that she'd dominate more and more easily, the longer they continued to play.

When they were finished, Gordon wiped the sweat from his forehead and met Liz at the edge of the net. They walked over to rest on the bleachers, where they'd left towels, extra balls, energy bars and some water.

"I always knew you had talent," he said.

Liz might have asked why he hadn't continued to foster her ability. But she didn't. What was the point? She knew from what had passed between them in her kitchen that he wouldn't answer the question. He didn't want to be reminded of the past. He wanted to pretend that everything was fine; that it had always been fine.

She wondered if they ever would have played again

had Luanna not left him. The obvious answer was no, but the little girl in her didn't want to accept that.

Passing a Thermos of water to him so he could drink, she was about to comment on how difficult it had been to beat him, especially early on. But movement at the edge of her peripheral vision stole her attention. Glancing toward the small building that housed the restrooms, she smiled as her brother's tall form separated from the shadow of the closest tree and came toward them.

"Isaac, what are you doing here?" she asked. "Where's Reenie?"

"She's helping her mother organize a charity auction for breast cancer. I was on my way to the feed store when I spotted your car and wanted to see how you're playing these days."

"She's good," their father volunteered. "She's improved a great deal."

"Since when?" Isaac countered. "Since last year? Since ten years ago?"

Gordon glanced away. Liz thought he'd let the comment go without a response, but after an uncomfortable silence he stood up and met Isaac's stony gaze. "I admit that I wasn't always the father I could've been," he said.

"*Now* you admit that? How many times did I come to you, begging you to step in when Luanna was mistreating Liz? Where was all this self-realization then?"

"Isaac—" Liz started. She was an adult. She didn't need him to defend her anymore. She wanted him to base his feelings toward their father on the merits of their own relationship, not on what had happened to her. But Isaac wasn't listening.

"And where's Luanna now?" he went on. "She was all you cared about. The only person you'd listen to."

"I cared about you, too," Gordon insisted. "Both of you. I—" He seemed to search for words. "It isn't always easy bringing the different parts of your life together, Isaac. I didn't choose to lose my wife. I didn't choose—" his eyes cut briefly to Liz "—some of the other stuff I've experienced. I've been dealing with my challenges the best way I can."

"By not dealing with them at all?" Isaac countered. "God, what do you think? That you can show up after fifteen years and pick up as though you didn't abandon us both in favor of the shrew you married?"

Gordon's hands had begun to shake, but he managed to keep his voice level. "I was a good father to you, Isaac. Maybe I wasn't the best I could be to Liz. Maybe I ignored too much of what went on—because of my own inadequacies. But you…you shouldn't have any complaints. Liz was the only thing that ever came between us."

"Liz? How could she come between us? She's your daughter!"

"No, she's not!" he shouted.

Liz's heart flew into her throat. She'd put one hand on her brother's arm and one hand on her father's, hoping to act as a mediator. But she let both men slip out of her grasp. Had Gordon just said what she thought he'd said?

"What do you mean?" she whispered, staring at him. Panic began to spread through her veins. The world around her seemed to slow to a crawl, until everything appeared to be happening in slow motion.

Gordon wouldn't even look at her. He was still glaring at Isaac. "What did you expect me to do?" he said, his voice tinged with bitterness. "Love another man's child as my own? As much as I love *you?*"

"You son of a bitch," Isaac whispered, obviously as stunned by this revelation as Liz.

Gordon didn't wait to hear any more. With a curse—at Isaac? at himself? Liz didn't know—he stalked across the grass to the road and headed down Main Street on foot.

LIZ SAT ALONE ON THE FLOOR in the back corner of her shop, where she couldn't be seen from the windows, hugging her knees to her chest. She didn't want to go home, in case her father—or the man she'd always thought was her father—was still there. She didn't want to go anywhere else, either, for fear she'd run into someone she knew and have to smile and pretend she was fine. She couldn't maintain the unaffected demeanor that generally hid her true feelings. She was too broken, too vulnerable right now.

It had taken some effort to convince Isaac to let her drive off on her own. He'd urged her to sit on the bleachers with him and talk, let out the pain. But she'd had nothing to say. She couldn't verbalize what she was feeling, couldn't even cry.

And now, at last, she was alone. It was her only consolation. She needed the silence, the absence of prying voices and looks of empathy....

She dug at her cuticles, ignoring a promise she'd made to Isaac—that she wouldn't fall back into her old habit—and somehow finding satisfaction in the pain.

uch a self-destructive tendency didn't make any sense, even to Liz, but the compulsion was there and the fresh ting reminded her she was still alive, still breathing, even though she felt numb in every other part of her body.

Slowly, her mind began to function properly again. Closing her eyes, she buried her face in her arms, allowing the questions that bombarded her to begin to arrange themselves in her mind. If Gordon Russell wasn't her father, who was? Why hadn't anyone, especially her mother, ever told her the truth? And how was it that Isaac belonged to Gordon, but she didn't? Her mother and father had been married for ten years when she was born.

Which meant there had to be more—reasons, excuses, explanations. She was afraid to hear them, to know them. All the same, what her father had said at the tennis courts explained a lot. In at least one way, this was a relief. But she couldn't bear the thought that the mother she'd always admired might not be quite the woman Liz had assumed she was. That was too much. That would rob her of the one person she'd loved beyond any other—as well as her more fallible father.

A chill ran down Liz's spine. Hugging her knees even tighter, she attempted to combat the cold seeping through her by rocking back and forth. But her clothes were still damp from playing tennis. And the temperature was dropping outside as a storm moved in. Clouds gathered in the sky and blocked the sun; the chimes outside Mary's shop tinkled wildly in the rising wind.

So much for Keith's barbecue, Liz thought discon-

nectedly, and tried to rouse herself enough to head ove
to his place, in case Mica and Christopher wanted to
come home. She had children. She had to take this or
the chin, along with everything else she'd been through

But she couldn't do it. Not yet.

"Liz? Liz, are you in there?" It was Reenie, knocking
on the front door. Judging from the worry in her voice
Isaac had filled her in.

Liz told herself she had to let her sister-in-law know
she was okay. But if she answered, Reenie wouldn't le
her be alone any longer. She and Isaac would gather
round with sympathy and well-meaning words, forcing
her to insist, over and over again, that she was fine
Dealing with them would take emotional reserves Liz
simply didn't possess right now. So she kept silent and
waited, hoping Reenie would give up.

"She's not here," Liz heard her say at last. "The doors
are locked and the lights are off."

Isaac responded that her car was in the parking lot
and then Reenie said, "She must've walked somewhere."

They moved on as rain began to patter on the roof. Liz
concentrated on the steady drumming so she wouldn'
have to think anymore—and she must have dozed off
because, when she came to, it was raining harder than
ever and someone was banging on the front door again.

"Liz? Hello? Open up!"

It was Carter. Immediately recognizing his voice, Liz
bit her lip as she listened. She didn't want him, of all
people, to find her. How could she explain what she was
doing, sitting alone in the dark?

She held her breath, waiting for him to go away, as Reenie and Isaac had done, and finally the calls and the knocking stopped. With a sigh of relief, she laid her head back on her knees. Even if her children weren't planning to come home until later, she should probably head that way to see what had become of Gordon. Life had to go on, whether she was ready for it or not. She knew that. She'd been in a similar place before. She just needed to give Carter time to leave first so she could make her exit unobserved.

"Liz? Let me in."

Great! Now he was at the back door. And he seemed so sure she was inside.

Covering her ears, she tried to block out the sound. He'd leave soon, she told herself. Reenie had given up. Why would Carter be any more persistent?

The pounding subsided and Liz relaxed again—but not for long. A moment later, there was a terrible scraping and popping, and the back door flew open.

Liz screamed and shielded her face as if an army was about to attack. But it was only Carter. He stood in the doorway holding a crowbar, his wet hair dripping down his neck and onto his shirt.

When his gaze settled on her, Liz waited for him to ask why she hadn't opened the door. Or why she was sitting on the cold, hard floor. But he didn't say a thing. He simply pivoted and walked away.

There was a distant jangle as he dropped the tire iron in his trunk, and then the thud of a car door. After which came silence.

Was he leaving? For a moment, Liz thought so. She

almost got up to make sure. But he returned with a blanket, which he wrapped around her matter-of-factly.

She supposed she should stand and offer some excuse for her behavior. But she didn't have the strength or the energy.

"Thanks," she murmured.

Carter didn't reply. Easily lifting her into his arms, he carried her out to his car as if she were a child. Then he left her bundled up in the passenger seat, while he hammered two boards across the door he'd broken.

When he finished, he climbed in and put the car in gear.

Liz glanced over at him. "What made you come looking for me?"

"I was over at the senator's house when Reenie called."

He didn't volunteer how much he knew and she didn't ask. "You broke my door."

"You wouldn't open it."

She sank into her seat as they drove through town. "How'd you know I was inside?"

"Your car was parked in the lot, for starters."

"And?"

"It's your favorite place in the world."

He was right, she realized. She'd never really identified it as that, even in her own mind. But it was the embodiment of her dreams, the only place that was entirely her own. Evidently, Carter was far more perceptive than he pretended to be.

"You're probably wondering what I was doing in there," she said at last, feeling as if she needed to make the inevitable explanation.

But she was talking to Carter Hudson, who didn't approach life in quite the same way as everyone else. "No," he replied. "I'm not."

CHAPTER TWELVE

LIZ SAT ON CARTER'S SOFA, wearing a pair of his sweats. She had a warm quilt wrapped around her and there was a fire crackling across the room. A glass of wine sat on the coffee table. Carter was in the kitchen, making dinner. He hadn't told her what they were going to eat, but she was guessing something Mexican. She could smell the steak and onions, even the lime.

She thought about fighting the sluggish state that had slipped over her so she could return to the real world. It was Sunday evening. The kids would be coming home soon. But she wasn't ready to leave just yet. She felt safe in Carter's isolated little cabin, surrounded by the tall, quiet forest. She was even comfortable with his tinkering around the place. She wasn't quite alone, but he didn't invade her space in the way that Reenie or Isaac would have. He didn't require anything from her. He'd simply put on his music and gone about his business.

"Do you mind if I use your cell?" she called out to him.

"Go ahead."

While they were in the car, he'd contacted someone, probably Senator Holbrook, to let her family know she was okay. She wasn't sure Keith had been made aware that anyone was looking for her, but she needed to let him know she'd pick up the kids on her way home instead of having him drop them off.

Retrieving Carter's silver camera phone from the lamp table, she opened it, and a picture of Carter with a woman appeared on the screen. They were at some kind of sporting event. The woman was the same person who'd been in the wedding photo. She held her cheek to Carter's so they could both fit inside the frame and she was smiling—but rather distantly.

Who was this woman? And what had happened to her? Liz wondered. Had they split up? If so, it was rather strange that Carter kept her picture on his phone.

"Did you find it okay?" Carter called from the other room.

"Yeah, it's right here," she replied and dialed her ex-husband's number before Carter had time to wander out and see why she wasn't talking to anyone.

"Where are you calling me from?" Keith asked as soon he heard her voice.

Carter's number had probably popped up on his caller ID. "I'm borrowing a friend's cell."

"A friend," he repeated.

"Yes. How are the kids?"

"They're fine. They're always fine when they're with me, aren't they?"

"You're a good father." He knew that, but every once in a while he acted as if he needed to hear it again. She supposed it was because his relationship with the kids was the one thing he hadn't screwed up.

Still, he paused as if it shocked him that she'd agree

with him so readily. "What's going on?" he asked. "Reenie called here earlier, asking if I'd seen you. She seemed worried."

Liz thought of what her father had revealed. Despite the problems she and Gordon had experienced after her mother had died, he'd been a tether of sorts, simply by virtue of living and breathing and being. Their relationship hadn't been good, but at least Liz had belonged to someone. Now, with her mother dead, her father coming forward to say he wasn't her father after all, and Isaac happily married and immersed in his own life, Liz felt as if she were drifting into space by herself. "My father and I had a disagreement."

"About what?"

"Same old stuff," she lied. She couldn't tell Keith what she'd discovered, because it wouldn't reflect well on her mother. Broadcasting the truth wouldn't help, anyway. What would it bring? Curiosity? Maybe a little sympathy? Certainly nothing that would improve the situation. She'd already decided not to delve any deeper into the mystery. If her real father knew she existed, he didn't want to be part of her life, or he would have contacted her long ago. Even if her real father *didn't* know she existed, she couldn't imagine he'd welcome the surprise at this late date. It was better to leave the past alone. Then she wouldn't have to address the part her mother might have played in what had happened. She could protect her memories of Chloe Russell—could salvage that much.

"Are you okay?" Keith asked.

"I'm fine." She just needed a few hours to come to terms with the shock and that was where Keith came in. "Can you keep the kids a little longer?"

"Where are you?"

Trying to sidestep the question would only increase his curiosity, so she told him the truth. "Carter's."

"What are you doing there?" he asked, his voice full of jealousy and suspicion.

"We're about to have dinner."

"Oh." A sudden drop in pitch told her the news had hit him like a punch. But she was no longer in love with him. He had to let her move on sometime.

"I thought you didn't like him," he said.

She wasn't sure how she felt toward Carter. He had a commanding presence, yet he wasn't arrogant, as she'd first believed. He was confident—and he was generous, even if he didn't seem that way. She was afraid to examine his nature any more than that.

Perhaps he was an unlikely friend, but he seemed to offer Liz exactly what she needed at the moment: a bit of space, some quiet and plenty of creature comforts. She knew from experience that he could also offer her a heady dose of pleasure. But letting herself slide further down that slope didn't seem wise.

"Actually, I do like him," she admitted, realizing that it was true.

"How much?" Keith asked.

"We're friends."

Liz could hear Jennifer in the background, talking to Mica or someone else. Keith lowered his voice. "You wouldn't sleep with him, would you?" he asked quietly.

The memory of Carter's mouth on her breast flashed through Liz's mind, instantly burning away the numbness she'd felt since she'd left the tennis court.

She wouldn't sleep with him *again*—but not because she didn't want to.

"That's not your concern," she said. "I'll see you later."

Her ex didn't say good bye, but Liz hit the end button anyway. Then she sat staring at the photograph on Carter's cell phone.

"You ready to eat?" Carter asked, poking his head into the room. Liz didn't set the phone down and pretend she hadn't seen the photo, as she had with the wedding picture. She studied the woman's face while he watched her.

"She's beautiful," she said.

He came farther into the room, took the phone and closed it. "I know."

"WHAT ARE YOU GOING TO DO?" Carter asked. He was sitting on the other end of the sofa, sipping his wine while Liz finished her fajitas. He hadn't touched her since they'd arrived, but the atmosphere was intimate, as if they were the only two people on earth.

"About what?" she asked.

"Gordon."

"I don't know what you mean. What *can* I do?"

"You could kick him out, if he's still around."

So Carter knew everything. Reenie had probably confided in her father, who'd confided in his trusted aide. Liz didn't want anyone else in town to hear about all this, but somehow she didn't mind that Carter was aware of the situation. He'd whisked her away when she'd needed it most, given her a reprieve before she had to deal with any questions. It was a bit strange she felt no inclination to tell Keith, who'd been such a big part of her life, however. How was it that she preferred to share her secrets with a man she'd met only a few days ago?

Liz set her plate aside. The food Carter had made smelled delicious, but she could scarcely taste it. "That's what you think I should do?"

"There's no *should* or *shouldn't*," he replied.

"There's restraint and forethought, as opposed to a knee-jerk reaction," she said.

He seemed to consider her response. "Do you always look at every situation from the opposite perspective?"

She pulled the quilt higher. "I try. How else can I be fair?"

"Judging from what Isaac has to say, Gordon hasn't been too fair to you."

"Who knows?" she said, toying with the edge of the blanket. "Maybe the situation has been difficult for him. Especially if he felt betrayed or *was* betrayed." Which must've been the case, although she didn't want to add that. "I would've been a daily reminder of his heartache. No wonder he let Luanna take charge. He probably didn't want to see my face." She stared at her wine. The wine she'd already drunk was turning sour in her stomach, so she set the glass next to her plate. "Maybe he's something of a hero."

"A hero?" Carter echoed. "Now, that's generous."

"He could've given me up, right? He kept a roof over my head, let me remain in the family."

"Isaac never would have forgiven him."

"That might be true. But that doesn't change the fact that those years could've been even worse. Maybe I should be grateful."

"I'd have to say that the amount of gratitude you owe Gordon Russell depends."

She rubbed her cheek against the worn quilt. The sensation was comforting, but no more so than the smell of Carter on the fabric. She didn't want to make love right now, but she wanted to be with him, just as they were. "On what?"

"Did he know you weren't his from the beginning? Or did he find out later?"

Liz had wondered about that herself, and had already guessed at the answer. "I'm betting he learned about the time my mother died."

"What makes you think so?"

"Prior to that, he doted on me. Afterward…" She let her words fall off.

"How old were you when that happened?"

"Fourteen."

Carter stared at the carpet, shaking his head.

"What?" she prompted.

"How'd he expect you to interpret his sudden withdrawal?"

"Chances are he never considered that. He was busy filling his life with other people."

"Like his new wife."

"And her spoiled stepson."

Carter drained his wineglass and set it aside. "Do you think your mother told him you weren't his just before she died?"

Liz covered her toes, which had slipped out from beneath the quilt. "It's possible. But I doubt it."

"That wouldn't have done you any favor," he agreed. "Especially if she was depending on him to take care of you."

"Maybe my real father turned up at my mother's funeral. Or Gordon found some old love letters in her closet. Or…"

"What?"

She couldn't prevent the slight hope that crept into her voice. As disappointed as she'd been in her father over the past eighteen years, she still loved him, still wanted to *belong*. "Through the years, a lot of people have told me we look alike. Do you suppose it's possible that he could be mistaken?"

Carter studied her for a moment. "Do you want the truth?"

"Maybe," she said cautiously, knowing if anyone would give it to her, he would.

"I can't imagine he'd tell you all this unless he knew for sure."

"Right." She pinched the muscles in her right shoulder, hoping to thwart the headache that was building.

"Would it be easier to know how it happened?" he asked. "To explore all the details?"

"Where would I start?" she asked.

He leaned forward, resting his elbows on his knees. "I could help you."

There was something significant about the way he presented this offer. "How?"

Sitting back, he put his feet on the coffee table. "By talking to the right people."

"My father?"

"Friends of your parents, neighbors, coworkers."

"Why do I get the impression you'd be more effective at piecing together the past than most other people would be?" she asked.

He shrugged. "Because it's true."

Liz's heart began to pound. There were depths to Carter she wasn't sure he'd ever let anyone fully explore. Somehow his darker side was connected to his mysterious past and to the woman in the pictures. But Liz couldn't see how, and she doubted he'd tell her why he'd closed himself off.

"You'd help me, but you won't let anyone help you. Is that it?" she said.

"Help me with what?" he asked.

"With whatever it is that's haunting you." She motioned toward the boxes. "The reason you won't unpack. The reason you're in Dundee, Idaho, instead of somewhere closer to home. The reason you make love like a starving man but refuse the kind of deep, lasting relationship you really need."

Her reference to the way he made love suddenly charged the room with sexual energy. His eyes met hers, but she couldn't read what was going on behind them. She only knew he was still hungry; they both were.

"I carry my burdens alone," he said at last.

She pushed her hair away from her face, threw off the

quilt and stood. It was time to pick up her kids and head home. "Well, to answer your question, no, I don't want you to help me figure out where I came from," she said. "My mother's gone. I won't ruin what I have left of her by digging through the past."

He'd stood when she had. "Okay."

He didn't seem to judge her decision. He just accepted it.

"Thanks anyway."

He caught a lock of hair as it fell back into her eyes and tucked it behind her ear. It was such a tender gesture, she thought he might draw her toward him. When she imagined the taste of his lips, his tongue moving against hers, her earlier ambivalence about making love instantly disappeared. She wanted to turn off the lights, remove their clothes and let him carry her away as she knew he could. But Carter would only be generous with his body, and that type of fulfillment wouldn't last.

"Some things are better left as they are," he said softly.

She wasn't sure if he was talking about her decision not to investigate the past, or about what had occurred on Friday night. But she took a long look around the cabin, just in case she never saw it again. Making love with a man who'd move on soon, leaving her with only a few heated memories, wasn't a part of real life. Facing the fact that she suddenly had no father, continuing to make school lunches for her kids, folding laundry—that was real.

At least Carter had provided a refuge for her when she'd needed it most. She was grateful to him for that.

"What would you do if you were me?" she asked, as

he grabbed his keys off the counter. "Would you search out the truth?"

"Definitely," he said. "But I'm one of those people who can't leave well enough alone."

Carter met her at the door, but didn't open it right away. He lifted her chin with one finger, letting his gaze fall to her lips. He wanted to kiss her; she could feel it.

Desire coiled within her gut and shortened her breath, but she didn't lean forward or make it easy for him and he dropped his hand. "Let's go."

WHEN LIZ RETURNED HOME with her kids, Gordon was gone. He'd left no note. He'd just taken his bags and disappeared.

Now that her children were in bed asleep, she walked through the house feeling empty and alone. Finally she stopped in front of her mother's picture in the hall. "What happened?" she murmured.

Chloe stared back, looking secretive and mysterious for the first time in Liz's life.

Liz remembered the boxes of family pictures and papers in the attic of her father's house. Was there something stored there that would tell her more? A letter? A journal? An apology?

Covering her eyes with her hands, as if that could block out anything she didn't want to acknowledge, Liz shook her head. *I don't want to know, remember?* But other faces appeared before her mind's eye—those of the men in the neighborhood where she grew up, and at the church her family had attended, even the teachers she'd had in school. Had her mother slept with one of them? Was Jeremy Lamph from down the street her father? Or maybe Ryan Sudwick's dad?

It was horrible to imagine her mother with any of those men, especially because they were all married. But Liz couldn't remember any others. Except for old Mr. Winter. And she couldn't picture her mother touching him in a romantic way.

Regardless of who her father was, her mother would've had to let a man sneak over to the house while Isaac was only a toddler and Gordon was at work.

Or had Chloe slept with a total stranger?

The concept of a stranger, a brief encounter, seemed more acceptable to Liz than any other scenario, but she didn't want to entertain the questions that naturally arose from there: Where did Chloe meet this man? Where did they go? How did he convince her to break her marriage vows? Did they stay in contact? If her mother hadn't told her lover about the pregnancy, was it because he'd have been angry? Uninterested? Upset?

Despite her reluctance to dwell on the various possibilities, Liz couldn't seem to stop them from whirring through her head like tickertape. So she was grateful when the phone rang— despite the fact that it had been ringing all night. She'd talked to Isaac and Reenie. Then Carter had called to tell her he'd replaced the door at the shop with one they'd removed from the apartment and Keith had phoned to ask all the questions he couldn't ask in front of the kids—if she'd enjoyed herself with Carter, if they were planning to see each other again. By the time she'd managed to convince her ex that she and Carter were merely friends, Senator Holbrook was calling to check on her. Reenie's dad seemed especially understanding because of his own experience. He and Celeste shared a few of the details of the affair that had resulted in Lucky, Reenie and Gabe's half-sister, and their story gave Liz hope that her mother could make a tragic mistake and still be an honorable person.

Reaching the cordless phone on the fourth ring, she brought it to her ear without bothering to check the caller ID. It had to be Dave. He was the only one who ever called her this late. "Hello?"

"Hey," he said, "I thought I'd hear from you this weekend."

Was the weekend over already? Liz could hardly believe it. Of course, she'd been pretty preoccupied....

"I tried to reach you on Friday," she said, remembering, with some relief, that she had tried to call him at least once.

"You didn't leave a message."

"You were out."

"On Friday? Oh yeah, I have a friend who's really into foreign films. He twisted my arm into going to see some artsy flick at a theater in Westwood."

He. Liz felt a twinge of guilt. "Was it any good?"

"Not bad. What'd you do this weekend?"

"Worked. Mostly," she added so that her answer wouldn't be a complete lie.

"That's why you didn't answer my e-mails?"

"I haven't even been on my computer."

"Did Keith come through for you, then?"

"No. He's been unavailable."

"How are you managing?"

"Someone else has been helping out."

"Who?"

"Carter Hudson."

"You've never mentioned anyone by that name before," he said. "Who is he? Some old cowboy?"

Not exactly. Liz moved into her bedroom and turned down her bed. She had to get some sleep. Carter was supposed to meet her bright and early in the morning. Father or no father, she had a business to open and run. "He's new in town."

"Is he a contractor?"

"No, he's Senator Holbrook's new aide."

"How'd he start working for you?"

"The Senator asked Carter to help me."

"Because Carter knows how to do what you need?"

Liz gulped, thinking about the meaning *she* might attach to those words. "He grew up building houses, and he's a hard worker," she said, trying to steer her mind away from the more interesting images racing through it.

There was a long pause during which Liz feared she'd shown a little more admiration in her voice than she'd intended. At last, Dave said, "Are you paying him?"

"No, I just told you. He's doing it as a favor to the senator."

"Really."

Dave wasn't typically the jealous type, but this wasn't his happy-go-lucky tone. He was obviously trying to figure out how significant Carter was to her. In some ways, Liz wished she could answer the same question for herself. It had been difficult to leave Carter's cabin without visiting his bedroom first—she knew that much "Is something wrong?"

"No," he said, then seemed to reconsider his response "I mean, not unless...You're not *seeing* him, are you?"

Liz didn't know how to respond. She hadn't expected Dave to be the one hoping to achieve an exclusive relationship. They'd had that one weekend together, but they'd made no promises.

"We...went out to dinner," she said, throwing that much out there to see how he'd respond.

"You did?"

She stood in front of the mirror. Instead of undressing, she simply stared at her own reflection as though—if she looked hard enough—she'd be able to understand exactly how she'd gotten involved with Carter and why she was still thinking about him almost every minute She'd been attracted to Dave. Why did he suddenly seem so forgettable? "Yes. Is that okay?"

"As long as you're just friends," he said.

Her eyes widened. *Friends?* How could she claim she and Carter were just friends?

On the other hand, how could she claim they were more? Their relationship didn't fall neatly into any category. He'd been her lover on Friday. He'd been her best friend today. But she wasn't sure they'd be anything to each other tomorrow.

"It's not serious," she assured him. Then she told him about her dad. She didn't really want to discuss Gordon and the past when her feelings were still so raw. But as painful as the subject was, it was better than talking about Carter—at least with Dave.

CHAPTER THIRTEEN

GORDON REACHED SALT LAKE via a circuitous route and an overnight stay in Wyoming, arriving at three in the afternoon. He continued driving south, toward Vegas. He wasn't sure where he was going. He hadn't thought that far ahead. All he wanted to do was drive—as if he could outdistance what he'd done and escape the look of accusation he'd seen on Isaac's face. He'd been such a fool. Blurting out what had been eating at him for the past eighteen years had been stupid, selfish. It was a plea for Isaac's sympathy and understanding at Liz and Chloe's expense. He knew his son would instantly recognize that—and he was embarrassed he'd done it.

If only he didn't see his best friend every time he looked at Liz. If only he didn't feel so robbed....

But what Randy's wife had told him the day she'd appeared in his office had tarnished his late wife's memory *and* cost him his daughter. There was no way around it.

Clenching his jaw, Gordon sped up. The miles passed in a blur of dark countryside. He was beyond the Wasatch Mountains and into the desert almost before he knew it.

When the sun began to set, he could see the glittering Vegas skyline in the distance. It was beautiful, rising above its flat, dusty surroundings. He considered stopping again. But the glitzy hotels, frenetic gambling, opulence and overindulgence held no appeal. There was nothing for him here. He wasn't sure *where* he belonged. He had no job, no house, no family—no anchor.

How could he have let his life end up this way? He'd always dealt with what had happened as honorably as he possibly could. *He* was the injured party, right? Maybe his relationship with Liz hadn't been the same as before, which made him bitter at times. But he'd provided for her. And he'd managed to keep Chloe's secret for all these years.

He rolled down his window to let the cool early morning air rush into the car. He should've taken his secret to the grave. Or maybe he should've told Liz at the time, and given her the opportunity to go live with Randy and Kristen.

Would she have been better off? He didn't think so. Luanna had never liked her. But Kristen wouldn't have been any kinder. Kristen had even more reason to resent her. Once Chloe died, Randy must've decided he could finally unburden himself by telling her the truth. Because Chloe was no longer a threat, he probably thought Kristen would be able to deal with it. But she hadn't taken the news well. Maybe she didn't leave him, but she was vengeful enough to retaliate by telling Gordon—so that Randy would lose his best friend.

Anyway, Gordon doubted the Bellinis would have taken Liz, even if he'd tried to send her to them. They didn't want their family, friends, their own children to know what Randy had done. They'd already been struggling to preserve their marriage.

Gordon hadn't wanted anyone to know that Chloe had betrayed him, either. His pride was all he'd had left.

He shook his head. What had happened was painful and confusing. Even after so many years.

Pulling to a stop at the first light on the edge of Vegas, he gazed at the string of casinos up ahead, trying once more to convince himself to lay over. But when the light turned green, he drove past all the gambling establishments, the restaurants, the homes and businesses. Eventually, he'd have to stop for food and gas, but he was leaving the glitz and glamour in his wake because he finally knew where he was going.

EXCEPT FOR THE SINK, the chocolate shop was basically finished. Liz couldn't believe it. After Carter packed his tools and left, she took a final walk around, admiring their accomplishments. The shop would look even better in a few more days, when the rest of the display cases and appliances were in and she had all her supplies on hand. But she could do that on her own. Carter had gotten her through the difficult part.

She was so grateful to him, she could almost have wept. But she knew that had to do with how emotional she'd been the past two days and she refused to let herself break down. Feeling indebted to Carter was a little dangerous if she planned to keep her distance from him in the future. So she focused on the fact that she'd probably be able to open next weekend, and tried not to think about how much what he'd done meant to her. If the shop required all her time and energy, she couldn't dwell on what her father had said, or on what she'd done Friday night.

She had to collect Mica and Christopher from their grandmother's house and get dinner started. But she could allow herself five or ten minutes right now to savor the positive.

Sinking wearily but happily onto the hardwood floor they'd put in the kitchen, Liz checked the phone sitting next to her to see if her service had been hooked up. Sure enough, a dial tone hummed in her ear.

"The Chocolaterie. How can I help you?" she said as though a call had just come in. She imagined selling whoever it was a box of her homemade fudge and pictured how prettily she'd wrap it.

Decadent. That would be the buzzword for everything she did here. Her shop would reflect the joy in life. And why not? There was enough disappointment and disillusionment in the world.

"I'm a chocolatier," she said aloud, marveling at the fact that something so good could have come out of the past eighteen months. As much as she still missed having a "complete" family, she never would have opened her own shop if she'd stayed married. Keith wouldn't have been friendly to the idea. He'd had her quit the airlines right away because he wanted her to be the pampered wife, to spend her time playing tennis and planning social outings.

Reenie poked her head through the back door— Carter had taped a Wet Cement sign to the front—and eyed the improvements. "Wow!"

Liz stood. She knew she was wearing a silly smile, but she didn't care. "I love it."

"For good reason."

"Where are the girls?" she asked, hoping to see Jennifer, Angela and Isabella.

"With Isaac, on their way home from school. I'm heading over to Gabe's house to check on Kenny and Brent."

"How have they been handling their parents' absence?"

"Better than I imagined they would. Of course, they think Gabe and Hannah are on vacation. I'm sure they wouldn't be doing quite so well if they knew the truth."

"It's hard to believe Kenny's responsible enough to take care of Brent."

"Hannah calls him at least twice a day. And my parents and I are staying in close touch. But he's just back from his first year at college and doing a fine job on his own. He's a good kid."

Liz glanced at her watch. "So what made you stop here?"

"I was in the neighborhood and wanted to check on your progress."

"Do you have time to see the rest?" she asked, smiling proudly.

"Sure." Reenie slipped all the way inside, and Liz let her have a look around.

"Carter helped you do all this?" she asked. "The fancy paint...the floors?"

"In only three days," Liz said.

"He's *good*."

How good, Reenie would never know. A wisp of a memory—the scent of the candles they'd burned on Friday evening—came back to Liz and, as a result, her smile probably grew sillier.

"Liz?"

She pulled herself out of her private thoughts. "What?"

"I said, he seemed pretty concerned when we couldn't find you yesterday."

"What's 'concerned' for Carter? A sympathetic grunt?"

Reenie laughed. "No, a very solemn expression. And he went out to look for you right away."

"He's a nice guy," Liz said vaguely. She didn't want to explain how he'd found her or that he'd had to break the shop door to get in, so she quickly changed the subject back to Gabe. "Have you heard from your brother?"

"Last night. His surgery is scheduled for this Thursday."

"He's still set on going through with it?"

"Yeah."

"Sometimes it's hard to give up on a dream," Liz said.

Reenie clenched her fists. "Sometimes you need to be happy with what you've got."

Liz nodded. She could understand Reenie not wanting her brother to risk his life. She didn't want Gabe to have the operation, either. But she could also understand his burning desire to walk again. "Have you told Lucky what's happening?"

"I wasn't going to, but…" Reenie twisted her hair around one finger. "She's been taking food to Kenny and

Brent. And I know how much she cares about Gabe, even if the two of them don't have the best relationship."

"What'd she say?"

"She wanted to call him and plead with him to come home."

"Did you let her?"

"Are you kidding? He wouldn't be happy that I included her in the secret."

"I thought the two of them were beginning to get along."

"Gabe's coming to terms with the fact that Dad made a mistake, and that Lucky is the result. But it hasn't been easy for him to accept her as part of the family. He does better in some encounters than others."

"He's been through a lot. If he hadn't found out about Lucky at such a vulnerable time—"

"We didn't know she existed until three years after the accident."

"He still hadn't come to terms with his losses, Reenie. When Lucky returned to town, he was living like a hermit in that cabin of his, remember?"

"I remember. I just—I wish he'd let himself care about her."

Liz gave her friend a sympathetic expression. "I'm sure he will in time."

"You haven't had any more trouble with that vandal who tore your sink from the wall, have you?" she asked.

"No," Liz said, but she couldn't remember telling Reenie about the sink. "How'd you know about that?"

"Keith mentioned it to me. He was upset you thought he was behind it."

"I'm not positive he wasn't," Liz admitted.

"He's made mistakes, but he's not destructive like that."

Liz turned back to the phone. "That reminds me. I still haven't heard from the plumber."

Reenie paused to look inside the bathroom. "What do you need him for?"

"So I can get the darn thing reattached."

"It *is* reattached."

Surprised, Liz retraced her steps and peered over her sister-in-law's shoulder. Sure enough, the sink was just as it should be. Even the wall had been patched and painted. "It wasn't that way this morning," she said.

"Carter must've fixed that, too. But weren't you here with him all day?"

"I left for a little while, to pick the kids up from school. I wanted to help them with their homework and buy them an ice cream cone before dropping them at Keith's parents' house."

"He must've done it while you were gone. But you'd think he would have told you."

Most men would've been eager to collect the praise they deserved for such a good deed. But not Carter. "He's different," she said.

Reenie narrowed her eyes suspiciously. "Now you're sounding as though you like different."

"Not necessarily," she said. But deep down she knew she liked it, maybe even too much. She had a lot of resolve, but she wasn't sure how she'd avoid visiting Carter's cabin over the ensuing weeks and months. Friday had been far too satisfying—and they'd gotten away with it far too easily.

There's always the other school of thought...Taking advantage of something while it lasts...

THAT NIGHT, LIZ SIGNED ON to the Internet while Christopher and Mica sat next to her creating a pyramid out of sugar cubes for Mica's school project. Mary Thornton had said she'd send some information regarding a joint ad they might run in the newspaper, and Dave had mentioned a couple of messages, too. Once she caught up on her e-mail, she wanted to search the Internet for some ideas. She planned to introduce one new chocolate-covered goodie each month as a "featured" item. For Valentine's Day, she already had in mind a special mix of chocolate-covered coffee beans, marshmallows, raisins and pecans. She wasn't positive it would work as an aphrodisiac as well as Vianne's special chocolates had, but it would certainly keep folks from falling asleep at an inopportune time.

Mary's message was brief. She described the various sizes of ads they could purchase and listed the cost of each. She also noted that they'd have to submit their information to the paper by Wednesday. Liz figured she should participate, and she decided to work on the layout in the morning. She sent Mary a response telling her as much, then opened her next message.

It was from Dave who said he missed her and asked if she'd come to L.A. in a few weeks. In the back of her mind, Liz had been considering a visit. But now she'd probably be so busy with the shop she wouldn't have a chance.

She found it interesting that being too busy came as a relief instead of a disappointment.

Unsure of the best way to break the news, she put off

her response and clicked on Dave's other message, which turned out to be a questionnaire.

1. What's the one thing you admire most in the opposite sex?

She considered her answer. *Honesty*. She wasn't sure she'd have chosen that particular trait before the whole disaster with Keith, but these days it topped her list.

She went on to question two. Would you rather be with someone good-looking or someone who made you laugh?

Laugh. Definitely.

3. Would you rather be with someone who told you how they felt or showed you how they felt?

Showed. Keith had been generous with his words, but his actions had nearly destroyed her.

4. If you could talk to one person right now, who would that be?

Liz considered everyone she knew, including Isaac, Reenie, Keith and Dave. Carter was the only one she excluded from the group, but he wasn't much of a conversationalist, anyway.

Dave.

5. What's your favorite part of a man's anatomy?

Carter's unusual eyes came immediately to mind. But she couldn't remember Dave's with that much clarity, so she went for what she could recall more clearly—a pair of muscular legs.

6. If you could reach out and touch one person, who would it be?

Dave again, right? Of course. Dave, Dave, Dave. Not Carter. Carter was too close and too alone in that cabin of his. And the answer to every other question had been Dave. Carter didn't make her laugh. He was too focused, too intense. He didn't have much to say, either.

But he communicated well enough with his hands. And he was more honest than anyone she'd ever met.

"What's wrong, Mommy?"

Liz glanced up to see her two children studying her curiously.

"Nothing, why?"

"You were frowning," Mica said.

"I was?"

"Like this." Christopher pulled his eyebrows together and scowled deeply.

"Are you sad that Grandpa left so soon?"

Mica and Chris didn't know what had happened with Gordon. Liz preferred to keep it that way, at least until they were older. They barely knew him anyway. "No, I was concentrating."

"On your e-mail?" Mica asked skeptically.

"It's nothing important," Liz replied, but she couldn't focus exclusively on Chris or Mica because her eyes had already skimmed down the page to the final question: 10. If you could make love with anyone right now, who would it be?

Oh, boy. She wasn't about to consider that one. She didn't want to know the answer.

Moving her cursor to the X, she closed the window and smiled at her children. "Shall we go read?"

Mica and Christopher responded eagerly. They were in the middle of Christopher Paolini's *Eldest*, which Mica particularly found riveting. But when Liz returned to her e-mail after her children were in bed, so she could formulate a reply to Dave, she came across one other unopened message with the subject header, The Lady of Shalott. Perplexed, she opened it to find only one line.

You'd rather remain safe in your tower and let life pass you by while watching in a mirror?

There was no signature, but the sender's e-mail address let her know who it was from: CHudson1973@aol.com. Carter. But she couldn't remember ever giving him her e-mail address.

"How strange," she muttered, pondering his question for several seconds. Obviously, he'd read the poem and correctly interpreted her earlier allusion. The Lady of Shalott had risked everything for love and lost. Liz was afraid of such a risk. But was safety worth the cost?

She imagined herself watching the people out on the street from behind the window of The Chocolaterie. Was she preparing for a life alone? A life devoted solely to her work and her children?

She didn't think so. Not even subconsciously. When she really thought about it, the Lady of Shalott didn't remind Liz of herself so much as it reminded her of Carter. He was the one working tirelessly to wall everyone out. The one watching life pass him by. She might've been hurt before, and maybe she was a bit skittish as a result, but she was still willing to risk her heart.

Hitting the reply button, she responded with one line of her own:

Are you sure I'm the one in the tower?

A JINGLE ALERTED CARTER to the delivery of a new e-mail message. Clicking over from his word processing program, he saw that Liz had finally returned his message.

He opened it to see what she had to say, blinking several times as the meaning behind her cryptic response sank in. Was she crazy? He'd lived life so up-close and personal that he'd been unable to separate his job from his private life. He'd risked his skin, known the darkest side of human nature, discovered truths that would disillusion even the most idealistic person. He'd tracked a twisted psychopath day and night and managed to put him away. And he'd fallen in love with the one victim who'd survived.

Maybe those things were in the past. But Liz didn't understand that it was all no good. What was the point of embracing life so fully? Of sacrificing so much? Of loving so hard?

"That's bullshit," he said and closed her message. But only a few seconds later he opened up Tennyson's poem and read it again, gravitating to one particular phrase.

I am half sick of shadows, said the Lady of Shalott.

"I am half sick of shadows...." he repeated aloud.

Well, maybe Liz was in a position to eschew the dark, but as far as Carter was concerned it was the shadows that made life bearable.

He glanced at the envelope that had come by overnight courier—and once again he refused to open it.

RANDY AND KRISTEN BELLINI still lived next door to the house in Long Beach that Gordon had owned with Chloe. Gordon had bumped into their oldest son at a restaurant a few months back and had learned that much. He'd also learned that Randy and Kristen were emptynesters. Their two daughters had graduated from college and were married; their youngest boy was living on campus at UCLA.

Their lives seemed ideal—and completely unaffected by the past. Even their house was the same. With the moon shining brightly, Gordon could see that it was still painted light blue with dark blue trim, or something close. The bougainvillea that had always grown against the chimney continued to thrive. The planters in the small turret surrounding the front door remained, and

Kristen's favorite petunias lined both sides of the path leading up to the entrance.

The garage had a different door. That was all. And now that the kids were gone, only a single car—a new Audi—occupied the drive.

Gordon sat at the curb, staring at the well-kept home. He hadn't showered in two days, had slept only a few hours at a rest stop on the drive from Salt Lake. He knew he probably looked like hell. But he didn't care. After a brief "stutter" in his relationship with his wife, Randy had gone on as if he'd done nothing wrong. Except that he couldn't meet Gordon's eyes again.

Dropping his head into his hands, Gordon rubbed his temples. He'd served in Vietnam with Randy. How could his best friend have betrayed him with the one person Gordon had loved beyond any other?

He'd wondered that for almost two decades. He'd confronted Randy right after Kristen had told him the truth, but Randy had refused to say anything. He'd just stared down at his feet. Now, maybe after all this time, he could explain why he'd done what he'd done. It wasn't as if Gordon could ever achieve resolution by confronting Chloe. By the time he'd learned the truth, all he'd had left of her was memories and pictures.

Getting out of his car, he strode purposefully to the front door. It was nearly midnight. But that wouldn't stop him from knocking. If he had to drag everyone in the whole neighborhood out of bed, he'd do it.

He banged on the door. When there was no response, he pounded more insistently. "Open up!"

After several minutes, a lamp was turned on inside,

and the porch light soon followed. He heard movement in the living room. Then Randy cracked open the door, leaving the security chain in place.

"Gordon," he said, his dark eyes narrowing with caution.

Gordon managed a bitter smile. His old friend had lines around his eyes and his mouth that hadn't been there eighteen years ago, and a surfeit of gray in his hair. But he was as handsome as ever. If Gordon had his guess, Randy hadn't gained a pound.

"That's some greeting, Randy," he said. "After so long."

"It's late. What are you doing here?"

"It *is* late," Gordon agreed. "Eighteen years late. I should've knocked your head off back then. But I didn't, did I? I accepted the knife you'd planted in my back and walked away."

"No, you let it fester."

"And you could've handled the news better?"

Randy bowed his head as if he couldn't bear the shame of what he'd done.

"Anyway, I just told Liz I'm not her daddy. Thought you might like to know that."

This made Randy look up. "You told her?" He shook his head—either in disgust or disbelief, Gordon couldn't tell until Randy spoke again. "You stupid bastard."

"I am stupid," Gordon snapped. "I trusted *you*, didn't I? I believed you were my friend."

"I loved you like a brother," Randy said.

Gordon hooted with laughter. "You had a funny way of showing it. I wish I'd never met you."

Randy flinched as if Gordon had slapped him, but

Gordon wasn't finished. "Are you sure you want to leave me standing out here?"

"You're not yourself tonight, Gordon. I don't want to let you in. Kristen's asleep and it's not fair to her that—"

"Fair to her? What about me, old friend? I think you should remember your manners. Otherwise, I might tell the whole damned neighborhood…" Now that the idea had occurred to him, Gordon turned and shouted the rest of what he had to say "That you cheated on your wife and screwed mine, that you fathered my only daughter. Can you believe it, folks?" he yelled. "This upstanding member of your community, this admirable father of four—no, it's five, isn't it? Including the daughter who should be mine?—betrayed his very best friend."

Behind him, the chain scraped and Randy yanked the door open. "Get in here," he snapped.

Gordon chuckled as he stepped across the threshold, but he felt only pain and anger. He hated the fact that Liz had Randy's coloring, his height, his broad forehead, high cheekbones and full lips.

It wasn't supposed to be that way….

"Randy, what is it? What's going on?" Kristen sounded frightened as she tied the belt of her robe and peered at them from the hallway. Then recognition dawned and even across the room, Gordon could see the color drain from her face.

"I've got it, honey," Randy said gently.

"It's just me," Gordon said. "You do remember me, don't you?"

She stared at him for several seconds, then disappeared.

"She's going back to bed?" he said in surprise. "Damn, that woman will put up with anything."

"Not quite," Randy said, his voice low. "She told you, didn't she? She did it, knowing it'd ruin our friendship. An eye for an eye. And she's never trusted me or loved me the same since."

"Gee, I feel terrible for you," Gordon replied.

"I'm not asking for your sympathy."

"What *are* you asking for?"

"Nothing. I don't deserve your friendship any more than I deserve her love. That's why I haven't come around."

"You were around for fourteen years after you screwed my wife!"

Randy rubbed his jaw. "I have no excuses to offer you. Is that why you're here? So I'll grovel and tell you how terrible I feel? So I'll plead for your forgiveness? If I thought that would help, I would've done it years ago. God, how I've missed you. But I knew you wouldn't want to see me."

"A little groveling might have been nice," Gordon said, as if he hadn't heard Randy's other words. "To see that it's affected you at all would be a step in the right direction."

"I'm sorry," Randy said. "I've been sorry since the day it happened."

"The *day* it happened?"

"Yes."

"You slept with her only once?" Gordon knew he shouldn't ask, but he'd be damned if he could stop himself.

Randy cleared his throat. "I said one *day*."

"A whole day." Gordon folded his arms. Those words

hit him like pointed darts, but he refused to show it. "You're right. Sorry doesn't help."

"So what are you doing here?" Randy asked in confusion. "To tell me you just destroyed Liz?"

"No, to tell you—" Gordon couldn't speak because of the lump in his throat. Blinking back the tears that were burning his eyes, he swallowed and tried again. "To tell you if she contacts you, you'd better be kind, you hear? You'd better give her what I couldn't give her. You owe me that much, you son of a bitch."

"You told her it was *me?*" he gasped.

"Not yet. But she'll get around to asking. Some day. She'll find out."

Tears welled in Randy's eyes. "It's been so long, and you love her so much. Why'd you give her up now? Why would you do that?"

"Why'd you sleep with my wife in the first place?" Gordon murmured in response, but the hard shell that had protected him so far was already slipping away, revealing his vulnerability and pain. As much as he hated that, he couldn't seem to help it.

"I wish I had an answer for you," Randy said.

"Then, maybe you can tell me about Chloe's part in...in what you did together."

Straightening up, Randy dashed a hand across his cheeks. "Chloe didn't want to get involved. I—I thought I was in love with her and I kept trying to get us alone. It was my fault."

Gordon clenched his teeth, trying to dismiss the image that had already done damage to his soul, and nodded. It wasn't much, but it was something.

Turning around, he stepped outside. He had to get out before he broke down completely. What had happened thirty-three years ago was Randy's fault. He'd admitted it. If he hadn't pressed her, flirted with her, cornered her, Chloe would have remained true—just as Gordon had tried to tell himself so many times.

But in his heart he knew Randy had taken more of the blame than he deserved. And as he stood on the stoop, Kristen's voice from inside the house confirmed the fact.

"That isn't what you told me, Randy," she said.

"No," he replied. "But if it brings him any peace…"

Wincing at this small bit of proof that Randy still cared about him, Gordon let the tears run down his cheeks as he walked to his car.

CHAPTER FOURTEEN

"HAVE YOU HEARD FROM GORDON?" Isaac asked.

Liz cradled the phone against her shoulder, as she stirred the melted chocolate. Her appliances and the remaining fixtures had been installed at The Chocolaterie the day before. Brent Price from Price Dairy had delivered an order of whole milk, unsweetened butter and heavy cream. All Liz had left to do was stock her display cases and refrigerators with what she hoped to sell this weekend, and that was the fun part. As mixed-up as the week had been, she was moving beyond it, immersing herself in activities she loved. "You can call him *Dad*, Isaac. He *is* your dad, you know."

"Not anymore."

"That's not fair," she protested. "Why should he lose both of us?"

"He's the one who shoved us away."

"He shoved *me* away. But he also tried to hold me close, in his own way. I couldn't see that before. Now that I know the truth, I...can understand, to a degree."

"Then, maybe I'm the only one, but I don't get it. So what if you're not his biological daughter? You're his daughter in every other sense of the word. Or you could've been, if only he'd been man enough to rise to the challenge."

Liz rested her arms on the large bowl she was using for dipping strawberries in chocolate. "What if it was Reenie?" she asked. "What if you thought she was giving you a child? And then—" Liz couldn't say the rest. Her words fell away and Isaac reacted with a long silence.

"It wouldn't be easy," he admitted. "But I'd never allow anyone's child to be hurt. None of it was your fault."

Liz watched the swirls her large rubber spatula made in the chocolate. "Do you ever wonder about Mom's role in what happened? How she could've gotten pregnant by another man when she was married to Gordon?"

"I don't want to think about it," he admitted. "I resent what Gordon did to her, too."

"*He* didn't do it, Isaac. He's reacting to pain, just like you are."

"And what are *you* doing?" he asked. "How's this affecting you?"

"I'm devoting myself to other pursuits."

"The kids?"

"And the shop." She smiled, looking at the large, ripe strawberries she'd already dipped. She was going to drizzle white chocolate over some of them and add coconut or chopped nuts to others. "I open this Saturday. Mary Thornton and I are running a joint ad in the paper."

"There should be plenty of tourists from the Running Y."

"I'm hoping it'll be a success."

"No more vandalism?"

"No. I'm beginning to think it was just some kids, screwing around."

"Probably," Isaac agreed. "Anyway, that was pretty nice of Carter Hudson to get you up and running."

She thought of the message she'd sent Carter the night before, and wondered if he'd gotten it. "I don't know where I'd be without him."

"Do you have any plans for summer?"

"I'll be working."

"Jeez, are you going to open *every* day?"

"Until tourist season is over. Then I'll close on Mondays and maybe Tuesdays, and see how it goes. If it's worth it to stay open, I will."

"Makes sense. What's your feature for opening day?"

"Chocolate-covered cinnamon bears."

"Never had them."

"You'll have to come in for a free sample."

"I'll be there," he assured her. Reenie said something in the background and Isaac covered the phone. A moment later, he came back on the line. "Reenie's parents are having a dinner at their place tomorrow night. They wanted us to invite you."

"I should spend some time with the kids."

"Don't they help at the shop every afternoon?"

"Yes, but I've been so preoccupied with getting The Chocolaterie up and running, I haven't been able to give them much attention."

"The girls were hoping Mica and Christopher could spend the night."

"They stayed with Keith last weekend."

"It's your big day tomorrow. Let us take care of them. Anyway, Jennifer has a new rabbit to show them."

Liz dipped another strawberry. "Who'll be babysitting while we have dinner?"

"Monique Harper from down the street."

"They love Monique," Liz said, warming to the idea. "What time are you going to the Holbrooks'?"

"Eight."

Liz felt a fair amount of stress, but she had to eat, didn't she? "What can I bring?"

"Nothing. Just yourself."

She supposed she could take a break, go for an hour or so, and then return to the shop if she had to. "Okay."

"Carter will be coming," Reenie called out in the background. "So dress sexy."

"Did you hear that?" Isaac asked.

Liz bit her lip, considering her options. Should she play it safe and back out?

She opened her mouth to do just that, then thought of the Lady of Shalott and changed her mind. Better to face temptation and rise above it.

"I heard," she said. "I'll see you soon."

LIZ SAT ACROSS FROM CARTER at the Holbrooks' elegant dining table, trying not to let her eyes automatically gravitate to him. The senator was talking to her about See's Candies and how much that company had grown. He told her there was a lot of money to be made in franchising and asked if she might ever be interested in doing something like that with The Chocolaterie. But she wasn't ready to think about expanding. Part of the appeal of her shop was the hands-on aspect, the fact that she could change anything at any time, run it her own way, provide a product completely unique to Dundee. If her new enterprise ever grew into a chain, she knew she'd definitely have to sacrifice some of that.

There were worse fates than getting rich, however, and she wasn't ruling out the possibility. But for now she was more interested in hearing what Carter and Reenie were talking about than in discussing something so far in the future, and so unlikely.

"I don't understand the compulsion to rape. There are so many nonviolent ways to satisfy sexual urges," Reenie was saying.

From what Liz could gather, the others were talking about three recent rapes that had occurred in Boise, which had been in the news.

"It's not about sexual satisfaction," Carter said. "It's about domination and control. Many rapists are married and could have all the sex they want."

"Could you imagine finding out that your husband has done something so horrific?" Reenie asked Liz.

What Keith had done was bad enough. Liz couldn't imagine what it would be like to deal with something so much worse. But she didn't have the chance to reply before Isaac jumped in. "I don't get what drives those men."

Now that everyone at the table had been served, Celeste took her seat beside the senator. "I saw a show last night about a rapist who abducted little girls from their bedrooms at night. He'd climb through an unlocked window and simply carry them away," she said. "The police thought they knew who it was. They even talked to the guy and made an appointment for him to come in and give a DNA sample. But then, of course, he skipped town."

"Why wasn't someone keeping an eye on him?" Reenie asked. "Isn't that what surveillance is all about?"

Celeste shook her head. "He was staying in a neighboring trailer, as a guest, so he had access to the little girl. He was the only stranger in the area. But I guess they weren't sure it was him until he disappeared."

"Did they ever catch him?" Isaac asked.

"Not until he'd raped another fifteen women, some of whom were just girls, in several more states. He even tried to kill one of his victims, a woman in her twenties. He slit her throat twice."

"She lived?" Liz said.

Celeste nodded. "She told her own story. I think it was brave of her to be so honest about what happened, don't you?"

"I do," Reenie said. "I wonder if she got married since then."

"I don't know," Celeste replied. "But I hope so. I hope she'll be able to live a normal life."

Carter was staring off into the distance, at a point on the wall beyond Liz's shoulder. "It'll stay with her," he said. "Every time she locks up her house at night or comes home to an empty place, that sick feeling will crawl up her spine and lodge in her gut. The scars left behind by that kind of violence can run—" he paused "—very deep. Some women never recover."

"You talk as though you know a lot about violent

crime, Carter," Celeste said. "Have you worked with rape victims or something?"

Carter shifted his gaze to her. "I was married to one."

The clink of silverware on china abruptly stopped. Like the others, Liz sat completely still. She'd just taken a bite of her dinner, but she couldn't seem to swallow as she thought about the woman in that wedding photo.

"When Congressman Ripley called to recommend you, he said you'd spent some time in law enforcement," the senator said. "He didn't give me any details."

Carter glanced at Liz. "I worked for the FBI."

"I'm sorry to hear about your wife," Reenie said.

Everyone except Liz murmured similar sentiments. She couldn't speak. The *FBI?* That was what he wouldn't tell her? She wondered how he'd met his wife; where she was now.

Carter continued eating. Liz knew that everyone must be curious to hear the whole story, but he volunteered no further information and no one dared to ask.

Reenie exchanged a quick look with Isaac, as though she might pursue the subject. But Isaac warned her against it with a slight shake of his head and, after a strained silence, Celeste tried to smooth over what had become an uncomfortable moment.

"I'm so sorry, Carter. We shouldn't have been discussing such an upsetting subject at the dinner table."

She was sincere, as only Celeste could be. And Carter offered her one of his rare smiles. "Don't be sorry."

"Some things are beyond tragic," she said. Then she cleared her throat and turned to Liz. "On a happier note, how is your shop coming along?"

Liz finally managed to wash down her food with a sip of water. "Great. Thanks to Carter."

She felt his eyes on her but didn't meet his gaze.

"I can't wait to see it," Celeste said.

"I'll open at ten tomorrow."

"I'll be there. I want to be one of your first customers. Then, someday I can say, 'I knew her when.'"

Liz laughed. "I'm going to be a little nervous," she admitted. "It'll be good to see a friendly face."

"We'll be there, too," Reenie said. "With all the kids."

"Good. I promised Mica and Chris they could come." Liz focused on Carter. "What about you, Carter?"

"I'll be there if I can," he replied, but there was a noncommittal quality to his voice that told her not to count on it.

With a nod, Liz stood. "I hate to leave early, but I have to finish up at the shop. I hope you'll forgive me."

"Of course," Celeste said.

Liz picked up her plate, but Celeste motioned for her to leave it. "Don't worry, Liz. I'll take care of the dishes."

"I'll help her," Reenie said.

Liz smiled. "Thanks for watching the kids."

"No problem. You'll see them at the store in the morning."

"Good luck," Celeste called, and Liz left, her mind half on the hours to come—during which time she'd make the shop perfect for tomorrow's big event—and half on the life Carter had left behind.

LIZ HAD JUST FINISHED arranging her window display for the tenth time. She moved away to take a look at it—

and heard a sharp knock on her back door. Surprised that she had such a late visitor, she glanced at the large round wall clock that she'd bought at Mary's shop earlier in the day. One long, ornate hand crept another minute closer to eleven o'clock. Reenie and Isaac had probably decided to stop by and say good-night on their way home, she guessed. But when she opened the door, she saw Carter standing in the dim light of the parking lot, wearing the pullover sweater, jeans and loafers he'd had on at dinner.

"It's late, and you answered the door without even checking to see who I was," he said.

Liz blinked in reaction to the confrontational tone in his voice. "I thought you were Reenie and Isaac."

"Next time, make sure."

She might have challenged his right to tell her what to do, but she knew he meant well—and that his concern undoubtedly stemmed from the violence that had touched his life. Was his wife one of the women he'd talked about, who couldn't completely recover? What would it be like to love someone who was a victim of such evil?

"Okay, I will," she said, clasping her hands in front of her while she waited for him to tell her why he was here.

He leaned against the door frame and watched her steadily.

"Are you just checking up on my safety skills?" she asked when he didn't state his purpose.

"You asked me to drop by, remember?"

The roof's shadow made it difficult to see the expression on his face. "I meant tomorrow."

"Everyone else will be here tomorrow."

"Exactly."

"That's why I figured this was a better opportunity."

"For what?"

"To offer you a ride home."

She unclasped her hands and raked her fingers nervously through her hair. "I have my car, and I only live a few blocks away."

"I'm not talking about *your* home. *I* live a lot farther."

Remembering the close, private atmosphere of his cabin, Liz felt a rush of hormones course through her body. He was asking her to sleep with him again. And they both knew she could if she wanted to. Her kids were at Isaac's. "We decided that we wouldn't press our luck."

"*You* decided that," he said. "*I'm* ready to venture out of the tower again."

The Lady of Shalott. Had her e-mail provoked him to issue this challenge?

"What about your promise?" she asked, searching for something to support her decision. "When it's over, it's over."

He moved closer. "Does it feel over to you?"

No. It didn't feel anywhere close to being over. She could barely look at him without melting inside. She'd spent six agonizing days trying not to think of him in anything other than a friendly light—and had ended up dreaming about him every time she closed her eyes.

"Someone has to play the Johnny Depp role," he said, his breath warm against her cheek.

He was talking about *Chocolat?* "How do you know

what role he played?" she asked. "You've never seen the movie."

"I rented it last night."

"You did?"

He nodded. "Watched it twice."

"Did you like it?"

"It made me hungry."

"For chocolate?"

His hands slipped around her waist, drawing her up against him. "For you."

Liz could remember all too clearly how well his body fit with hers. If she let him kiss her now, they'd never make it to the cabin. But his lips were only a hair-breadth away, and *she* closed the distance.

Pressing her mouth to his, she met his tongue with her own, relishing the taste of him, letting her fingers explore the thickness of his hair and hold him fast.

He groaned and walked her backward, closing the door behind them. She told herself he should be the one to start stripping away their clothing, but he wasn't. She couldn't get his shirt off fast enough, couldn't wait to feel the warmth of his chest against her breasts.

"Not so fast," he murmured. "I want to take you home and treat you properly."

But she was too impatient. Now that she'd let her resolve slip, she had to take what she wanted, before her inhibitions could override her desire. "Do you have a condom?" she murmured.

"In my wallet."

"Then right here," she said, fumbling with his zipper.

He didn't argue. Lifting her onto the closest table, he

slid her skirt up to her waist, watching as the emotions played across her face.

When he touched her, Liz closed her eyes and let her head fall back, trying to capture each dizzying sensation. There were reasons she shouldn't be doing this, she knew. But it was no use. She was lost to all coherent thought. And Carter wasn't helping to remind her.

"Take me," she whispered.

Freeing himself long enough to don a condom, he gathered her in his arms.

Liz locked her legs around his hips and ran her tongue along his neck, gasping as he pushed inside.

"You're perfect," he murmured and kissed her eyelids, her cheeks, her breasts. Then he started to move and the world seemed to spin out of control. Around and around, faster and faster until...

Liz was about to cry out, but Carter found her mouth and plunged his tongue inside, as if he longed to swallow her response, to absorb it along with the shudder of her body.

A moment later, he set her back on the table, bracing himself with one hand as he recovered from bearing their combined weight amid such a frenzy of need.

Reaching out, she smoothed the hair from his forehead. She knew it might give too much away, especially if he looked into her eyes, but what she was feeling was too powerful to dismiss. She was falling in love with him.

He didn't seem to mind. He traced a finger reverently over one breast, as if he'd never seen such a beautiful sight. Then his mouth curved into a boyish grin. "I think we can go now," he said and helped her down.

LIZ TOYED WITH CARTER'S HAIR as he slept with his cheek against her shoulder. Once they reached the cabin, he'd made slow, gentle love to her—a completely different experience than the frenzied passion they'd shared at the shop and, ultimately, far more challenging to her defenses. Afterward, he'd insisted she get some sleep for her big day. He'd kissed her neck and pulled her into the cradle of his body as if it were the most natural thing in the world, as if they were both exactly where they should be.

She'd managed to doze for a couple of hours. But it was nearly three in the morning and she was staring at his ceiling, wondering what she'd gotten herself into. She could tell Carter expected her to share his bed on a frequent basis from now on. But she didn't know what that would do to her life or to her children. She didn't want to steer any of them into rough water. Not after everything they'd been through.

"What's wrong?" he asked, his voice thick with sleep.

She didn't have an answer. How did a woman, especially a mother, find a balance between living in a tower and abandoning all caution?

"I'm excited about the shop," she said.

"It'll be great," he promised. "Now that I've seen the movie, I can make the place look even more like Vianne's. You'll love it."

She smiled. Maybe he needed her, needed someone to care about again.

"I appreciate what you've done," she said.

He muttered, "No problem," and went back to sleep.

Liz lay still until his breathing deepened, then slipped out of bed. Pulling on one of his T-shirts, she wandered around the cabin, trying to arrange her thoughts. What kind of man had she fallen in love with?

Someone who was living in a cabin cluttered with boxes, so he could leave at his earliest convenience. That didn't bode well. And yet, if she could help him in some way, maybe by fulfilling that lonely yearning she sensed inside him, she knew she would.

Carter's office was down the hall. It was the only room not filled with boxes, and eventually she gravitated there. Sitting down at his computer, she went on to the Internet to check her own e-mail and found a new message from Dave.

Wincing against a surge of guilt for sitting there in Carter's T-shirt, still warm from his bed, she opened it.

Jeez, where are you lately? I know you're busy, but it's like you dropped off the face of the earth. What's going on? Are you still coming out this summer? Or should I come there?

By the way, where's my questionnaire?

Liz opened his previous saved message, the one that included the questionnaire, and quickly glanced down the page.

What's the one trait you admire most in the opposite sex?

Honesty. Which was Carter incarnate.

If you could talk to one person right now, who would it be?

Carter.

If you could make love to someone right now, who would that be?

Carter.

She couldn't fill it out and send it back because as much as she'd tried to convince herself otherwise, every answer was tied to Carter.

She had to tell Dave, didn't she? She couldn't continue to lead him on.

Taking a deep breath, she hit the reply button and tried to explain.

I'm sorry I've been so out of touch. This is a difficult e-mail to write, but...I think it's only fair to be up-front with you. I've met someone else. I didn't mean to fall so hard or so fast, and I'm probably making a big mistake, but...

Hitting the backspace key, she erased most of her last sentence.

I didn't mean for this to happen, she corrected.

I certainly don't want to disappoint you, but I feel as if I should tell you before you buy a plane ticket. You've been a wonderful friend. I couldn't have made it through the past eighteen months without you, which is why this is so hard for me. You made me feel attractive and desirable when I needed it most, gave me someone to think about and laugh with when there weren't too many things I considered funny in my life. I hope you'll continue to be my friend. I know I'll always remember you fondly.

I wish you much happiness.

Love always,

Liz

She stared at the message. She was cutting her ties with Dave. Carter would run the senator's campaign and move on, with all of his boxes in tow and then she'd have no love life at all. But she had to be fair.

Forcing herself to send the message, she shoved away from Carter's computer. So many things were changing. She felt out of control and more than a little lost.

But when she made her way back to Carter's bedroom and looked in on him, she smiled. Maybe, like the Lady of Shalott, she was making a catastrophic mistake.

Carter rolled over and the moonlight that filtered through the window lit his handsome face.

But it was a heck of a way to go.

CHAPTER FIFTEEN

"WHAT ARE YOU DOING HERE?" Luanna asked, hugging the door even tighter than Randy had when Gordon made his previous surprise appearance.

Gordon took a good look at the woman who was still technically his wife, and scratched his whiskery cheeks. He'd gotten her out of bed. He could tell that easily enough. Her reddish hair—a color that came out of a bottle—stuck up on one side. She had a faint waffle impression on her cheek and mascara was smeared on the puffy bags under her eyes.

He knew he didn't look much better. He hadn't shaved for a few days. His beard itched unmercifully. And he'd slept in his clothes the night before. But somehow his appearance didn't matter to him half as much as it usually did. After leaving Randy's, he'd rented a cheap motel and drunk himself into a stupor. Problem was every time he sobered up he felt even worse. So that didn't last. He'd awakened this morning with a raging headache, a cotton mouth and fresh determination to change his life.

"I came to get some stuff out of the attic," he said.

"You'll have to come back when Pete's here."

Her new lover. She'd met him at church, ironically enough.

"I've never laid a hand on you," he said in disgust. "And I won't touch you now. I just want to get Chloe's things."

"Chloe's!" she blurted, obviously surprised.

"What's wrong with that?" he asked. "After all, I was married to her once, remember?"

"How could I forget? She cheated on you, and I'm the one who got stuck raising the daughter she had as a result."

"I wouldn't pride myself on that if I were you," he said. "You did a pretty shitty job."

Her eyes widened. "She turned out okay, didn't she?"

"Compared to your son she did."

"I didn't hear you complaining when I was the one doing all the work!"

"That was when I could see some good in you."

Her jaw dropped, as if she didn't quite know how to respond to his apparent change of heart. When she'd asked him to leave a few weeks earlier, he'd still been reeling from the shock of discovering Luanna had a boyfriend.

"You're no better than I am," she said.

He had to agree with her there. He'd wanted to blame Chloe and Randy for what had happened eighteen years ago. Lord knew he'd tried. But as muddled as his mind had been over the past several days, there had also been moments of clarity. Moments when he remembered flirting with his secretary at the law office and taking her out to lunch instead of inviting his wife. Moments when he remembered working extra long hours for the recognition he'd receive, instead of going home to spend time with her or give her a break from taking care of baby Isaac. Moments he remembered using what little money they had in those early years on golf with Randy instead of treating Chloe to the new dress she deserved. He'd taken her for granted and trusted she'd always be there for him, no matter what.

Those were painful memories. They showed him that he, too, was responsible for what had happened, even though, in his weaker moments anyway, he still worked hard to deny the fact. It was easier to feel sorry for himself and place the blame on others than to acknowledge the role he'd played in creating the vacuum that surrounded Chloe during their early years together. He'd learned and improved as a husband. By the time Chloe died, they'd become quite close. But Liz had been fourteen by then.

"All I want is five minutes in the attic. I bought this house. Surely, you can give me that much."

She hesitated, then stepped back and swung the door open. "Fine. Five minutes."

He swept past her, took the stairs two at a time and accessed the pull-down ladder that led to the attic. Holiday decorations and some of the household items Luanna had owned before she'd married Gordon crowded the floor, but off in the corner he found several boxes labeled Chloe. Sliding them over to the ladder, he hauled them down one by one while Luanna watched.

"What are you hoping to find in all that?" she asked.

He studied her for a moment. "The reasons I loved her in the first place."

"What about me?" she asked sulkily.

Gordon felt as if he was seeing Luanna clearly for the first time. "I don't know why I loved you," he said honestly and left.

THE CHOCOLATERIE WAS CROWDED. Along with the senator, Celeste, Isaac, Reenie, Jennifer, Angela, Isabella, Mica and Christopher, half the town had turned out, including Kenny and Brent, Gabe's kids. As the initial babble of voices grew to a low roar, Liz grinned excitedly at Carter, who'd gotten up early to drive her to town. He'd spent two hours just before she'd opened The Chocolaterie at the hardware store, and had come back to show her what he'd bought and what he could do with the materials at the shop. He'd told Liz his first project would involve some more built-in cabinetry. She knew she couldn't afford it and she tried to tell him so, but he told her not to worry about the money. He also brought her breakfast from the diner and insisted she eat.

"You did all this, Mommy?" Mica said, her voice full of awe.

Liz hugged her daughter to her side. "Me and Mr. Hudson."

Mica could hardly contain herself. "It looks so beautiful!"

"I love the chocolate gummy worms," Christopher said. The smeared chocolate on his face confirmed the fact.

Liz almost told him not to overdo it with the candy, but simply laughed instead. She had trays of samples circulating. She knew she should probably be trying to sell the treats she was giving away. But these people were her friends, and she was anxious for them to try everything she'd created. As she poured cup after cup of hot cocoa and heard the moans of pleasure and the compliments echoing around her, she was certain this was one of the best days of her life.

She felt Carter noticing her every move and turned to smile at him again. When their eyes met, their encounter late last night came rushing back to her. She could tell by his crooked grin that he was probably remembering exactly the same thing. Or maybe he was thinking about what had happened in the shower this morning just after they'd woken up....

Shaking her head, she chuckled. He winked at her, then sobered and nodded toward the door.

She followed his gaze to see Keith and his parents come in. Her ex-husband was carrying a bouquet of flowers. When he saw her, he smiled widely, as if relations between them hadn't been strained, especially for the past ten days or so, and brought over his gift. "Congratulations," he said and gave her a hug.

"A dozen red roses," Georgia said, as if Liz couldn't see that for herself.

"They're lovely," she murmured. Aware of Carter's keen interest in the flowers, she cleared her throat, thanked Keith politely and used the excuse of finding a vase to slip away from him and his parents.

"You've attracted quite a crowd."

Liz looked up to find Mary hovering at her elbow. "Who's watching your store?" she asked.

"My mother."

"How's business over at your place?"

"Great. Standing-room only."

If that were true, Mary would be basking in the glory of it all rather than inspecting the competition. But Liz wasn't about to check up on her. If Mary wasn't having the same success, she didn't want to know about it. She didn't want anything to mar her happiness right now. "It must be that ad we ran, huh?"

"I guess." Mary studied the elaborate displays Liz had worked so hard on the night before. "Where'd you get these old-fashioned cabinets?"

"At a garage sale in Boise. I've been storing them in my garage."

Mary pulled her gaze away. "So, did you ever catch the person who ripped your sink from the wall?"

Liz hadn't thought of the vandal since Carter had repaired everything. "No, why?"

"Someone was lurking in the parking lot last night when I was closing up. He seemed to be keeping a pretty good eye on your place."

Was Mary simply trying to wreck the moment? "Who was it?" Liz asked.

"I didn't recognize him. He didn't look like he was from around here. He was wearing really baggy clothes and a hooded sweatshirt."

"Did you approach him?"

"I tried. I wanted to get his name. But the moment he spotted me, he got in his car and drove off."

"What kind of car was he driving?"

"An old Toyota truck."

That hardly narrowed down the list of suspects. Almost everyone in these parts owned a truck, and there were lots of Toyotas. "Thanks. I'll keep a lookout for suspicious activity."

"I drove by again late last night, just to make sure the place was secure."

A tremor of foreboding slithered through Liz. "Did you see anything?"

"Carter's car parked in the lot next to yours," she said and smiled as if she'd witnessed a lot more than that.

"He's been a lot of help to me," Liz said in an effort to throw her off the trail. She knew it hadn't worked when Mary responded. "I wish he'd lend *me* a hand every now and then." She laughed conspiratorially, but when Liz didn't laugh with her, her expression changed and she said she had to get back to her store.

Liz felt a little unsettled as she watched Mary go. Mary must've seen Liz and Carter kiss. Or maybe she saw them come out of the shop with their clothes askew. For all Liz knew, she could've had her skirt tucked inside her panties and her blouse buttoned the wrong way. She'd had eyes only for Carter.

In any case, Mary probably knew his involvement had extended to more than the chocolate shop, which meant it wouldn't be long before the whole town heard about it.

Liz wished she could keep her relationship with Carter private. She didn't want Keith to make an issue out of what was happening, didn't want it to adversely affect her children. Especially when everything was still so new and uncertain—and temporary.

"What's wrong?" Georgia asked, sidling closer.

Liz finished arranging the roses. "Mary saw someone lurking in the parking lot last night."

"*Lurking?*" she repeated.

"Her word, not mine."

"Why would anyone lurk in the parking lot of a store that hasn't even opened yet?"

"That's what I'd like to know," she said.

GORDON SAT ON THE BED in his dingy motel room, listening to the steady drip of a leaky showerhead as he opened the first box of Chloe's belongings. He felt as if he had a lump the size of a football in his stomach and he had a sudden reluctance to proceed. But he wouldn't let himself force Chloe back into the corners of his mind the way he'd shoved her belongings into a corner of the attic.

He'd showered—it had seemed irreverent to paw through her things without cleaning up a bit first—but he could still smell alcohol oozing from his pores and it sickened him. God, how had he let himself sink so low? Low enough to hurt Liz and Isaac. Low enough to say something he could never take back.

Briefly closing his eyes, he licked his lips, which were cracked and dried from sleeping with his mouth open, and pulled out the scrapbook Chloe had made for him before they were married. Inside, he found pictures of them both at eighteen, nineteen and twenty. Pictures with Randy and Kristen sitting on the hood of his first Buick. Pictures of him and Randy smoking cigarettes and laughing into the camera lens. Pictures of the cake Chloe had made him for his birthday—which he'd teased her unmercifully about because it had slumped to a half inch on one side.

She was so pretty in those pictures that she stole his breath....

The life in her bright smile was almost mesmerizing. He touched her image as if he could feel, once again, the softness of her cheek, the curl of her hair around his forefinger.

How he missed her. Such a terrible longing crept through him that he had to close the book in order to recover.

They'd started out right, hadn't they? They'd been in love, optimistic, intent on building a family.

He pulled out a different book, a baby book that showed Chloe just before Isaac was born. He'd been excited to have a son, he remembered, but not really ready for the change it'd make in their lives. Chloe had gotten pregnant so soon. They'd had to move across the country, away from both their families so he could attend school, and because she had so much difficulty carrying Isaac, she'd been bedridden most of the time. To make matters worse, they'd been extremely poor.

Gordon knew his wife had suffered from depression the first few years of their marriage. The reality of their lives had fallen far short of the dream, and Chloe hadn't had school and work to fill her days as Gordon had. But she never complained.

He wished now that she had.

Rubbing a thumb over his freshly shaved chin, he turned to the back of the book. Isaac, at one and two, stared back at him, his chubby face smeared with icing or Magic Markers or dirt, but always wearing a smile. Chloe was smiling right beside him, but for the first time, Gordon could read the strain in her eyes. He could see the way she was looking at him, when she didn't expect to be caught by the camera—as if she needed so much more than he was giving her—and his gut ached with regret.

He'd been young and stupid and too preoccupied with his own needs to love her as he should have.

Luanna's cutting words came back to him. *How could I forget? She cheated on you....*

Maybe that was true, but Luanna wasn't half the woman Chloe was. Deep down, Gordon had known that all along, despite what had happened with Randy. He'd just never wanted to deal with the pain that accompanied really thinking about the situation. And as long as he kept some semblance of a life going, he could avoid that easily enough.

But now he had no way to camouflage the truth. He'd let Chloe down even more than she'd let him down, hadn't he? Liz was the only true innocent of the three of them, and as Isaac had always said, Gordon had done nothing to protect her from Luanna's cruelty.

Gordon picked up a greeting card that was stuck between the pages of the photo album. It was an anniversary card from Chloe. He wasn't sure exactly what year she'd given it to him, but when he opened it, he realized the date didn't matter. It could've been from any year.

"I know we're not perfect, Gordon. I know our marriage could use some work. But I love you. And because I love you, I can give you this promise—I won't give up."

THE MEMORIAL DAY WEEKEND flew by for Liz. She kept her kids with her, helping out at the shop, and she was pleasantly surprised at how politely they greeted people and assisted her, even at their young ages. Tourists from the Running Y streamed through her store, along with the locals, and they bought so much that Liz had to stay up late each night to make enough candy to carry her through the weekend. Keith came by at closing time to pick up the kids so she could finish her work. Then, because they were already asleep at Keith's, Liz went to Carter's. She knew she risked giving away their relationship. Mary didn't seem to be spreading the word as rapidly as expected. But the fact that she was never home to answer her phone at night would be suspicious to Keith, if he ever tried to call her. Still, she couldn't stop herself. She didn't want to hear from Dave, knew it would be difficult to explain how quickly and completely she'd gotten involved with Carter. And she didn't want to waste the opportunity. The day when he'd leave town already seemed too close.

By eight o'clock Monday evening, Liz was happy but exhausted. The past three days had been beyond everything she'd hoped for. Now, she wanted to close up shop and take her kids home, but Mica had invited her father to try a treat she'd made herself—giant chocolate and caramel–covered graham crackers—and he'd only just arrived.

"You're the talk of the town," Keith told her, and she smiled as she thought of her favorite movie. Vianne had been the talk of the town, too. Fortunately, Liz had more support than Vianne had enjoyed.

"I think most everyone liked my candy."

"All except Mary. I heard her tell someone your chocolate isn't any better than what she's selling."

Liz was glad that was all Mary was saying. "I guess you can't please everyone."

"Carter sure spent a lot of his weekend here," he said.

"He'll be doing a few more projects for me around the shop."

"Is it anything I can do?"

"No, as fate would have it, he's a good finish carpenter."

"Mr. Hudson?" Mica asked.

Liz nodded.

"I gave him one of my own candies, and he said it was the best thing he's ever tasted." Mica adjusted her glasses. "Actually he said it was the *second* best thing he's ever tasted. He wouldn't tell me what the *best* thing was."

Liz couldn't help coloring. She remembered Carter saying that, and the significant glance they'd exchanged at the time. He'd been talking about her. *She* tasted better to him.

Turning away, she continued to clean the counters and put the unsold chocolates into the pantry. "He must've liked my hot chocolate, eh?"

"That's not it," Mica said, still trying to puzzle it out.

"He's been all over the country. Second best to a man like that isn't bad," Liz said.

"Second best always sucks," Keith said, his sullen tone indicating he was talking about his current status with Liz.

Facing him, she met his gaze squarely. "Tell me about it."

He flushed at how easily she was able to turn his own words back on him. "You were never second best," he argued.

Liz lifted a hand. "Stop. At least have the dignity to be honest about it. You loved Reenie best. If she were single now, you'd probably still be knocking at her door."

Christopher was oblivious to the conversation. He was too busy campaigning for more chocolate. But Mica's eyes grew round, and she glanced worriedly between them as if she expected an argument to erupt.

Liz regretted what she'd said, but only because she'd said it in front of her daughter.

An unfamiliar expression flickered over Keith's face. Ever since Liz had learned of Reenie's existence she'd felt Keith's partiality to his first wife. Ultimately his actions had established his preferences—in the minds of almost everyone. Mary Thornton was a case in point. But Liz had never stated it quite so matter-of-factly, as if it no longer mattered to her.

Because it *didn't*. Not anymore. Maybe that was what Keith sensed, why he looked so crestfallen.

"You have a thing for Carter, don't you?" he asked.

Liz angled her head toward their children. "We'll talk about it later."

"Just give me a yes or no."

"I—*like* him," she said, registering a moment's relief when she heard the back door open. She wondered if maybe Mary Thornton was coming over to assess the weekend and suggest future joint ventures in advertising. But it wasn't Mary. It was Carter.

He pulled up short when everyone turned to stare at him. Obviously, he was as surprised to see Keith there as Keith was to see him.

The resentment in Keith's face would have intimidated a less intrepid soul. Fortunately, Carter didn't seem bothered. His movements became more deliberate, perhaps, but he still crossed the floor and kissed Liz on the temple, as he would have done if they'd been alone. "I brought you some strawberries."

She'd sold out of chocolate-covered strawberries around noon, and Finley's Grocery didn't sell the large berries she required. "With the stem?" she asked, seizing this topic because it was entirely unrelated to Keith and Carter and the tension buzzing between them.

"I went to Boise," he said. "Got you some other stuff, too, while I was there and could buy in bulk. Sugar. Flour. Powdered sugar. They had a giant bag of pretzels, so I bought it, just in case."

Liz nodded. "Pretzels. Good. They'll be great covered in chocolate."

"Are you my mommy's *boyfriend?*" Mica asked, studying him closely.

The mention of a boyfriend finally caught Christopher's attention. He stopped wandering around the shop, greedily ogling all the goodies, and scowled at his sister. "Mommies don't have boyfriends."

"Yes, they do," Mica argued. "Angela's mom married Uncle Isaac, didn't she? Our mom could get married again, too, silly."

"To Daddy?" he asked, confused.

"You don't need to worry about it," Liz assured them. "Mommy's not getting married. Mommy's already married to her new business." It seemed like the safest response, but Keith didn't appear any happier despite her ingenious reply.

"He might look good to you now," he said. "But you don't know him very well. And everyone has their problems." He shoved away from the table and stood. "Maybe when he walks off and leaves you behind you'll be ready to forgive me."

He strode out without another word, leaving Mica and Christopher staring uncertainly at Liz. Carter gazed after Keith, his face a mask.

"Daddy's not happy," Chris said sadly.

"Daddy has no right to be mad," Mica told her little brother. The anger she'd felt toward her father when they'd first arrived in Dundee had dissipated, however, and now she was merely acknowledging the truth.

"Hey, we're celebrating," Liz reminded them, in an effort to recapture the festive mood. "I've launched The Chocolaterie and everyone seems to love it."

"Does that mean I can have another peanut-butter cup?" Christopher asked, immediately recognizing the fact that he suddenly had an advantage.

"I don't know," Liz said, trying to be firm. She didn't want her children to overindulge just because she was in the candy business. But still...

"Those peanut-butter cups are pretty big," Carter said. "Maybe they could split one."

Liz hadn't expected Carter to side with her son, but when Chris sidled closer to his new ally as if they stood together on the issue, Liz relented. "Okay."

Chris's mouth stretched into a broad grin that revealed two missing teeth. "Thanks!" he said to Carter, and as he and Mica ran over to the counter, they seemed to forget their daddy's angry departure.

With a sigh of relief, Liz met Carter's gaze just before he went to cut the peanut-butter cup in half. "He's right, you know," he said.

"About what?" she asked.

"Everyone has their problems."

She knew that. And she knew Carter had more than most.

CHAPTER SIXTEEN

AFTER SPENDING THREE DAYS at the shop and three nights at Carter's cabin, Liz's house felt unnatural to her, as though it had been shut up after a death in the family. The unpleasant things she'd shoved to the back of her mind floated to the surface—the way her father had left, what he'd said, images of her mother and what she must've been like at thirty-one, the age she'd been when she'd gotten pregnant for the second and final time.

Liz put her children down for the night, then tiptoed around the place, exhausted and yet reluctant to go to bed. She knew sleeping alone would feel odd after having Carter's warm body curled around hers. Besides, she felt obligated to check her e-mail to see if Dave had responded to her last message. He hadn't left anything on her answering machine. But, at her request, he typically didn't, in case Mica listened to the message before Liz could.

Taking a glass of lemonade with her to the computer in the guest bedroom, she sat down and signed on. Sure enough, there was a message from Dave waiting for her. Three, actually. There was also a message from Carter.

She opened Carter's first. It was short but sweet.

It's lonely in the tower tonight.

She grinned. Tennyson's poem. But he was right—his cabin was like a medieval tower into which the rest of the world did not intrude.

"The curse is come upon me," she quoted. The way Keith had stormed out of her shop and the confusion on Christopher's face afterward proved to Liz that seeing Carter was already complicating her life.

Should she tell him that she didn't want to continue seeing him? Or should she admit that she could still smell him on her skin, that she held her arm to her nose every now and then just to breathe him in? That when she closed her eyes, she remembered the warmth of his bare chest next to her cheek, rising and falling in his sleep? That she smiled whenever she pictured *his* smile?

"No to all of the above," she muttered. She knew she'd break down and be with him again, so telling him it was over seemed pointless. She wasn't about to volunteer what kind of an effect he had on her. That was a little too much information this early in the relationship. So she looked up "The Lady of Shalott," reread the poem and sent him a response to his lonely tower line.

The broad stream bore her far away, the Lady of Shalott.

After hitting Send, she took a deep breath and, figuring she might as well deal with the other messages in chronological order, opened Dave's first e-mail.

He'd written: You're joking, right? You've got to be joking....

That was it, but obviously it wasn't his final thought because he'd sent her two messages after the first.

The second one read: It's my age, isn't it? You've never really given us a chance.

Their age difference bothered her, but she had other concerns, as well. What amazed her was that she had concerns about Carter, too, and yet she'd just spent three nights making love with him until they were too exhausted to keep their eyes open another minute.

Dave's final e-mail was longer:

I want to talk to you before you make up your mind for good, okay? I'm not the same man you knew when you were in California. You should realize that by now. We're not talking about one quick weekend in Vegas. We've been calling and writing each other for a year and a half. That's a long time to get to know someone. A long time to establish a strong foundation for a permanent relationship.

Since you wrote, I haven't been able to think about anything else. Maybe I'm slow coming to this, but I'm in love with you, Liz. If you did this to see if I really care—I do.

Dave

Liz blinked and reread the second to the last line. *I'm in love with you, Liz....* She scrolled down, looking for one of his infamous jokes as a postscript, but he'd ended there. As if he was serious. As if he meant it.

She gave a low whistle. What could she say to that? She thought she probably "loved" Dave—but she knew she wasn't *in love* with him. Meeting Carter had cleared up any confusion in that arena.

She tried to form a reply, but she couldn't come up with a better reason for suddenly ending their relationship than the one she'd already given him. He lived too far away, he was too young for her, and she was already involved in what, at best, could be described as a summer fling with someone else. She and Dave had argued about his age and the distance between them enough. He wouldn't concede those points. And the last one…

Well, she didn't really want to go into that. She wasn't sure enough of the future to use Carter as a reason for anything. So she went back to the issue of distance.

Maybe it's a mistake to cut you loose. You're a great catch, a fabulous guy. And I'll always care about you. But my life is going in a different direction. I won't be moving back to L.A. for years. She thought of her shop and then added: *if ever*, and you certainly don't want to move to a small town in Idaho. What chance do we really have?

It was more of the same old stuff. But she sent the e-mail anyway, then checked, out of habit, to see if any messages had come in while she'd been deliberating.

To her surprise, Carter had already sent a reply: I can save you.

Chuckling, Liz rubbed her tired eyes. She wished *someone* would save her—from herself. Spotting an instant message on her screen, she dropped her hand.

CHudson1973: I bought some of the candles you like.

Carter. Her smile broadened. Vanilla?

CHudson1973: Vanilla *bean.* I guess the "bean" part is important. Makes them gourmet.

Luvs Chocolat: LOL Bet they smell great.

CHudson1973: Not as good as you.

Luvs Chocolat: You're just trying to coax me back into your bed.

CHudson1973: Is it working?

Luvs Chocolat: I'm thinking about it.

CHudson1973: Could you think over here?

Luvs Chocolat: If I had a babysitter.

CHudson1973: I could call Keith.

Luvs Chocolat: Right.

CHudson1973: Okay, maybe not. But I wanted you to see the place. I unpacked some boxes.

Luvs Chocolat: This *is* news.

CHudson1973: Figured I've got quite a while here. Months. Might as well get comfortable.

Luvs Chocolat: Are you mentioning that as another ploy to get me into bed?

CHudson1973: I must be more transparent than I thought.

Not exactly. She knew hardly anything about him, and he seemed content to keep it that way.

Luvs Chocolat: Maybe you're not the easiest guy in the world to figure out, but you're *good*. I have to hand you that.

CHudson1973: Good in what way? <G>

Luvs Chocolat: Fishing for compliments?

CHudson1973: Hoping you'll talk dirty to me.

Luvs Chocolat: Are you kidding? I know where that will lead. Thanks for the things you bought today, by the way. How much do I owe you?

CHudson1973: Getting uncomfortable with the conversation?

Luvs Chocolat: With what the conversation is making me feel.

CHudson1973: What if I'm feeling the same way?

Luvs Chocolat: There are other considerations.

CHudson1973: There don't have to be. I could come to you.

Luvs Chocolat: I wouldn't want Mica or Christopher to wake up and find a man in the house.

There was a slight delay, but Carter finally responded with an Okay.

Luvs Chocolat: You didn't tell me how much I owe you for the supplies.

CHudson1973: Dinner.

Luvs Chocolat: When?

CHudson1973: Tomorrow night.

Luvs Chocolat: I have to work.

CHudson1973: You also have to eat. Close up for an hour. I want you.

Luvs Chocolat: You mean you want to see me?

CHudson1973: Both.

He appeared as invested in what was happening between them as she was. But could it be true? He'd be in Dundee for a while. Might as well make himself comfortable. He'd said that himself. So was it a matter of making do, of passing the time?

Luvs Chocolat: I won't be so busy once I hire someone to work evenings.

CHudson1973: The sooner the better.

Luvs Chocolat: Carter...

CHudson1973: What?

Luvs Chocolat: I don't think we should become too involved.

CHudson1973: We're already involved.

No kidding. Liz sighed as she stared at the screen. She'd never been swept away in a whirlwind romance like this one. It was frightening and exhilarating all at once. When she'd gone to the cabin with him Friday,

Saturday and Sunday, she'd told herself it was one weekend, no big deal. Deep down, she'd probably known that they'd see each other again. Maybe a few weekends before he left. But the reality was far more consuming. She couldn't get enough of him. Which made her contemplate inviting him over, after all. Which made her realize that she had to get off the computer at once.

Luvs Chocolat: I'm exhausted. Talk to you tomorrow?

She expected him to tell her good-night, but he didn't.

CHudson1973: Before you go, have you heard from Dave?

She sat up taller. Luvs Chocolat: You remember Dave's name?

CHudson1973: I remember that he wants to get together with you.

Luvs Chocolat: I cut off the relationship.

CHudson1973: How'd he take the news?

Luvs Chocolat: He told me he loves me.

There was a long pause.

CHudson1973: That comes as a bit of a surprise. Last I heard he was *calling* you.

Luvs Chocolat: It was a surprise to me, too.

Chudson1973: How do you feel about him?

Luvs Chocolat: I'm not sure.

CHudson1973: So he's giving me some competition?

Luvs Chocolat: Was there supposed to be a smiley face after that sentence?

CHudson1973: In case you haven't noticed, I'm not a smiley-face kind of guy.

Luvs Chocolat: So you're serious? Having Dave call me bothers you?

CHudson1973: What do you think?

It did. Liz shook her head. Blatantly honest, as usual.

Luvs Chocolat: You don't have to worry. If he's smart, he'll wait until you leave. Win by default, right?

There was an even longer pause.

Luvs Chocolat: Hello?

CHudson1973: I'll let you go now.

Exactly. That was the problem, wasn't it? If Dave was really interested in her, all he had to do was bide his time for a few months. Liz would be on the rebound again soon.

But she had known that going in. She could hardly complain about it now.

Luvs Chocolat: Night.

CHudson1973: Keith hasn't bothered you since he left the shop, has he?

Luvs Chocolat: I haven't heard from him, why?

CHudson1973: Just checking.

CARTER RAMBLED AROUND the cabin. While sorting out the kitchen and living room and moving boxes around, he'd found a pair of Liz's panties. He remembered them from the first night they'd made love and chuckled to think that she'd gone home without them. Liz definitely wasn't the type to walk around without underwear. Yet she'd never mentioned they were missing.

He found that pretty amusing but, combined with what she'd told him online about Dave, that small scrap of fabric had him too distracted to focus on any additional unpacking. What was going on between him and Liz O'Connell was like a runaway train, he decided. It could only end in a major wreck, but he'd be damned if he could control the momentum that was propelling them toward their doom.

He was using her as a distraction, he realized. When he thought of her legs, her skin, her lips, he didn't think of Laurel. Or the man who'd tortured and raped Laurel before he could get her out of that damn hotel room. Or the package from Johnson that was still sitting on his desk. He could pretend nothing existed beyond Dundee, which had just cataloged another exciting day with the opening of The Chocolaterie.

He certainly wasn't living in the fast lane, but he liked it here. He liked what he'd done at the shop. It was good, it existed because he'd helped to create it, and it made Liz happy. She'd laughed and smiled all weekend.

He needed more positives—like her—in his life.

Maybe he should go back to building, after all. But he'd have to stay in one place to start a construction business. Even speculative building took time and could result in houses that wouldn't sell, which might turn into rentals...which would require some level of care and management. Carter supposed he could hire someone else to manage his properties, but owning real estate basically meant he'd be tied to a particular region. And he couldn't have that. He had to be free, in order to stay ahead of the ghosts that haunted him.

Dundee worked for now. But the ghosts would catch up with him eventually. They always did.

He went to his room and put Liz's panties in his drawer. Then he broke down the boxes he'd emptied and stacked them outside against the cabin so he could dispose of them in the morning. At last he cared whether or not his place looked lived in. But only so that Liz would feel more comfortable when she came to visit.

He wondered if she'd spend the next weekend with him. Keith had Mica and Christopher only twice a month, which meant she'd have her children with her. That wasn't promising. He was fine with having them all over. They seemed like good kids. But Liz didn't act as if she wanted them to get to know him.

He could understand, to a point. But that didn't make it any easier to carry on a relationship with her.

His cell phone rang. He'd left it in his office when he'd been talking to Liz on the computer earlier, so he headed down the hall, wondering who might be calling him so late.

When he scooped it off the desk and spotted the name on his caller ID, he laughed and punched the talk button.

"Mom, what are you doing up so late?" he asked.

"I'm not up late. It's four-thirty here," she said. "I'm up early. The rain woke me an hour ago and I haven't been able to sleep since."

He slid into his chair and started playing Hearts on the computer. "So you're calling me at, what, two-thirty my time?"

"I was going to hang up if you sounded groggy."

"A solid plan." Considering he slept so little. "What's up?"

"I just got back from a road trip."

"You never mentioned a road trip to me."

"It was only for a couple of days. I went with Suzanne. She's the friend I met at the antique store."

"I remember."

"Anyway, when I got home last night, there were several messages on my answering machine from a Special Agent Johnson."

Carter swiveled around to face the package on the corner of his desk. He'd nearly tossed it out. Wished he could do so now. But his innate sense of responsibility had stopped him every time he'd come close.

"Why'd he call you?" he asked, not particularly pleased to hear that Johnson had contacted his mother.

"He said you're not picking up your cell. He wanted to see if I had some other way of getting hold of you."

"Like hell."

"What's that supposed to mean?" she asked.

"He knows I'll pick up for you and that you'll tell me he's trying to reach me."

"You don't want to talk to him?"

Carter sank lower in his seat, feeling tired for the first time tonight. "No."

"What does he want?"

Carter was tempted to say *nothing*. But that package a few feet away called him a liar. It had only God knew what inside. He couldn't leave it there forever. Yet he couldn't throw the damn thing out. "Charles Hooper claims he wants to talk."

Silence met this response. Finally his mother said, "About what he did to Laurel?"

"No. He knows I'm not interested in that. I already got him for what he did to Laurel." He wondered if he'd been wrong to push Laurel to testify. Had the anxiety of the trial contributed to the hopelessness that had eventually destroyed her will to live? He'd been so sure he could help her—completely confident that once they were married they'd be able to put the terrible violence that had brought them together behind them. "Johnson thinks there are others."

"Like Laurel?"

"Worse."

"Murdered?"

"Yes."

"My God, what that man did."

Hearing the break in his mother's voice, knowing how much she'd loved Laurel, he clamped his jaw shut and waited, giving her a few seconds to rein in her emotions. He didn't want to deal with her tears. His stomach was already knotted. No matter how much time passed, he couldn't seem to gain perspective on Laurel's death. He'd loved her almost from the moment he'd tracked Hooper to the hotel where he'd been keeping her, and she'd risked her life to warn him that Hooper had had a gun. "He's an evil son of a bitch," he said.

"So what's he willing to talk about? To tell you what he did to the others? To lead you to their bodies?"

"That's what he's telling Johnson."

"You don't believe him?"

"I think he's trying to yank my chain."

"In what way?"

"He must've heard about Laurel's suicide. That's why he's asking for me. He wants to rub my nose in the fact that she's gone—that regardless of what I did, what I tried to do, I'm living a life sentence right along with him."

Another long silence met Carter's words, and then a sigh. "She was so good," his mother said. "She couldn't accept that there were people like Hooper, who could do what he did."

"And once her eyes were opened, she couldn't ever forget."

"It was tragic."

He said nothing.

"But with Hooper's cooperation, you might be able to close an unsolved case."

"That's true."

"And bring another family some peace."

"Just because you get answers doesn't mean you get peace," he said.

"It has to be better than hoping against hope that your child is alive somewhere," she said.

Carter didn't respond, but he knew it was true. He'd seen it too often when he'd worked for the Bureau. A family suffered until they could reclaim their loved one. They suffered, too, if that loved one was dead. But nothing was worse than not knowing.

"See?" he said.

"What?" she replied.

"Hooper's not the only one who's good at mind games."

"What are you talking about?"

"Johnson," he said and hung up after a brief good-bye. Johnson knew what he'd been doing when he'd placed that call to Sarah Hudson. Johnson was still dedicated, relentless and relatively untouched. He'd never had the evil he worked with spill into his personal life.

Carter sat in his chair, glaring at the package. What did it contain? Letters from some poor family, pleading with him to help? A sample of the information Hooper could provide?

"Shit," Carter said and reached over to open it. But there weren't any letters inside. Not even a note. It contained pictures of three women, three he'd never seen before, with the dates they'd disappeared and the locations from which they'd gone missing written on the back. One of the women was beautiful. One wore a pair of stylish glasses and appeared keenly intelligent. And one didn't seem to have quite so much to recommend her. She just looked lost.

It was the lost one that got him.

CHAPTER SEVENTEEN

GORDON GLANCED AT CHLOE'S CARD, which he'd stuck behind his sun visor. Over the past several days he'd gone through all of her journals and keepsakes, but nothing else had struck him as deeply as the message she'd written on that card.

The road became a blur of pavement beneath his tires, and the countryside changed from desert to high wilderness, but he barely noticed. He was too busy thinking, wondering if she'd ever thought about telling him the truth. Knowing her, she must have had a very difficult time keeping such a secret. As the years passed, they'd grown so happy, so close. When Liz had gone to kindergarten, Chloe had started working half days at a candy store and had often talked about owning her own chocolate shop. They were finally in the planning stage when she'd passed away. But regardless of the improvements in their relationship, she had never even hinted about Randy.

She'd kept her mouth shut for her daughter's sake. He knew that. She'd probably feared he'd behave exactly as he'd done.

He winced at the memory of the hurt on Liz's face at the tennis court. Her features still reminded him of

Randy's. They always would. But he loved her anyway. That was what he'd learned from all of this. That was the underlying truth he'd had to dig so deep to find. He loved her and he wanted her to be his daughter again, even if it meant dealing with disappointment on a daily basis.

A sign appeared on the side of the road. It was fifty-three miles to Boise, and Dundee was only another hour or so beyond that. He wasn't far now.

He opened Chloe's card and, splitting his gaze between it and the road, quickly read her words again. *I know our marriage could use some work. But I love you. And because I love you, I can give you this promise—I won't ever give up.*

I won't give up, either, he vowed in return and slipped the card back under his visor. *I'll make it right with Liz if it takes the rest of my life, Chloe. You have my word on that.*

CARTER HAD JUST HUNG UP after making arrangements to fly to New York when his phone rang. He expected it to be his mother, wanting to continue their earlier conversation. Although she wouldn't come right out and say it, she believed he should talk to Johnson. He believed it, too. Otherwise, he would have been able to throw that package in the trash without even opening it.

But it wasn't his mother. It was Senator Holbrook's daughter, Reenie.

"Carter?"

"Yes?" he said in surprise.

"I—I'm glad I caught you."

The wobble in her voice concerned him. "Is something wrong?"

"It's Liz."

Carter's heart immediately jumped into his throat. "What's the matter?"

When Reenie sniffed, his grip on the phone tightened, and the memory of a call he'd received two years earlier, telling him Laurel hadn't shown up for work, came crashing down upon him. "What is it, Reenie?"

"Someone broke into The Chocolaterie last night after Liz went home and trashed the place."

"What?" His first thought was of Keith storming out of the shop. Had this been his retaliation? "Anyone see who it was this time?"

"Not that we know of. But they wrecked the shelves you built her and tore the sink out again and spray-painted the floor and walls. They even poured water on the chocolate and smashed most of her inventory."

He squeezed his forehead, trying to absorb the news that this had really happened, in Dundee of all places. "Is she okay?"

"She's taking it pretty hard."

Running a hand through his hair, Carter told himself to breathe deeply. Damage to the store he could handle. Damage to—

He cut off his thoughts before they could progress any further. "Are you with her?"

"I'm in the parking lot. I didn't want her to see me cry, so I stepped outside." She sniffed again.

"Have you contacted the police?"

"I tried. Officer Orton was suppposed to be on duty, but he isn't even out of bed yet."

A lot of good he'd probably turn out to be. "Is he coming?"

"He'll be here as soon as he can make himself presentable."

"So did she call you when she found it or—"

"My dad spotted the door propped open on his way to the diner for breakfast and stopped to see what was going on. When he realized what had happened, he called her. He called me and Isaac, too, and I'm glad he did."

"What's she doing?"

"She's just…standing in the middle of it, staring at everything as if she's seeing all her hopes and dreams shattered on the floor. This place means so much to her."

Carter cursed under his breath. Whoever had done this would pay. Maybe Hooper had had the last laugh with Laurel. Maybe ugliness and violence had won before. But only because Laurel had quit fighting.

Maybe the vandalism at the shop was on a much smaller scale than the battle he'd fought for Laurel. But it was somehow very important that he win this time around. "I'll be right there."

LIZ COULDN'T SEEM TO GRASP the fact that she wouldn't be able to open for business today. She'd climbed out of bed so eager to arrive at the shop and get started….

And now this. Her eyes scanned the filthy words someone had painted on her wall—Go Home, Bitch. It was right there in front of her and still she couldn't believe it. Who would do something so mean? Who hated her enough to hurt her so carelessly?

Senator Holbrook turned in a circle and frowned at the wreckage. Isaac had a broom and dustpan and was already trying to clean up. And Reenie began to cry every time Liz met her eyes. Which made it that much more difficult for Liz to hold herself together. Reenie understood that the shop was more than brick and mortar to Liz; Reenie understood how deeply the damage cut.

Fortunately, Liz had dropped Mica and Christopher at their grandmother's house on the way to work, so Georgia could drive them to school. Liz didn't think she could deal with their questions or their disappointment. She couldn't even deal with her own. She felt as she had when her father told her he wasn't her father: numb. As if the whole thing was unreal and if she only waited long enough someone would say, "Just joking."

But no one ever did, did they?

"Your insurance will cover most of this, won't it?" Isaac asked.

Liz knew it would cover some of the damage. But because of the low crime rate locally, she hadn't been worried about this type of problem. So she'd purchased an inexpensive policy with a high deductible.

"Yeah, the insurance will cover it," she said. She opened her eyes but tried not to see what was there. The shop had been so perfect….

Isaac scraped mashed strawberry into the trash. "That's good."

"It'll be fine," Liz told him. What else could she say?

It wasn't Isaac's fault that she'd skimped on the insurance. Besides, Gabe was going into surgery tomorrow and might not come out of it alive. How could she worry Isaac and Reenie about the shop when Reenie's brother's *life* was on the line? "It'll just take time," she added. *A lot of time.* And where would she get the deductible?

Reenie scowled at her. "Stop it," she said. "You don't have to pretend this is okay for us."

Liz said nothing. It wasn't okay—not at all. She'd been crazy to stay in Dundee. She should've gone back to Los Angeles to rebuild her life. But she'd started to feel safe here, part of the community.

Until now.

Go home, bitch. She couldn't remember anything like this ever happening to anyone else in Dundee.

"If it's Keith, I'll beat him to a bloody pulp," she heard Isaac murmur to Reenie.

"I'll pile on," Reenie whispered back.

Liz pretended she couldn't hear them. She was in Dundee so Keith could be near his children. She knew he'd left upset last night. But would he really wreck the one thing that brought her joy?

The back door swung open with such force that it banged against the outside wall. Startled, Liz turned to see Carter stride in. The hard line to his jaw and the glitter in his eyes told her he was livid. He surveyed the damage, eventually focusing on the words written across the wall, and when she realized his anger was directed at whomever had done this to her, her vision blurred. She, who ordinarily couldn't cry even when she needed to, suddenly couldn't stop the tears.

Carter's expression gentled when he saw her. He crossed over to her and she buried her face in the soft cotton of his T-shirt.

Isaac and Reenie stared as Carter tucked her head under his chin. But Liz didn't have it in her to care. Her children weren't around. She could allow herself this small amount of comfort. She wasn't sure she could have stopped herself, anyway. In this moment, Carter was like the air she needed to breathe.

"Don't worry." He smoothed her hair away from her eyes and made her look up at him. "I'll fix everything, okay? I have to go to New York for a few days, but I'll start the minute I return. I promise."

As she nodded, he said, "You'll see," and wiped the dampness from her cheeks.

CARTER LEANED AGAINST the cinder-block wall that served as the back of Mary Thornton's Trinkets and Treasures Gift Shop. In less than an hour, he had to leave for Boise to catch his plane. Johnson was expecting him. But it was nearly nine o'clock, which meant Mary would be arriving soon and he wanted to talk to her.

Reenie came out of Liz's shop, eyes focused on the ground in front of her and car keys jangling. Carter said nothing as he watched her cut across the alley to her van. But then she glanced his way—and did a double take. "What are you doing here?" she asked in surprise. "I thought you had a plane to catch."

"I want to talk to Mary before I go."

Liz's sister-in-law lowered her voice and angled her head toward The Chocolaterie. "About what happened?"

"It's always smart to talk to the neighbors," he said vaguely. But a vague response was never good enough for Reenie Russell. From what he knew of her, she didn't like subtleties. She preferred to have everything spelled out. Maybe it came from being a math teacher. She had to be taken step-by-step through any equation that didn't immediately appear to add up.

"You don't think it was Mary, do you?" she asked.

"No." While Mary struck him as being a little more interested in Liz's business than she had any reason to be, she cared too much about her image to do anything that might reflect badly on her. Maybe deep down she'd love to sabotage Liz's chances of success, but Carter doubted she'd do it at the risk of embarrassing herself.

Of course, he could be wrong. He'd been wrong before—and it had cost Laurel an extra day in that hotel with Hooper. He'd always wondered if it had been that particular day that had left the deepest scars. Which was why he wanted to talk to Mary. Just in case he was tempted to focus too closely on Keith. After the way Keith had acted last night, it was difficult *not* to blame him.

"Isaac's going to take my classes today so I can stay here and help clean up," Reenie told him. "I can't leave Liz like this."

"He can handle yours as well as his own?"

"He'll have to combine them but that's okay for one day."

"Good. I'm glad you'll be with her," he replied, and he meant it. He supposed some schools would fire a teacher for missing a day at the last minute. But this was

Dundee. Reenie's brother had paid for the new football field, the library bore her mother's name, and according to the little old ladies he'd heard in line at the grocery store, she and Isaac were both excellent teachers. He supposed that gave them a little more wiggle room than some. Regardless, school was out in another week, so maybe it didn't matter too much. He'd heard Reenie tell Liz that she'd lined up a substitute for tomorrow, too, because she'd be too nervous to teach while her brother was in surgery.

"Are you heading to New York on business or pleasure?" Reenie asked.

Carter smiled. Reenie was always warm and friendly, but she was direct, too, and generally didn't hesitate to ask about anything that piqued her curiosity. He'd seen her husband try to warn her off now and then with a gentle look and a "don't do it" grin. But it was rare that Isaac managed to convince her.

"Business." His inflection indicated she'd be better off not to press him further, and he knew she'd gotten the message when she frowned.

To her credit, she let the subject go. "Oh, well, have a safe trip."

"Thanks."

She unlocked her car door, but hesitated before climbing in. "You know, Liz means a great deal to me."

It was Carter's turn to frown. He and Liz had only been seeing each other for a couple of weeks, but he suspected he was about to receive his first personal helping of the well-meaning interference he had witnessed so often since arriving in Dundee.

"And with Keith and her father, she's been through a lot." Reenie continued.

Carter was growing impatient. He'd face Hooper soon; he had a lot on his mind. "Is this where you warn me not to hurt her?" he asked dryly.

Reenie shook her head. "No, this is where I tell you that you'll never meet a more wonderful person."

Carter blinked in surprise. He opened his mouth to say something, anything to make amends for how gruff he'd just been, but Reenie didn't seem to expect a response. She climbed into her van and drove away.

The sound of the van's engine faded, but Reenie's words seemed to echo in his head. *You'll never meet a more wonderful person.* He wasn't ready to meet someone so wonderful, was he? He was still too angry, too bitter. And too much in love with Laurel.

Mary rolled past him in her Cabriolet, parked in the lot and approached the store.

"Liz's shop is that one right there, in case you're confused," she said, pointing in the direction of the chocolate shop. "Or have you decided to be friendly to some of the rest of us, too?"

"This isn't a friendly call," he admitted.

"Then why are you here?"

"I have some questions to ask you."

Confusion etched a series of lines on her forehead. "About what? I have a lot to do and I'm running late."

"Where were you last night?"

"Why do you want to know?"

"Someone broke into Liz's shop and trashed the place."

Her stride faltered for a moment, but then she unlocked the back door and stepped inside, flipping on lights as she moved toward the front. "Okay, I was with Lou Masters."

"Doing what?"

She gave him a suggestive grin. "How detailed would you like me to get?"

"A yes or no answer as to whether he'll support you in that statement will do."

"*Statement?* What, are you working for the police now?"

"No. But they should be next door. If you don't want to talk to me, you could talk to them."

Giving him an arrogant look, she set her purse and money bag on the counter. "Don't try to badger me. I could tell you to get lost and I'd be well within my rights."

"Is that what you're going to do?"

Her mouth puckered in a pout. "You deserve it."

He cocked a questioning eyebrow at her.

"For ignoring me," she said, flashing her dimples. "You've been hell on my ego."

"There's always Lou Masters," he replied.

"He's not quite the challenge you are." Her gaze moved down his body and back up again. "Anyway, I'm busy. Maybe we could discuss this over dinner tonight."

"I'll be out of town."

"Someone just trashed Liz's shop and you're leaving?"

"Do you know who's behind the vandalism?" he asked.

She stepped up to the cash register and started filling the drawer. "I have no idea, unless it's that guy I saw."

"What guy?"

"The one standing in the parking lot, watching Liz's place when I locked up the other night. I warned her about him the day she opened."

Why hadn't Liz mentioned this to him? "Who was it?"

"I didn't recognize him."

"But you'd know him if he was from around here, wouldn't you?"

"It was pretty dark, but, yeah, I'd probably know him. Or know of him. He wasn't familiar at all."

Which meant this guy had to be a tourist or someone from a neighboring town. But that didn't make any sense. Why would someone who wasn't even from Dundee want to hurt Liz? The fact that her shop had been damaged twice removed the possibility it was a random act.

"Can you give me a description of him?" Carter asked.

"He was tall. But he was wearing a pair of extra-baggy jeans and a sweatshirt with a hood, so it was difficult to see his face or even the color of his hair."

"What was he doing?"

"Just leaning against his truck, drinking what looked like a beer."

"What kind of truck?"

"I already told Liz. It was a red Toyota."

"Do you know the model? The year?"

"No. It wasn't new, that's all I can tell you." She thought for a moment. "And it was missing the back bumper."

"Did you see the license plate?"

She shut her cash drawer. "Jeez, were you once a cop or something?"

"Something." He rarely mentioned having worked for the FBI. It saved him from answering the Dreaded Question—why aren't you with them anymore?

"Did you get the plate number?" he repeated.

"No."

"Was it an Idaho plate?"

"Yeah, but an older one."

"What else can you remember? You said he was drinking a beer. How did you know it was a beer?"

"I recognized the bottle."

"Was he also smoking? Chewing tobacco? Listening to music?"

"No. Like I told you, he was standing there. When I came out, he tossed his beer into the Dumpster, hopped behind the wheel of his truck and took off."

So he didn't like being seen.... What was the link between this stranger and Liz? "Can you think of anyone who might have it in for her?" he asked. "Heard any good rumors lately?"

"I've heard she's sleeping with you," she said pointedly.

He refused to let her put him on the defensive. "I suspect you're the one spreading that rumor."

"Maybe. Maybe not. Is it true?"

"We're talking about the damage to the chocolate shop, not my personal life."

She scowled. "I definitely sense some loyalty there."

"Are you going to answer my question?"

She gave him a dirty look and started to tidy up behind the counter. "You want a list of her enemies, huh? Well, you'd think *Reenie* would hate her, that they'd hate each other. But no, they're best friends and have been since before Reenie married Isaac."

"Anyone else? Besides the obvious?"

"The obvious?"

"Her ex-husband?"

"You know, I would've bet money it was Keith. Until I saw that stranger in the lot."

"What about you?" Carter asked softly.

"What about me?"

"You're not very excited about having The Chocolaterie next door."

She glared at him for several seconds after she realized his intimate tone actually harbored an accusation. "I already told you. I was with Lou Masters last night."

"You could've done it together."

"Wait a second. Liz is selling a lot of the same stuff I'm selling, and I worry that she may cost me my business. But I'd never break in and destroy her property."

"Really?"

Mary folded her arms and held her chin at a defiant angle. "Really."

Carter knew the whole "stranger" sighting could be an elaborate lie meant to point him in the wrong direction. He'd had suspects try to mislead him in the same manner, many times. But Mary was more interested in trying to add him to her list of admirers, in feeding her ego, than in getting rid of him. If she was really the culprit, she'd probably be more eager to see him leave.

"I'm glad to hear that," he said, pulling a card from his back pocket. "Will you call me if you see that stranger again?"

"Why should I?" she asked in an injured tone of voice. "What have you ever done for me?"

He grinned as he held out his card. "I believe you. Doesn't that count for anything?"

She hesitated, but accepted it. "You're too good-looking. You know that?"

He chuckled and headed out.

When he reached the alley, there was a police car parked next to the building. He wanted to go back into the chocolate shop to see what the Dundee police had to say about the break-in. Maybe someone had seen the perpetrator running from the building and called in a tip, or better yet, a patrol car had spotted the mysterious stranger that Mary had mentioned. But if Carter didn't hurry, he'd miss his plane.

Checking his watch, he strode briskly toward the Jag. But then he spotted the Dumpster Mary had mentioned sitting on one side of the parking lot, and if only to check her story he spent a few minutes digging through it. He doubted he'd find many loose bottles in there, at least ones that weren't broken. The shop owners probably tossed their bottles in a recycling bin or bagged them up with their other garbage.

Carter found that to be true, for the most part. There were only two loose bottles. One was a broken vinegar bottle. The other was a Bud Light.

Being careful not to smudge any prints that might still be on the bottle, Carter carried it to his car and put it in his glove compartment. It wasn't practical to lift and run the hundreds of prints that would be inside Liz's shop. But he was doing the bureau enough of a favor that Johnson should be able to run one or two prints for Carter in return.

He doubted he'd get a hit. He knew of only three people who had a motive to do what had been done to Liz's shop—Keith, someone close to Keith, or Mary. Unless the culprit had a police record or had served in the military, he or she wouldn't be in the FBI's Integrated Automated Fingerprint Identification System. Running the print was arguably overkill for a case of vandalism. But Carter was meeting with Johnson anyway. And after what had happened to Laurel, he couldn't stand the possibility of a stranger lurking about....

Anyway, it was worth a shot. The local police weren't likely to do anything without an eyewitness. They didn't have the resources or the expertise to track down the offender through physical evidence.

So, yes, checking the fingerprints was definitely worth a shot.

CHAPTER EIGHTEEN

GORDON RUSSELL LEANED BACK and tried not to reveal how nervous he was while Dundee's only real-estate agent, Herb Bertleson, wedged his ample, pear-shaped body into a swivel chair on the other side of the desk. Gordon knew he was doing the right thing in returning to Dundee. But he couldn't believe how hard his heart was pounding. Or that, even now, he thought he'd just as soon drive off and pretend all was well instead of facing the mess he'd made, accepting the challenge to make it right, and confronting the fear that he'd be unable to do so.

Avoidance. That was his greatest temptation. He was good at shoving his messier emotions under the bed, so to speak. He'd done it for years.

But he wouldn't let those tendencies get the best of him this time. He'd made Chloe a promise. And he'd promised *himself*. Although recently the anger he felt toward Chloe and Randy ebbed and flowed between outrage and betrayal on the one side and understanding and forgiveness on the other, no matter where he stood on that continuum he had only to think of Chloe's anniversary card to remember his purpose.

Liz and Isaac. He was robbing himself by not trying

harder to bridge the gap between himself and his children. Anyway, they deserved more than he'd given them so far, regardless of what their mother had or hadn't done. Gordon couldn't change the past, but he could change how he reacted to it.

He thought of Luanna standing at the door, gaping after him. She'd been shocked by the change in him. But she was the one who'd opened his eyes. Had she never left him, he'd probably be playing golf. Or traveling with her, talking about her son and what Marty needed, while ignoring his own children.

Maybe, in the long run, it was a blessing that she'd found someone else, he decided. Certainly, it was going to make a better man out of him.

"I'm afraid we don't have a big rental market here in Dundee," Herb explained apologetically.

"I don't need anything fancy," Gordon said.

"And you'd like how long a lease?"

Hoping it'd help him stay put and deal with his children, even his grandchildren, Gordon planned to lock himself in for a good stretch. "A year at least."

"Okay. Let's see here." Herb thumbed through a file, then placed a couple of calls. "I've got two properties to choose from," he said at last. "One's a duplex, and the other is a trailer."

Gordon pictured the lovely home he'd left behind in L.A. But that wasn't important to him anymore.

"Which one is nicer?" he asked.

"The trailer sits on a beautiful piece of land by a running creek. You could have horses, dogs, whatever you want."

Horses? Gordon had never considered owning a horse. But that wasn't a bad thought. He could learn to ride. Become a cowboy. A cowboy grandpa with a huge dog for the kids.

He stared at the picture Herb shoved across the desk. He'd never imagined himself living in a dilapidated mobile home on the outskirts of a small Idaho town. Yet he was excited about it. He suspected it was the chance to start over that made him feel so free.

"I'll take it," he said and chuckled as he imagined showing the photo of his new home to Liz.

THE DAY AFTER THE BREAK-IN at her shop, Liz sat on the couch at her brother's farm with Reenie and Lucky Hill. Lucky was Reenie's half sister—the daughter Garth had learned about only a few years earlier. The truth about the senator's relationship to Lucky had caused a huge scandal in Dundee, had disrupted his bid for a congressional seat, and had threatened to tear the Holbrook family apart. But thanks largely to Celeste and the way she'd handled the situation, they'd all recovered. Now Reenie, Garth, Celeste and Lucky were close. Gabe seemed to be the only one still struggling to accept her.

Obviously, she didn't feel the same reluctance toward him. From what Liz could see, Lucky admired Gabe a great deal and was as worried as Reenie was about his impending surgery.

"He'll be okay," Liz murmured to them both, patting Reenie's dog Spike, a black lab–chow mix, who sat at attention in front of her.

Reenie nodded in agreement, but even so she had her

hands clasped tightly in her lap, and Lucky kept glancing at the clock. Isaac's substitute teacher had backed out at the last minute, so he'd had to go to school. But he'd already called several times to check in, and they'd promised to let him know the moment they heard any news.

"Hannah was beside herself when I talked to her on the phone this morning," Reenie said. She'd put on one of their favorite DVDs, *The Last of the Mohicans*, but no one was really watching it.

"With worry?" Liz asked.

"With anger because she couldn't talk him out of this!"

"That would be frustrating."

"I can identify," Reenie grumbled.

"I can't imagine what we're going to tell Mom and Dad if something goes wrong," Lucky added.

Hearing Lucky call Celeste Mom had, at first, struck Liz as strange. But she'd grown used to it. Lucky's mother was dead, and not so fondly remembered in this town, and Celeste included Lucky in the family as wholeheartedly as she included her other children.

Only someone as generous as Celeste could pull it off, Liz thought. In the beginning, she'd probably done it out of love for Garth. Lately, however, Liz sensed a real fondness between the two women.

"They'll never forgive us for not telling them when they could still have stopped it," Reenie said.

In the movie, Daniel Day-Lewis led Madeleine Stowe and various other actors into the fort. Liz glanced at the flashes of cannon fire as Spike nudged her hand for more affection.

Garth and Celeste had a right to know that their son might not make it through the day, didn't they? she mused. As a mother, she would definitely want to be privy to that information. But it had been Gabe's decision. And he hadn't given Reenie a choice.

"Do you think I should call them?" Reenie asked, her expression mirroring the anxiety churning inside her.

"No!" Liz and Lucky responded in unison. Even Spike barked and wagged his tail as though he agreed.

"They can't change the situation now," Lucky said.

"But he's been in there more than eight hours. Something must be wrong. And if the operation ends badly…"

Reenie could hardly get the last word out, let alone face the possibility. "I'm sure it's going fine," Liz said, hoping she sounded convincing. "Some surgeries take forever."

Reenie stood and went to stare out the window. "I have a plane reservation, just in case Hannah needs me. If we lose him—" her voice cracked "—someone will have to help her bring him home."

Liz walked over and put an arm around her shoulders. "Come on, Reenie," she said, giving her a squeeze. "I know the waiting is getting to you. But don't let yourself think the worst."

"I'm a realist." Reenie rubbed her eyes, which were already mottled and puffy from the tears she'd shed earlier. "Caught between what he wants, what I want, and what I know my parents would want. He's put me in a terrible spot."

"If he survives, I'm going to kill him," Lucky

muttered, joining them at the window. "And I'm just the person to do it. He doesn't like me, anyway."

Reenie tossed her a sympathetic smile. "That's not true. He cares about you. But he has too much pride to let you know you've finally won him over. That's all. Gabe doesn't like being wrong."

Lucky's expression revealed how much she longed to believe Reenie. As she blinked quickly, battling her emotions, Liz felt a lump swell in her own throat. She was infinitely relieved, however, when Lucky managed to hold back her tears. After so many hours of waiting and wondering, they were all on edge. If anyone started to cry now, they'd all break down.

"We have to keep up the positive energy," Liz said. "Imagine Gabe walking off the plane."

"It won't be like that," Lucky said. "Even if today goes well, he'll probably be looking at several more surgeries."

"Can't he see what that'll do to Hannah?" Reenie asked.

On the television, Daniel Day-Lewis was arguing with the character who played Madeleine Stowe's father. Liz frowned. Another stubborn character.

"Hannah's boys still think their parents are on vacation," Lucky said, adding that into the mix.

It had all been said before, of course. But they couldn't help going over the worst of it again and again.

Reenie dropped her head in her hands. "I should never have let him do this."

"If Hannah couldn't stop him, you couldn't either," Liz told her.

"I know but..." She threw her hands in the air. "God, this waiting is driving me nuts."

Kneeling, Liz scratched Spike, who'd migrated to the window with them. "Let's change the subject."

"To what?" Reenie asked, and Liz knew that for her nothing else existed. Not right now. The conversation had grown more and more stilted as the day dragged by.

"The Chocolaterie," Lucky said. "Your grand opening was fabulous."

Reenie and Liz exchanged glances. Evidently, Lucky hadn't heard about the vandalism. "Not such a great topic," Reenie warned.

Lucky's eyes went wide. "What's wrong?"

"I'll tell you about it later." Reenie pulled them both back to the couch and flopped down on it. "I want to hear about Carter."

"Carter?" Liz echoed in surprise.

Lucky muted the TV. "Hudson? The new guy?"

Liz tried to outmaneuver them. "Wait, I like this part," she said, referring to the movie. "The scene with Madeline Stowe meeting up with Daniel Day-Lewis after tending the wounded is my favorite."

"You're stalling," Reenie accused.

"I just want to watch that scene."

"You've seen this movie a dozen times. I know because I've watched it with you." She nudged Lucky. "She must really like him."

"We're dating," Liz said. "That's all."

Reenie slumped lower in her seat and pinned her with a level stare. "Not quite."

Liz folded her arms and stared right back. "What's that supposed to mean?"

"I bumped into Dickie Robinson at Finley's Grocery yesterday. He said you never came home last weekend."

"What?" Dickie Robinson was Liz's closest neighbor. An older widower who lived alone, he took it upon himself to instruct Liz's children on putting their bicycles away and staying out of his flowerbeds. But he'd never struck her as particularly nosy. "Now we've got Dickie telling tales?"

"He wouldn't share what he knows with just anyone," Reenie said. "He trusts me. Isaac asked him to look out for you."

"Oh, brother." Liz rolled her eyes, but Reenie was undeterred.

"So?" she prompted, rubbing her hands together.

"So what?" Liz repeated.

"So get to the good stuff. I was waiting until I thought you might be ready. But I need to hear it now. What's really going on?"

Liz wished she knew. She and Carter had had a wonderful weekend together. But she didn't know if it meant anything. She didn't even know where he'd gone or why. Or when he'd be back. She hadn't heard from him since he'd left twenty-four hours ago. Carter had many wonderful qualities—and more sex appeal than any man had a right to possess—but he told her only as much as he wanted her to know, and she doubted he'd ever let her get any closer to the private person that his rough exterior protected.

"Didn't you once tell me Liz was involved with her old tennis coach?" Lucky asked Reenie in confusion.

Reenie waved a careless hand. "That's old news. At least I've been told it is." She looked pointedly at Liz.

Liz glanced forlornly at the movie. "Are you sure you want to miss the part where Madeleine Stowe and Daniel Day-Lewis hook up?"

"We can always rewind it," Reenie said and snapped off the movie.

Liz sighed. Evidently, she was the entertainment now. But as long as talking about her screwed-up love life kept Reenie from thinking about Gabe…"Dave told me he loves me," she confided.

"That's the tennis coach?" Lucky asked.

"That's the tennis coach," Reenie confirmed. "But Liz doesn't love him in return. Right, Liz?"

"Right."

"You're sure of that at this point?"

"I'm sure." If meeting Carter had done nothing else for her, she was grateful for that bit of clarification. Except she'd have no love interest at all once he moved away. She couldn't imagine how lonely that was going to be. But she couldn't string Dave along. If she hadn't fallen in love with him by now, it was likely she never would.

"That's quite an admission, for someone who likes to play fast and loose," Reenie said, referring to Dave.

"He claims he's a changed man."

"Do you believe him?"

"I do," Liz said. "Whether or not it'd last might be another issue. But he swears he loves me."

"What does Carter have to say about him?"

"Not a word. He doesn't have much to say about anything. That's the problem."

A flash of concern drew Reenie's eyebrows together, and Liz realized that absolute honestly would only add to her friend's burden of worry. So she smiled brightly. "But it's okay. We're just enjoying each other while it lasts. It's a summer fling," she added indifferently.

Reenie studied her for a moment. "I think he's a good man."

"He is a good man."

"But—"

"What?" Liz asked.

"He's guarded. And if he can't get beyond that—"

Liz shrugged carelessly. "He doesn't have to get beyond it. We're having a little fun together, that's all."

Reenie opened her mouth to say something else, but the phone interrupted them. The three of women stared at it as if it were a live wire. Then Reenie jumped up and ran to answer before the ringing could stop.

"Hello?" she said breathlessly, cradling the receiver with both hands.

Liz and Lucky grabbed each other, squeezing until their knuckles turned white.

As they watched, Reenie closed her eyes. Several tears squeezed out from beneath her lashes to roll down her face.

"Thank you," she murmured, letting those drops fall from her chin without bothering to wipe them away. "Thanks for letting me know." When she hung up and turned, she looked as white as chalk, but she managed a tremulous smile. "He's alive. They don't know if he's better or worse off than he was before, but he survived the operation." She shook her head. "The tough son of a bitch."

The three of them laughed and hugged all at once.

"He is a tough son of a bitch," Lucky murmured. "How could we ever have doubted him?"

Liz wiped the tears from her own cheeks. She felt heartsick about what had happened at The Chocolaterie and confused about her relationships with her father and Carter. But this day had put a few things into perspective.

CARTER SAT IN A SMALL SQUARE room across a metal desk from Charles Hooper. At Carter's request there was no safety glass to separate them. Hooper wasn't cuffed or shackled. It was important to Carter that the man he'd put in prison for murdering eleven women and raping and torturing Laurel know that he wasn't afraid of him. On the contrary, part of Carter—a large part, actually—hoped Hooper would attack him. He was certain Hooper knew that, just as Carter knew Hooper wouldn't give him the chance to exact the revenge he craved.

Besides, Hooper was a coward. He stalked only women—and little girls. Once he had lured them to his car with some seemingly innocent question, he dragged them inside and cuffed them to him. What happened after that was too horrid to contemplate.

Carter remembered Laurel's halting testimony in court, the way her gaze kept sliding toward him for strength—and felt sick inside.

"Nice of you to break up the monotony of this shit hole," Hooper said, leaning back and crossing his legs under the table.

Carter watched him beneath half-closed eyelids, trying to quell the revulsion and anger rising up inside him like bile. Special Agent Johnson stood outside the room, watching them through a one-way mirror. Ostensibly, he was there in case Hooper stepped out of line. But Carter knew Johnson was more worried about having to save Hooper from Carter.

Interestingly enough, however, Carter's anger wasn't directed solely at the tall, narrow-shouldered monster sitting across from him. He was mad at Laurel, too. Why had she let this demented bastard win? After all Hooper had done to her, why had she handed him the final victory?

"What have you got to say to me?" Carter asked without preamble. It was difficult enough to be sitting in the same room with Hooper. He didn't want to have to say anything beyond what was absolutely necessary.

But he knew Hooper didn't want it that way, knew it wouldn't be that easy.

"How's Laurel?" Hooper responded with a grin that showed teeth as yellowed as fifty-year-old newspaper.

Carter clenched his jaw. Hooper knew about Laurel's suicide, as he'd suspected. He could tell by the insolent light in the other man's eyes. But he refused to give Hooper the enjoyment he was looking for by letting him know that he'd just hit his target. "Better now," he said.

Hooper's bushy eyebrows shot up at the lift in his voice, the longer gray hairs falling into a deep groove on his shiny forehead.

"And you?" Carter pressed on. "How's life on the inside?"

Hooper quickly rallied. "Not as bad as I thought."

"Glad to hear it. So are we past all the bullshit? Or did you want to inquire about my health?"

Hooper folded his hands in his lap and didn't respond for a moment. "You're an interesting man," he said at last.

"I won't say what I think of you."

Hooper laughed softly. "Come on. No need to be so...*malevolent*," he said as if it was his new word for the week. "Your lovely wife must've been confused when she told you it was me, because she fingered the wrong man."

"And the DNA evidence?" Carter asked dryly.

Another laugh. "Oh...that." He drummed his fingers on the desk, then sent Carter another piercing gaze. "Tell me, does it bother you to know I was inside her? That I got there before you? And she was moaning." He closed his eyes as though the mere memory excited him. "Right in my ear..."

Every muscle in Carter's body bunched, but before he could react the door banged open and Johnson came in. He wore an apologetic expression and waved Carter out of the room, but Carter shook his head. "I've got it. Get out of here."

"Come on, he's playing games."

"Get out," Carter said.

Several seconds passed, but then Johnson backed out and the door clicked shut. "Does it bother you to know you'll never be inside a woman again?" Carter asked Hooper.

Hooper sobered and sat up straight, looking agitated and glancing in the direction of the people he knew were standing behind the one-way mirror.

"What's wrong?" Carter questioned.

"My mother abused me when I was young," Hooper said. "How can you hold me accountable for what I did? When she was so cruel?"

"Cruel?" Carter echoed. He managed to laugh, as if being around Hooper was merely entertaining and not causing every nerve he possessed to burn with the most negative of emotions. "You're kidding me, right? She coddled you, doted on you. And we both know it. She sobbed through the whole trial. You're a terrible disappointment to her."

Hooper glowered at him, the mirror, then the floor. "She still writes," he mumbled. "She knows there's been a mix-up. That I'm an innocent man, wrongly imprisoned."

Carter made a show of yawning. "We're back to that, are we?"

"What did you expect?"

"I thought you were finally going to get it right for a change, make your mother proud."

He stared at the wall.

"Hooper?"

He blinked.

"Tell me where you buried Rose Hammond, Hilary Benson and Vanessa Littleton." Pulling their pictures from a file folder, he spread his documentation over the table. Hooper had been charged with eleven murders, but these were three more that hadn't been connected to him at the time.

Three more...And that probably wasn't all of them.

His face void of expression, Hooper scanned the photos. "What made me do it?" he whispered to himself, then louder, to Carter, he said, "Why am I so different from everyone else?"

There was no regret in his voice, just a distant curiosity. "I wish I had an answer to that," Carter replied.

"If only I knew." Hooper shook his head. "Because I could, I guess. Because the desire fed on me like a...a compulsion, a craving."

"You do remember these women, don't you?" Carter said, drawing Hooper's attention back to the photos.

"I'm trying," he said, scratching his head.

As Carter watched the other man glance from face to face, he couldn't help thinking how pathetic Hooper was. Hooper was a lost creature, locked up and alone for the rest of his life. He'd traded the lives of others, and his own future, for his deeply sick obsession.

Maybe the only thing sadder than being one of Hooper's victims was being Hooper himself, Carter thought. What would it be like to live, knowing you weren't worth the air you breathed? That you were held in utter contempt by everyone around you?

Abruptly Carter gathered up the pictures.

"What are you doing?" Hooper asked in alarm.

"I'm leaving."

"But I haven't told you what you want to know."

"You had your chance." Carter knew Johnson was probably having a coronary on the other side of the glass, but he didn't care. Hooper remembered these women. He was just drawing out the visit, because there was a certain intimacy involved in the hatred Carter felt toward him. Hatred wasn't a positive emotion, but at least Hooper had achieved a reaction. A strong reaction.

Hooper was so desperate to matter to someone that he was willing to accept the most negative form of interest. But because of what he'd done to Laurel, Carter wouldn't let him. Why bother hating him, when that was exactly what he wanted?

"Wait, it's coming back to me now," Hooper said the moment Carter's hand reached the doorknob.

"Too late."

"But they promised me a few packs of cigarettes. And some chocolate."

Carter paused. "You have ten seconds. Then I leave."

Hooper cursed and glared at him, but when Carter shrugged and turned the knob, effectively ending Hooper's dog-and-pony show, he blurted out what Carter had wanted to hear all along. He'd buried all three women in upstate New York, near the cabin his uncle had owned when he was growing up. The police knew of that cabin, had searched it many times, but Hooper had claimed the bodies were buried on a neighbor's property, near a creek, where the ground was softer.

Carter had Hooper circle the spot on a map, and then he turned to the mirror. It showed him his own grim reflection, with Hooper sitting just beyond him, disappointed and grim himself.

Carter managed a tired smile for Johnson who he knew was watching. He'd gotten it. He'd gotten what he'd come for. And maybe, in seeing how pathetic Hooper was, he'd gotten a little more....

"Tell my mother I helped you out. She'll be happy about that," Hooper said as Johnson came in.

"I'm not telling her anything," Carter replied. Hooper hadn't told them where the bodies were out of a sense of contrition or guilt. He'd done it to feel a measure of power, a measure of control in a place where he typically had none. He'd also done it to break up the monotony of prison life, to taunt Carter, and to enjoy some cigarettes and candy. A man like that didn't care about his mother. Hooper probably never had. Or he wouldn't have broken her heart in the first place.

"Want to know why I think you did it?" Carter asked, pausing at the door.

Hooper looked up at him in surprise. Then his eyes narrowed. "Why?"

"Because you can't identify with anyone else. You can't feel their pain or their suffering because you don't care about them. You care only about yourself."

Hooper's thin lips curled into a "you got me" grin. "Tell Laurel I said hello," he said in a singsong voice.

This time, Carter didn't clench his jaw. He actually managed to smile. "You should see where I'm living now," he said. "It's beautiful. Wide open country. A small café that serves pancakes the size of dinner plates. Rodeos every summer. And a *chocolaterie*."

"A what?"

"A chocolate shop. Best chocolate you ever tasted."

Hooper glanced from Carter to Johnson, as if he didn't quite know what to make of Carter's friendly tone. "Maybe you could get me some of that," he said tentatively.

"Maybe," Carter replied. "You should really see what you're missing." With that, he started to walk out, but Johnson called him back.

"Don't go anywhere, Carter. I've got some good news for you."

Carter's mind was still so engrossed in what had just transpired that he didn't immediately realize what Johnson was talking about. "News?" he repeated in surprise.

"Yeah. We got a hit on that print you brought in."

CHAPTER NINETEEN

SOMEONE WAS INSIDE THE CHOCOLATERIE.

Liz was sure of it. She'd left all the lights on, hoping to discourage further problems, but the back door stood slightly ajar and she knew she'd locked up before she'd left last night. Maybe she'd been reeling after learning about the damage, but she hadn't walked off and left her shop open.

Hesitating halfway between her car, which she'd already parked in the lot, and the building, she glanced up and down the darkened alley. She should go to the police. But they'd been so little help, she didn't have much confidence in them. Besides, she didn't own a cell phone and if she left, whoever it was might get away. She was tired of not knowing who was targeting her, of blaming Keith without proof. He always denied it, as he had again when she'd called him this morning, leaving her nothing more to say. And she couldn't run next door and ask Mary or another neighbor to watch out for someone. The shops on either side of hers were closed. She'd stayed at Reenie's until well past eight. Isaac had picked up the kids when school had let out and they'd had dinner, together with Lucky's family, to celebrate the fact that Gabe had pulled through his operation.

Mica and Christopher were still at Reenie's. But Liz had grown anxious about getting back to her shop. Now that she'd had a chance to begin to recover emotionally, to realize what had happened wasn't the end of the world, after all, she was ready to tackle the cleanup and repairs.

Whoever had done this to her might have set her back a few days, but she wasn't about to let one person destroy her dream. Not Mary. Not Keith. Not anyone remotely connected to either of them. She loved The Chocolaterie and would make it a success if it was the last thing she did.

But that didn't mean she wasn't frightened to confront whoever it was inside. Mary had mentioned a stranger watching her place, someone in a red Toyota. Was it him?

She took slow, careful steps as she approached the back door.

Movement inside made her knees go weak. What did this person have against her? Hadn't enough damage been done?

Squatting, so she could run her hands over the ground, she searched for a weapon of some kind. Chances were good she'd know whomever it was. Chances were also good the vandal wasn't dangerous in a bodily harm sort of way. But there was always that remote possibility…

When her fingers encountered the sharp edges of a large rock, she hefted it in one hand and rose, wishing her heart would quit making such a racket. It sounded louder than a jackhammer in her ears and made it difficult to believe she was approaching with any stealth.

The door creaked as she swung it wider. She almost called out to see if anyone would answer. She desperately wanted to hear a familiar voice, so she could be angry—instead of angry *and* scared. But the element of surprise was really her only advantage.

She crept through the opening, gripping the rock so hard it hurt her hands. In her panicked state, she couldn't identify any new damage. But there were noises coming from the bathroom. What was it with that bathroom?

The door stood open but blocked her view of whoever might be inside. Light glimmered through a tiny gap by the hinges and Liz could just make out a body and some shifting shadows.

Whoever it was looked large. She was almost positive it was a man. Was it Keith, then? Or the stranger Mary had mentioned?

The hardwood floor creaked as she moved closer. Maybe she was being foolish, confronting this person alone. But she had to stand and defend what was hers while she had the chance.

And now was her chance....

Springing around the door, she lifted the rock and nearly brought it crashing down—on her father's head. Or make that Gordon's head. She didn't quite know what to call him anymore. Not after thirty-two years of calling him *Dad*.

"What are you doing here?" she asked, momentarily frozen.

He'd automatically shielded his head with an arm, but once he realized it was her he jutted his chin toward the rock she still held in one hand. "You've got every right to be angry, but there's no need to get violent," he said, offering her a sheepish grin.

She relaxed into a less-threatening position. "I'm sorry. I was afraid—"

"That I was the bastard who did this?" He waved at the destruction around them. "No, I'm just the bastard who said something I sincerely regret."

She could see now that he wasn't ruining anything. He was trying to repair the damage. There was a toolbox at his feet. But she didn't know how to respond to his comment about regretting what he'd said. Did he think he could announce that he wasn't her father and then pretend he'd never mentioned it?

"How'd you get in?" she asked, stalling for enough time to sort out her feelings.

"I had to break the lock, but I can fix it."

"Why didn't you call me?"

"I wanted to surprise you."

He'd definitely done that. "Why?"

"Herb over at the real-estate office told me what happened here, so I thought I'd come in and see if I could help clean up. I'm starting by reattaching the sink."

"That doesn't explain—what are you doing *in Dundee?*"

The way Gordon shifted on his feet revealed a fair amount of nervousness. "Maybe you should put down that rock before I tell you the rest," he teased.

She set the rock on a table. "Go ahead."

"I live here."

Her jaw dropped. "You're not serious."

He rubbed his hands together. "'Fraid so. I'm now the proud tenant of a rather dilapidated mobile home. But it's not far from Isaac's farm."

"Does *he* know you've moved to town?" she asked.

"Not yet. I just settled in this morning. Not that it took me long. I'm traveling pretty light these days."

"I see," she said. But she didn't see at all.

One second stretched into the next as they stared at each other. Gordon seemed to be waiting for some sign that it was okay with her he was living in Dundee. But she couldn't imagine why that would matter. She didn't even belong to him. He'd made that perfectly clear.

"I'm sorry," she said at last. "I'm guessing you came back because you don't want things between you and Isaac to stay the way you left them. But I don't think I can act as mediator, if that's what you're expecting."

"I don't expect that at all."

"Then I'm at a loss to know what you want from me."

"I'm here to fix what I broke, if I can."

"That makes no sense. Since Mom died, you've wanted only to be rid of me—"

"That's not true," he argued. "I've always wanted you. I just…couldn't deal with the truth. It was easier to stay busy and move forward as if nothing had happened." His eyebrows knitted together in a rueful expression. "I told myself nothing *had* happened. But I'm afraid you might've received signals I didn't even know I was sending."

Liz moved some rolling carts out of the sugar that had been dumped on the floor. "So what's changed?"

"Everything."

"Everything," she repeated, disbelieving.

"That's why I'm here. That's why I'm staying. I'm going to make it up to you and Isaac. I swear."

Liz had never seen her father so contrite. Where was the big, plastic smile that usually hid what he was really thinking? The pretenses that allowed him to lie, even to himself? The subtle inference that if a problem existed he had no responsibility for it?

"How long?" she asked.

"How long what?" he replied.

"How long will you be here?"

"As long as it takes."

Liz covered her mouth. She'd wanted this man's love and attention since she could remember—had worshipped him from afar when he wouldn't let her any closer. And now, just when she'd given up hope, he was here?

Could she really trust what he was telling her? Obviously, the past still bothered him, or he wouldn't have acted the way he'd acted for the past eighteen years. That type of thing didn't change overnight.

"I don't know if I can deal with this," she admitted, her heart racing. "I'd like you and Isaac to be able to have a relationship. What Mom did with me...I mean, it shouldn't impact *him*."

"I shouldn't have let it impact you, either," he said. "It wasn't your fault."

She gazed earnestly up at him. "Whose fault was it, Gordon?"

He winced when she used his name. "Mine," he said without blinking.

She tried to accept his answer. But it was exactly

what she wanted to hear, and he probably knew it. "How can that be true?"

He studied her with an air of sad resolve. "You'll have to trust me."

Despite his words, all the questions Liz swore she'd never ask nearly rushed out of her mouth all at once. Questions about how and when and why. But she permitted only one.

"Do you know who my real father is?"

She watched his Adam's apple bob as he swallowed; could see him struggling with the question.

"I do," he said.

"How long have you known?"

"In a way, I just found out this weekend."

Her heart skipped a beat. *Let it go,* she told herself. She knew she might not like what she learned, that it could be a friend's father, an enemy's father, or someone who worked on her parents' cars or their yard or their house. It could be someone she'd never liked and wouldn't want to belong to. It could even be someone too old or far too young. Beyond that, if she achieved a name and could put a face to the stranger who'd help create her, she'd forever picture her mother in the arms of this other man and wonder if she'd ever really known Chloe. Besides Isaac's love, her mother's memory was the only positive thing she had left from her childhood. She needed to safeguard it so she could pass on Chloe's legacy to her children.

For all those reasons, Liz knew she shouldn't ask. But how could she let it go, now that she had the chance? In any case, the word escaped before she could consciously form it. "Who?"

"Me, in all the ways that count," he said with a smile.

She clamped her hands together. "Does that mean you won't tell me?"

"Can we recover from what's happened first? Get to know each other again and then, if it's important to you, talk about it later?" he asked hopefully.

Liz knew that, someday, she'd ask again. As frightened as she was of the answer, it was a question that was going to eat at her. But she didn't have to know now. They both needed time.

She nodded.

"Thanks," he said, and then he surprised her by adding, "I love you."

WHEN LIZ WENT BACK TO COLLECT her children, Lucky and her family were gone, and Reenie and Isaac were cleaning the kitchen together. They touched and kissed and smiled at every opportunity. It always made Liz happy to see them so in love—but tonight it also made her miss Carter.

She told herself she was crazy for feeling as strongly about him as she did. How had she been stupid enough to let herself fall for the wrong guy—again?

Maybe it was because she wasn't fully recovered from her divorce. Or she was lonelier than she'd realized. Or she was, quite simply, a fool. But she missed him terribly and he'd only been gone two days.

She pictured the woman smiling cheek-to-cheek with him on his cell phone. Had he gone to see her? Were they considering reconciling? Or had he returned home to visit his mother or sisters or both?

He'd given her no clue. She wasn't even sure she'd hear from him. Or that he'd be all that interested in seeing her again when he got back.

. And now her father was back in town, and she couldn't trust her heart in that situation, either.

"What's wrong?" Isaac asked.

Liz was gathering together Mica's jacket and Christopher's sweatshirt as she waited for them to put on their shoes. They'd been begging her to stay a little longer, so they could see the end of the movie they'd been watching, but after the shock she'd received at The Chocolaterie, Liz craved the solitude of home. "You know Reenie will let us borrow the video tomorrow," she told them for the third time.

"What's wrong?" her brother repeated, when Liz didn't give him an answer.

"Nothing," she said. She'd already decided she wouldn't tell him about Gordon tonight. She needed to ponder how she'd handle the fact that the man who wasn't really her father had just moved to town. She wanted Isaac to have a good relationship with Gordon, told herself it would be petty to hope for less. And yet, if she was being perfectly honest, she was frightened by the thought of the two of them growing close and somehow increasing her sense of isolation.

In any case, she figured she could give herself one night to sort out her emotions before dealing with Isaac's reaction to the news.

But, as usual, he could tell that something was going on. He'd always been able to read her so well. "You seem upset."

"Just tired."

"Is it the shop? Because school will be out soon, you know, and I plan on helping you clean up whatever's left."

"You'll be working on your book, remember? You spent all that time in Africa. You need to publish your research before it's out of date."

"I will, but I can still help. And I know Carter will help, too."

Carter had promised he'd fix the shop the moment he returned. But she didn't know when that would be. "I'll muddle through," she insisted.

"Do the police have any idea who's responsible?" he asked.

Liz shook her head. "I called them earlier this afternoon, just after we heard the news about Gabe, but Officer Orton didn't have anything new to tell me. He said he's been trying to track down the stranger Mary saw in the parking lot. He's been asking around to see if anyone might know him, but so far, he's come up empty."

"Mary was probably trying to throw you off the track," he muttered.

"Maybe," Liz said.

Reenie, finished with wiping off the counter, joined them.

Catching his wife's eye, Isaac jerked his head toward the hallway. "Should we tell her?" he whispered, his change in tone and manner indicating they were talking about a whole new subject.

Liz glanced over at the children. Jennifer, Angela and Isabella hadn't moved since she'd returned from the shop. They were completely engrossed in the movie. Her own children had finally managed to put on their shoes, but they were sitting on the floor, watching, too. "Tell me what?" she asked Isaac.

"We have a little secret." Reenie smiled widely. "And we'd like you to be the first to know."

Liz put the jacket and sweatshirt she was carrying on a chair along with her purse. "What is it?"

Reenie tugged on her arm. "Come in here. We don't want the kids to know until we've had the chance to tell my parents. And we were waiting to do that until we knew how Gabe was going to fare."

"Have you heard from him?" Liz asked, as she followed them both into the small living room that looked out over a wide expanse of lawn.

"Hannah put him on the phone just before you got back. The painkillers have made him loopy. His words were so slurred I couldn't understand him. But at least I heard his voice. And Hannah said he's doing better than the surgeon anticipated. If he recovers as quickly as planned, she should be able to bring him home in another week."

"How will you explain such a long delay to your parents?" she asked.

Isaac closed the door separating the living room from the family room. "When Gabe's able to speak coherently, Hannah plans to have him call and tell them about the operation. Kenny and Brent too. It's in the past, and he pulled through, so there's no reason to be upset."

Liz remembered Lucky saying Gabe would require a *series* of operations, but she figured she didn't need to mention future hurdles. For the moment, they could take heart in the fact that Gabe was okay. "Won't they be angry that he didn't tell them?"

"Of course," Reenie said with a wave of her hand. "But that's between them. I'm going to play dumb and stay out of it."

Liz guessed the fact that Reenie had known all along would come out at some point. But she knew the Holbrooks would deal with it. Right now, she was more interested in the other secret they'd mentioned. The one they seemed so excited about—especially because she was fairly certain she'd already guessed what it was. "So what's going on?" she asked eagerly. "What did you want to tell me?"

Reenie slipped her hand inside Isaac's. "You tell her."

His face filled with pride and excitement. "Reenie's pregnant," he said. "We're expecting our first baby together."

Liz had been right. It was a baby. Covering her mouth so she wouldn't squeal and draw the children's attention, she hugged Reenie. "How wonderful," she said. "I'm so excited for you both. There's nothing like having a child."

"We tried to get pregnant for months, but it never happened," Reenie explained. "Then we got so busy we gave up hoping and counting the days and making sure we timed everything right. And just a few weeks ago I realized that it had been almost two months since I'd had a period."

"Have you been to the doctor?" Liz asked.

"No, but we've confirmed it with one of those over-the-counter tests."

"Twice," Isaac added.

"And I'm always regular."

Liz was regular, too. Like clockwork. With Mica and Christopher, she'd been able to tell right away, almost the day she conceived—

Suddenly, her knees went weak and terror shot through her chest like a javelin.

"What is it?" Reenie asked.

Liz couldn't speak. She was too busy thinking, trying to remember. When was the last time *she'd* had a period? She'd been inactive for so much of the previous two years that she'd gotten out of the habit of keeping track. But it had certainly been more than her usual twenty-eight days....

"Liz?" Isaac prompted, a heavy dose of concern in his voice. "Maybe you should sit down. You look like you're about to pass out."

Because she was. A buzzing sound inside her head, what sounded like a horde of bees, seemed to be growing louder by the second.

Her period should have started several days ago. Deep down she knew that, even if she didn't want to admit it. But several days weren't so many. Maybe she'd miscounted. Or she was only late. She'd been under a lot of stress lately. There was her father, and Gabe's operation, and the shop, not to mention having Mary copy everything she did and Keith constantly pressuring her to reconcile.

Then there was Carter, of course.

He was the real problem, wasn't he? He'd been inside her several times. They'd always used a condom, but in the middle of the night they'd been half-asleep. Had they been as diligent as they thought they'd been?

And even so, a condom was no guarantee...

"Liz, you're scaring me," Reenie said, her voice reflecting her worry.

Convincing herself that there had to be some other reason for her body's tardiness, she managed a feeble smile. "It's nothing."

"That's not true," Isaac said. "I know you too well. *We* know you too well."

"I'm thrilled for you, really." She hated how reedy her voice sounded.

"But..." Reenie said.

Liz told herself to breathe, to smile, to lie as convincingly as she'd ever lied in her life. But she wasn't particularly good at pretending, especially when she was reeling as though someone had just blindfolded her and run her around in circles. So she used the only excuse she could think of that might cover for her strange reaction. "Dad's moved to town," she said. "He's leased a trailer not far from here and he plans to stay."

CHAPTER TWENTY

LIZ SAT IN HER LIVING ROOM alone, with all the lights off, thankful that Mica and Christopher were finally asleep. Because she couldn't pretend to function normally any longer. Not since she'd checked the calendar.

She'd had her last period the day she went in to help with Chris's class. She remembered because she'd had to run to the store on her way to school to pick up some tampons. And that was thirty-five days ago. *Thirty-five!*

She needed to buy a pregnancy test. Only she couldn't do it in Dundee. Marge over at Finley's Grocery would tell everyone in town. Besides, Liz was too frightened of what the truth might be.

What would she do if she was pregnant? She and Carter barely knew each other.

With a helpless groan, she imagined herself eight months along, trying to prepare for the arrival of a baby while running the shop and taking care of her two other children—and nearly broke into a cold sweat. How would she explain the situation to Mica and Christopher? To everyone else?

She'd be a pariah in this conservative town. And she couldn't move away. She'd just opened The Chocolaterie. Besides, where would she work if she was pregnant? And where would she go? Back to L.A. to face Dave?

No.

She buried her head in her hands, trying, without luck, to avoid the worst thought of all—telling Carter. What would he say? He wasn't even planning to stay in Dundee, let alone become a *father*.

The phone rang. Liz eyed it suspiciously, then picked up the receiver. She was fairly certain it was going to be Reenie or Isaac. They'd asked her to call once she got home and was settled in for the night. They still believed she was upset about having Gordon in town.

"Hello?"

"There you are."

She let her breath seep out very slowly. It was Carter. "How's it going?" she asked, gripping the phone far too tightly.

He hesitated for a moment, which made her fear he'd already read something amiss in her voice. "Good. You?"

"Fine."

"You sound tired."

"It's been a long day." And then, because she didn't have anything else to say, she added, "Gabe underwent surgery in Boston."

"I thought he was on vacation."

The sarcasm in his voice would've made her smile, had she been capable of it. He'd known they were harboring a secret all along. She'd seen it on his face that night at the Holbrooks'. He was so perceptive, which only increased her anxiety. There was no way he could guess the truth—was there?

"He didn't want anyone who might tell his parents to know," she said, hoping to keep him talking about other things.

"So how'd he do?"

"He's still alive. That's all we know so far."

"That man doesn't give up easily."

Liz curled her fingernails into her palms. She was willing to bet Carter was a lot like Gabe in that way. "No."

"Reenie must be relieved."

"She is."

"Is that where you've been? At her place?"

"Yeah. Have you been trying to reach me?"

"I've called a few times. I tried the shop, too—and I couldn't believe it when Gordon answered the phone."

"He's back," she said simply.

There was another lengthy pause. "Is that why you're so subdued?"

Hoping to improve the blood flow to her brain, Liz put her head between her knees. She was subdued because she might have gotten herself into the biggest mess of her life. She was almost sure of it.

"I guess," she managed to say. She would've asked him where he was and when he was coming back. That was what she'd been wondering since he'd left. But if she was pregnant, there was little point in that. Once he found out about the baby, he'd feel trapped and the re-lationship would be over.

"Liz?"

"What?" she replied, but she was only half listening.

She was too busy remembering a snatch of conversation they'd had the first day they'd been together at The Chocolaterie.

Do you have children?…A little boy?…Maybe a girl, as well?

Did I bring any children to town?

They could be with their mother.

You were certain at the restaurant that I've never been married.

Some men have children without ever marrying.

Not me.

Not him. He'd said it so matter-of-factly. So positively. Which meant the relationship wouldn't be over. He'd marry her whether he wanted to or not. Or maybe he'd ask her to get an abortion. But for Liz that wasn't an option.

"Are you okay?" he asked.

"I'm fine. Really." Her second line beeped and she immediately latched on to the excuse it offered. "I'm getting another call." She hoped he'd say she could get back to him later, but he didn't.

"I'll hold. I have some news on the vandal that's been giving you so much trouble."

He had news? He'd been gone since right after the break-in. And the police certainly hadn't been able to tell her anything.

"Okay, um, just a second." She bit her lip and switched over. "Hello?"

"Liz?"

It was Dave. Did everything have to go wrong at once? "Now's not a good time, Dave."

"Fine. If you won't talk to me over the phone, I'll fly out there."

"No!"

"What else can I do? You won't even give me the chance to speak to you."

"It's not that. It's…it's been a horrible few days." She felt tears burn the back of her eyes but refused to succumb to them.

"Why?"

"For starters, someone broke into the shop and nearly ruined it."

"You're kidding."

"No."

"Is it the same person as before, the one who ripped the sink from the wall?"

"I think so, because they did the same thing again. And a lot more. They spray painted the walls, poured water all over my inventory, broke a few cases and shelves, upended the sugar and spread it all over the floor. I haven't been able to open since."

He cursed under his breath. "I guess Dundee's not so different from L.A., huh?"

"The worst part of it is that I can't name even one enemy. So…who's doing it?"

"It has to be Keith."

Keith had been angry over Carter when he'd left that night. But he seemed so sincere when he said it wasn't him. "Maybe."

"I'm sorry, babe," Dave said. "I know how that must've felt. When you figure out who's doing this, I'll come up there and kick some ass."

"*If* I figure it out," she said glumly.

"Do you want me to help you clean up the mess?"

"No, I've got it. Anyway, I've got to go. Reenie's on the other line," she said so she could get off the phone with him more quickly.

"Call me back?"

And say what? That she was probably pregnant with another man's child? "Dave—"

"Please?" he said. "Come on, Liz. If you care about me at all, you'll do that much."

Biting back a sigh, she promised she would and returned to Carter. She thought he might ask about her caller's identity, but he didn't. She didn't know if that meant he respected her privacy, he wasn't easily threatened or he didn't care. He'd once let her know that he didn't like having competition, but he hadn't mentioned Dave since, so maybe that had changed.

"Do you have any connection to a Rocky Bradley?" he asked.

"Who?"

"Rocky Bradley. He's an ex-con living in Boise, currently on parole for grand larceny. But he's done time for drugs, assault—a variety of charges."

"I've never heard of anyone by that name. The only people I know who live in Boise are the Howells. They moved from here last fall."

"Do they have any reason to dislike you?"

"None. I spoke to them occasionally when I worked at Finley's Grocery. That's it. Why?"

"Rocky Bradley is the stranger Mary saw in the parking lot."

"How do you know?"

"She told me he was drinking a beer, and I retrieved the beer bottle from the Dumpster. His prints are all over it. Besides that, his mother told me he drives a 1985 red Toyota truck, without a bumper. And he fits Mary's description of a tall, lanky man who wears baggy clothing."

"So it's not Keith who keeps breaking in."

"I don't think so."

"And Mary was telling the truth."

"About a stranger."

"What's that supposed to mean?"

"Since there's no apparent connection between you and Bradley, I'm guessing she or someone else hired him to do what he did."

She leaned her head back on the couch and stared up at the ceiling. "Have you talked to him?"

"He wasn't there when I called. He's living with his mother. I'm planning to drop by their house when I fly into Boise tomorrow."

"You're coming home?"

"Early in the morning."

"Where are you now?"

"My sister's place."

She tossed a lap blanket over her legs because her toes felt like blocks of ice. "You went to New York to visit your family?"

"No, I had unfinished business here."

Liz wanted to ask if that business included the woman whose picture was on his cell phone. But she knew that would probably come off as too possessive, and she definitely didn't want to sound like a jealous lover. Especially if she was pregnant. Relations between them would soon become difficult enough.

How was she ever going to tell him?

She wasn't, she decided. Not yet. First she'd pray that she started her period.

"Have a safe trip," she said.

"Liz?"

Her breath caught at the way he said her name. Before, he'd been all business, trying to figure out who had broken into The Chocolaterie. It was easier to keep him at an emotional distance when he spoke that way. But this sounded as if he was about to get more personal. "Yes?"

"Will you be okay having Gordon around?"

It touched her that he was concerned. But at this point, she felt as if *anything* would be okay—so long as she wasn't having a baby. "He's the least of my worries."

"Is it the shop that's got you so upset?"

"Yeah," she lied.

"We'll get it open by next weekend."

"Okay."

"What else is going on around there?"

"Reenie's pregnant," she said, just to see his response.

"I'm sure your brother's happy about that."

"Thrilled. Between Gabe pulling through the operation and the pregnancy, he and Reenie have a lot to celebrate tonight. But I'm the only one who's supposed to know about the baby at this point, so don't mention it to the senator."

"I won't. Where will you be tomorrow afternoon?"

"I don't know. Probably the shop."

"I'll drop by when I get in. I want to see you."

"Right, okay. Good night," she said and hung up. Then she curled into herself. She was supposed to call Dave, and Reenie and Isaac, too. But she couldn't muster the energy.

Unplugging the phone from the wall so it wouldn't ring, she headed down the hall and fell into bed. She didn't even bother to undress. Such details hardly seemed important when she was pretty sure she'd never be able to get up again.

"MOMMY...MOMMY." A SMALL HAND tapped Liz's shoulder. "Mommy, wake up."

"What?" she muttered into her pillow.

"I think we're late for school."

Jerking her head up, Liz squinted at her son, then took in the glowing numerals on her alarm clock. Sure enough, it was almost nine. They'd overslept.

Liz might've cursed, but she'd been taking extra care with her language these days. Christopher was at the age where he mimicked everything he heard, and she definitely didn't want him running around school saying, "Shit!"

Staggering to her feet, she shoved a hand through her hair and tried to gather all her faculties together. "Where's Mica?"

"Eating."

"Eating what?"

"Cold cereal."

She would rather have made her children a healthier

breakfast. "What about you?" she asked, starting down the hall. "Can I make you some oatmeal?"

He trailed behind her. "I've already eaten."

"Why didn't you wake me sooner?"

"Grandpa Russell said not to."

"Grandpa Russell!" she said, her voice loud enough to make her head throb.

"He's the one who rang the doorbell earlier," Mica volunteered as Liz entered the kitchen.

Liz hadn't heard any doorbell. She glanced around. "Is he still here?"

"No. He just came by to tell you that he put a new lock on the back door of your shop and to drop off the keys." Mica waved toward the counter. "They're over there."

Was this really Gordon they were talking about? "That was nice of him," Liz mumbled.

"He's in a real good mood," Mica told her. "He went home to shave, but he's coming back to drive us to school. That's why he said to let you sleep. He said he'd take us today."

Liz could hardly believe it. "I can manage."

"No, Mom. He promised us we'd stop for doughnuts if we get ready quietly." She made a face at Christopher. "I guess I'm the only one who gets one, though, since big mouth over there woke you up."

"I'm not a big mouth!" Christopher said.

Liz put a hand on her son's shoulder, since he was already hugging her leg and she could reach him easier. "Stop it, you two. It's good he woke me, Mica. I needed to get up. I have a lot to do." But then she remembered the fact that she might be pregnant and nearly groaned out loud.

Mica grimaced at Liz's wrinkled T-shirt and skirt. "Weren't you wearing that outfit yesterday?"

"I fell asleep before I could change for bed."

"You've never done that before."

"Not that I can remember."

Mica shoved her glasses all the way up to the bridge of her nose. "Are you sure Angela's uncle Gabe will be okay?"

"He'll be fine," Liz assured her. "And I'm fine, too."

Mica's thoughtful expression indicated she wasn't totally convinced. But then Gordon knocked at the door and she and Chris rushed off to gather their backpacks.

"He's here! We gotta go!" Chris cried, as if they weren't already in motion.

Liz made her way to the front door. "You don't have to take the kids to school," she said once she let Gordon in.

"I don't mind," he replied. "You looked a little strung out last night. I figured you could use the rest."

"I looked that bad?"

"Why not take a hot bath and relax?"

Obviously, she didn't look any better this morning. "Do you know where the school is located?"

"I can show him," Mica said confidently, pulling Christopher along as she tried to squeeze between Liz and the door frame.

Liz moved back to make more room.

Once they stepped outside, Gordon put a hand on Mica's shoulder. "This one reminds me so much of you," he said with a twinkle in his eye.

Liz blinked in surprise, then returned his smile. "Thanks for your help."

He started to leave, but pivoted to face her again halfway down the walk. "By the way, I'm almost finished with the shop. You should be able to open tomorrow. So you might want to make some candy this afternoon."

"Almost *finished?*" she echoed.

He shrugged. "Once I got going it was tough to stop."

"You must've been up all night."

"I had a goal in mind."

He waved, and the three of them climbed into his car and drove off.

Liz closed the door. She needed to go to a neighboring town to purchase a pregnancy test. To put her mind at ease, to know exactly what she was facing.

But just as she finished getting ready and was about to grab her purse and car keys off the counter, someone rang the doorbell.

And this time it wasn't her father. It was Dave.

CHAPTER TWENTY-ONE

LIZ'S EX-TENNIS COACH still looked stunning, with his golden hair, broad smile and tanned face. She'd forgotten how handsome he was. Her memory of him certainly didn't compare to the flesh-and-blood version standing on her doorstep. But he wasn't Carter, and he didn't affect her in the same way.

"Dave, what are you doing here?" she managed to ask once she'd recovered from the shock.

"You never called me back last night."

"I was exhausted. I fell asleep."

"I need to talk to you."

"Why? I've already explained that—" she didn't know how to put it any more gently "—it's over."

Dickie from next door came out of his house to water his lawn. When Liz glanced over at him, he was eyeing Dave suspiciously, which made her realize that she should probably encourage Dave to vacate her front porch, so Dickie couldn't eavesdrop.

"Here, come in," she said, holding the door.

When Dave brushed past her, she could smell his cologne. The scent was familiar—from Vegas and from when they used to play tennis together. He could be sweating buckets and still smell like a cologne card from some magazine. She supposed she should find that attractive. There was a time when she had. But at this point, she felt only panic concerning her situation and the desire to get rid of Dave as soon as possible. Evidently, meeting Carter had completely doused the small flame she'd once carried for Dave, which was crazy. Only a few weeks ago, she'd been convinced she was falling in love with him.

"This place is exactly how I pictured it," he said.

Liz didn't think it required much imagination to conjure up an image of the rental house in which she lived. At least fifteen years old, it was a basic four-bedroom, two-bath starter house. But The Chocolaterie was special. She wanted to show him that. Except she knew Carter would be looking for her there this afternoon and she hardly wanted the two of them to meet. Not that she anticipated trouble. Carter probably didn't care enough to act out, and Dave wasn't the type. She just preferred to avoid the whole awkward situation.

"Have a seat," she said.

He sat on the couch but leaned forward, resting his elbows on his knees and smiling at her. "You're not really mad at me for coming, are you?"

"No, of course not. It's good to see you. I'm just… with what happened at the shop, I'm pretty stressed out."

"I understand that and I'm sorry."

"It's not your fault. Anyway, this is your busy season," she said. "How'd you get time off at the club?"

"I told them I was taking a vacation."

"How long did you tell them you'd be gone?"

"I didn't get specific."

"I'm sure they weren't too pleased to hear that."

"They'll put up with it because they don't want to lose me." He rubbed his hands lightly together. "Anyway, I had to come. I couldn't let things fall apart between us at the last second."

"Dave, you don't…I mean, we're not…"

"What?" he challenged, and for the first time she realized that he was nervous. She'd never seen him at a loss. It made her feel guilty in terms of the past few weeks. Surely he'd be shocked to know that her relationship with Carter had become so intimate. She couldn't imagine what he'd say if she told him she was probably carrying Carter's baby….

"Compatible," she finished.

"What do you mean? We get along great. We've never even had an argument."

Liz wasn't sure anyone *could* argue with Dave. He was too easygoing, too fun-loving. And he didn't hold himself or anyone else to a strict standard of behavior. "You know what we're up against."

"An age difference that's meaningless. My reputation, which doesn't matter either, because I've changed. And too much distance, which could be rectified."

That wasn't all. There was Carter. But Liz didn't volunteer that piece of information. She and Dave faced enough obstacles without another man added to the mix, which was why they hadn't gotten together before. "Exactly."

"Liz, I'm asking you to move back to L.A."

"Dave, you can't really expect—"

He raised a hand so she'd let him finish. "I'd offer to move here, but the only place I could coach tennis is at the Running Y Ranch, and I've already called them. They're happy with who they have and don't need my help."

"You called the Running Y?" she echoed.

"I did, and I didn't get anywhere. Which means, if I moved here, I'd either have to commute to Boise, which isn't exactly the tennis capital of the world. Or—" he gave her a rueful grin "—I'd have to work at the hardware store with Keith."

Liz couldn't help chuckling. She liked Dave. Being with him was starting to bring those comfortable feelings back to her. But she couldn't see him living in Dundee, and she wasn't about to leave. "I can't move back, Dave. There's the shop and the kids—"

"Even if I asked you to marry me?"

She gaped at him, unable to formulate a response. Finally, she said, "You can't be serious."

"I am," he said earnestly. "I know it would be difficult to take Mica and Christopher away from their father, but I'll be the best stepdad I can be, and we'll let them come out here as much as possible."

Instinctively, Liz cupped a hand to her stomach, horrified by the fact that she was actually tempted by the escape he'd just offered her. If she married Dave and moved to California, no one would ever have to know about Carter's baby. Even Carter.

She wasn't sure she could really leave Dundee without telling him. She couldn't imagine doing that. But she couldn't imagine confronting him with the news, either. At the very least, she'd have to be honest with Dave. She couldn't marry him without telling him the truth. As terrified as she was, as panic-stricken as she was, she knew that much.

She shook her head to try and clear her thinking. Before she made any decisions, she needed to discover the truth herself. "I'd lose a lot of money on the shop."

"We could sell the business."

The mere thought of letting The Chocolaterie go into the hands of someone else nearly broke Liz's heart. But it would be preferable to closing it down. "Can I have some time to make up my mind?"

He blinked and sat up straight, as if he was surprised he'd gotten this far. "Sure. Think about it. Meanwhile, I'll rent a room over at the Running Y and help you get the shop open again, just in case you decide to sell."

Gordon had said The Chocolaterie was nearly finished, so it wouldn't take much, besides making more candy to replace what had been lost. But that information wasn't quite so important right now.

"Okay," she said. Then she showed Dave to the door and walked back to the telephone to leave a message for Reenie at the high school.

As HIS PLANE LANDED IN BOISE, Carter stared at Laurel's picture on his cell phone. He'd wanted to stop by her grave, to pay his respects and tell her about Hooper, but he'd been too worried about Liz to delay his return. Liz hadn't sounded like herself on the phone. And then there was the issue of Rocky Bradley.

What was Bradley's connection to Dundee? To Liz?

Carter had racked his brain trying to come up with one, to no avail. But there had to be some reason Bradley had driven into the middle of nowhere to vandalize a chocolate shop—twice.

What did an ex-con living in Boisc havc to gain by such an act? Why violate his parole and risk going to prison over a petty crime such as this?

Carter snapped his phone shut and shoved it into his pocket. He'd figure it out sooner or later. Since he was heading to Bradley's house, maybe it would happen today.

When the Fasten Seatbelt sign went off, he pulled his single carry-on bag from the overhead compartment and followed the flow of people off the plane. It didn't take long to retrieve his car from long-term parking. And only a half hour later he was standing on Bradley's mother's doorstep.

"Who are you?" Mrs. Bradley asked when she saw Carter.

"Carter Hudson. I'm the one who called you yesterday."

She stood behind a locked screen door. "I remember. You were asking questions about Rocky."

"That's right. He around?"

She hesitated. "I told him that you think he wrecked a candy shop in some small town, but he said you're crazy. He can't leave Boise without notifying his parole officer."

"He's not *supposed* to leave town without notifying his parole officer."

He glanced at the red Toyota truck in the driveway. It had no back bumper.

"He didn't do it," she said.

"I'd like to hear that from him."

She yanked on the collar of a big dog that was trying to wedge itself in front of her. "Who are you with again?"

"The FBI." After quitting the Bureau nearly two years ago, it was a stretch to claim the connection now. But the fact that Carter was no longer an official employee hadn't bothered Johnson when he'd asked for help with Hooper.

"We don't want any more trouble," she said as the dog pressed his nose to the screen.

"Then I suggest you get him."

Sighing in resignation, she yanked the dog back again. "Let me see if he's up."

Carter waited for several minutes. He was just beginning to wonder if Bradley and his mother had slipped out the back door and left him and the dog to stare at each other from opposite sides of the screen, when the man from the mug shot he'd seen in New York stumbled sleepily into view. His hair stood up on one side and he wasn't wearing a shirt—just a pair of jeans belted well below the top of his boxers. Tattoos covered his arms and chest.

"Since when is vandalism a federal crime?" he asked, unlocking the screen door and holding it open with his foot as if he were some kind of tough guy.

The dog squeezed outside and proceeded to sniff Carter. But he didn't seem dangerous. He wagged his tail and ultimately licked Carter's fingers. "I could call the local police, if you'd rather," Carter said.

Bradley pulled a smashed pack of cigarettes from his pocket and lit up a smoke. "Don't make a damn bit of difference to me," he said with a shrug. "You've got the wrong guy."

"Have you ever been to Dundee?"

"No."

"Never?"

"Never. I don't even know where it is."

"That's interesting, because I've got your fingerprints all over a beer bottle you left there," he said. "I've also got a witness who can place you in an alley near the main drag and a good description of your truck."

Rocky's face lost a great deal of its color. "So I visited the place. So what? That doesn't prove I did anything wrong."

"It proves you violated your parole."

"That's bullshit, man. I took a drive. That's no reason to send me back to prison."

"Tell me why you were there and what made you choose that particular shop, and maybe I'll forget that your name has turned up in all of this."

Bradley exhaled, blowing the smoke in Carter's face, but Carter could tell it was all an act. The guy was scared.

Jerking the cigarette away from the younger man's mouth, Carter tossed it to the ground and crushed it with his foot. The dog danced around, barking at Carter, but Bradley didn't move.

"Do you really want to serve time for spray painting someone's walls?" Carter asked.

Rocky's eyes darted to the smashed cigarette, and his mother came out to calm the dog.

"Tell me you haven't done anything wrong," she said to her son, holding the dog's collar. "Tell me you haven't gotten yourself in trouble again."

"What if someone paid me to do it?" Bradley asked, nervously rubbing his knuckles along the bottom of his chin.

Carter nudged the cigarette butt off the cement stoop. "Who?"

"If I tell you, will you go after him and forget about me?"

"That depends."

Rocky sent a fleeting glance toward his mother, as if he hated letting her overhear him. But she didn't look like she was going anywhere. "A guy named Keith paid me a hundred bucks to do it," he said. "That's all I know. He didn't want anyone hurt. He just wanted me to mess up the place."

Carter couldn't believe it. He would've bet money that it wasn't Keith. Keith had acted so indignant about being accused. But how else would Rocky know Liz's ex-husband's name? "Where'd you meet Keith?"

"At a bar here in town."

"At a bar."

"Yeah, man, he and I played a game of pool, okay?" Bradley jammed his hands in his pockets, and his voice revealed a touch of panic as he asked his next question. "So, are you gonna turn me in?"

Bradley's mother gasped and pressed a hand to her heart. "I can't take no more," she muttered.

Carter felt sorry for her. Her son clearly didn't amount to much and would probably cause trouble again. But Carter decided to give him one more chance.

"If you can pay for the damage, I'll let you do that instead."

"He'll pay," the mother said, pushing Bradley out of the way and dragging the dog inside. "He helps his father with the lawn service four days a week. We'll take the money out of his checks."

Carter nodded and gave her his card. "Fine. I'll send you the bill." He craned his head to catch a final glimpse of Bradley. "Stay away from Dundee," he said. "Or next time I won't be so nice."

LIZ STARED AT REENIE, who'd just arrived at her house with a brown paper sack. She knew what was inside. She'd asked Reenie to get it for her.

The moment of truth had arrived.

"I can't believe this," Reenie breathed, her eyes filled with worry.

"Neither can I." Liz pulled the pregnancy test from the sack. As she gazed down at it, the anxiety sitting low in her stomach turned painful. She'd asked Reenie not to tell Isaac about this and hoped against hope that her sister-in-law had respected that. She needed Reenie to be her best friend and not her brother's wife. But she knew it wouldn't be easy for Reenie to keep quiet. "Are you sure this kind of test will give me accurate results? I'm probably only a week or two along—"

"A week *or two?*" Reenie cried. "You just started dating Carter a couple weeks ago!"

Liz winced at the shameful reminder. How did she explain? She couldn't. Life and loneliness had simply gotten the best of her. And now she was floating down the river, just like the Lady of Shalott, doomed to de-struction. "I don't know what happened. I dated Keith for months before I slept with him. And my high-school sweetheart and I were together a year before we did anything. But it was different with Carter." She didn't mention Dave, but she'd known him a long time before she'd slept with him, too.

Reenie squeezed her arm. "What will you do if you're pregnant?"

"I'm not sure."

"Whatever happens, I'll help you."

Liz let Reenie pull her into an embrace. What Reenie had said was exactly what she needed to hear—that she wouldn't be completely alone. "Somehow I'll get through it," she said as she drew back, but she certainly wasn't convinced.

"Of course you will." Reenie hurried her toward the bathroom. "Go see. Maybe we're freaking out over nothing."

Liz wanted to believe that was the case. But she knew she was pregnant before she even took the test. She'd never been so late before.

And the test confirmed it.

THAT AFTERNOON, Liz went through the motions of making her mother's special fudge, caramel apples, rocky road and other candies, but she wasn't sure there was much point in it. Unless all this candy-making helped her sell the shop. She'd already decided she'd marry Dave and head to California. *If* he'd have her after she told him about the baby. She couldn't imagine he'd want a real marriage at that point. But she hoped he might be softhearted enough to lend her his name for a few months. That would help. It would give her the appearance of respectability, for her children's sake, and it would provide an excuse to leave Dundee. It would also guarantee that no one would ever suspect the truth. Especially Carter.

Guilt made her gut twist. She hated the fact that she'd be keeping such a secret. But maybe it was best for now. It wasn't as if Carter *wanted* to have a baby. She'd have to tell him eventually, of course, but she had nearly nine months to decide how and when. And it would be easier if she didn't live in the same town.

She gazed at the shop she loved so much. Her father and Dave had been there all day, painting over the writing they'd been unable to remove from the walls, and now the place looked as good as new.

Her future could have been so different, if only she'd been more careful. But it wasn't as if she'd *planned* on having an extended affair—with anyone—or she would have gone on the Pill.

"You're quiet today," Gordon said, ducking out of the bathroom, where he'd been rinsing off his brushes and rollers.

Dave looked up from where he was fixing a piece of baseboard that had been pried loose. "She's thinking," he said and winked at her.

She smiled, even though she felt sick to her stomach, and wondered if she'd be able to work for the airlines again, so she could support her little family.

The back door opened and Carter strode in. Liz had

been expecting him, waiting for him, and still the sight of him stole her breath. He was wearing an amber-colored shirt that brought out the gold flecks in his eyes and a pair of blue jeans.

He smiled when he saw her and came toward her as if he'd kiss her, but she quickly put the table between them. "You're back," she said, forcing another friendly, if strained smile. "Good to see you."

He couldn't miss her standoffish reaction, and then he caught sight of Dave, who stood up and dusted off his hands before offering to shake.

"I'm Dave Shapiro."

Carter said nothing. Neither did he accept Dave's hand.

Liz cleared her throat. "Dave, this is Carter Hudson."

Carter's mouth tightened at the edges, but he finally shook hands. "Dave's from California?"

She couldn't seem to formulate any more words at the moment, so she nodded.

"And what are you doing here in Dundee?" Carter asked.

His voice was amiable enough, for Carter. But Liz could sense the blunt question beneath his calm tone: *What the hell is going on?*

Dave might have sensed it, too. He hesitated for a second before answering. But then his easy smile returned and so, evidently, did his confidence. Or maybe he was making sure, now that he was here, to stake his claim. "I came to ask Liz to marry me."

Gordon, who'd been gathering up the last of his tools, straightened and stared.

"And what answer did she give you?" Carter asked, stone-faced.

Dave grinned warmly at Liz. "She hasn't told me yet."

Carter's cheeks flushed with some emotion, but Liz was at a loss to identify it. In any case, she knew he couldn't be experiencing anything more painful than what she was feeling.

"I see. Well, presuming she says yes, I hope you'll be happy together," he said and stalked out.

THAT NIGHT CARTER STOOD at the window of his cabin, staring out at the view he'd shared with Liz. He had one hand in his pocket. The other clasped a beer—but it was warm. He hadn't taken a sip of it in probably thirty minutes. He couldn't seem to move.

He knew it was Keith who'd vandalized Liz's shop. And yet he hadn't told anyone. In his mind, it hardly mattered if Liz was going to marry Dave and head back to California.

*If she married Dave...*How could she even think about being with Dave after what they'd shared? Had she told him that they'd been sleeping together? God, he could still smell her on his sheets!

He glanced at the phone. He wanted to call her but wasn't sure he could trust himself not to say something cruel. Evidently, he'd had different expectations of their relationship. He wasn't sure what those expectations were, exactly. He hadn't thought them through. They'd only just started seeing each other. But he'd considered the two of them a couple. Even if he hadn't communicated that to her, he was pretty sure it went without saying, when they'd had sex so many times within a two-week period.

Picking up the phone, he called information. He was completely confused and angry and had no answers on his own. But maybe Reenie could help him.

"Hello?" She answered on the first ring, but he could tell he'd called too late. She sounded half-asleep. He almost hung up, when she lowered her voice to a whisper and said, "Liz? Is it you? I'm here, honey, if you need to talk. It'll be okay. You have to believe that. It's the only way to get through this."

Carter pinched the bridge of his nose. "Get through what?" he asked.

Dead silence.

"Reenie?"

"Carter?" The sharpness with which she'd said his name told her she was far more awake now.

"Yeah. Remember me? The guy who works for your father? The guy who was dating your sister-in-law three days ago?"

"It's late, Carter."

"I know that."

There was an awkward silence. "So why are you calling me?"

The panic in her voice confused him as much as Liz's strange reaction had when he'd arrived at the shop today. Reenie wasn't easily intimidated. She would have no trouble telling him to go to hell if she wanted to. But she felt bad about something. He could tell. "When I left we were friends. Has that changed?"

"No," she said, drawing out the word.

"Good. Because everything else has."

There was another long pause. "I'm sorry."

"Does she love this guy?" he asked. "Does she *want* to marry Dave Shapiro, or whoever the hell he is?"

A long sigh greeted this question. "I don't know what to tell you," she said at last. "Because…I—that's up to Liz."

"Just tell me if she's in love with him," he said.

Silence. Finally, "No, she's not in love with him."

He blinked in surprise. "So that means she's going to turn him down." The anxiety tightening every muscle eased and Carter felt as if he could breathe again.

Until Reenie answered.

"Actually, I'm pretty sure she'll say yes."

"What?" He sank onto the couch. *"Why?"*

"I've already told you too much. I can't say any more," she said and hung up.

CHAPTER TWENTY-TWO

THE PHONE RANG, but Liz ignored it. She'd already spoken to Dave. She'd explained the whole painful situation, and now she was giving *him* time to think. She had no idea what he'd say. He'd grown quiet when she'd told him, and revealed little of what he was feeling.

But she could easily imagine his disappointment. He loved a woman who was pregnant with another man's child. Although she hadn't cheated on him—they hadn't had any commitments between them—her news couldn't have been a pleasant surprise.

Liz felt drained from the decisions she'd had to make and the tears she'd shed. She wanted to sleep. Sleep and forget the look on Carter's face when Dave had announced that he'd proposed and that she might accept. But she'd barely dozed off when a knock on her door jarred her awake. Grabbing her robe, she tied it as quickly as possible and went to answer before whoever it was could wake her children.

It was Dave. Sweeping her into his arms, he kissed her passionately. "I've decided," he said, smiling broadly. "I want you badly enough to make this work."

She returned his hug. This was the first time she'd been in his arms since Vegas. But she felt none of his enthusiasm or eagerness. Just a vague sense of relief that she had a plan. She would not allow herself to think of Carter.

LIZ'S FATHER WAS WAITING for her when she arrived at the store the following day. "What are you doing here so early?" she asked curiously.

"I came to help out. You need someone else around for the busy times. And for when you go to lunch or take a break."

She wanted to tell him how grateful she was for his support. He'd been wonderful the past few days, perfect. But she was still afraid to trust his change of heart. And now that she was moving out of state, she saw little point in struggling to voice the appreciation she felt. He'd be in Dundee with Isaac and everyone else that she loved. And she and her children would be in L.A., trying to make a new marriage work.

She cringed, but it was the best way out of her predicament, and she knew it. At least it seemed like her best choice. Her thoughts were so muddled she couldn't be entirely sure. "Thanks for all you've done," she said simply.

He studied her face and frowned, as if he definitely didn't like what he saw. So Liz focused on unlocking the front door. "If you have something to say, say it," she said as she drew back the bolt.

"I will," he replied. "But I'll wait until we're inside, because you won't like it."

"I know what it is. I look tired, I need to take better

care of myself and get more sleep. You've been saying it since you moved here."

"That's true. But that's not what I have to say this morning." He held the door so she could go in ahead of him. Then he followed her inside.

"What?" she said when the door swung shut behind them.

He took a rather combative stance. "Are you going to marry Dave?"

She clasped her hands in back of herself so he couldn't see them shake. "Yes."

"Which means you're moving to California."

"It does."

"When?"

"Soon. As soon as we sell The Chocolaterie, if we *can* sell it."

"What about Mica and Christopher? If I remember right, you wanted them here close to their father."

"I've done my best. They'll…" Knowing how badly she had let them down caused searing disappointment. They were going to hate being dragged away from Keith, Isaac, Reenie, Jennifer, Angela, Isabella—and Reenie's new baby. They didn't even know about the baby yet. Liz had accidentally ruined Reenie's good news by getting pregnant herself.

"They'll adjust," she finished weakly. "But please don't tell them about it just yet. I need some time to come to terms with my decision. Dave's promised to go to California and wait for me. He needs to get back to work, anyway. So I don't need to explain his presence or anything he says. I'll break the bad news in a few weeks."

He gaped at her. "*Bad* news? Isn't a wedding supposed to be good news?"

"Bad news to them," she said, trying to cover her mistake.

"I don't think so."

She scowled at him. "What are you talking about?"

"You don't want to do this. I can tell. What I can't figure out is what's behind it."

She headed to the kitchen and started pulling trays of truffles, chocolates, brownies and caramels off the rolling cart so she could arrange her displays. "Sometimes you do what you have to."

"No one's making you do this."

"Dave's in love with me."

"So? You're not in love with him. You told me so, remember?"

"I said I was infatuated. That's close."

"You said 'a little infatuated,' and you didn't sound particularly sincere."

"Dad—" She hesitated. She'd been calling him Gordon, for the most part, but he was acting like her father and the word had slipped out.

"I *am* your dad," he said. "And that gives me the right to say this."

"I know who you are. But don't worry. We'll be fine."

"Liz—"

The urgency in his voice made her look up even though she didn't want to. "What?"

"Don't do it."

"I have to."

"Why? What are you running from?"

She didn't respond. Because the answer to that question had just walked through the door.

CARTER TOLD HIMSELF he shouldn't care about Liz. If she could make love to him one weekend and marry someone else the next, she wasn't the woman he thought she was. But that kind of thinking hadn't lasted once he'd spoken to Reenie. Her words troubled him because they hinted at something deeper. And as he entered her shop, he decided it was time to find out what was going on.

"Mr. Russell," he said.

Liz's father nodded a greeting, but it was clear Carter had just interrupted a private conversation. He would've asked Liz to call him later and left, so that Russell and Liz could continue whatever it was they were discussing, but he couldn't trust that she'd ever give him the audience he craved. He'd sent her several e-mails and tried to call her, too. She seemed determined to avoid him.

"Would you mind giving me and Liz a few moments alone?" he asked.

Before her father could respond, Liz said, "I'm sorry but now's not a good time. We're about to open."

Gordon Russell's gaze shifted between his daughter and Carter. Then he smiled as though he'd read something in their expressions that finally made sense. "Actually, I think now would be ideal. I'll be down at the doughnut shop if you need me."

"I'd like a doughnut," Liz called after him. "Maybe I'll go with you."

Carter felt his eyebrows slide up. What was she so afraid of? "He can bring you one. Right, Mr. Russell?"

"You bet." Her father scooted out, and Liz's eyes went wide when Carter locked the door behind him.

"What are you doing?" she asked, putting the table between them for the second time since he'd been home.

Carter remembered them using that table in a very different way, not as a barrier to keep them apart. If she didn't remember that encounter as fondly as he did, maybe he could accept what she told him and leave her alone, as she obviously wanted him to do. "Insuring our privacy so we can talk."

"We don't have anything to talk about."

"Sure we do. For starters, I know who's been vandalizing your shop."

Basic curiosity seemed to war with her desire to be rid of him. "You already told me. It was the stranger, Rocky somebody."

"Rocky Bradley did the damage. But he claims your ex-husband paid him for his trouble."

Genuine surprise lit Liz's face. "You're kidding."

"That's what he says."

She took a moment to work through it, but she eventually drew herself up. "Well, good!"

"Good?" he echoed.

"It'll make what I'm doing a whole lot easier."

Carter rounded the table and she backed into a corner. "Somehow I thought you'd be angry. Don't you want to see him punished?"

"No. I have too many other problems right now to be angry with Keith. Obviously, if he'd do something like that, he needs help."

"Okay, let's talk about the other problems in your life."

Liz's throat worked as though she was struggling to swallow. "Why?"

"How are you going to answer Dave's proposal?"

"I've already given him my answer."

Dread filled Carter. "What was it?" he asked softly because his voice couldn't seem to go any louder.

Her gaze dropped to her feet. "I'm going to marry him," she mumbled.

A fresh wave of jealousy screamed through Carter. He'd been jealous ever since he'd returned to find Dave with Liz, but hearing those words on her lips gave the ugly emotion razor-sharp teeth. "Then tell me you love him."

"I'm doing what I think is best."

"I said, tell me you love him. And look me in the eyes when you do it." He drew closer, invading her space just to see how she might react. If she wanted Dave, she'd have no trouble telling him to get lost. "We made love just last weekend, Liz."

She squeezed her eyes closed. "I know. But it's over when it's over, remember?"

"It's over for you?" Lifting one finger, he ran it lightly over her arm. He feared she might recoil, but she didn't. She watched him touch her, as if mesmerized by the goose bumps that rose in the wake of his hand. "I thought about you the whole time I was gone," he admitted. "I imagined your skin brushing against mine, the taste of your lips, your legs wrapping around me as I—"

"Stop it," she said, covering her ears. "I'm engaged."

Carter could see the desire in her eyes, the blush of warmth his words brought to her cheeks. "That's bullshit. You want to be with me."

She looked up at him then, searched his face. "And what do you want?"

"I want to be with you, too. Why do you think I'm here?"

"But how long could we expect it to last?" she countered. "Until you leave next fall?"

Scowling, he jammed a hand through his hair. "Hell, I don't know. We just met a few weeks ago."

"And that's the problem."

"It's a problem that I can't make a commitment after *three weeks?*"

Her hands clutched the fabric of her Give Me Chocolate and No One Gets Hurt apron. "I'm not asking you for a commitment. I'm not asking you for anything."

"I'm asking *you* for something! Tell me what's happening," he said.

"Carter..." She grabbed his arm and he felt heartened by her touch, hopeful. It was all he could do not to pull her to him and kiss her deeply, to reassure himself in the quickest manner possible. But he still wasn't sure she'd let him.

"What?" he said.

"I'm pregnant."

She'd barely whispered the words, but they hit him like an arrow in the throat. He even staggered back a couple of steps.

"And please don't ask me if it's yours," she added, blinking against the tears filling her eyes. "I haven't been with anyone else in months."

*Pregnant...*The word seemed to echo around the room.

"Does Dave know?" he managed to ask even though he could barely breathe.

"Do you think I'd marry him without telling him about the baby?"

"How could you marry him anyway?" he demanded. "Especially now?"

Frustration contorted her elegant features. "I'm letting you off the hook, in case you haven't figured that out!"

Carter didn't know how to respond. He and Laurel had wanted a baby, but Hooper had injured her too badly. She couldn't conceive. Carter had been eager to move forward with the adoption process. But then…Laurel had overdosed on Valium and had left him completely alone.

He struggled to suck in enough air to speak. "*I'll* marry you," he said. What other choice did he have? He knew it wasn't the most romantic proposal in the world, but…he was too shocked to think beyond the practical. He knew that he wanted do the right thing, to take care of his child. That was all.

She surprised him by stepping out of his reach and shaking her head. "No."

"Why not?" he asked, amazed that she'd reject him. "I'm the baby's father. Surely marrying me is better than marrying *Dave*."

"No, it's not."

He gaped at her. "You don't love him!"

"But he loves me. You're still in love with whomever that woman is on your phone."

"Laurel," he said softly.

"Is that her name?"

He nodded.

"Did you see her while you were in New York?"

He'd meant to visit her grave and take her flowers, but he'd come straight home to Liz. "No."

"Maybe you should try and reconcile with her," she said.

"She's dead, Liz. She killed herself two years ago. You're threatened by someone I can no longer see or touch."

There was a long pause, then, "That doesn't mean you don't love her," she said.

Carter had no answer for that.

"Anyway, Dave wants to marry me in spite of the baby. You're willing to marry me because of it. There's a difference. I've been second best before, Carter. I can't live with that again. Not even to a memory."

Carter didn't know what more he could offer. He was reeling too badly to sort anything out. "I'll send money."

She winced but nodded. "Child support is only fair, I guess. I certainly didn't do this on purpose."

"I know that." He was just as much to blame, and he felt terrible about it. But did she really have to marry somebody else and move away? Wasn't there room in this town for both of them?

He didn't get the chance to answer his own question because Mary Thornton knocked on the door and Liz took advantage of the interruption to briskly usher him out.

"Thanks for stopping by," she said, her tone suddenly formal and her head held high, as though she was building some emotional fort he'd no longer be able to breach. "I'll keep in touch."

THE NEXT SEVERAL DAYS crept by with agonizing slowness. Carter passed Liz's chocolate shop every time he drove to work. Senator Holbrook's district office was finally up and running so at least he could keep busy. But if she saw him, she looked right through him as if he didn't even exist.

Meanwhile, he missed her. Terribly. He'd just started living again. Feeling like a human being instead of an empty shell. And now his days were more meaningless to him than before.

He still had Laurel's pictures, and her memories, of course. But they weren't the sacred objects they'd once been. He didn't stare at them and ache for her voice, her touch. He actually tried to go back to that. At least Laurel was a loss he'd grown used to. Instead his mind automatically shifted to Liz. The way she made love. The sound of her laughter. The scent of the candles she liked so much. She was passionate and responsive and—in his more honest moments, he had to admit—much stronger than the Laurel he'd known.

But Liz was out of reach. Everyone in town knew she was leaving. Keith was furious and claimed he'd petition the court to make sure she couldn't take his kids so far away. But it was painfully clear he didn't really have the money. And no one felt particularly sorry for him after what he'd done to Liz's shop. Carter had notified the police that he'd found the culprit so they could stop looking. He'd heard the prosecutor had issued a formal complaint giving Keith a court date for his arraignment.

But even if Keith was convicted, he probably wouldn't go to jail. Carter didn't care what happened to him. Not anymore. As far as he was concerned, it was punishment enough that Officer Orton had spread the word all over town.

Liz wasn't pressing the vandalism issue. She didn't seem to want to bother with it. She was too busy trying to placate her children. Mica and Christopher were terribly unhappy about the impending move, but Liz was going ahead with her plan anyway. There was a For Sale sign in the window of The Chocolaterie, just to prove it.

Gossip suggested her father might buy her out. Carter had also heard Celeste talking about throwing Liz a bridal shower. It upset him to think of Liz receiving lingerie to wear for someone else. And that sensation became almost painful when he imagined her big with *his* child and sleeping in Dave's arms.

He wished he could convince her that he'd make a better husband. But as much as he wanted it at times, he wasn't sure that was true. What if they couldn't make it work? What if she'd be happier, in the end, with someone like Dave? Dave was still young and unscarred.

Two weeks after the day she'd told him about the baby, he was on his computer late at night when he saw her come online. Was she instant messaging with Dave? Making plans for where they'd live? Arranging the sale of the shop? Talking about the baby? *His* baby?

How could he care so much about someone he'd known for such a short time? It didn't make any sense. But he supposed it was like the first sweet taste of chocolate. A person didn't have to eat a whole box to know it was good.

Unable to stop himself, he clicked on her e-mail address and hit the instant message button.

CHudson1973: Have you been to the doctor yet?

He could ask about the baby, right? The baby was his, too.

She took so long to answer him, he was beginning to doubt she'd respond. But then a blue line of text appeared.

Luvs Chocolat: Not yet. I'm waiting until I get to California.

CHudson1973: When are you leaving?

Luvs Chocolat: In three weeks.

CHudson1973: Does Dave have a place for you yet?

Luvs Chocolat: He's looking.

Carter wasn't sure why he'd initiated this conversation. Every line she sent cut him deeper than the one before.

CHudson1973: I think you're making a mistake.

Luvs Chocolat: Keith wants to meet Rocky

Bradley. He says he wants the chance to clear his name, that he didn't do it.

She'd ignored his comment, which didn't surprise him. Neither did it surprise him that Keith would request an audience with Bradley. He'd been swearing by all that was holy that he was wrongly accused.

CHudson1973: I know. He already asked me if I'd arrange a meeting.

Luvs Chocolat: What do you think?

CHudson1973: To be honest with you, he comes off as innocent.

Luvs Chocolat: But he must have done it. How else would Rocky know his name?

CHudson1973: Right. Unless there's another connection.

Luvs Chocolat: How could there be? I don't know anyone in Boise.

CHudson1973: I want to see you.

That statement came out of nowhere. Carter knew he shouldn't have typed it. Or if he did type it, he shouldn't have sent it. But he couldn't stop himself. He wasn't getting over Liz. He was growing more obsessed with her by the day.

Luvs Chocolat: I won't reply to that.

CHudson1973: Can I come over? We need to talk.

There was a long pause.

Luvs Chocolat: No.

CHudson1973: Why not?

Luvs Chocolat: You know we won't end up talking.

A surge of hope and arousal shot through him. If he was that much of a threat to her fidelity, she had to feel something for him.

CHudson1973: I hate the thought of you with Dave. I hate the thought of you with anyone but me.

Luvs Chocolat: Stop. We already had this discussion. Things are better this way.

CHudson1973: For who? You? No. Me? No. The baby? Definitely not. It's only better for Dave.

Luvs Chocolat: You had your chance. I've already given him my word.

CHudson1973: Your *word?* So? Take it back.

Luvs Chocolat: I can't. That wouldn't be fair.

CHudson1973: You're not striking a business deal, damn it. You're talking about a marriage. Till death do you part.

No response.

CHudson1973: You still care about me.

Luvs Chocolat: That's not a question.

CHudson1973: I know.

When she didn't answer, didn't deny it, Carter's heart began to beat faster.

CHudson1973: If it still matters, I'm in love with you. I can't think of anything else that would make me feel this terrible. I'm dying without you.

He'd poured his heart out in that last line, but she didn't write back.

CHudson1973: Liz?

Luvs Chocolat: What?

Carter stared at the screen. Maybe the future's uncertain. Maybe I can't make you a lot of promises. I won't pretend I'm as easy to get along with as Dave seems to be. I've had experiences that have left some marks. But I want to try. I didn't know that the day you told me, but I know it now. I want to try. He nearly added that he wanted to help raise his child, but after what she'd said, he was afraid she'd misinterpret that to mean he wanted to marry her because of the baby. That's something, isn't it?

Again, it took her a long time to respond, but at last, she wrote, Yeah, that's something...

Maybe he hadn't lost her completely. Taking a deep breath, he typed his next line: Is it enough?

Luvs Chocolat: Carter, don't.

CHudson1973: Is it?

Luvs Chocolat: You're asking me to take a huge risk.

CHudson1973: And what's marrying Dave? A guarantee?

Luvs Chocolat: At least he can't hurt me.

CHudson1973: We're talking about the Lady of Shalott again.

Luvs Chocolat: If so, the mirror has already cracked.

CHudson1973: Liz, listen to me. We could change the ending. I always thought that ending sucked, anyway.

He felt as if she was tempted, as if he was close to convincing her. But then she withdrew.

Luvs Chocolat: I can't. What would that do to Dave?

Liz, he started to write, but she signed off.

CHAPTER TWENTY-THREE

"DADDY DIDN'T DO IT."

The following morning, Mica sat at the kitchen table glowering at Liz, who was standing at the toaster, waiting for her bagel to pop up. Christopher was already watching cartoons.

Thank goodness school was out, Liz thought. Summer was easier. But it was getting late in the day and Liz needed to shower. Her father had taken over opening the shop for her each morning, but she wanted to be there by noon. She needed to make more candy. They were running low on coated strawberries and cherries.

"We've already been through this, Mica," she said gently. She was glad that Mica had something to say to her this morning. Her children had barely spoken to her since she'd told them they'd be moving. But Liz didn't want to argue. She hadn't been able to sleep last night. Carter's words had left her too agitated.

What's marriage to Dave, a guarantee?...I'm in love with you...We could change the ending...

"He *promised* me," Mica insisted.

"Honey, adults do some really weird things some-times, and for some really weird reasons," Liz said, trying to explain. "And they don't always tell the truth about it. Occasionally, they lie even to themselves."

"Daddy's not lying! He loves you. He told me he does. Why would he want to hurt you?"

"Maybe he thought if I couldn't make it on my own, I'd marry him again."

"Why not marry him?" she asked, throwing all of her emotions behind those words. "Then we could stay here. Please, Mom? *Pull-eze?*"

Mica and Christopher's unhappiness felt like hundred-pound weights attached to each leg. "Mica—"

"If we leave, I won't get to see Reenie's baby."

Liz hadn't told them they'd be getting their own baby. That was news that could wait until she was married. Maybe when they grew older they'd count the months and realize her marriage to Dave hadn't preceded the pregnancy. But that would be years from now.

"Don't make the situation any more difficult, okay?" she said. "Please?"

Mica looked as if she'd continue to plead, but the phone interrupted before she could, and Liz raised a hand to indicate silence.

"Hello?"

"Hi, babe. You up and moving around?"

"Yeah." It was Dave. Of course. He called her several times a day.

"I think I found a house. I'm going to tour it tonight."

Feeling intensely guilty for messaging with Carter the night before, Liz drew a deep breath. Since agreeing to marry Dave, she'd tried so hard to avoid contact with Carter. Just looking at him felt like a betrayal, because her whole heart ached with longing. But it was Dave who'd come to her rescue when she'd needed him most. She owed Dave her loyalty, even if she couldn't give him all her love.

"Where is it?" she asked.

"Laguna Hills. The real-estate agent said it's been neglected. But a fixer-upper might be fun. It'll give us a project, you know?"

A fixer-upper was all they could afford in L.A. But Dave always painted everything in a positive light. "Sounds great."

"You feeling okay?" he asked at the lack of enthusiasm in her voice.

Liz quickly rallied her spirits. "Fine. Good. Why?"

"You seem tired."

"I am. For some reason, I couldn't sleep last night." For some reason? She knew exactly why....

"Maybe you should grab a nap today. Will you have time? What do you have planned?"

"I've got to make more strawberries and cherries for the store."

"And the kids?"

"They're going over to Reenie's. Now that we're moving, they want to spend every minute they can there."

"Is your father at the shop again?"

"Yeah. He's been opening for me."

"How are he and Isaac getting along?"

"Not so good. Isaac still refuses to talk to him. He's being stubborn."

"He'll come around."

"I know." Isaac was too kindhearted to hold a grudge for long. His issues, at this point, dealt more with trust. If Gordon could remain consistent, he'd eventually win Isaac over. But that would probably happen after she left.

Liz shook her head. She'd miss Isaac and Reenie. She'd miss her father, too. They'd been working together quite a bit lately. Walking away from that relationship, which was growing in a healthy direction for the first time in eighteen years, wouldn't be easy. But she'd told him about the baby. He understood what she was doing. He just didn't agree with it.

"By the way, you can tell Mica I bought her a good tennis racket," Dave said. "I think it's time to teach her how to play."

Liz glanced at her daughter, who had rested her cheek glumly on one fist the moment she realized Liz was talking to Dave. "I'll tell her. She'll be excited."

"I've got to go," he said. "I'm supposed to be at the club. Call you later?"

"Okay."

"I love you."

Liz's chest constricted. She wanted to say it back. He deserved to hear it. But she hadn't been able to yet. And today wasn't going to be any different. Whenever those words rose to her lips, she pictured Carter. "Talk to you soon," she said and hung up.

"I don't like Dave," Mica announced.

"What do you think of Carter Hudson?" Liz asked.

The question obviously caught Mica, who'd been readying herself for an argument, off guard. She opened her mouth, closed it, then tried again. "He seems nice," she said.

He wasn't *nice*. Dave was nice. Carter was enigmatic and complex, and he could be difficult. Carter was a huge question mark.

But he was everything Liz wanted.

CARTER SAT ACROSS FROM KEITH at Jerry's Diner and shoved his cup to the edge of the table so the waitress would refill it when she came around. Over the past few weeks Keith had requested several times that they meet, but Carter had always turned him down. He'd been too engrossed in his own problems, in trying to figure out how he felt about Liz and his baby, and whether or not he'd be able to withstand losing them. The vandalism at the shop was no longer a priority. Because he didn't feel sorry for Keith, it was easy to let that go.

But there was something at the back of his mind that was bothering him, something that didn't sit quite right, and he couldn't ignore it any longer, regardless of what Bradley had told him.

"So you didn't do it," Carter said, leaning back and folding his arms across his chest.

"No, I didn't," Keith replied. "I don't know how to prove it to you, but I swear I'm not the one."

"Where do you think Bradley got your name?"

"I have no clue." Keith raised a helpless hand. "That's the crazy thing. I've never heard of him before in my life."

Carter took the mug shot he'd brought from New York out of his shirt pocket and slid it across the table.

"This is him?" Keith asked.

Carter nodded. "Ever seen him before? Maybe at the Honky Tonk or some other bar?"

"No."

"What about a bar in Boise?"

"I haven't been to Boise in over a year."

Maybe that was what bothered him. Carter couldn't see Keith at a bar in Boise, hanging out with Bradley. Maybe if Keith's other friends were Bradley's type, yeah. But they weren't. He had Reenie's kids one weekend and Liz's the next. And he worked during the week. "Where were you the night the shop was trashed?"

"If it happened late, I suppose I was asleep."

He lived alone, so he had no one to back up his story. And yet...

Carter rubbed a hand over his jaw. He'd shaved this morning, but he could already feel the stubble that would turn into a dark shadow by dinnertime. "Do you remember what was written on her wall?"

"I won't play dumb," Keith said. "Everyone knows it said *Go home, bitch.* But why would I have anyone write that? I don't want Liz to go anywhere. Especially with my kids."

Carter had assumed those words had been meant to upset and intimidate. He hadn't taken them literally. But what if they *were* meant literally?

Tossing a few bucks on the table, he stood.

"You're leaving?" Keith said.

"You're coming with me," he replied.

"Where?"

"Boise."

CARTER BANGED ON the Bradleys' door, waited a few seconds and banged again. It was noon, so there was a good chance Rocky would just be rolling out of bed.

Mrs. Bradley opened the door before he could knock a third time. She was wearing a flowery dress and had curlers in her hair. And she wasn't happy to see him. "Oh, no. It's you."

"Sorry to trouble you," Carter said. "But I'd like to speak to Rocky again, if you don't mind."

She adjusted the kerchief that covered her pink sponge rollers. "What's he done this time?"

"Nothing that I know of. I'm only hoping for a few details."

"He's not home."

Carter glanced at the driveway. There were still two cars parked there, but one looked more like a hunk of junk that hadn't been used in a long while. The red Toyota was gone. "When do you expect him?"

"I sent him to the store for a gallon of milk fifteen minutes ago."

"Mind if we wait?"

He could tell she did mind, but she shrugged anyway. "Suit yourselves." Locking the screen door, she left the inside door open and proceeded to vacuum. Then the clink of dishes and the sound of running water rose from the house. After thirty long minutes, Carter knocked again.

"How far away is that store you mentioned?"

"Not far. But we have a wedding in the family, so I told Rocky he needed to pick up my best dress from the cleaner's this week. Maybe he decided to do it today, since he was already out."

"Who's getting married?" he asked, just to keep her talking.

Her expression brightened. "My nephew. He's a tennis pro," she confided proudly.

Carter's gaze locked with Keith's. Keith opened his mouth to say something that, from his expression, was bound to be indignant, but Carter silenced him with a look and smiled affably at Mrs. Bradley. "He's good at tennis, huh?"

"Yeah. He lives in L.A., so we rarely get to see him. But I'm going down for the wedding."

Carter's blood began to rush through his ears. *Go home, bitch.* Who wanted Liz to return to L.A. more than anyone else?

"I'm from Southern California," Carter said. "What's your nephew's name? Maybe I've heard of him."

"Dave," she replied. "Dave Shapiro."

WHEN CARTER WALKED IN to Liz's *chocolaterie*, she was busy helping two customers. Her eyes flicked his way, and she licked her lips as though she was suddenly uncomfortable, but she didn't acknowledge him.

"Maybe you'd enjoy one of my French creams," she said to a couple decked out in brand new cowboy hats, western belts and shiny boots. Obviously, they were tourists who'd already visited the gift shop at the Running Y.

"Is a French cream like a butter cream?" the woman asked in obvious confusion.

"No, a good butter cream is made with water, sugar and butter. My French creams are made with whole milk, ultra-heavy cream and butter." Liz shot Carter another glance. "Turning creams on a marble slab is sort of a lost art, but that's what I do here."

"They sound great," the man said and bought half a dozen. Then the other customer, an older woman, stepped up to the register.

"What do you have with cashews in it?" she asked.

Liz led her to a section of various chocolate-covered nuts and proceeded to explain that she used no peanuts or peanut products. Only the best tree nuts. "Tastes like heaven!" the woman exclaimed as she bit into a sample.

Liz grinned, and Carter couldn't help smiling proudly. When their eyes met and she blushed prettily, he *knew* he loved her. Maybe they'd only met five weeks ago, but it didn't matter. He wanted her. Regardless of the baby. Regardless of Laurel. She offered him what he needed most. Love. Acceptance. Change.

A rebirth.

He supposed he should accept the fact that he'd be spending many years in Dundee, because he could never take Liz away from her shop. If Dave truly loved her, he wouldn't be able to do it, either.

The woman paid for a pound of chocolate-covered nuts and some caramels, and then the bell rang over the door and he and Liz were alone.

"Where's your father?" Carter asked.

"At the diner, having dinner."

"What about you? Have you eaten?"

"He said he'd bring me something."

"And the kids are—"

"At Recnie's." She pulled her gaze away from him as though it took some effort and started straightening up. "Since they found out we're moving, they beg to stay there as much as possible. I can hardly get them to come home."

"Then you'd better call them up and tell them you're not moving, after all," he said, stepping up to the glass case that separated them. "At least not very far."

She tucked a stray lock of hair behind her ear. "I'm engaged, Carter."

"You belong to me."

"Carter—"

"And I belong to you," he finished.

Wariness entered her eyes, as if she was afraid of how good that sounded. "And what would I tell Dave? That you came through for me after all? That I don't need him anymore?"

"You can tell him if he ever sends Rocky to Dundee again, I'll break his jaw."

Liz's eyebrows gathered above her hazel eyes. "What?"

"It was Dave," he said. "He's the one who had Rocky Bradley do what he did in here."

"But Rocky's from Boise—" Recognition dawned on her face. "His *cousin?*" she gasped.

Carter nodded.

"Wait, Dave's not like that. Why would he want to hurt me?"

"I guess he was getting tired of waiting for you to return to L.A. And he feared the shop would keep you here indefinitely."

She brought a hand to her chest. "Poor Keith! He got blamed."

"That's what Dave told Rocky to do if he was caught."

He watched the emotions flicker across her face—surprise, disbelief and then anger. "How could he pin it on an innocent party?"

"Figured you'd believe it, I guess."

"But how could he do it to me in the first place? He knows how much I love this shop!"

"Maybe we should ask him," Carter said. "We can do that when we call to tell him that you're marrying *me*." Moving around the display case, he pulled her into his arms. She hesitated for a moment, as if she'd resist. But he took her chin and tilted it up so she had to look at him. "Take a chance on me," he said.

"What about Laurel?"

"She won't stand between us. I'll probably never stop loving her. But she's gone, Liz. And I've accepted that. Loving her doesn't mean I can't love you just as much."

"You're sure?"

"I've spent the past two weeks making sure, missing you just as badly as I ever missed her."

A smile lit her face.

"It's true," he murmured.

"You wouldn't say it if it wasn't."

He chuckled. "See? You know me pretty damn well."

She slipped her arms around his neck and snuggled closer. "Where will we live?"

"Here. I'll build you a house with a white picket fence and a large yard for Mica and Chris. And I'll make a cradle for our child." He touched her flat stomach, finding it hard to believe there was already a baby growing inside.

"What will you do once the campaign is over?"

"Maybe I'll build houses."

"You're good with your hands," she breathed, grinning suggestively.

"I do believe you're coming on to me," he said. "Maybe we should close up shop for a few minutes so we can reacquaint ourselves with what we've been missing."

She brushed the hair out of his eyes, then sobered. "What about all those boxes in the cabin? Could you really be happy staying in one place?"

"As long as I have you," he said, and then he kissed her.

EPILOGUE

CARTER SAT IN THE ROCKING CHAIR at the rental he and Liz would soon vacate in favor of the house he was building, and stared down at the bundle in his arms. His son was nearly four months old. Jeremy probably would've slept through the night; he was starting to do that. But Carter had slipped into his room and jiggled him so he'd have an excuse to pick him up. The child's sweet innocence, his complete trust and dependence, even the feel of his downy head, satisfied something Carter couldn't even begin to understand.

He knew Laurel would've loved having a baby. A child might have made up for some of the ugliness she'd experienced. It had certainly made a difference to him. Slowly but surely he could sense his old idealism returning, could feel the taint of Hooper's crimes fading as he became more and more involved in his family, his new construction business, Liz's shop, and the small town he'd never dreamed he'd call home. He had too much to be grateful for to lament the past. He'd always be sorry about what had happened to Laurel, but the love he felt for his first wife was becoming a pale shadow next to what he felt for Liz, Mica, Chris and Jeremy.

After kissing his son's head, he returned the baby to

his crib and walked down the hall, eager to climb into bed with his wife.

"What is it?" Liz asked when he entered the room. She muted the television and looked up at him as if she could tell by his expression that he had more than their nightly routines on his mind.

"I'm just thinking."

"About what?"

"The Lady of Shalott," he said.

Her smile broadened. "What about her?"

"I like our ending better."

She pulled him into her arms and let him kiss her deeply.

"So do I."

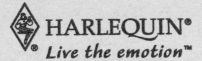

Harlequin Historicals®
Historical Romantic Adventure!

From rugged lawmen and valiant knights to defiant heiresses and spirited frontierswomen, Harlequin Historicals will capture your imagination with their dramatic scope, passion and adventure.

Harlequin Historicals... they're too good to miss!

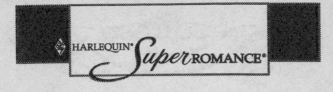
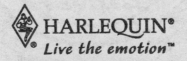

HARLEQUIN®
Presents

The world's bestselling romance series...
The series that brings you your favorite authors,
month after month:

Helen Bianchin...Emma Darcy
Lynne Graham...Penny Jordan
Miranda Lee...Sandra Marton
Anne Mather...Carole Mortimer
Susan Napier...Michelle Reid

and many more uniquely talented authors!

Wealthy, powerful, gorgeous men...
Women who have feelings just like your own...
The stories you love, set in exotic, glamorous locations...

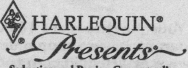

HARLEQUIN®
Presents

Seduction and Passion Guaranteed!

HPDIR104